THOSE WHO
LOVE NIGHT

Also by Wessel Ebersohn

THOSE WHO LOVE NIGHT

WESSEL EBERSOHN

Minotaur Books

New York

THOSE WHO LOVE NIGHT. Copyright © 2011 by Wessel Ebersohn. All rights reserved. Printed in the United States of America. For information address St. Martin's Press, 175 Fifth Avenue, New York, N.Y. 10010.

www.minotaurbooks.com
www.stmartins.com

ISBN 978-0-312-65596-9

First published in South Africa by Umuzi, an imprint of Random House Struik (Pty) Ltd.

First U.S. Edition: January 2012

10 9 8 7 6 5 4 3 2 1

For a kind and gentle man, my brother Joe

Things that love night
Love not such nights as these

—WILLIAM SHAKESPEARE, *King Lear*

THOSE WHO
LOVE NIGHT

1

She had heard the sound made by engines for at least five minutes now. By her reckoning, they should already have arrived in the village.

On most evenings, especially on Fridays, someone would arrive from Bulawayo or Plumtree, and you could hear their approach from the time they came round the low hill on the far side of the open stretch of savannah where the cattle grazed. The sound would start as a soft humming, then gradually grow louder. It would be perhaps two or three minutes before the vehicle arrived in the village.

Tonight was different. The sound was clearly that of more than one vehicle, and she had been hearing it for longer than she would have expected on other nights. It also had a deeper note. She knew the sound made by diesel engines and thought that must be the reason for the sound's rumbling nature. It was much louder than that made by just a single car or even a truck.

Janice had been asleep, but now that she had children, she found that she was woken by anything unusual. A new sound or a change in a familiar one, an unexpected smell of smoke, a movement in the house—anything that should not be there, no matter how minor, was enough to rouse her from her sleep.

Someone was shouting, the voice deadened by distance and the clay walls of the houses in between. The house was one of only two in the village with both wooden floors and ceilings, but the walls were of the same clay as the others. Both had been built in colonial days, one for the district administrator and the other for the village police officer. The voice was male, but young and not fully formed: possibly Benjamin, the teenage boy from the next house up the track. She could not yet make out the words, but his agitation was unmistakable.

For the first time she saw that Wally was not in bed. His place was vacant and the sheet had been pulled back into position. The only blanket had been pushed off much earlier, doubtless as unnecessary in the warm summer night. Wally did not seem to have left in a hurry. The jacket of his uniform was still carefully hung over the chair where he had left it when he got undressed, but his trousers were gone.

None of this was surprising to Janice. He spent hours on most nights wandering the house or sitting outside on the veranda. She had long since given up trying to lure him back to bed at such times.

She got slowly out of bed, turning carefully and allowing her feet to slide gently to the floor. No matter who was coming, she could not afford to hurry and risk falling. The precious cargo, already eight months old, the child she was carrying inside her, could not be put at risk.

Once on her feet, wearing the knee-length nightdress in which she usually slept, she crossed the room, reaching for the door frame to steady herself, and entered the hall. Through the glass panel in the front door she could see Wally in the faintest of moonlight. He was wearing only the trousers of his uniform. His head was raised, like an animal sensing the wind, and he was staring in the direction of the main road from which the sound was coming. He was holding on tightly to the wooden rail that ran along the edge of the veranda, and seemed to have risen to the balls of his feet. To Janice, it was the posture of a man ready to take flight.

As she opened the door, the sound increased in volume. In the distance and below them on the flat ground, she could see the first of the headlights, sending twin beams back and forth through the darkness as the track twisted. Acacia bushes and clusters of hard veld grass stood out in momentary, sharp silhouette as the lights flashed over them. "Is it . . . ." she tried to ask. "Is it them?" Wally's attention was held so closely by the approaching column that he could not respond immediately. "Is it them?" she asked again, this time touching his naked back.

"Yes, I think so. It must be." She could hear the breathless sound of fear in his voice. "Get the children. I'll get the truck."

There was only one track into the village. It passed alongside the house and would now be blocked by the column. She thought she could make out at least five, perhaps six sets of headlights, the ones at the back obscured by the dust stirred up by those in front. "Where will we go?"

"Into the bushes; just into the bushes. Get the children."

"They'll see our lights."

For the first time he turned to her. "We'll go without lights. Please, get the children."

All over the village, people were appearing from their houses. Most were women. Some had children in their arms. The boy whose voice Janice had first heard was crying now, loud enough to be heard above the voices of others.

Both children were asleep when Janice reached them. The girl was four and the boy not yet three. They were sharing a bed, their heads at opposite ends. She bent to pick up the boy, but she felt the child inside her move, and shook them both instead. "Wake up—wake up quickly. We have to run away."

She pulled the girl by one arm until the child, not yet fully awake, slipped from the bed, landing gently on her knees. "Mama?" The word came out as a question.

"We have to go. We have to run away."

"Why?" She was slowly wakening. "Where's Papa?"

Outside and below them, Janice thought she heard the sound of their pickup starting. The boy was sitting up now and seemed to be blinking in the darkness. "Come." She dragged them toward the door, the girl in a white ankle-length nightdress and the boy in underpants. "Come, we have to go."

"But my clothes," the girl said.

"You don't need clothes. Come."

She got back to the veranda with the children stumbling sleep-ily next to her, the boy hanging on to her nightdress for support. The column was much closer; more than halfway across the flat ground, the headlights of the back trucks turning the dust of those in front into clouds of light. They were coming fast. They knew that their approach would be heard in the village and that they had to come fast to prevent the villagers escaping.

The veranda was only a few shallow steps above the ground. The boy was holding tightly on to one of his mother's legs, but his sister was moving on her own now. People were running past the front of the house. Janice thought she heard Wally's voice, but she was not sure. It was only as she reached the ground that she realized he was trying to get into the driver's seat, but that the truck was swarming with people. They had filled the back and another three or four had somehow crowded into the front, leaving no room for him to drive. And no room for Janice and the children either. "You can't all . . ." Wally was shouting. "No."

The instinct to protect the children and the child inside her drew her away from the truck and down the side of house. Staying in the cover that the house provided, she moved deeper into the village. She knew that Wally was wrong to be fighting over the truck, but that he had been right about the direction in which to flee. Disappearing into the bushes was the only way to keep them all safe. If she could get only a few hundred meters away from the village and lie down with her children in the long grass, they would not see her. They would have to stumble over her to find her. She would far rather take her chances with the snakes than with the men of the approaching column.

The convoy was moving toward the main track where it went through the center of the village. Janice had taken the rougher path on the other side of the huts. If she moved farther to her right she would be out of the village and the huts would shield her for the moment. The headlights were her enemies. If they fell on her once, she would become a target. The soldiers would see her and probably pursue her. But how far away were they now? How long before they reached the first row of houses where, when she had last seen him, Wally was struggling to get people off the truck?

The girl was running next to her mother now, her eyes open so wide that the whites were visible right round the irises. The boy was stumbling and had to be helped.

"Papa?" Janice heard the girl ask. "Where's Papa? Why isn't he coming?" Her voice sounded even more fearful than Wally's had.

"He's coming in the truck."

"I want to go in the truck too."

"Papa will fetch us."

"When will he fetch us?"

"Run, Katy, just run."

In a moment, as if with the throwing of a switch, the bouncing beams of headlights were lighting up the track in the center of the village. Janice glanced at the girl. In her white nightdress she looked almost luminous in the darkness. She knew that she must also be as conspicuous.

"Give me your dress." She was already pulling it off the child.

"But Mama, I haven't even got pants on!"

"Give it to me."

Janice tore the nightdress away from her daughter and slipped off her own. She rolled the clothes into a tight ball and pressed them into the child's arms. Now they would be much harder to see. "You carry our nightdresses. I need my hands to help you two."

"But everyone can look at us," the girl wailed.

"It doesn't matter. Be quiet now. Don't look back."

As they passed an opening between two houses, Janice saw people in the headlights running up the track. An old man, Mr. Makaleka, wearing a pair of shorts that reached almost to his knees, stumbled and went down in the dirt. Janice suppressed a momentary impulse to go to his aid. The children were more important.

"What about Papa?"

"Be still, child. You must be still."

At that moment Janice heard what she thought was the engine of their truck. It was racing unmercifully. Then she saw it flash between the houses, traveling parallel to them, but much faster. The angle was wrong for her to see who was driving. Perhaps it was Wally. Too many people were pressed into the cab. The frightened faces of those on the back were lit by the headlights of the first vehicle in the approaching column.

Janice stopped, out of breath, in the shadow of a shack made largely of corrugated iron. She was not conscious of the boy wrapping both arms around one of her legs. From her position she could see the first of the personnel carriers as it entered the village. It continued up the main track, engine roaring. Almost immediately, the second vehicle in the convoy came to a halt. Soldiers leaped from the back, their rifles held in both hands, the fixed bayonets flashing in the lights of the next vehicle.

She knew who they were. This was Five Brigade. Everyone knew about them and what they were doing in her part of the country. She had been told that their orders were to crush all dissidents. They were doing it in the most fundamental way. She had heard about their bayonets and the way they used them. The orders by which they functioned demanded that, if the rebel women were pregnant, they were to be killed and their dissident sons with them before they were born.

Could such a thing be true? she had wondered.

The main track through the village was brilliantly lit by now. The driver of each invading vehicle had left his headlights burning after he brought it to a halt. She could see the soldiers, but they were not yet coming in her direction. The first wave, perhaps twenty of them, was moving straight down the track. The rest would probably spread the net wider.

The dense bush was too far away for her to reach it unnoticed. There was only the shed that the young Anglican priest had built. It was twenty or thirty paces away across open ground. But it was an obvious place for someone to hide. On the far side of the shed, the remains of a pigsty, rimmed by light scrub on the near side, were barely visible. It had not been in use since the pigs had sickened and died.

Night sounds that had consisted only of internal combustion engines, the grunting of people running and the occasional crying of a child, changed into something entirely different. The first scream was followed almost immediately by another, and then a third. But there had been no gunshots. They're using the bayonets, Janice thought. They're using them not to waste bullets or to make a noise.

The crash came from beyond the edge of the village. It was in the direction taken by Wally's truck. There were too many crowded into it, she thought, just too many. Why could they not have found their own way? Why did they have to crowd into our truck?

But where was Wally now? Had he been driving?

There was more screaming from the center of the village. The people were not dying quietly.

The pigsty was the only possibility. It meant they would have to cross open ground. They would be in clear sight for a minute, maybe less. If the soldiers' attention was on what they were doing, the chance of them reaching the sty safely was good.

Outrunning anyone was impossible. The very act of running was impossible. The only chance was to walk quickly and carefully to the shelter of the pigsty and then sit down on the nightdresses in the densest possible cover.

Janice carefully unfolded her son's arms where they held her leg. Taking her children by the hand, she stepped into the open. Katy was still holding the nightdresses against her chest. She was running a step ahead, pulling Janice. The screaming from the village had intensified, but Janice tried not to hear it. Let me concentrate only on picking my steps carefully, very carefully, she thought.

The possibility of snakes flitted through her mind, but only for an instant. She looked back for the first time when she reached the light scrub at the edge of the sty. There was no sign of pursuit. She could also see nothing of Wally's truck, but her view was obscured by the nearer huts. She wondered about the time. Dawn would bring light, and perhaps light would not be in her interest. She sank carefully into a crouching position, one arm holding the boy close against her and the other around her distended stomach. She could feel the girl pressing against her on the other side. Perhaps tonight darkness would be her good friend.

2

For an ambitious woman who had risen so fast in the organization that most of her male colleagues felt uncomfortable in her presence, Abigail Bukula was surprisingly unhappy. She felt that recent government decisions that affected her work were both wrong in principle and operationally unsound. She had just spent half an hour explaining her position to the director general of the Department of Justice in which she worked.

"The decision was not yours and it was not mine, Abigail," he had said. "It was made by other people for us to implement. We simply have to abide by it."

"But we were so successful. Everyone says so."

"The media says so."

"But we were."

"Maybe so, but the decision is made."

"Could I speak to the minister?"

The director general sighed. He had been Abigail's senior for not much more than a year, but already he knew her well. "Don't be foolish," he said. "The minister himself is carrying out policy that has been decided in cabinet. You can't debate policy with him. I can't debate policy with him. Even he can't change this."

She had tried to argue the matter further, but he had ended the discussion with: "This is no time to choose the wrong side."

That was where it had ended. As the director general had explained, that was where it had to end.

The arm of the justice system that had been closed was the Directorate of Special Operations, known to the public as the Scorpions. Their cars were black and each bore a large white scorpion on either side. The organization had been made up of both police officers and lawyers. And their success rate had been almost as good as their sense of drama.

They had loved to make arrests in major cases in the bright light of television cameras. Not all heroes of the liberation struggle admired that characteristic, but they seemed to have decided to live with it. It only turned out to be an unforgivable sin when some of those arrested came from their own ranks.

The Scorpions were being replaced by something called the Hawks. In Abigail's view, the leadership of the new body had been carefully chosen, not for their effectiveness, but because they would give their political overlords the least trouble.

For the last year she had served under a talented, but little trusted, senior advocate by the name of Gert Pienaar. He and Abigail had formed a formidable combination. Gert's matchless investigative skills had combined brilliantly with Abigail's singular presence in the courtroom. "I provide the facts and you tear the enemy apart," he had once said to her. She was not sure that she liked the inference that she was the bulldog while he was the brain, but had forgiven him a week later when she heard that he had described her as the finest analytical brain in the country in the field of criminal law.

Pienaar was, in his own words, "a refugee from the old regime," having played an almost identical role in the apartheid government. "There were criminals in those days too," he had told Abigail with a shrug.

The leaders of the new regime had decided that if they wanted to keep some sort of rein on organized crime they had better retain people like him. Now that he, and others like him, had started arresting some of their own members on charges of corruption, they were no longer sure of the wisdom of their decision. "We have given this apartheid spy the chance to attack us," a party functionary had said in a recent speech, and the papers had reported it countrywide.

Damn, Abigail thought, how is it I always get involved with

problem people? Why did he have to be a white Afrikaner and, most especially, why did he have to come from employment in the justice department of the old regime?

She knew that he was a good man. She had met others; men as good, who had stayed in the employ of the old regime right to the end. She had never understood any of them.

Pienaar's sin had been the single-mindedness with which he had gone after the corrupt practices of a certain group of politicians. She had worked next to him for all of twelve months. They had dug through evidence together and she had agreed with all his conclusions. The difference between them was that Pienaar had only seen it as his job, while she had been outraged that people who had been her seniors during the days of the liberation struggle should be behaving in this way. Pienaar had wanted to collect the evidence and pass it on to someone else to handle. She had wanted to prosecute them herself.

"It's different for you," he had said. "You have a history in the struggle."

"This is not about politics," she had told him, admitting later to herself that it was a pretty naïve statement.

If Pienaar had characteristics that would always keep him an outsider, Abigail had a few of her own. Chief among these was the fact that growing up in exile in the United Kingdom had resulted in English being her primary language. She had spent a year in Matabeleland, the province of Zimbabwe's minority Ndebele. Those were the latter years of the apartheid regime and she had not felt safe in her own country. Her time there had given her a knowledge of Zulu that was less than rudimentary. All of the country's other African languages were unintelligible to her. When approaching a group of her colleagues engaged in conversation in one of the vernacular languages, they would switch to English for her benefit. She was grateful for the considerate way she was dealt with, but it also emphasized the differences between them.

She got up to go in search of Pienaar. For a long time, the rumors around the closure of the Scorpions had been threading their insidious way through the passages of the department, some of them even reaching the press. Today, for the first time, it was official. By the time the evening papers were out, the whole country would know it.

Before she reached the door, her phone rang. Johanna, her trusted and irrepressibly curious PA, was on the line. "A call from Zimbabwe."

"Put it through."

"It's a man. He wouldn't tell me who he is."

"Damn it, Johanna. Just put him through."

"I'm putting him through," Johanna said.

There was considerable background noise on the connection. "Abigail Bukula?" The voice reached her across an insecure connection. "Is that Abigail Bukula?"

"Yes, it's me."

"Abigail Bukula of Zimbabwe?"

"No, I'm not a Zimbabwean. I practiced in your country for a year . . ."

"My name is Krisj Patel. I . . ." The voice faded in a shower of static and only returned when the crackling faded. ". . . are hoping you would be able to come to our country to represent them in this matter."

"Mr. Patel, I can barely hear you. I think you want me to represent you in some matter?"

"Not me, my clients. I am Krisj Patel, of Smythe, Patel and Associates, attorneys at law. My clients were hoping . . ." Again the voice faded and the crackling grew, but not for as long this time. "I think we can get a high court injunction to have them released."

"And you said you are . . ." Abigail was writing it down.

"Krisj Patel of Smythe, Patel and Associates."

"You're the Patel of Smythe, Patel and . . ."

". . . Associates," he said. "Yes, I am. Will you call me Krisj?" he asked. "People here are proud . . ." Again the voice was gone. When it came back, she heard him say, ". . . your cousin. So we thought you may want to help . . ."

"My cousin?"

"Tony Makumbe. As I understand it, he's your Aunt Janice's child."

"No, she had a daughter."

"She also had a son."

"Mr. Patel, I don't think . . ."

"He's one of the seven dissidents. Our people . . ." Again the crackling rose, but the phone went dead, even the crackling disappeared. Abigail waited a few minutes for him to call again, but the phone remained silent. Mr. Patel was wrong about everything. As far as she knew, her Aunt Janice only had a daughter. In any event, she had no doubt that Patel could find an advocate in his own country. And the closing down of the Scorpions was, to her, a matter of far greater importance.

Usually, when Abigail left the building, she had Johanna send an e-mail to both Pienaar and the director general to keep them informed of her whereabouts. This time she walked past Johanna without responding to her question: "Is it true about the Scorpions?" The offices of the department were just too damned constricting this afternoon.

Abigail was a good-looking woman, a little above average height, with the leanness and easy stride of an athlete. Most men, when seeing her for the first time, took special interest. Her African curls were cropped close to her head. Time spent at the hairdresser was, in her view, time lost.

She was wearing a lavender-gray trouser suit, relieved only by an inexpensive turquoise brooch. Robert had given her many presents of jewelry that she felt were far too expensive. And this was neither the town nor the country in which it was wise to flash high-priced baubles. Robert's paper had recently carried an incident in which a woman had lost a ring on which a large imitation diamond was mounted—and her finger along with it. It seemed that a pair of garden shears had been used. The result had not been a neat cut.

Abigail's own diamonds stayed safely in the bank's safe deposit box, only to be used two or three times a year for various state banquets. The only three skirts she possessed were part of the evening wear she had reluctantly invested in for those occasions.

Robert's office was only a few blocks away, but Abigail took her 7-series BMW. It was something else Robert had insisted on paying for. She was not intending to return that afternoon.

The security man at the basement parking in his building recognized her immediately and opened the boom to let her in. She brought the car to a stop in the parking space Robert had reserved for the odd occasion when she visited him.

In the lift on the way to the top floor, two people, whom she was certain she had never seen before, greeted her with "Good afternoon, ma'am."

The top floor of the building held only Robert's office, that of the chairman, the deputy chairman, the financial director, the marketing director, the human resources director and the editor of the group's major weekly, together with their personal assistants, of course. Before Abigail's first visit to the building, she had heard what she thought were exaggerated stories of corporate extravagance—that on the executive floor the pile carpet was so deep you had to wade through it. It was only when she visited Robert for the first time that she realized her husband's office was inherently a subject for satire. And the carpet really was so heavy that it slowed you down.

Until this moment, Abigail had not seen Robert's new PA. She would have been a surprise to most wives. It was not just the long blond hair, the milky-white complexion, the neckline that allowed her boss a view of just enough breast to keep him interested, the petite waist, the trim legs and tiny feet that fitted into stiletto-heeled shoes—the kind that showed both the toes and the heels, narrow leather bands encasing each ankle. Abigail was sure she had read somewhere that women who wore such shoes were on the hunt. It was not just the PA's appearance, though. As she came round the desk, a question in her eyes, Abigail saw something insufferably confident in them. If these offices were the caricature of corporate splendor, this girl was the caricature of the trophy PA.

How did we come to this? she asked herself; our ostentatious cars, our ridiculous home with its acres of garden, three entertainment lounges and five bedrooms—for two people. And now this PA . . . worst of all, this PA. And to run into her today, after what she had already been through. On what did Robert base his hiring criteria? she wondered. Pictures in *Cosmopolitan*? More likely, *Playboy*.

Something had brightened in the PA's face. "Oh, you must be Mrs. Mokoapi?"

Mokoapi was Robert's surname. Abigail had never adopted it. "I'm Abigail Bukula," Abigail said. "Is my husband here?"

To Abigail's satisfaction, the clear white skin deepened till it reached a full pink around the eyes and in patches on the neck. "I'm sorry, Mrs. . . ." She was visibly casting around in her mind. Clearly, Mrs. Bukula was not going to work either. "May I call you Abigail?" she asked.

But Abigail had not yet finished with the PA, she of the neat little white breasts peeping out at Abigail's husband. "Ms. Bukula will do," she said. "Where is my husband?"

"Robert is . . ." she started, but stopped immediately. "Mr. Mokoapi is in a meeting with the chairman and some of the institutional investors. They should have been out already."

"Tell him his wife was here." As she turned to go, another thought, or perhaps just a barb, came to her. "Tell him also that I'd appreciate him being home on time tonight."

"Yes, Mrs. . . . Ms. Bukula."

Abigail stopped in the doorway of the office and looked back at the still pink face of the PA. For the first time she realized that the kid was no more than twenty-two or twenty-three. Jesus, Robert, she thought, what were you thinking? What part of your body were you thinking with?

3

The gates of Abigail and Robert's home opened at the touch of a button. The house was set back perhaps fifty paces into a garden that required two gardeners to keep it in trim. Abigail had tried to persuade Robert that neither a property that size, nor a house that magnificent, were necessary, but he had said the company expected it. If you were the beneficiary of an empowerment deal of this size, the company expected you to behave that way. What sort of impression would it make if the CEO lived in an ordinary town house? Where would he entertain clients and investors?

She still felt the same, but Abigail admitted both to herself and to Robert that she loved the garden. There was a beautiful lawn kids could play on, if there ever were going to be kids. There were summer seats in cool shady corners, hooks for a hammock, also in the shade, a spot in one corner that was sheltered from any wind but caught the winter sun for most of the day. She loved the flowers, the trees, the ponds with their frogs and crickets, and the birds that visited daily. She loved them not because they were hers, but because they were beautiful and they were alive.

The house too, needed two servants, both of whom had soon learned that the fact that they shared skin color with the madam did not mean that they were going to get away with anything. To Abigail it was not a family relationship. They were well paid by the standards of the city in which they lived, their hours were reasonable and they were expected to work well. The first one to overstep her boundaries by extending three consecutive weekends by an extra day each, without permission or satisfactory reason, had been fired, bringing home the nature of the relationship to the others. They, in turn, would have passed on the news to the replacement. Since then, Abigail had no real staff problems.

She poured herself a glass of fruit juice and sat down in her favorite recliner on the patio. From where she was sitting, she had a view of the drive so that she would see Robert's car when the gate opened. She could also see much of the garden where the two gardeners were busy closing up for the day. They were packing their implements onto the wheelbarrow to take them to the garden shed.

The worst thing about this huge house was being in it without Robert. When he was at home its absurd spaces did not seem that ridiculous. She hated being alone in the house, even if it was just for an afternoon. Very often she escaped into the garden or onto the patio on such days.

Abigail was a reader. She read novels, poetry, books about famous people and infamous ones, historical texts, wildlife studies, law reviews, case histories and newspapers. The newspapers she read were mostly those published by Vuna Corp., Robert's company.

She had brought a book of Robert Frost's poems out to the patio, but this afternoon the words made no sense. The picture of Robert's so-called personal assistant rose in her mind, but she dismissed it. Worrying about this kid was foolishness.

The other matter was not. Oh God, she thought, how could they do this? She knew that this was not just an objective assessment. The liberation struggle, in which both her parents had died, had been intensely personal for her. Now, she felt, its legacy was being sullied. In the Scorpions they had created a crime-fighting force that, Abigail believed, was second to none anywhere in the world. They had delivered leaders of organized crime to the asset forfeiture unit, where the criminals had lost their ill-gotten fortunes. More than three-quarters of their cases had been successfully prosecuted. But then they had started to root out corruption in the state machinery. And, seemingly, that had been unforgivable.

Abigail put aside Frost's poems and took up the afternoon

paper. The front-page story was about the end of the Scorpions. Her eyes flicked across the columns, taking in the broad outline of the article. Opposition politicians were quoted as saying that this was a sure sign that government had no interest in bringing down the high crime rate. No spokesperson for either the Department of Justice, which was losing a division, or the police, which was gaining one, were available for comment at the time of going to press. A table compared the Scorpions' excellent record to the relatively poor one of the regular police. In a sidebar, a criminologist she had never heard of compared the Scorpions to the FBI, coming to the conclusion that they were in the same category.

As she turned to page two, her cell phone rang. The voice on the other end told her that the caller was Sipho Dabengwa of the *Sunday World*. Abigail switched off her phone and went back to the newspaper.

It was on page five that she saw a story that she did read carefully. The headline read "Seven Zimbabwean Dissidents Still Missing." Krisj Patel had managed to get in something about seven dissidents before the lines had gone down. This seemed to be his reason for calling her.

Abigail knew Zimbabwe well and loved it more than any place other than her own country, having lived there for a little more than a year, before the first democratic election made it possible for her to come home. She knew as much as any outsider about the Zimbabwean people's struggle for their own democracy. Power was now being shared between the old dictator who had reduced the country to ruins, and the popular leader who, everyone hoped, despite the handicap of an unequal coalition, might have the strength and will to rebuild it.

According to the article, a few days earlier seven dissidents who had been particularly active before the power-sharing deal came into effect, had been picked up by the Central Intelligence Organization. She understood this body to be the political police that had often, during the previous twenty-nine years, been accused of providing violent solutions to the ruling party's political problems.

The head of the CIO was quoted in the article as saying that the whole thing was a vicious slander; that they had not touched the seven in question. Even a representative of the popular co-leader had said that it was possible that the seven had left the country. One of the dissidents, who had asked not to be named, had said: "They were picked up by the CIO. We have witnesses to the arrests. The agents who arrested them are known to us."

Abigail closed her eyes and lowered the newspaper till it came to rest over her face. Oh, my Africa, she thought. I'd hoped we were getting past this sort of thing.

It was almost dark when she was woken by Robert's hand on her shoulder. He was bending over her. "Don't sleep out here," he was saying. "Let's go inside."

"Oh, you're here." She scrambled to her feet and into Robert's arms. "Thank God you're here."

"Sorry about the Scorpions," he said.

"Oh, Robert, what are they doing?"

"Let's go inside," he said. "It'll soon be cold."

4

Given the chance, Abigail was quick to tell others that she was never late for work. And her boast was close to being true. She was almost always first into the office. Being at her desk an hour or two before the others arrived gave her a chance to assemble her thoughts and her documentation for the day ahead. On the other hand, if she did come late, she seemed to be trying all day to catch up.

This morning she was late though, not just five or ten minutes, but almost forty. The powerful drive that comes with having a purpose had deserted her. She had been up too late the previous evening, arguing with Robert about the problem of working for an organization she did not believe in.

As soon as she passed the open door of Johanna's office, she knew that something had happened to disturb her loyal assistant. Johanna was on her feet in a moment, her hands massaging each other in the way she had in times of crisis. "Gert's been arrested," she said.

"Arrested? What the hell are you talking about?"

The anxiety in Johanna's face was so intense that she might have been the one who had been arrested. "The police were here; a lot of them, ten minutes ago. They took him away."

"Where to?"

"I don't know. There were plenty of them. I saw one body-search him, right up between his legs. Then they marched him away, three or four in front and three or four behind. But I demanded to know what they were doing. I went right up to the head one and said, "What do you think you're doing?" It was a habit of Johanna's, when retelling an incident, to spend far more time on what she had done or said than on the other parties involved.

"So what did they say to that?" Abigail wanted to know.

"They said I should mind my business and go back to my work."

"Sound advice," Abigail said.

"But I didn't let them get away with that. I told them when my boss, Abigail Bukula, got back they would be in trouble."

"Thank you, Johanna, but I'd rather you didn't try to build my reputation in quite that way."

"But you should have seen them. The one behind even pushed Gert as they went to the lift."

"I can't believe it," Abigail muttered. Seeing Johanna's crestfallen look, she corrected herself. "Coming from you, I know it's true, but I still have difficulty believing it." She was already on her way down the passage in the direction of the director general's office.

The director general's PA reacted as if she had been expecting Abigail's storming entrance. "He's not here," she said, as she rose from her chair. "He's out, holding high-level . . ."

But Abigail was already past her and had thrown open the door to the director general's office. One step into the office revealed that it was indeed empty. The PA, a middle-aged woman of Indian extraction, had not moved from behind her desk. "Abigail, I told you he's not there," she said. "I'm not one of those who lie about such things. You should know that by now."

"Where is he?"

"I believe he's with the minister of police, trying to negotiate for Gert's release."

"Negotiate?" Abigail said the word as if it had just developed a repulsive new meaning. "You don't negotiate for the release of innocent people. You demand it."

"I'm just telling you what my boss told me."

Abigail studied the other woman's face for a moment longer, then turned abruptly to leave.

"Wait. The minister is, in any event, the right one to deal with this," she called after Abigail. "He's gone to the same meeting. There's no point in trying to see the DG." Abigail had stopped in the doorway. "It's true. They're trying to free Gert."

Abigail passed Johanna without saying anything. "What did they say?" Johanna was following close behind her.

"They say the minister and the DG are talking to the police."

"But why . . . ?"

Abigail waved her away. "Johanna, I don't know the answer to any of these questions. Don't ask me. And I want no calls this morning. None. Do you understand?"

Johanna retreated, closing the door behind her. After working with Abigail for some years, she knew when avoiding her boss was the best course of action.

Abigail hated the feeling of helplessness. She was not one to let the winds of fate decide her course. She felt that she was in charge of her own destiny and was determined to have an effect, wherever it was needed, on the destinies of everyone who crossed her path. And this was one of those occasions. She could not bear the thought that the DG and the minister were going to pretend to be defending the rights of one of their senior officers, arguably their best officer. Neither man, in her opinion, possessed the inclination to stand up to those in authority on matters of principle, or any other sort of matter.

She thought of calling Freek Jordaan, the deputy commissioner of police for the province, who had had helped her in the past. When she had first been given the job as Gert's junior, she had asked Freek for his opinion of her new boss. She remembered that Freek had thought about it for a while before answering. Eventually he had said: "You have to understand that in the old days I often had problems with the system, but Gert seemed to be all right with it. He seemed to like prosecuting, as long as he was prosecuting some wrongdoer. The system never seemed to matter to him."

"I don't think he's that uncomplicated," she had told Freek.

Working had become almost impossible. And if Gert was vulnerable, who else was? There were other staffers, including herself, working on the same set of cases. Or will my party membership card protect me? she wondered. And is that the sort of protection I want? Thank God for Robert, she thought. He was the rock she had always been able to rely on. For the moment, she had forgotten the petite, blond PA.

They had pushed Gert as they went toward the lift, Johanna

had said. She got to her feet so suddenly that her chair crashed to the floor. Before she reached the door, Johanna had opened it. "What happened?" It was a standard Johanna question. Just as she loved to recount her role in any crisis, she always had to know what was happening.

"It was my chair."

"Is it broken?"

Abigail took her by the arm. "Forget the chair, Johanna. You mind the shop. I'm going out."

"Where to?"

Abigail stopped and looked at her. There were times that the younger woman's insistence on being informed was a little too much for her. But this was not one of those times, she told herself, not with everything that was happening around them. "Police headquarters," she said.

"Should you?" Johanna's eyes had grown to twice their normal size.

"Do I only do what I should? Do you know me that way?"

"No," Johanna said. "But the DG won't like it."

"Never mind the DG. I'll probably be back in an hour or so."

"What if Mr. Patel from Zimbabwe phones again?"

"Tell him he's wrong. Tell him I have no male cousin in his country."

5

Freek Jordaan would usually have been pleased to see Abigail. This was not the case today. He had cursed silently when he heard she was downstairs in reception, but sent for her immediately. When she entered his office, she was wearing that superficially restrained, determined look he knew well.

Christ, she looked fabulous, Freek acknowledged. He found it interesting that in the days of apartheid South Africa he had never found any black woman attractive, but now there were some who could stop him in his tracks.

"Abby, I'm delighted to see you, but to what do I owe the pleasure?" Now that he saw her in front of him, the question held more pleasure than irritation.

"As if you don't know."

"Of course I know. Come any time, but right now you can do nothing. After forty-eight hours, Gert Pienaar has to be either charged or released."

"I just came to deliver a message," Abigail said.

"A message?" They were still standing, Freek still considering whether the pleasure of her company was worth the accompanying aggravation. "Your presence here is a message to everyone in the building. You won't be out of the door before the national commissioner will want me to explain what you were doing in my office on this day of all possible days."

Abigail ignored Freek's speech. "I want you to tell everyone all day that, if Gert is not out of here in twenty-four hours, I'll be seeking an urgent interdict against the minister of police."

"You want me to tell everyone that. Why?" Freek waved her to a seat. He had given up the idea of being rid of her soon. "Sit down, you foolish woman," he said.

"I want the minister to know what sort of fight he's going to be involved in."

"And what will your minister say about it?"

"I'm an officer of the court. I don't need his permission."

"Yes, you are an officer of the court," Freek said. "But you are also an employee of the government. Even I can see that there's a conflict of interest there." She had accepted the offered seat and was looking steadily into his eyes. Seeing her this way, as he had on other occasions in the past, Freek thought she was magnificent. He had no doubt that she would try to do what she threatened to. "Don't do this, Abigail," he said. "It just won't fly, not with you representing Gert." They were seated at a round table in a corner of Freek's spacious office. "Tea or coffee?" he asked gently.

"Coffee will do. Thank you."

Freek crossed the room and opened the door into the passage. Five senior officers were scattered along the length of the passage, all looking in the direction of his office. "Thank you, gentlemen," he said. "I'm sure you all have work to do." Then he raised his voice half-a-dozen decibels. "Miss Mofokeng!" He had spotted the tea lady peeping out from her cubicle. "I have a guest. Coffee please." When the passage had been emptied, Miss Mofokeng to make the coffee and the officers to phone other officers, no doubt to tell them who was visiting Deputy Commissioner Jordaan, he returned to Abigail.

"Gentlemen, I'm sure you all have work to do?" Abigail asked, as Freek sat down. "How many gentlemen were there?"

"Enough to spread the word through this building in the next ten minutes. Your minister will know about your visit to me before you get back to the office."

For the first time since arriving in Freek's office, Abigail both looked and felt apologetic. "I've embarrassed you," she said.

"Your timing could have been better."

"Will you forgive me?"

He looked at the smooth skin of her face, more like that of a twenty-year-old than a woman in her late thirties, the trim figure and the natural poise. "There's nothing to forgive," he said, acknowledging to himself that this may not be altogether true. "I will tell everyone that you came here to protest Gert's arrest, no more than that," he said. "I will even tell the national commissioner himself."

"Thank you, Deputy Commissioner," she said sweetly.

When she got back to the office, Abigail was relieved to find that both the minister and the director general were out for the afternoon. She had been careful not to advertise her presence, taking the longer route to her office and coming up the fire escape from the floor below. That way she did not pass the door of either the minister, the director general or the deputy director general.

The tactic was not perfect. A message from the deputy director general was waiting for her on Johanna's desk, a politely worded order to see him as soon as she came in. But Abigail reasoned that as an officer in the Scorpions she did not report to him yet, and that although that agency had been disbanded, she had not yet been redeployed. She could argue that there was no reason to believe that she was obliged to report to him now. He phoned once during the afternoon to see if she was in, but Johanna told him only that Abigail had gone to police headquarters that morning.

One message Johanna did pass on correctly came from Krisj Patel. He had eventually gotten through on a better line and left his number, asking that Abigail call back.

He answered on the first ring. "Smythe, Patel and Associates." This time the connection was good.

The boss operating the switchboard? Abigail wondered. "Krisj," she said, "Abigail Bukula here. You've been trying to reach me again."

"Oh, Abigail, I'm so glad I found you. May I call you Abigail?"

"Of course, but I . . ."

Patel, who sounded more like an English schoolteacher than an Indian settler in Africa, was eager to tell his story before listening to objections. "I've been phoning one number after the other for two days, trying to track you down. I tried the Law Society, a few law schools and almost everyone else I could think of."

Abigail interrupted him. "My mother told me that my aunt was killed by soldiers of Five Brigade during the Gukurahundi massacres. She had a daughter. I don't know what became of her husband and daughter. But you're wrong about there having been a son. My mother never mentioned a son."

"Perhaps she knew nothing about him," said Patel. "I believe that Tony Makumbe is your cousin, and he is one of those abducted on Tuesday night. And he is such a talented boy, a writer of international potential. My clients hoped . . ."

Abigail had heard enough. "Mr. Patel . . . Krisj . . . there are two issues here. First, I am not in private practice. I am a government prosecutor and therefore not free to take on private work."

"Oh." Patel was silent, probably looking for a way round this new revelation. "Apparently you were in private practice while you were here in Zimbabwe."

"That was fifteen years ago. I'm sorry, Krisj. And second, you're wrong about the family connection."

"I don't think so." Patel, it seemed, was as persistent as Abigail herself. "We know the woman who brought up the children of Janice Makumbe. And we know that Janice died in the Gukurahundi killings in 1982, as you said, in a village called Bizana, near Plumtree in Matabeleland. Her husband was a man called Wally. He was also killed. Two children survived, a girl called Katy and a boy called Anthony."

It was Abigail's turn to be surprised into silence. The names of her aunt and uncle were correct. Long before, she had heard the name of the village. Patel had that right too.

"I'm sure they're your family." He had sensed a weakness in her defenses. "They need you now."

"Don't try that emotional blackmail on me. It won't work."

"No, I meant . . ."

"Listen, you have plenty of advocates in Zimbabwe. Use one of them." Abigail was angry. The problem, she knew, was that his emotional blackmail was already working.

"The good ones won't touch it. The pro-government ones don't dare upset their bosses. That's not surprising, I suppose. But the opposition is in a coalition with the regime now. They also don't want to upset the government. They say that maybe the seven just fled the country. But we know they were taken by the CIO, the Central Intelligence Organization. You may have heard of them?"

"Yes."

"Well, they took them. The only advocates we can get are either scared or useless . . ."

". . . or both," Abigail added thoughtfully.

"Exactly, exactly," Patel said. "They're both scared and useless and they require lots of money, in American dollars."

So this is strictly pro bono, Abigail told herself. And the real problem is one of payment.

"And we've heard about your reputation. I am sure with your help we can get the government to hand them over to us."

Abigail knew there was no point in the conversation continuing. "Whatever the truth, I am not a free operator. I am in full-time employment. I work for a salary. I'm sorry."

"Will you think about it?"

"No, Mr. Patel." The more formal note seemed appropriate now. "You're not listening to me. The conditions of my employment don't allow me to think about it. I'm sorry."

"Before you go, before you go . . ." His voice for the first time took on an anxious tone. "It is so important. Those young people were just taken away. If we don't act, they may never be seen again. You don't know what our prisons are like, especially Chikurubi, where they are. And Tony's not strong."

6

Abigail waited twenty minutes after the usual knock-off time. She told herself that this way she avoided the possibility of being killed in the afternoon stampede out of the building. But, more important, she would avoid running into the deputy director general who usually led the four-thirty charge.

Robert was not at home when she got there. That was not unusual. She was tired, with a tiredness of the soul that had overcome her with the arrest of Gert Pienaar and the disappearance of seven apparently young dissidents in a country she knew and loved. And what about Katy and Tony . . . her cousins, according to Krisj Patel? Her mother had told her about Janice and Janice's daughter. If Patel was even halfway right, that would have been Katy. But Tony was news to her. Her mother had never spoken about him.

She went upstairs to the master bedroom she shared with Robert and lay down. It made no difference what Patel said. And, as for the fuss she may have caused in police headquarters this morning, that probably made no difference either. The newspaper had been delivered, but she had left it downstairs. She wanted to read no more speculation about Gert Pienaar and no more reporting on the Harare Seven, as the media had started calling them.

She had lived in Zimbabwe for half a year before she heard about the Gukurahundi killings for the first time. A Ndebele woman who had been crippled in one of Five Brigade's attacks had told her what had happened in their village. In the months that followed she learned that the incident the woman had told her about had been one of many. Very few people of the Shona majority had ever agreed to talk about it. Only a few admitted even hearing about it. Everything she had learned had been from the Ndebele victims.

She had worked hard during her year in Harare. The signs that the country was coming apart were already visible. The leader was becoming increasingly paranoid and seemed to have convinced himself that he was the only answer to Zimbabwe's problems. Already his policies of political patronage disguised as Marxism were resulting in the country's economy shrinking by the year.

Apart from an ordinary caseload, Abigail had agreed to take two pro bono cases of political dissidents who had been disabled under the CIO's torture. One had a leg that had been damaged by CIO agents. Doctors had never been able to repair it fully, and now he had to wear calipers to walk at all. The other, a woman who had led resistance to the government in one of their strongholds, had developed a respiratory problem after a month in which she had been held under water too long and too often. Abigail had won substantial compensation for her clients in both cases, but the government had simply ignored the court orders and her clients had never received their money. The woman whose lungs were damaged had died the next year, and she had lost contact with the man.

She allowed her eyes to close. The thoughts blurred in her mind, and the troubled face of a young man she had never met rose and hung expressionless before her.

Her consciousness had just started to dissolve into warm but troubled oblivion when the phone rang next to the bed. She did not recognize the voice of the woman on the other end of the line.

"Abigail Bukula?"

"Yes," she murmured, not yet fully awake.

"I'm a friend, someone with your best interests at heart."

Abigail heard only hypocrisy in the voice. "Who is this?"

"My name is not important. I'm phoning as a friend."

Abigail already knew what the anonymous voice was going to tell her. Almost every part of her soul screamed at her to hang up. Only a few traitorous corners of her mind kept her listening. Her imagination had already raised the image of Robert's gorgeous, pinkly blushing little PA. "What do you want?" she heard herself ask.

"I don't want anything from you. I just want to tell you something you should know."

"And what would that be?" her voice said into the mouthpiece. Stop, the wise part of her was saying. Hang up and unplug the phone.

"First, I'd like to ask you if you know where your husband is at this moment. And if you know where that sweet little secretary of his is, and what they're doing."

It had become impossible to respond in any way. She could also not hang up. She could only listen.

"Perhaps you know the Sheraton, the one right opposite the Union Buildings. They have such comfortable suites there. I understand the mattresses are very soft." A pause was followed by a question in the same soft, gently destructive voice. "You are still there, aren't you, Abigail?" Again a pause to allow her the chance to answer. "I believe you are. I can hear your breathing. It seems to have become heavier in the last few minutes. I hope it has nothing to do with what I'm telling you."

Jesus, Robert, Abigail was thinking—not this, and not today. Please, not today.

"They booked in just about half an hour ago. I don't know what name they used. They've probably had enough time to get it done by now, don't you think?"

At last Abigail hung up. In almost the same movement she unplugged the phone. She was sitting on the edge of the bed now, dry-eyed, her face expressionless. There had been little love-making in the last three or four months, maybe even six. Christ, Robert, was this the reason? She was still in the same position when, almost two hours later, she heard Robert's car come up the drive.

She went down the stairs carefully, a hand on the banister for support. She needed to be downstairs when he arrived. The thought of waiting in the bedroom for perhaps an hour while he poured himself a drink and sampled the cook's gammon steak dinner could not be entertained. She needed to know, and she needed to know now. She was in the hall when he came through the front door.

Abigail had not planned it, but she moved quickly into his arms, her arms around him and her face pressed against his shirt. Her eyes found what she would rather not have seen, a dark smudge in the area of his shirt pocket, just at the right height to be mascara.

She broke away from him, till she was almost the width of the room away. The surprise that showed on his face when she rushed into his arms had doubled with her sudden retreat. "Abby?"

"Is it true?" she demanded. "Were you in the Sheraton tonight with that woman?"

"What are you talking about?"

She could not decide whether the bewilderment in his face was that of innocence or guilt discovered.

"You know damned well what I'm talking about. Were you in the Sheraton with that blond kid from your office?"

"Don't be absurd."

"Don't tell me how to be. Just tell me. Were you in the Sheraton this evening?"

Robert was looking straight into her eyes. He was speaking, and she had to listen carefully to hear him through the haze of her anger. There was sound but she struggled to make sense of it.

"This is ridiculous. Of course, I was in the Sheraton. I told you last night that those Australians are here. I was with them, so was my PA and so were the chairman and Pete and Kgomotso. But you knew about it."

The mark on his shirt was just visible where his suit jacket hung open. "What's that mark on your shirt?"

"On my shirt?" He looked down, then threw off his jacket in irritation. "Oh Christ, look at this." The expensive pen she had bought him was in his pocket and, as he drew it out, the nib was sticky with heavy black ink where it had leaked. "Jesus, look at this mess."

There was now no doubting the reality of his reaction. This was no performance. "Oh, Robert," she said. "I'm such a fool."

He looked up from the ruined shirt and waved a dismissive hand. "It's okay. Listen, that girl, she's a temp. I wouldn't hire that little cotton-wool brain as my PA. What do you take me for?"

"Did you eat?"

"No. I'm hungry as hell."

"Let's eat then. Bintu's food looks good tonight."

And so it was over. She had received a call from a troublemaker and had fallen right into the trap and attacked Robert, who had never given her any reason for doubt. But, on the other hand, it was not over. Robert had been there, and the chairman and Pete and Kgomotso and Robert's PA. No other PAs seemed to have been at the meeting with the Australians, only Robert's cotton-wool-brained temp. Or were the other PAs present? She almost asked Robert, but succeeded in restraining herself.

That night, once again, they slept without making love. Robert got into bed half an hour after she had. She was reading, and did not look up from her book as he slipped in between the sheets. For his part, he rolled onto his side, faced away from her and was asleep in a few minutes.

Before they came to bed, Abigail had noticed that he looked tired. Despite herself, she could not help wondering if the tiredness was the result of a tough day at the office or vigorous exercise in one of the Sheraton's bedrooms. She could always call Pete or Kgomotso about the meeting and, if they confirmed that there had been such a meeting, she could ask them about which PAs had attended. But would they tell? Men closed ranks, she had heard. They covered for each other. Other women had warned her that men never ratted on each other, because they knew that some other day they would be needing the support of the one who was in trouble.

What the hell am I thinking? Abigail asked herself. That was not Robert. That had never been Robert. Let me not direct my anger at my husband. He is not the one who has arrested an innocent man. It makes no sense to exercise my anger on him.

And that damned smudge had turned out to be ink, not mascara.

She put down her book and turned away from Robert. She had not mentioned Krisj Patel's call and his insistence that a cousin of hers, one whom as far as she knew did not exist, had fallen into the hands of Zimbabwe's CIO. She had also not told him about Gert Pienaar and what the police were putting him through. She felt ashamed that the matter of the PA and the Sheraton had been more urgent.

I will not be able to sleep tonight, she thought, not with all this keeping me awake. But she was wrong about that. On this night, her consciousness sought rather to escape it all. Soon she was asleep.

7

Seventy-two hours had passed, twenty-four more than the law allowed, and the police were still holding Gert Pienaar. The weekend had been of the sort that people usually refer to as a nightmare. Abigail had spent Sunday with senior counsel at her own expense. The next morning she ignored two messages from the director general to see him in his office. "He should be doing what I'm doing," she had said to Johanna. "Screw him."

"Not me," Johanna had said.

"Not you what?"

"Not me. I'm not going to screw him."

For a moment Johanna had managed to dissipate the tension that surrounded the Gert Pienaar matter. They clung to each other, laughing at the thought of Johanna screwing the director general. He was not a man either would ever have thought of in those terms.

By nine o'clock though, a message came from the minister himself. Brought down by one of his assistants, it said simply, "Be in my office in five minutes."

"Nomsa brought the message," Johanna told her. "He wants to see you alone."

"Alone?" Abigail tried not to let her relief show.

"The DG won't be there. That's what she said."

Nomsa's information had been accurate. The minister was alone when she entered his office. Because he was new to the post, Abigail knew little about him. She did know that he was a stalwart of the party from the days of the liberation struggle. Like so many of the present leadership, he had been a political prisoner on Robben Island. In his case, the sentence had been ten years for smuggling young party members out of the country to join the liberation army. He had the reputation of being one of the hardest-working cabinet ministers, and also a great football-lover. On the side of his office farthest from his desk was one of the standard, government-issue round tables for meetings. But this time he remained seated behind the broad oak desk where he did his work. He gestured for Abigail to sit down opposite him.

He seemed to be examining every shade of expression on her face, but said nothing for a period that was far too long for Abigail's comfort. As for her, she had decided to follow Robert's advice: restraint and control would be more likely to work in her favor than her usual frontal attack.

"Good morning, Abigail," the minister said at last.

"Good morning, sir."

"You've been very busy lately."

"Yes, sir." There was much else she wanted to tell him, in fact, was determined to tell him. But stay away from the rapid-fire onslaught, she warned herself. Slow and rational will yield better results.

"Not all of it in the service of this department, I believe."

"That depends on how you look at it," Abigail said. The self-restraint tactic was becoming increasingly difficult to implement.

"How do you look at it?" he asked.

Could it be, Abigail thought, that there's the slightest smile somewhere in that stern countenance? "I look at it that a colleague of mine was taken into police custody for no real reason and I am trying to do something about it."

"You are?"

This was the moment, and no, there was no smile. "Yes, I am."

"Defending your colleague?"

"Yes, sir."

"Your colleague, and my staff member."

"Yes, your staff member." Abigail was aware that she was nodding emphatically.

"And you don't think you could have trusted me with the matter?"

"Well, of course, but . . ." Her explanation had nowhere to go. The truth was that she did not trust him with the matter.

"You know that there's nothing I could do for the first forty-eight hours. But you started talking to outside counsel yesterday, I believe."

All of that was true, but he was missing the main issue. "I know, Mr. Minister, but now seventy-two hours have passed since they picked him up."

"That's true." The minister nodded slowly, seeming to concede the point.

"And so?" Abigail demanded. "Where is he?"

"In his office," the minister said. "They did hold him too long, and I have sent the Minister of Police a written objection."

Abigail had looked in at Pienaar's office an hour earlier and it had been empty. Now it was difficult to say anything at all.

"Would you like to go down the passage to check on the accuracy of that statement before we continue?" he asked gently.

"No, Mr. Minister, of course not." The relief brought on by the knowledge that Pienaar had been released was competing with the humiliation caused by the feeling, perhaps the certainty, that she had acted in a way that revealed her reservations about the workings of the system and the effectiveness of the minister himself. She was, after all, a senior executive of the government and a card-carrying member of the party.

The minister looked searchingly at her the way he had when she first entered the office and, again, too long for her comfort. "Would you like coffee?"

"Strong and black," she said.

"Like some of my staff members," he said, and this time he did smile. After he had called his PA to order the coffee, he again gave his attention to Abigail. "When I was deployed to this position, I was told that in you I had my most talented staff member, but also the one least amenable to discipline."

Abigail breathed in deeply. The moment to tell the minister what had been driving her actions over the past two days had come. "It's not a matter of discipline," she said.

"What is it a matter of, then? Tell me."

"It's a matter of justice." She was ready to let it all flow out at last. The flow of words came out quickly and emphatically. "Gert Pienaar has served this government well. You have a no more diligent staff member. If some of his investigations embarrassed certain senior people, it is only because they have something to hide. I will stake my life on the fact that he is guilty of nothing. He is also a white Afrikaner. His being taken in for questioning for seventy-two hours by some of the very people he was investigating gives the impression of justice being ignored and a racist element creeping into our actions. The whole matter was simply not right. And it all comes on the back of their closing down our unit, the most successful in the history of crime-fighting in this country. And the first thing they do after closing us down is to start taking us into custody."

"Is that it?" the minister asked.

"In essence." So, now that you know how unrepentant I am, tell me my fate and get it over with, she thought.

The minister took off the glasses that he usually wore indoors, wiped the lenses on his tie, and laid them down on the desk in front of him. "I share your concerns," he said. Sensing the possibility that she was not finished, he raised a hand to ward off another Abigail broadside. "The unit you have been working in has been closed, it's true. But criminal justice has not ended with it . . ."

"But, Mr. Minister . . ."

The forbidding hand was still raised. "No. I have listened to you. Now, you listen to me." He waited until he was sure that Abigail was ready to listen. "The Scorpions are dead, but the Hawks are alive. I am offering you a deputy director general position in the new organization. It's a well-earned promotion. You deserve it."

For someone who had expected to be disciplined, perhaps even demoted, the minister's offering her a promotion and telling her that she deserved it was enough to upset her equilibrium. And Abigail was ambitious. The idea that she would, before the age of forty, be one step away from heading a government department was a powerful temptation. But, for her, it was not that simple. "And Gert?" she asked.

"The department's negotiations with another employee are simply not your business."

She would not be that easily diverted. "But are you offering him a post?"

"I will tell you that, but only once I have discussed it with him."

Abigail wanted the promotion more than anything, except perhaps faithfulness from Robert. And she was afraid that her desire was probably obvious to the minister. "I'll have to think it over, Mr. Minister," she said.

Every trace of friendliness had left his face when he spoke again. "I'm afraid it's this or nothing."

"I understand."

"There's one more thing. If you accept, and I hope you do, I am giving you a six-month sabbatical."

"Six months? But I haven't earned it."

"I'll tell you the truth. The restructuring of the Scorpions into the Directorate of Priority Crimes, or the Hawks, as people are calling it, is going to be a delicate affair. I want you on leave while I do it. After your activities of the last seventy-two hours, I need you out of the picture for a while. After that, you can return, with my blessing. And remember, the new body is probably going to fall under the Minister of Police, not me." Again that searching look seemed to be examining her every thought and motive. "I want you in the new organization, the Minister of Police wants you, the government wants you. Please consider the offer carefully."

There was only one question left. "When will my sabbatical start?"

"Right now."

8

It was early afternoon when Abigail arrived home. Thirty partly completed cases had been put aside, a crying Johanna had been hugged, a probably smug director general avoided and her office cleaned of personal items. Then she had left the building, driving slowly through the suburbs, a woman who no longer had a purpose in life.

At home, a parcel that had been delivered by a courier company was waiting for her. The sender was shown as Mr. K. Patel of Smythe, Patel and Associates, Harare. She tore open one end and shook it. The first items to fall out were two photographs.

The first was of a small African girl, not more than six or seven. She was wearing a school uniform and standing proudly erect, facing the camera, her heels touching and her hands at her sides. A school bag hung from one shoulder. The expression on her face was one of the simple pride that went with a first day at school.

The second picture was of the face of a young man, his main characteristic being his extreme leanness. The flesh seemed to have retreated around his eyes, making them seem unnaturally large. The whites were visible right round the pupils, giving him a frightened, even pursued appearance.

He was the one who, according to Patel, was being held illegally by the Zimbabwean authorities. Abigail's eyes searched the face of the young man in the photograph for much longer than she would remember afterward. She saw something of strength and vulnerability, also boldness and sensitivity. She imagined that he was not uncomplicated, and it seemed that he was kin to her. What has brought you to this point? she asked the photograph. And would we have been friends, had we known each other? Yes, she thought. I know we would have. I can feel it.

She laid the photographs down and reached into the parcel, bringing out a letter from Krisj Patel and two files of what seemed, at a glance, to be newspaper articles. She opened the letter first. "Dear Abigail," she read. "These are the only photographs I have of Katy and Tony. As you can see, the one of Katy was taken many years ago. I'm afraid we've lost contact with her. The one of Tony is recent.

"He is a great writer and a real force in the democratic resistance to the dictatorship—a person of real quality. He writes wonderful, brave words for our underground Web sites, strong words to expose the regime's thugs. I have included some of his writings so that you can judge for yourself.

"Over the last year he has been very ill. We have seen him grow weaker, and we don't understand what the problem is. We feel that a prolonged stay in Chikurubi prison could have a permanent effect on his health. It could even result in his death. I'm afraid people are very poorly fed in our prisons. As far as we can make out, Chikurubi is the worst of all. And of course there are six others with him, all of whom are wrongly imprisoned."

The letter ran on for six pages. Abigail's eyes skimmed over them quickly. She already understood what Patel wanted. Two hours before, it would have been out of the question. But now? No, it was still absurd. And this thing of Tony being a writer? What had he written?

That question was answered in the two files. Among the hundreds of pages in the first file were printouts from Web sites, pages of uninterrupted text from a computer and what appeared to be photocopies of newspaper articles, some of which carried Tony Makumbe's byline . . .

The articles had headlines that were filled with a young man's anger. "The Gukurahundi slaughter remembered," said one.

Another screamed at the reader: "Thousands left homeless after Murambatsvina." A third article was headed "More MDC dissidents arrested without cause."

The language of the articles themselves was filled with phrases that would have found an echo in all Zimbabwean dissidents and minorities. "Freedom will not come until every right-thinking Zimbabwean is willing to lay down his life," Abigail read in one. "Death is preferable to our continued suffering," the article screamed at the reader. "Many of us are willing to make the ultimate sacrifice."

Abigail had the general idea after only a few minutes. She was not sure that she agreed that Tony was a great writer, but she could see why people who were involved in the Zimbabwean freedom struggle might think so.

She had almost finished skimming the first batch of articles when the phone rang. Gert Pienaar was on the other end of the connection. "Abigail, I'm just calling to say goodbye," he said. "I've decided to move on." Despite the three days he had spent in police custody, he sounded surprisingly relaxed.

Gert did not stay on the line for long. Abigail tried to extend the conversation, seeking to persuade him to stay, even going over to the argument put forward by both Robert and Gert himself. "It's not a perfect world," she told him, "but we can do a lot of good within those imperfections."

Now that he had tasted them, Gert seemed to have changed his mind about those imperfections. He told her that, as far as he could see, this was payback time, a warning that he was overstepping his limits. "I was on the wrong side then. Maybe I'm the wrong color now."

"That's bullshit," Abigail had told him, "and you know it."

"Do I?" he had asked. "Maybe I do, maybe I have some doubts."

After Gert hung up, it was some time before Abigail could go back to her reading. The events of the last few days had brought back memories that she would rather have left hidden. She had been in a safe house in Lesotho when the house was attacked and her father murdered by soldiers of the old regime. Two years later her mother had been killed by a parcel bomb.

In some ways, the way they had died was easier for her to accept than the death of her aunt. Her parents were victims of the racist regime that she had accepted as being evil, an enemy of the people. Her aunt's death, on the other hand, had been at the hands of what she had been taught was an army of liberation. She was nine years old at the time and altogether unable to grasp this new reality. How had the heroes of the liberation struggle become murderers?

It was her father who had told her what had happened. For an hour or more she had questioned him, trying to understand something that was beyond all understanding. Eventually he had said, "Abigail, I really don't know the details. I was not there. All I know is that they were killed by the same soldiers who in the last year have killed a lot of Ndebeles."

"But why, Papa?" she had asked. "They fought for freedom too, didn't they?"

"Perhaps that's not quite what they were fighting for, but you're too young to be wrestling with these things now," he had said. "Later, when you're older, we will discuss them. I promise you that."

It was a promise he had been unable to keep. Six years later he was killed by soldiers of the apartheid regime.

The second parcel of Tony's work was quite different than the strident pamphleteering of the first one. So absorbed was Abigail that she found herself reading every word of every page. Robert came in and was surprised by how quickly she returned to her reading.

Most of the pages were straight from a computer printer, seeming to indicate that their contents had never been published. A few were photocopies from a publication that carried its name, *Kultur Zimbabwe*, in small letters at the bottom of every page. A few were copies of standard-size magazine pages, and others of trade paperback pages.

By the time Abigail finally laid aside the last page, Robert was asleep. She looked at the bedroom clock, saw that it said a quarter to one and wondered if it was too late to call Yudel. Apart from the lateness of the hour, it had been nearly four years since she had last seen or spoken to him, and she was not sure how she would begin the conversation.

Although she barely admitted it to herself, Abigail felt uneasy about the differences in the paths her life and Yudel's had taken. Yudel had been retrenched from the Department of Correctional Services in order to bring about what government considered more acceptable representation, without ever specifying what sort of representation they were talking about. On the other hand, Abigail's Robert had been the beneficiary of an empowerment deal of such excessive proportions that she still did not feel comfortable in the seemingly endless expanses of their home.

It was true that when the department discovered how short they were of the requisite skills, Yudel was brought back on a generous contract. But, if her memory served her well, that too was about to expire.

She reached twice for the telephone on her side of the bed, but eventually did not make the call. The matter of Tony Makumbe's writing could wait till morning. Anyway, Yudel would probably not be able to contribute much.

9

Yudel Gordon sat at his desk in the office the head warder of C-Max high-security prison had allocated to him. Two hours before, it had taken him ten minutes to get through the gate at the outer perimeter, park his car in the lot outside the walls of the prison itself, pass through the security check at the main entrance and then gain access through another two heavily barred gates before he reached his office.

None of this was unusual. Changing shifts in C-Max took at least half an hour, sometimes longer. The system had been designed to keep the inmates within its walls. A little inconvenience to the personnel had to be expected.

Yudel was not a patient man. He hated queues, inept bureaucrats, dithering people who were slow to make decisions and any person or body that seemed to be conspiring to waste his time. That he spent so much of his life entering and leaving prisons, all of it without resentment, was a reflection of how much he was absorbed by his work.

This was not something to which he readily admitted. He was aware that it seemed crass to enjoy imprisoning other people. It is not the act of imprisoning people that I enjoy, though, he thought. It is the crawling through the channels of their minds, even if I sometimes get lost in the worst of those sewers.

He had often asked himself how enjoyment could be defined. He did enjoy his work, but, on reflection, that often seemed absurd.

The petty thief, the white-collar swindler, the political loony, the serial killer, the family murderer: Yudel dug into the minds of every one of them with equal dedication. Perhaps enjoyment came from fascination, he thought. At least, in his case, this was probably so.

Yudel was physically a small man, in a nation of large ones. The unruly fuzz of his hair had been graying for some years now. He would have loved to have been a man whom women remembered after one meeting. The truth was that often they had to be introduced to him more than once. He was aware though that an occasional woman found his untidiness and absentmindedness somehow endearing. He was grateful to them.

In many respects Yudel lacked confidence. He was never sure how much to tip waiters, whether to expect a porter when arriving at a hotel, how to address his seniors in the department, or how to deal with what he saw as the impenetrable solidarity of his wife's circle of female friends.

It was for his work that Yudel was noticed, and then as much for his irregular forays into the territory of the detective branch as for his efforts at bringing sanity to a corner of the nation's prisons. Unconventional activities had, on occasion, brought him to the attention of the minister. Because of some of these activities he had been passed over for promotion a number of times under the old government and had been retrenched once by the new.

For most of his adult life, Yudel had worked for the Department of Correctional Services in a segregated prison system in which black prisoners were sometimes hired out at slave wages. Down the years he had been asked on many occasions how he squared working in such a place with his conscience. It was a question to which he had never found an answer to satisfy even himself. He imagined that it probably had to do with the fact that the prison system had an endless supply of criminals with which to satisfy his curiosity about this subgroup of humanity.

He also told himself that his presence there and his well-known readiness to rock the departmental boat was a threat to that category of warder who was attracted to the prisons for the chance to employ violence against men who could not retaliate. But most of all, he knew that his presence in the department had to do with the sheer stimulation of it. He was fascinated by the forces that turned men into criminals. Yudel hated the thought that he loved it all, but he loved it all the same.

He also knew and understood the longer-term prisoners better than anyone else in the service. An hour before, a lockdown had been initiated, because, after the prisoners had been returned to their cells, one had seemed to be missing. Yudel had directed the search to cell D22, where the warders found an extra prisoner. "He just wanted to be with his wifey," Yudel had told the warders. "He'll go back without any rough treatment."

The pile of paper in his in-basket was topped by a few requisition forms which, when signed, would go to admin to be processed. He expected to see the required equipment some time within the next eighteen months. They were followed by a letter from the director of human resources, telling him that he was owed ten days' leave. The letter went on to add that his contract was due to expire in three months. If he had not taken his leave before that date, he would forfeit it. It ended in capitals: NO LEAVE CAN BE PAID OUT!

After the admonition from human resources, a pile of self-evaluation forms of staff members were clipped together by a large paper clip. Yudel had to assess the way they had evaluated themselves and give his opinion. He lifted what remained in the pile and slid the self-evaluations to the bottom.

The next item was a letter to him personally, from the minister. She wanted him to shed light, if any light could be shed, on the matter of allegedly terminally ill prisoners being released on compassionate grounds and recovering to such an extent that they returned to their former criminal activities. One had even been released twice on compassionate grounds and the police were looking for him, because his trademark way of entering a safe had been used on a big job in Cape Town, a city he was known to favor. The minister went on to add that only thirty percent of compassionate parolees had the good grace to die within six months of release. It was shocking. Did Yudel have any suggestions?

The letter was irresistible. Yudel started his response immediately.

Dear Madame Minister,
May I suggest reinstating the death penalty for the limited use of deal-
ing with these problem cases. Any of these allegedly terminally ill pa-
rolees still alive after six months could be picked up and brought to
Pretoria Central for administering the coup de grace. Their prompt
demise would, after all, be an element of the agreement we had reached
with them. A short period of the zealous implementation of this policy
should have the effect of limiting frivolous claims of terminal illness.
Your avenging and enthusiastic servant, Yudel Gordon.

The temptation to print the letter was almost overwhelming. He would have referred to such an urge in others as a pocket of immaturity. A more sensible and sober part of his personality intervened. He reached for the delete button and dispensed the message to cyber heaven. Then he took the tried-and-tested civil-servant route of passing the responsibility to someone else.

The reply he sent to the minister read like this:

Dear Madame Minister,
My own concern for this phenomenon is, if possible, as intense as
your own. Accordingly, I have forwarded your letter to the two func-
tionaries whose signatures appear on these parole documents, the head
surgeon of our department and the District Surgeon for Tshwane. I
shall insist on speedy replies from these gentlemen and will forward
them to yourself as soon as I receive them.
Yours faithfully, Yudel Gordon.

He was answering a mail from the department's director general, wanting his opinion of stun belts that temporarily disabled the wearer, when a knock on the open door of his office revealed a young warder, carrying a box file. "From the Department of Justice for you, sir," he said.

Yudel reached for it. "What's it about? Any message?"

"No message. Only that it comes from the Department of Justice and that it's urgent."

Yudel put the director general's mail aside. He would deal with it later. Receiving the file had surprised him. He had few dealings with that department.

Yudel was a man who, for all his many eccentricities and his readiness to champion unpopular cases, was concerned that in certain matters people should think well of him. First among these was in his relationships with younger women. He could not tolerate the idea that he might be thought of as an old fool who chased after any woman young enough to be his daughter. He also prized his relationship with Rosa, his wife of many years, and was determined to do nothing to upset that. Despite all that, he was pleased, too pleased for his own peace of mind, to see that the file had come from Abigail.

He had only had dealings with Abigail once, some years before, over a period of little more than a week. But the period had been so intense and the stakes so high that it had brought them closer than they would have been had they been lovers; far closer than either expected. Yet, when it ended, neither had made any attempt to contact the other.

Dear Yudel,
How are you? It's been a while. I trust that both you and Rosa are in good health. I have a little matter that interests me and I hope may interest you. This file contains some of the writings of a Zimbabwean relative who is in trouble with their authorities. I discern personality elements in his writing that surprise me and that I do not understand. Please have a look and tell me what you think.
Love to Rosa—Abigail.

After years of silence she wants me to be her literary critic, he thought. Nevertheless, he turned the page to the first of Tony Makumbe's writings, read it slowly, then read it again.

Yudel knew something about the state of Zimbabwe's prisons. He also knew that almost all the waiters in restaurants in the province he lived in came from Zimbabwe's Ndebele minority. They had flooded across the border in their millions to escape the political and economic devastation of their own country. Nurses, journalists, businesspeople, hotel night managers and whatever other kind of occupation they held back home, they had found a living of sorts in South Africa's restaurants. At least in their adopted country they could afford food. Beyond that, what he knew about Zimbabwe came from newspaper reports and the occasional professional tidbits reaching him from its prisons. It was a place to avoid.

Yudel was surprised to find Rosa waiting for him in his study when he came in. It was the one room in the house that she rarely visited. "Abigail phoned," she said, rising to meet him.

He offered the usual perfunctory kiss. "She sent me a file that she wants me to read."

"Yudel, what does she want this time?"

Yudel knew that his wife's anxiety had nothing to do with Abigail's charms. "It won't be like that this time," he said. "Nothing like that."

"What, then?"

"I thought you liked Abigail."

Rosa lifted a threatening finger. "Yudel, don't you try to dance around me that way. You know that this has got nothing to with what I think of Abigail. I think she's a wonderful person, but what does she want?"

"As far as I can see, she wants me to analyze someone by reading his writing."

"His handwriting?"

"No, his prose."

Rosa's puzzlement showed on her face. "Why? Shouldn't the person be present when they're being analyzed?"

"As far as I can make out, the person is not available. Abigail wants my opinion."

"I hope that *is* all she wants."

"I'm sure it is," Yudel said. Perhaps not, he thought, but that is what you need to believe.

After she had left, he opened the file again. During the next four hours, stopping only for a half-hour break during which he consumed in silence the dinner Rosa had prepared, he read everything in the file. Then he paged back, searching again for the sections that interested him most and reading them more slowly. Of those passages, he studied every word, looking for a meaning that, he was aware, may not be there. A section that seemed to be photocopied from a book drew his attention:

Never pausing, never yielding, the arm of night sweeps across the city. The people would rise, but they are smothered by the cloud that comes with darkness. There is no sight. There is no thought, no gentleness in this our lovely land. We live within the depths of this fortress of dusk.

A passage printed directly from a computer had a theme with some similarities:

I have no life, but the life of this darkness. I have no light, but it is covered by the cloud of this reality. I see no stars, no moon, only the blankness of this fog, only the blank, featureless cloud. Even by day, the fog haunts me. Trees and mountains disappear, friends fade into its depths, only fear remains.

On the next page another paragraph needed rereading:

All of life is a pretense. We spend every hour of every day pretending to others that we are more than we really are. Everything we do, every word we speak: all are aimed at misleading others as to our virtue, our bravery, our competence, our attractiveness. Truth and honesty are beyond the grasp of any human being.

On the very last page he found something altogether different, and lingered over it longer than he had over any other section:

The fertile seed brings forth much fruit. The corrupt seed too results in a harvest, but what is the value of such a harvest? Only death, decay and fear are the fruits of the evil seed. The failing harvest is not to blame. The decaying fruit is not at fault. Nor should the dead growth stand accused. Look only to the seed for that is where the guilt lies.

At the back of the file, lying loose inside the back cover, was the photograph of a young African man. It was the photograph Abigail had studied the night before. Extreme leanness, slightly bulging eyes and hollow cheeks gave the impression of malnourishment. The whites that were visible right around the pupils gave his face a startled look. His forehead was broad, his cheekbones high and his jaw firm. Despite everything, it was a strong face. Yudel believed that the state of mind of any person was reflected on that person's features. The slight smile reflected a self-assurance that stood in contrast to the rest of the face.

He looked at the back of the photograph. Someone had written his name, Tony Makumbe, there. He thought about the young man's state of mind and what the contents of the parcel revealed. It was possible that the photograph could be deceiving. He believed that the writing could not.

He remained motionless behind his desk for longer than he had intended. Eventually he reached for the phone to call Abigail.

Robert Mokoapi answered. There had been occasions in the past when he had called Abigail later than Robert had considered appropriate—or reasonable—or both. Yudel paused too long before speaking. "Is that you, Yudel?" Robert asked.

It's been years and he still remembers that episode, Yudel thought. "Yes, I wondered . . ."

"She's still awake. I'm passing the phone to her."

"Yudel," Abigail said.

He was surprised at the joy he felt at hearing her voice. "Yes, it's me." To find some pleasantry as an introduction to the conversation was not within Yudel's scope. "Your man . . ." he began. "I believe he could be a schizophrenic."

"My God. Are you sure?"

"No, I'm not sure. Who is he?"

"He seems to be a cousin of mine."

"Let me meet him. I'll be able to make a better assessment."

"That won't be possible. Listen, Yudel, I need to speak to you to discuss this—soon, tomorrow."

"Tomorrow's not possible, I've promised Rosa . . ."

"It must be tomorrow." There was still the same insistence on getting her way that he remembered. Perhaps that was not fair.

Perhaps it was simply her determination to get things done. And they were always important things. "Tomorrow evening. Robert and I have been invited to the Tikkun SA launch of an art exhibition to support a project of theirs. Will you be there?"

"No."

"But you're Jewish. Didn't they invite you?"

"I didn't respond to the invitation."

"Come anyway. Please come. It'll be the only chance I have to speak to you."

"I don't know." The thought of the meaningless chatter of a cocktail party and the speeches that were bound to be made was too much. He had done what she asked, spent hours on it, and told her what he thought. Was that not enough? "I don't think I . . ."

"Please, Yudel, please. You and Rosa come. I have to speak to you. Say you will."

"I . . ." It was almost impossible to avoid her.

"Say you will."

"I . . ."

"You will come."

"All right, Abigail. I'll come."

Rosa was usually a good sleeper, but tonight when Yudel entered the bedroom she was in bed, but not asleep. "You're still awake," he said.

"Tell me what's in that file."

He sat down on the edge of the bed and took one of her hands in his. "Just the writings of a very disturbed boy. Nothing else."

"Is there a case against him?"

"He's a Zimbabwean and he's one of those who oppose that government."

"But everything's changed there, hasn't it?"

"I don't think so. Those who have controlled the real power all along, still control it."

"So he's in trouble."

"It sounds that way."

"At least it's not here."

"No."

She sighed. "I know I sound selfish. But I was so afraid last time."

"I know. Will you be able to sleep now?"

"I think so."

"I think you should take a pill. I was given some samples of the best sleeping pill in existence. I'll get one."

When he came back from his study, he had the pill in one hand and a glass of water in the other. Rosa was looking searchingly at his face. "Yudel?" Her voice had acquired a surprisingly sharp tone.

"Yes, my dear."

"You're not giving me a placebo, are you?"

"Of course not."

"I'd hate to think that I was allowing myself to be deceived by a sugarcoated pill."

"Rosa, I would never do that," Yudel said sincerely. "I would never patronize you by giving you a placebo. It would be an insult to someone of your intelligence. This pill will put you to sleep inside thirty seconds. It's the most effective sleeping drug available on the planet."

"Thank you, Yudel."

Yudel handed her the water and the placebo and she swallowed them. She was asleep with ten of the thirty seconds to spare.

Yes, my dear, he thought. Your mind is the most powerful drug of all.

10

The mist had stayed away for more than twenty-four hours. The little light there was in the cell came from a lamp somewhere beyond the cell's only window. By this faint glow, Tony Makumbe could still see the length of it and the seven men in it. Since at least four that afternoon all had been lying down. No one had moved in that time, except to roll over to give another part of the body the chance to do battle with the concrete floor. They had sleeping mats woven from reeds, but the mats did little to soften the unyielding surface of the floor.

He had tried to get up around midday, but had gotten no further than raising himself onto his hands and knees, and then only for perhaps five minutes. He wondered how much he had eaten. He remembered the food coming and thought that he had offered some of it to others in the cell, but none of it was clear. Anything that happened while the mist was around him was lost to memory. Not eating would account for his weakness. But the other men were all weaker. With the sparseness of their rations, it was not surprising. A few of them had tried to talk through the inspection flap in the door to prisoners in adjoining cells. None had made the effort more than once.

The big man he had noticed before was on the mat next to his. "Tony, my man, you awake?" He spoke softly to avoid disturbing the others.

"I'm sorry," Tony said. "I don't remember your name."

"Jacob. People say Big Jake when they talk to me."

"Hello, Jake." It was always difficult to look for the sort of information that he wanted from Jake now. "Have I been here . . ." He looked at Jake and saw only a sort of fatherly, stern-faced sympathy. "Have I been here long?"

"Yes, you were sick. A week, maybe a day or two more."

"Could you tell me, have I been eating?"

"A little. When you didn't eat, some of the others took your food. You get better food than us and . . ."

"I know. It's all right."

"Me also, I took some of your food too. I hope you don't mind. None of us are strong anymore."

"Jake?"

"Yes, my brother."

"Why are you here?"

"Armed robbery. Awaiting trial."

"What did you rob?"

"A supermarket." Tony waited too long, thinking about the reasons a man robs a supermarket. Big Jake spoke again: "Not to feed my family or anything like that. Wife and children died last year. I was just tired of all this. I wanted to take the money."

"I understand."

This seemed to surprise Big Jake. "You feel like that too, an educated man like you?"

"Sometimes. We all do."

Big Jake seemed to think about that for a while, but when he spoke again his mind had been seized by something altogether different. "Tony?"

"Yes."

"You see the man in the corner, over there on the other side?"

"The old man with the gray hair?"

"You see him? He lies very quiet."

"I see him."

"He died yesterday."

"Do they know?"

"I told them."

"Are you sure he's dead?"

"I went up to him to see. He's not breathing. Heart's not beating."

Tony looked at the body of the gray-haired man for a while, then he closed his eyes to cut out the sight.

"Tony?" It was Big Jake again.

"Yes."

"If we stay here, we're all going that way."

For Tony, there was no point in taking the matter further. Conversation was both pointless and too great an effort. Everything was.

Eventually the fog again rose from the ground until Tony could see none of the other men or even the far walls of the cell. Nor could he hear Jake's voice when the big man spoke again.

11

The exhibition was at the Sheraton, directly across the road from the gardens of the Union Buildings, the same place where, according to Abigail's anonymous friend, Robert had dallied with the PA, the pretty blond temp with the milky-white breasts.

These were Abigail's thoughts as they neared the hotel, Robert driving the BMW four-by-four, while she sat silently, her hands folded in her lap. He had tried to make conversation a few times but, with little response from her, had given up.

Abigail had been surprised at the invitation to what she thought was an all-Jewish affair. "No," Robert had told her. "They're looking for donations wherever they can get them. And the work they're doing is genuinely good."

Joshua Berman, the chairman of Tikkun SA, eighty years old and near the end of an active business career, greeted them as they stepped from the lift. He was wearing a tuxedo and smiling warmly at all new arrivals. He read their registration tags very skilfully without them being sure that he was doing so. "Robert," he said, beaming, "and Abigail, I'm delighted you could come."

Berman's speech, delivered a few minutes later, was short. The artists had donated their paintings and the money was all going, every last penny, to an antipoverty initiative in an impoverished part of the Eastern Cape. The hotel had donated the venue and Tikkun SA's donors had picked up the administration costs.

The paintings were not being auctioned. Like any other exhibition, they carried prices, personally inflated by Berman, "for a cause that is second to none for social impact." The guests, perhaps a hundred representatives of the region's wealthier families and most profitable businesses, milled among the works of art making appreciative sounds. Berman, who had little interest in art, but much interest in publicizing his efforts to alleviate poverty, watched the scene through benevolent eyes.

Abigail had just begun examining the paintings when she saw Yudel and Freek approaching from the direction of the lifts. Yudel looked as distracted as ever. Next to him, Freek was smiling at her in that way he had that was part friendly uncle and part alpha male. It was Yudel who had introduced her to Freek, at a time when she needed police help badly. "Hello, boys," she said.

Robert had come up behind his wife while Freek took one of Abigail's hands and held it a little too long. "May I suggest, in the presence of your husband, that you look most charming tonight?" he said.

Robert looked past him. "I suppose we'll survive it."

Abigail tilted her head in Freek's direction. "Thank you, sir. By the way, where are Rosa and Magda?"

Freek explained, "Magda's out of town and Rosa is . . . I believe powdering her nose is the commonly used term."

"You both look very handsome tonight."

Yudel looked at Freek. To his eyes, Freek did not look especially handsome. He felt sure that he personally did not look handsome to anyone. Perhaps Abigail's remark was not meant seriously.

Rosa arrived and Abigail hooked an arm into hers, guiding her away from the men and through the crowd of businesspeople who were, for the evening, connoisseurs of African art. It was already clear that, from an income-generation point of view, Berman's exhibition was on its way to success.

Rosa stayed close to the younger woman. "My dear, I'm afraid Yudel and I can't possibly afford these prices."

"You're not here to buy paintings, Rosa. You're my guests, not old Berman's."

If the prices of the paintings were weighing on Rosa's mind, there was something that bothered her more deeply. "Abby, this other thing—it won't bring Yudel into danger, will it?"

"I just want his thoughts." The way she spoke, Rosa knew this was the truth. "Only that."

"Thank you, Abigail."

Opinions, of greater and lesser enlightenment, were being offered in every corner of the room; none more loudly and insistently than that of a politically well-connected and newly rich woman who called herself Baroness Drubetskaya. Ten years before, at the age of nineteen, she had married her sixty-year-old employer, who claimed to be descended from a line of Russian barons. Since his death a year later, she had only ever allowed herself to be addressed as Baroness. She wore a close-fitting red evening gown that was a size or two too small. She had already bought two paintings. In a penetrating voice she was lecturing one of the other guests on the convergence of line, color and texture that had attracted her to the works. As she paused for breath, her eyes fell upon Yudel. "Professor Gordon," she yelled. "Professor Yudel Gordon. I heard a talk you gave at university while I was still a student. It was on rehabilitation, I believe. You said it was impossible to rehabilitate anyone."

Damn you, Yudel thought, mangling my work at the top of a voice that has all the elegance of the screeching of brakes on the Blue Train. What did I do to deserve you this evening?

The baroness swarmed up to Yudel in predatory fashion. "And who is the handsome man with you?" She looked coyly at Freek.

"Police Commissioner Freek Jordaan," Yudel said, taking a step back to leave the field to Freek.

"I'm Baroness Gaynor and I love a man in uniform," she said archly, although Freek was wearing a suit. It seemed that she saw herself as so well known to the other guests that the rest of her name was unnecessary.

Yudel's attempt to leave her with Freek turned out to be a failure. Before he could back away any further, she rounded on him, waving a hand at one of her purchases. "I would love your impression, Yudel. May I call you Yudel?"

Yudel ignored the question. Abigail was standing close to Robert on the other side of the painting, and Rosa perhaps a step behind them. To his surprise, the entire mezzanine floor fell silent, waiting for his reply.

To hell with it, he thought. She's the one who asked. "As far as the arts are concerned . . ." he began. Rosa raised a hand to cover her eyes.

"Yes Mr. Gordon . . . Yudel?" The baroness was encouraging him to continue.

"As far as the arts are concerned, I enjoy music that is melodious, prose that makes rational sense, poetry that rhymes . . ." The baroness was beginning to feel uneasy, her eyes casting around in the direction of some of the other guests. Yudel had moved to get a better look at her purchase. ". . . movies that feature movie stars and visual art in which the colors go well with the curtains."

The silence continued for longer than the baroness would have liked. Rosa had covered her face with both hands now. Freek was grinning and Abigail was laughing softly.

"You're a Philistine," the baroness murmured in a stunned voice that was still too loud.

No one else spoke. Rosa, who after many years should have grown accustomed to Yudel's inappropriate remarks, had not come out from behind her hands. It was Joshua Berman who broke the silence with a loud chuckle. "No, he's not a Philistine. He can't be. He's a good Jewish boy." The guests, seeing that it was in order to laugh, joined in. "Mr. Gordon's just joking, folks. He loves the paintings."

Yudel took a last look at the picture in which the convergence of line, color and texture had made such an impression, before moving away. As for the exhibition, it returned to its earlier confusion. He was at the balcony rail, looking down into the lobby when he heard Abigail's voice at his shoulder. "Come on," she said. "I need to talk to you."

He followed her to a small lounge just off the mezzanine. She closed the door behind them and they stood facing each other. In his mind, Yudel ran through possible things to say. He wondered if he should offer her a seat, ask what this was all about, thank her for inviting him, shake her hand, hug her, or just look at her. He just looked.

"That was entertaining," Abigail said. Her smile showed that there was nothing sarcastic in the observation. "Thanks for coming. It's great to see you again."

"Yes"—Yudel stumbled over possible responses, settling on— "me too."

"Let's sit down," she said. She was already sinking into an arm- chair, one of a few arranged around a coffee table. Yudel sat down opposite her. "So what've you been doing?" Abigail asked.

Yudel was glad to see her, but this was not the kind of conver- sation he made. "You want to know about this young man, Tony Makumbe?"

"Same old Yudel," she said. "No small talk."

"I don't know what to say. I'm not skilled in that area."

"Or interested, either. Let's talk about Tony, then. You said you think he's a schizophrenic?"

It had been asked in Abigail's most businesslike way, but she had not changed and he could see the anxiety behind it. "Yes. He doesn't perceive things the way the rest of us do."

"I saw that too."

"In fact, he sees the world in a way that we cannot comprehend."

Abigail's face had become very still. "Yudel, he's in prison in Zimbabwe, with six others."

"Not Chikurubi, I hope."

"Yes, I think that's the name of the place."

Yudel looked at her without saying anything. It was a look Abigail had difficulty reading. She was not sure whether it was sympathetic or portentous, or both. "What do you know about that place?" she asked.

What should I tell you? Yudel wondered. "It's not a good place," he said eventually. "I visited it fifteen years ago. It was not a good place then. It's worse now. Food may be the main problem. Even Zimbabweans who are free have little food."

"I know," she said.

"A few months ago, inmates were being fed a slice of bread and a bowl of thin sadza porridge a day."

Abigail's face was very still. "How long do they live?"

It was a question he hated having to answer. "I'm told that in the last five years more than half their prisoners have died, either of hunger or of diseases they were not strong enough to resist— often cholera. The cells are overcrowded. I believe sometimes cells contain three or four times the number they were intended for." He decided against telling her about the cemetery that had been created on the prison farm or that the prison had the month before contracted a company to undertake mass burials. He had told her too much already.

"Oh God, Yudel. What are you saying?"

"Is he a sturdy boy?" Yudel asked. "Many schizophrenics are not."

"The letter I received said he'd been sick."

"They may have been talking about the schizophrenia. How long has he been there?"

"Just a few days."

"Are you sure he's still alive?"

"No. Are you sure he's a schizophrenic?"

"No, but it's a reasonable guess. How long is his sentence?"

"He's not sentenced. They're just holding him. They haven't troubled the courts. In fact, they deny they have him."

"And he's in Chikurubi?"

"The activists there say so."

"Ah," he said. "Not always the most reliable source of information." He asked himself what there was to say about this sort of African catastrophe. There were enough of them. Then he remembered that there may be some good news. "International bodies have been asking us to help. I don't know if we've done anything, but I understand there's a World Food Program shipment on the way to Chikurubi. It was due to land in Beira yesterday."

"That's a blessing."

I suppose you'd better know the rest of it though, Yudel thought. "That food will have a street value. And it has to get through some of the most corrupt officials and the most desperate crowds on the planet before it reaches them."

"Oh, Yudel," she said.

"He'll have to get out of there soon." He looked at her face and saw that this was not all she had to tell him. "There's something else?"

"Just that they've asked me to come there to help them get a court order, forcing them to free my . . ." She paused a moment to rearrange the sentence. ". . . to free Tony's group."

Before she could continue, the door was thrown open and

Robert came into the room, arms swinging in agitation. Abigail was on her feet quickly. Yudel followed uncertainly.

"Robert?"

"There's an entire party out there, wondering where you are." He was gesticulating in staccato fashion.

Rosa and Freek had followed him into the room, Freek having the presence of mind, always a strong characteristic of his, to close the door behind him.

"You slip away. Why aren't you with me?" His words were again accompanied by furious gesticulations. "After you laughed at his feeble joke—if it was a joke."

Abigail's eyes blazed with the light of battle. "You're out of your mind."

"Am I? It was like this last time, too."

"No, Robert. I'm not the one holding business meetings with the opposite sex in the Sheraton."

"This *is* the Sheraton," he snarled.

Rosa had followed the exchange between Robert and Abigail from close by, her head swiveling like a spectator at a tennis match. She placed a comforting hand on one of Robert's forearms. "Robert," she said gently, "you don't need to be concerned. Abigail doesn't feel that way about Yudel. I am the first to sense these things and it's not like that at all." She turned toward Yudel, perhaps looking for confirmation, but her eyes widened. "As for you, Yudel, take that smug look off your face."

"Smug look . . . ?" Yudel tried to protest.

"My God, Yudel." Abigail rounded on him. "Your relationship with me gives you nothing to look smug about."

"I've got no smug look," Yudel tried to say.

"I know the Yudel Gordon smug look," Rosa said.

How did I so quickly become the villain of the incident? Yudel wondered.

Freek came up to Yudel, and leaned heavily on his friend, an elbow on one of Yudel's slight shoulders. He could scarcely keep the amusement out of his voice. "You've got it wrong, Robert. Yudel's not the old white guy lusting after your wife. I am."

Robert looked from one to the other. He turned suddenly and

strode from the room, as angry as when he had entered. "What a fucking ridiculous pair," he muttered.

"Thanks awfully, Freek," Abigail said. "That was very helpful."

Abigail and Robert drove in silence. This time neither attempted conversation. Abigail could see that Robert was holding the steering wheel far too tightly. His jaw was set in a way that reflected his anger. She had seen it before, not often, but often enough to recognize it.

And what was that all about? she asked herself. As if I didn't know. Oh, Robert—all that fuss about something you know to be innocent, you foolish man. It's all so clear. You are fucking her, aren't you? I'm afraid it's all too obvious now. You really are. There is simply no doubt about it.

12

By the time Robert had signed off the afternoon edition of his paper, Abigail's flight to Harare was airborne. Her decision to go had been taken in bed the night before. The idea of putting a thousand kilometers between herself and Robert had considerable appeal. And, of course, there was Tony. Thinking about his imprisonment in that awful place instead of falling asleep, she had come to the conclusion that she had to go.

But even that is not entirely true, she thought. I knew from the start that I had to go. I tried to avoid it, but I knew from the moment Krisj Patel first called.

She had waited till this morning before telling Robert. He had looked straight at her for too long, an expression on his face that she could not read, before suddenly turning away and going to work without replying. At least, for you, your wife will be out of the way, leaving the field to the opposition, Abigail thought.

From a businesslike flight attendant Abigail had received a glass of wine and a small packet of salted nuts. She had brought a book to read, but it had stayed in her luggage. With thoughts of Tony Makumbe and the tragedy that was Zimbabwe on the one hand, and Robert and his foolishness on the other, reading was impossible.

Suddenly, without warning, Abigail found that she was weeping silently. It was not for Tony or Zimbabwe. She may yet weep for them, but so far she did not even know Tony and it had been many years since she had last lived in Zimbabwe. She was weeping for herself and Robert. To Abigail, it was much more than her husband weakening with this pretty white girl. Pretty? Abigail asked herself. She was much more than pretty. It was no wonder Robert had not been able to resist her.

Her sadness went much deeper than that. Abigail had hated her first experience of sex. The rape had taken place when she was fifteen years old on the night after her parents had died. It had been so much worse for being at the hands of a man who many in the movement saw as a hero. For ten years after that she had recoiled at the possibility of a man, any man, desiring her physically. Then Robert had come.

Apart from that one incident she had endured against her will, Robert had been her only sexual partner. He had taken everything in sexual intercourse that had been repulsive and frightening, and replaced it with something so wonderful that it filled her with a joy that she had not believed possible. She loved Robert with the love of a woman for a man, but also with the gratitude of the rescued for the rescuer.

Oh, Robert, she thought, you damned fool. Did this have to come now? Did it have to come at all? Would I be on this flight had you not screwed that kid?

She closed her eyes and oblivion came quickly, blotting out all the unpleasantness in her own life and the tragedy of the country to which she was returning. When she woke, she turned for the first time to the newspaper she had bought at the airport in Johannesburg. The front-page headline was set in massive, bold, seventy-point type. It read: "MDC pulls out of unity government." The subhead, immediately below that, expanded on the theme: "Zimbabwean moderates claim their right to disengage from a dishonest and unequal partnership." In the article, the leader of the moderate partner in the coalition was quoted as saying: "They arrest our members without reason. They pack the key cabinet posts with their members. They only tolerate us because it gives them credibility."

And where does that leave me? she wondered.

Almost before she realized how long she had been first asleep, then in thought, the two-hour journey was ending. The aircraft made a slow circle around Harare airport, tilting slightly toward the side on which she was sitting. Down below, she saw the runways and the terminal buildings off to one side.

On the far side of the airport in the middle distance, she could see the sprawling tangle of business premises, houses, shacks and official buildings that made up Harare. She was still too far away to see any of it clearly. But she had read about the shops where shelves had stood empty for years, the many businesses that had closed, and the white farmers who had been attacked, arrested and driven off their land.

But for now, it was better not to think about any of that. It would do no good. She was coming for one reason and one reason only.

Disembarking was delayed while a party of dignitaries in suits emerged from first class and were ushered out of the aircraft. From her window, Abigail saw that a red carpet had been spread at the foot of the stairs. At the end of the carpet a small delegation, its members also wearing suits, had gathered to welcome them. Judging by the fleet of Mercedes sedans and the motorcycle policemen waiting behind them, this group would not have to bother about formalities like passport control.

After the two groups had completed their handshaking and been driven away in the Mercedes motorcade, the red carpet was rolled up and a professionally smiling hostess thanked everyone for using their airline and ushered them toward the stairs.

Abigail noticed Krisj Patel as soon as she passed through customs. He was a tall man, but his narrow shoulders and hips would have fitted well on a much smaller one. As Abigail crossed the concourse, she could read the sign he was holding: "ADVOCATE ABIGAIL BUKULA."

Patel was wearing clothes that seemed to have been intended for a stockier man. The trousers, especially, were baggy and held up by a belt that was pulled tight, but not threaded through the loops provided for that purpose. The shoulders of his short-sleeved white shirt hung halfway down his upper arms. Sleeves that should have ended above his elbows were at least a hand's breadth lower. As a sop to corporate conformity he wore a broad, red necktie. He swallowed heavily when Abigail stopped in front of him. "You're Krisj Patel," she said.

"That's right, Ms. Bukula. Certainly, that's me, Attorney Krisj Patel of Smythe, Patel and Associates."

"Suddenly, we're formal, Krisj."

Abigail was wearing a dark pantsuit and white blouse with ruffles down the front. Her expression was serious and unsmiling. "Over the phone it was all right to call you Abigail," Patel said, "but now that I see you face-to-face I can see that you are actually Ms. Bukula."

"Don't be absurd." He was leading her toward the doors. "You call me Abigail, or I'll be on the next flight back."

"Of course, Ms. . . . Abigail."

The airport was in a better state of repair than Abigail had imagined it would be. She could see none of the cracked tiles, broken windows and discolored paintwork she had been led to expect. What was missing was the range of food outlets that you found in the airports of more prosperous countries.

As they reached the exit to the parking area, Abigail's attention was drawn to a woman of perhaps thirty. She was alone, leaning against a pillar, her thumbs hooked into the pockets of her jeans. Her skin was the deep brown of many equatorial peoples. She seemed to be watching them. When their eyes met, she held Abigail's gaze for too long before looking away.

"Who's she?" Abigail asked. "Do you know her?"

"Who? Oh, that girl." To Abigail's ears, Patel sounded like someone who had memorized the line. "Just a local."

Perhaps, Abigail thought, and perhaps you're not telling me everything. Abigail glanced once more in the direction of the woman, but she had her back to them and was moving away in the direction of the departures section.

Stepping out of the building, Abigail was enveloped by the warmth of the Harare afternoon. Suddenly she remembered Zimbabwe's perfect days and how she had enjoyed her years in the country. Somewhere she had read that Harare had the best climate of any city on earth, and she had experienced it.

Two taxi cabs occupied a rank intended for more. Krisj Patel had his own car, an ancient Nissan that seemed to have been repaired many times, always with more enthusiasm than skill. Sections had been touched up with paint of three slightly different

shades. The other cars in the parking looked to be in better condition, not too different from those at any other airport.

"I'm afraid this is my car," Patel said. "I have to get in first to
open the door on the passenger side. There's no door handle on
that side. I hope you don't mind."

"Not at all." Abigail looked doubtfully at the car.

Once inside, Patel had to lean all of his weight against the passenger door to get it open and allow Abigail in. Despite the car's
appearance, the engine started easily and it pulled away smoothly
enough. As they drove, Abigail turned to look back. The woman
from the concourse was outside now, watching them go.

"As I was saying on the phone . . ." Patel spoke quickly, as if fear-
ing that he might be interrupted or that his message might not be
favorably received and that he should deliver it quickly before there
could be resistance. ". . . my clients want us to get an order releasing
the prisoners, and Tony, of course, is one of them. When we get to
court, I will appear with you. I am the attorney who will brief you."

"And is Smythe happy with you spending a lot of time on the
case?"

"Smythe?"

"Your partner, the Smythe of Smythe, Patel and Associates."

"Oh no. Blake left after the 2000 referendum when the people
voted against the government and the old man really went crazy."

"And the Associates part of your firm's name?"

"No associates either. Just me. I am the whole of Smythe, Patel
and Associates."

Absurd as it seemed to her, Abigail thought she heard a measure of pride in the statement. He seemed to be saying that as long
as Krisj Patel was alive, the firm of Smythe, himself and the associates would be alive too. "Things have not been going too well
here, Krisj," she said.

"Not well at all, Ms. Abigail. I have more cases now than last
year, though. I'd have still more if people were braver. Many
would like to sue the government, but few have money. And most
of those who do have money are afraid."

As they traveled, the airport property gave way to open fields,
fringed with trees. Both trees and grass were a deeper green than
she remembered. It felt like a homecoming.

Perhaps it's not the way the newspapers say, she thought. And yet she knew that the beauty of the country was only one part of her memory. There was also the other part, and that had not diminished with the years. She expected that she would soon be confronting it again.

Spanning the road, a sign announced: "Zimbabwe Independence 1980." A little farther on, a billboard bore a bank's suggestion to "Bring money back to Zimbabwe."

Without warning and with an open road ahead of him, Patel braked sharply, swung the car onto the grass verge and switched off the engine. Cars on either side of the road were doing the same. It was a moment before she heard the sirens and some seconds longer before their source came into view. Three uniformed motorcyclists were followed by an armored personnel carrier. Through its darkened windows she could just make out armed soldiers. Close behind it, a black limousine flew the national flag. A second armored car and an ambulance brought up the rear of the motorcade.

As the sirens faded, cars started moving again. Patel restarted the engine and accelerated gently away. "What in hell was that?" Abigail asked.

"The old man's motorcade. He must be on his way to the airport to meet some bigwig."

"Does it happen often?"

He shrugged. "Quite often—twice a day on Borrowdale Road, as he comes to the office and returns home."

"And everyone has to stop?"

Patel smiled. "Only if you don't want to be shot."

"I've heard of this. I thought it was an exaggeration."

"A lot about our country must seem like an exaggeration."

They were passing through the outskirts of the city now. Over the years, Abigail's memory of Harare had faded like an old photograph that had been left in the sun. Those had not been the worst years. The bloodletting of the Gukurahundi was past, and the other lunacy was still to come.

Despite fading and blistering signage and discolored paintwork, the doors of small enterprises were open for business. A man was adding fuel to the tank of his car at a small filling station while two others stood in line. That these enterprises had survived at all was, to Abigail, a sign of the indomitable spirit of ordinary Zimbabweans. In contrast, a few stripped bodies of cars rusted at the roadside.

"Can people afford to buy food?" she asked Patel.

"We pay in American dollars now. It's much better than it was in the days of the Zim dollar, when inflation was so high that some prices changed twice a day. In those days we had to barter to survive. Even now, some of my clients pay me in food—maybe some eggs, a chicken if I'm very lucky. I handled the transfer of a house last month for ten pockets of potatoes, to be paid at the rate of one pocket a month."

Patel cleared his throat in the manner of a man about to say something important. "Our clients, the Organization for Peace and Justice in Zimbabwe, are very pleased that you're here." It was said in the same proud way that he had when telling her that he was the sole member of his law firm.

"Do they have any money?"

"Very little, I'm afraid." He glanced quickly and anxiously at her. "Does that make a difference?"

"I can work without being paid," Abigail said. "I hope we have no major expenses though." She looked at this serious man in his ill-fitting clothes, driving his old car. "How many members do they have? Thousands, I hope." She already had a fair idea of the answer and realized that the question was cruel.

"Thirty-one, actually."

"And you're among them?"

"Yes."

"So you're both attorney and client. That's an unusual situation."

She could see a line of perspiration forming along the top of Patel's forehead. "I'd hate to be cross-examined by you in court."

Like all good cross-examiners, Abigail was not easily distracted. "And the missing seven, are they also members?"

"Yes."

"So twenty-four remain—you and twenty-three others."

"Yes."

"Any of them over the age of thirty?"

"Oh, yes. Me and Paul Robinson, a commercial farmer who had his land confiscated, and one or two others. And our group also has solid overseas connections." When she kept looking at him, he added, "In Europe."

"I'm relieved to hear that we have allies ten thousand kilometers away." Abigail sighed deeply. "You're not putting my head into a noose, are you, Krisj?"

"If I am, my head will be right next to yours."

It was not much consolation, but she could see he meant it. "Why are there so few members?"

"We're not a political party, Ms. Abigail. We don't go looking for members. We are just committed Zimbabweans."

They had turned away from the main artery into town and had entered a pleasant suburb. The gardens were wooded and the houses did not have the worn look of the buildings she had seen so far. Patel stopped the car at the glass front door of a small hotel. The brick walls on either side of the main building carried electrified wiring along the top. A modest sign attached to the wall next to the motor gate gave the establishment's name as McDooley's Inn.

"It looks like a nice place," Abigail said.

"Yes, and the owner's an opponent of the dictatorship."

Good for them, Abigail thought. I will be living in a guesthouse whose owners oppose the dictatorship, and surrounded by a bunch of kids with the same sentiments, seven of whose colleagues have disappeared off the street. And the dictatorship is still in place and, according to the papers, whatever moderating influence existed in the coalition has now been withdrawn. On top of all this, there is little doubt that they are already aware of my presence here. What other favorable factors could I have forgotten? she wondered.

"Ms. Abigail," Patel said uncertainly. "I suppose you'd like to rest before we meet our clients tomorrow?"

"What I'd like is to be home in Johannesburg with my husband." The car had come to a stop and Abigail leaned toward Patel. "As that is not a reasonable possibility, I'll see these clients of ours today. Get them together for a meeting this evening."

"Ms. Abigail, I don't know if it's possible to assemble them all so quickly. I do think . . ."

"Do you want me in, or don't you?" she interrupted him.

"I do, but . . ."

"Then get them together this evening. I'm not here on leave."

13

The old scout hall was situated on the edge of one of the city's shack suburbs. The day had passed, but the building had no ceiling and it had retained much of the day's heat.

Abigail had not known what to expect when she first met her clients. Krisj Patel had already told her that most of them were young. There were also very few of them, so clearly they were brave. Her experience of political activists, especially those who were young and radical, was that they were good at shouting slogans, but not good at viewing their own behavior introspectively. Most of the activists she had contact with since being an adult had been active in places where there was no danger to themselves. She had seen them protest outside the New York offices of companies that did business in apartheid South Africa, or take part in marches in London to draw attention to Mugabe's Zimbabwe. They were always loudly certain of the correctness of their causes and passionate about righting the wrongs they had read about or seen on television.

The twelve people who had gathered in the old scout hall were altogether different. They were quiet, talking in undertones, knowing that they could not afford to draw attention to themselves. They had come in just three cars. The cars had been parked in separate places, none of them within a hundred meters of the hall. By Abigail's calculation, the organization had another twelve members in addition to those present and the seven who had been detained. The other twelve seemed to have thought better about gathering with their fellow conspirators in a season when government had decided to come after them.

They were a disparate group. The one man who, like Patel, was over forty, was introduced as Paul Robinson. He was a gray-haired farmer who had lived in the country since childhood. She would learn later that six months earlier he had been driven from his farm by a heavily armed gang of fifty, who had claimed the land in the name of redistribution to the masses. He had won a court order instructing them to vacate the farm, but they had stayed and the police had shown no interest in his court order. His nose was discolored with the red-blue tint of the habitually heavy drinker.

A man called Prince, no older than twenty-five, was concerned for his wife, who was among the seven who had been taken. A university student, who had recently been barred from the campus because of her political activities, was hoping that Abigail would help to get her sister released. Most had no such direct link to the missing seven. They were just brave people who believed in justice and wanted to see it done in their country.

Two serious-faced young women had been introduced as Tanya and Natasha, the Makwati twins. Both shook hands solemnly with Abigail and thanked her for coming.

"This can't go on forever," said Tanya.

"We won't be staying long," the other twin said. "We have to relieve Abel."

"Abel?"

"It's our shift to watch the gate at Chikurubi. We all take turns. If they move our people, we'll know."

"Do be careful." Abigail had not been able to stop herself. That was so damned obvious, she thought. Of course they would be careful.

"We are very careful," Tanya said.

Abigail immediately recognized the woman in T-shirt and jeans. While the others had crowded around Abigail, she had hung back, leaning against a wall much as she had at the airport, her thumbs again hooked into the pockets of her jeans. To make contact, Abigail had to approach her. "Helena Ndoro," the woman said, as they shook hands.

"You were at the airport this morning."

"Yes, I wanted to get a look at the person who's come to save our friends."

Abigail heard the faintest trace of mockery in her voice. "You don't believe that I'll be able to?"

"I believe you'll do what you came to do. Perhaps you'll even win your court order. But it'll make no difference. Some of our members have had court orders awarded to them by brave judges before this."

"Maybe we'll be lucky," Abigail said.

"Maybe we will." Unexpectedly she reached out, her fingers brushing one of Abigail's arms. "I came tonight, didn't I?"

The hall had no table. Abigail and the members of the Organization for Peace and Justice in Zimbabwe sat in a circle on folding chairs. The chairs had long since lost whatever varnish they once had and creaked when anyone moved. They all looked at Abigail, waiting for her to start. "The first thing I need to know is under what conditions the authorities picked up your colleagues."

Prince was first to speak, explaining that when he had returned from work his wife was gone. The neighbors told him the CIO had taken her. The student whose sister had been taken, had a similar story.

"Helena, you tell." It was Robinson, the farmer.

"I'm not sure what I saw," Helena said.

"Tell us anyway," he said.

"I was a block away when I saw one of their double-cab pickups with the CAM registration pull away from outside the flats where I stay. They travel only in those vehicles and no one else has those registration plates." Her voice was flat, altogether without emotion. "I don't know why, but I followed. They went straight to Chikurubi. I didn't see who was in the back. When I got home the other people in the building told me they'd taken Petra. I never actually saw it, though."

"Petra's your friend?"

"Petra's my partner."

Oh, you brave people, Abigail thought, following CIO and prison vehicles, watching the prison gate, holding clandestine meetings in this ruin that was once a scout hall. You're so brave and your opponents are so ruthless and your chances of victory are so slim. Unbidden, a different thought entered her mind. And you, Abigail Bukula, what are you doing here?

"Tomorrow," she said aloud. "Tomorrow Krisj and I will prepare our papers and the day after we'll serve them on the government. The fact that we are acting openly, in front of many witnesses and that I am a South African, may help to protect us. I think the rest of you are in greater danger than we are. Please be extra careful."

"There's one other thing," Helena said. "They seemed to be trying to pick us all up that day. They just missed me. I should have been with Petra when they came. They went to the homes of all the others."

It was a possibility that had never occurred to Abigail. "They came to the homes of everyone?"

"Everyone," Helena said.

"But they haven't tried since?"

"No."

"Is there anything else I should know?"

"There've been assassination attempts," Helena said.

"On your members?"

"Yes. We've been fired on."

"How many times?"

"A number of times."

"Which of you?"

"I'm not sure how many . . ." Helena began.

"Just Tony," Prince said. "They shot at him twice."

The last thing Patel said to Abigail when he dropped her off at the hotel was to ask if she was afraid. She seemed to act without even a trace of fear, he said.

"There's no fear while I'm active," she said. "Tonight when I'm alone and I start thinking, then the fear will come."

"Ms. Abigail . . ."

"Krisj . . ." She paused to make sure that she had his attention. ". . . can't we make it just Abigail?"

"Yes, I'm sure we can. I believe we can."

"Good."

"Abigail, it was wonderful of you to come. Now that I know you feel fear too, it is so much more wonderful. After all, doing something that does not scare you is not very heroic."

"You're a sweet man, Krisj. Thank you."

14

Inside, the hotel was comfortable and clean, but with the cleanliness of desperation. Carpets worn down to the webbing had been carefully vacuumed. Cracks in tiles had not been allowed to gather dirt. The pictures on the walls had probably been produced by local craftsmen and bought along the roadside, making up in brightness for what they lacked in originality. In the foyer and the dining hall, photographs of the stern-faced president looked down watchfully on the hotel guests.

The dinner the hotel served was passable. For a country in which most were underfed, it was outstanding. The proprietor, a white woman who introduced herself as Marjorie Swan, made a point of coming to talk to Abigail. "It's a real honor having you here," she said. Her smile deepened the lines on a face that showed the signs of being much exposed to the African sun.

What the hell have Krisj and the others been telling people? Abigail wondered. "Thanks for having me," she said.

"We would always find room for someone like you."

With only three other people in the hotel restaurant, making room did not seem to be much of a problem. "Nice of you to say that."

After the proprietor had gone, she ate only a little of the dinner. The thought of so much hunger being so close had spoiled her appetite. One look at the roast pork and potatoes on her plate was enough to bring the meal to an end. She asked for coffee to be served in her room and went upstairs.

The room was one floor above the street, and large by the standard of most hotel rooms. Like the rest of the hotel, its furnishings looked as if they were being cared for to make them last. Anything that broke was repaired, not replaced. In a corner near the window a vividly painted plaster moulding of a snarling tiger doing battle with an equally angry elephant added color to the room.

Abigail switched off the light and went to the window. The day's heat had been replaced by the enfolding warmth of the African evening. She swept the curtain aside. For perhaps half an hour she stood still, looking down into the street, trusting her skin color and black suit to make her, if not invisible, at least not readily noticeable.

Abigail's eyes stopped at every shadow, studied every walking figure and every window on the far side of the street. The few cars that she saw came slowly past, perhaps in fuel-saving mode.

Could they be watching? Everything she had learned about this country had told her that the CIO had informants everywhere and knew all there was to know about anyone who was in the country. She had no way of knowing just how accurate the stories of killings and torture might be.

She considered that she could be spending the night in her ten-million-rand house, as comfortable and well-served as any human being on the planet. So she was on a forced sabbatical, so what? Gert Pienaar had been arrested on spurious grounds, but released pretty quickly. None of it looked that serious now. What the hell am I doing in this place with its worn carpets and old cars and hungry people, just down the road, on every road? she asked herself.

The street remained empty, and eventually there was no reason to remain at the window. She closed the curtains and sat down in the room's one easy chair. Before she had left home, she had her cell phone enabled for international roaming. Now she dialed her home number. It rang for too long before she heard her own voice encouraging her to leave a message. "Robert, please call me before you go to bed," she told the recorder. Then she tried Robert's cell phone, but received no response.

Abigail's thoughts tumbled toward an internal tirade that had to do with Robert's current whereabouts and who he was with. But an effort of will drove them back to the task that lay ahead of her. She realized that she could win her court order and that the government could pretend to comply, but simply claim not to know anything about the seven. We'd release them if we had them, they might say.

I'll have to find a way around that, she thought. I'll have to find a way to close off that escape route.

She tried to call home again, and again reached the answering device. She ended the call and, looking among the items in her briefcase, took out the photograph of Tony. The extreme leanness and the unnaturally large eyes bothered her, but she found the little smile around the mouth reassuring. It seemed to be saying that there really were no grounds for worry. Everything would yet be fine.

But damn you, Tony—where are you? What are they doing to you? And is it in any way possible that my efforts will make a difference to you?

Sleep came slowly to Abigail that night. She usually had a few sleeping pills in her bag for such occasions, but this time she had forgotten to pack them. When she did sleep, dreams that she thought had been left behind years before returned to disturb her night. It was years since they had last plagued her. Now menacing figures again peopled the gloom in the corridors of her mind. She tried to shake them off, even to bring herself back to consciousness, but found herself locked in passages that offered no chance of escape.

It was only when a hand closed around her throat, almost closing off her breathing, that she rushed upward through the darkness to full consciousness. With her eyes open she could still feel the place where the fingers of the hand had dug into her throat. She fumbled for the switch of the bedside light. It came on in a blinding flash, but she was alone in the room.

I shouldn't have said that to Krisj, she told herself. I should never have admitted that fear comes when everything is quiet and I'm alone and thinking. I should have told him that I have no fear and never have had. That's what I should have done.

According to what she had heard that evening, the CIO had come in the daytime to make their arrests. But more often they came at night. She remembered that in her own country in the apartheid days, the security police had usually come in the night. So did the army when conducting the cross-border raid in which her father had died. These were the purveyors of violence who loved the night. They loved it because of the cloak it drew over their activities.

At night, the sleeping victim was disoriented, unable to counterattack or even to flee. The only other time when a human being was as vulnerable was during love-making. That thought brought Robert to her mind, so she tried to dismiss it.

Surely the CIO would already know about her presence in the country? If they were detaining members of this organization, they would be watching them closely. Such organizations often had informants in their ranks. Telephones could be tapped, and other listening devices used. She was certain that they would know that she had arrived and where she was staying, right down to the room number. Whatever Marjorie Swan said about it being an honor to have her stay, would she really be able to refuse the CIO access to her register? Would she even try?

And Krisj Patel, why had he put her up in this damned hotel? Did they not have a safe house somewhere, a place where the nights would not be haunted?

Abigail's watch told her that the time was just past two. She had slept for a little more than four hours. She reached for her phone to try to raise Robert again and had started keying in the number before she canceled the call and laid the phone down.

She got out of bed to go again to the window, but stopped herself before she was halfway there. A memory returned to her of Douglas Bader, a Battle of Britain hero who claimed that, as a child, he would walk slowly through woods at night, his only purpose being to overcome his fears, forcing himself never to look back no matter what he heard behind him.

Abigail returned to the bed, switched off the light and again tried to sleep. Just closing her eyes brought back the images from her dream. It's this room, she told herself. If they come looking for me, the register will tell them where I am.

Staying in bed, unable to sleep, unable even to close her eyes for more than a few seconds, was impossible. Without switching on the light this time, she made her way to the door, unlocked it and opened it, trying to make no sound. Except for a dim light on the landing three or four doors away, the passage was in darkness. She moved quietly into the passage.

Abigail carefully turned the door handle of each room in turn. The first three were locked. The idea that some man, also an insomniac, might see the door handle move and open it to find her there, was disturbing. It would be entirely reasonable for him to assume a special interest on her part. The fourth door was not locked. Abigail eased it open. The bed was empty and the curtains drawn.

She locked the door behind her. If they came during the night, they would not look for her here. And yet there was always a chance. Opening the closet, she saw that the floor space inside was wide enough for her. She removed the bedcover and spread it across the closet floor. Its extra width could be wrapped around her. Once inside, she pulled the doors closed. Lying down was not possible, but she could stretch out her legs and rest her body against the wall.

I'm being a fool, she thought. I'm allowing myself to be stampeded for no reason. I'm behaving like a child.

But, despite admonishing herself, that was how she spent the rest of the night. This time the dreams stayed away. By the time she woke, the room was already full of light and getting back to her own room was something of a challenge.

15

At breakfast, Abigail discovered that *The Herald* was already carrying the news that she had arrived to challenge the government over the so-called Harare Seven. A photograph of herself, taken all those years before when she was practicing in the country, smiled at the readers from page five. The article described her as an ambitious young lawyer, trying to establish a reputation. It ended by quoting a senior member of the ruling party as saying, "All indications are that the seven have left the country."

She was reading the article when Krisj Patel arrived. He was still wearing his ill-fitting clothes of the day before. "Would you like to join me?" she asked.

He glanced at the food on her plate, then back at her. She read the gesture to mean, yes, please, but I didn't dare ask.

"Come along, Krisj, we can talk while you eat your bacon and eggs."

"Do you think they'll have bacon?" he wondered.

They did have bacon and eggs, and sausages too. Patel consumed a fair portion of all three, while Abigail had scrambled eggs on toast. Then he wrapped a slice of toast, one of the sausages and a piece of bacon in a paper napkin and slipped the parcel into his pocket. He saw the curiosity in her face and explained, "I'd like to take it to Suneesha. We don't often have bacon or sausages."

"Your wife?"

"Yes."

Abigail hated other people showing excessive interest in her affairs. For this reason she automatically turned away from unnecessary interest in theirs. "Are we going to work in your office this morning?" she asked.

"I think so."

"Then why did we have to meet in that scout hall yesterday?"

"Not everyone agrees that it's safe at my office. My own feeling is that, when they really want to find us, the authorities will be able to."

The office building where Patel worked, like so much of Harare, was teetering on the brink of a desperate respectability. Spotless cleanliness was offset by cracked and even missing windowpanes on the staircase.

Prince, whose wife had been taken, Helena, and one of her neighbors were waiting outside the door of the offices of Smythe, Patel and Associates when they arrived. Not only is there no Smythe and no Associates, Abigail thought, but there's no receptionist either. Only one of the suite of offices rented by Patel's firm was in use. Another three awaited the return of Smythe and the associates.

Once in the office, Patel offered his usual seat behind the desk to Abigail. She looked at his face for only a moment to satisfy herself that the offer held no irony, before accepting. The others sat in chairs ranged round the desk.

"So, after all this, we have just three witnesses?"

"The others are either afraid or I didn't think their testimony would help," Patel said.

Slowly, with great deliberation, Abigail listened again to the stories as told by her small group of witnesses. Patel sat at an adjoining, smaller desk, making notes from which he would draft the affidavits needed for court. Helena went first, describing the CIO vehicle she had followed and how she had seen it enter the gates of Chikurubi prison. Her neighbor completed her story, leaving no doubt as to who was responsible for the disappearance of Helena's partner.

Then it was Prince's turn. He described at length what he had found when he came home and what the neighbors had said, but he had found no neighbor brave enough to testify.

"Unfortunately, Prince, if the matter comes to court, all that you can really testify to is that you came home and found your wife missing," Abigail said.

"What about the neighbors? I can tell the court what they said."

Abigail shook her head. "Unless they are willing to testify, the enemy will object on the grounds that this is hearsay. The judge will almost certainly throw it out."

"But my wife," Prince said. "They took her. I don't know what they may be doing to her."

"How long have you been married?"

"Two months, only two months."

Only two months, Abigail's mind echoed, and the pain is unbearable. She imposed her most legalistic calm on her voice before continuing. "One thing we must remember, people, is that we are not preparing for a trial. No evidence will be led. We will simply be asking the court to release the prisoners. All we need is enough fact to make our request reasonable." She looked from one expectant face to the next. "I think we have it."

"I'll need you to come back in two hours while I complete the affidavits," Patel said. "Then I'll take you to a neighbor who is a commissioner of oaths. He'll be waiting for us."

After the others had left, Abigail and Patel worked on the affidavits. Lunchtime came and Abigail went downstairs to a roadside stall she had noticed earlier to buy fat cakes, little rolls that are fried in oil instead of being baked. "Do you have fillings?" Abigail asked the woman who operated the stall. "I'd like savory mince, if you have it."

"No fillings, ma'am. Sorry."

Abigail took them as they were, without fillings. She and Patel were consuming them, when the telephone rang. Patel answered in his best corporate voice, "Good afternoon. Smythe, Patel and Associates." His eyes widened before he said, "Certainly, I'll put you through." He handed the phone to Abigail, his wide-open eyes and pouting lips intended to convey his surprise to her. "For you," he whispered.

"Abigail Bukula," Abigail said into the phone.

"Good afternoon, ma'am," a strong, confident male voice said. "This is Director Jonas Chunga of the Central Intelligence Organization. We understand you have been briefed by clients regarding a matter in our courts. I wondered if we could meet before this matter goes any further. I am sure that we can straighten out any difficulty that exists and avoid a lot of unnecessary unpleasantness."

Really? Abigail thought. And exactly what do you intend to sort out? After a long moment's reflection, she answered. "Thank you for your offer. I would love to meet you. When did you have in mind?"

"Now," the voice said. "As your colleague Mr. Patel knows, we are just a few minutes away. Would that be convenient?"

Now would work as well as any time, she thought. "I look forward to seeing you," she said.

Patel watched her hang up. "He's coming here?"

"Yes."

"Do you know who he is?"

"He said he is Director Jonas Chunga."

"Abigail, we don't trust him at all. He is the public-relations face of the CIO. But people say he's the most ruthless of them all." Patel was clearly alarmed.

"Krisj." She reached out to pat one of his hands. "I can hardly avoid seeing him, can I? Rather this than have his henchmen pick me up."

Jonas Chunga's knock was surprisingly soft. At first glance she could see none of the bombast she expected to find. Chunga was an impressive man. Of slightly more than average height and broad in the shoulders, he was carrying a little extra weight. A strong, broad face, eyes that looked directly at Abigail and a firm jaw: all seemed to reflect a mixture of confidence and resolution tempered by restraint. His close-cropped hair was sprinkled with gray. He was wearing a dark, well-fitting suit and blue tie.

His first view of Abigail brought him to a dead stop in the doorway of Smythe, Patel and Associates. She had risen to meet him and the light was falling toward her from windows on two sides.

The neat cut of a suit that had cost Robert plenty showed off her figure to great effect.

Abigail saw his reaction and how long he took to recover. Despite herself, she found an unexpected excitement rising in her. "Good afternoon," she said, offering a hand. "I'm Abigail Bukula."

Chunga took her right hand in one of his. The palm of his hand was dry and the grip firm, but considerately gentle. He bent over her hand. Please don't let him kiss it, she prayed.

But his lips never touched her fingers. "Jonas Chunga, at your service," he murmured.

To Abigail it was like something out of a Viennese operetta in which she was cast as the soprano who had to be swept off her feet. Where were the violins? "Won't you sit down," she suggested.

Chunga accepted a seat opposite her. She had already arranged the seating so that Patel was now on her side of the desk, forming in her mind a united front against the danger this man represented. Chunga had nodded to Patel in a perfunctory way. The solicitor was clearly not a person who needed to be taken into the reckoning. This South African woman, with some sort of ties to her own government, was a different matter.

"You found out about my visit quickly," Abigail suggested.

"We try to keep abreast of who is visiting our country." Chunga was effortlessly genial, but she heard an unevenness, almost a hoarseness, in his voice. Something had changed since she had spoken to him on the phone. Only the knowledge of who he was and what he represented reminded Abigail that there was a need to be careful. "And when the visitor is someone as eminent as yourself, we are always eager to help."

Beyond the words, which may have been straight from a government manual, Abigail read in his face a different message entirely. His smile, deliberately warm and relaxed, seemed to be saying, I am a powerful man and you are an attractive woman. We should not be spending our time discussing such matters.

The words continued on their own course. "As for this visit, I am simply wondering if there is anything I can do to help." A slight hoarseness lingered in his voice.

"I don't think you can," Abigail said.

"Why don't you try me? We understand you are here to sue

our government, or something of the sort? We'd rather deal with it before it reached that point." If there was a threat in what he was saying, Abigail could not discern it.

She glanced at Patel and saw that his eyes were fixed on the CIO man, seemingly without blinking. She was reminded of a rat, cornered by a cobra. "It is my intention to file and serve papers on your country's prison authorities tomorrow morning." She could see no point in silence. Within hours of the papers being served, he would know why she had come. "We are appealing to your High Court to free the seven people arrested by your organization some ten days ago, the so-called Harare Seven, and held without trial since then." She was pleased that she had been able to keep her voice calm and even. She would like Chunga to believe that, for her, this was a professional matter that contained no emotional element.

"Do you have the names of these people?" Chunga was good at this. It was almost possible to believe that he did not know their names.

"I believe we have a list," Abigail said. Patel had already produced a sheet of paper with the names of the seven. Abigail slid it across the desk.

Chunga looked over the list as if this was the first time he had seen these names. "No, I don't believe we have them." He was looking seriously at Abigail, trying to hold her eyes with his.

"Oh, we know that you don't have them," Abigail said casually. She was aware of a quick movement from Patel's direction.

It should have been a victory for Chunga, but he showed no sign of celebrating. The directness of his gaze had not changed and he said nothing.

"We know you don't have them. But we are sure that the prisons department does."

"I don't think so, but I will establish that today."

I could argue the case with you, Abigail thought. I could tell you about my witness who saw your vehicle enter the gates of Chikurubi. But how would that help me? I too can use silence, she thought. Her eyes were fixed on Chunga's with a look as direct and uncomplicated as his own.

He waited for her to continue. Eventually, he spoke again. "How would it be if I put my resources at your disposal?" The hoarseness in his voice had increased. "You are, after all, a visitor to our country. Let me see what I can do to help. I am willing to contact every government agency to see if they have these young people."

"Young people?" Abigail asked.

Only the briefest flicker of confusion betrayed the possibility that Chunga had recognized his mistake. He immediately tried to cover his tracks. "It's usually the young who get themselves into this sort of trouble."

"I do thank you very much. Your help would be greatly appreciated." Abigail could play the game at least as convincingly as he did.

"Then we're in agreement," he croaked.

"Absolutely."

"Excellent. I will have our people look into the matter and report back to you tomorrow."

"Thank you, Mister Chunga," Abigail said.

He smiled again, but she imagined the expression to be more guarded now. "While you're here, why don't you let me show you around the city?"

Was it possible that his voice now held an element of breathlessness? "Would you do that?"

"Certainly I would."

"Perhaps in a day or two, when this matter has been sorted out."

"It would be a pleasure. It's not every day we have a person of your standing visiting us." He paused and his voice deepened, but the slight weakness was still present. "Nor one as attractive."

"Thank you," she said. Despite herself, she felt a growing warmth in her face and neck, and just the smallest tremor of excitement. God, Abigail, she asked herself, what are you thinking? Has this thing of Robert's derailed you to this extent? Get yourself together, girl—quickly, very quickly.

He was talking again. "Where are you staying?"

As if you don't know, she thought. "The Holiday Inn," she lied.

The look of surprise that crossed Chunga's face was momentary, but it was clear to Abigail. "In that case, we'll get you there." His eyes dropped, seemingly unable to maintain the contact. "You'll hear from me tomorrow." He took a card from one of his jacket pockets and passed it to her. "The number of my cell phone is on it, in case you need me."

"Thank you."

After he had left, they had to draw aside a curtain before they could look down into the street. The black double-cab pickup with the CAM registration plates was parked half a block away. Chunga appeared from the front door of the building and walked quickly toward the vehicle. He was accompanied by two other men, both also in civilian clothing.

"They must have waited for him outside," Patel said.

"Yes."

"He likes you—sexually, I mean."

"Perhaps." The warmth in her face was draining away.

"Without a doubt. And do you think he'll try to contact you at the Holiday Inn?"

"No. He knows I'm not staying there."

"Why did you tell him that you are?"

"To test that statement, to see if he does know better. And he does."

"Yes, I could also see that. And are you going to wait for him to report before serving the papers?"

"No, but he also knows that I'm not going to." She stepped away from the window. "Give me our submission, Krisj. I want to go over it again tonight."

"I didn't think things would happen so fast," Patel said. "How did he know? Do you think someone in our circle told him?"

"Don't spend any time thinking about how the authorities know what they seem to know. It'll mess with your mind. People used to do that in my country in apartheid days. Eventually no one trusts anyone else. Forget it." She reached out and gave the shoulder closest to her a reassuring squeeze. "There's no point in delaying anything. The faster we get it done, the sooner it'll be over."

"Yes."

"Now I want you to take me back to the hotel. I've got work to do." She looked at him. Standing next to her in his ill-fitting clothes, he looked so vulnerable. Increasingly, Abigail felt the need to pat him or stroke him, not as a lover, but perhaps as a parent.

"God willing, I'll see you tomorrow, Krisj. We'll let them know they're in a fight."

Patel looked straight into her eyes. He may have been thinking about the cio. "God willing," he said.

As they left the office, she wondered why she had used that expression. It was not usually one of hers.

16

Dad, as Yudel called Rosa's father, was waiting for him. He had been waiting all day. The thought of being taken out and having something to eat in one of the city's restaurants and simultaneously escaping a meal or two at the home was a source of endless anticipation.

The strengths of the home's staff lay in qualities like cleanliness and orderliness, not imagination. To compensate, Dad had his own small refrigerator packed with yogurt, muffins, cold meats and other snacks. He had filled his room with reminders of his identity. Family photographs were everywhere. Group photos of picnics, grandchildren performing in school concerts, himself with a ten-year-old Rosa, holding hands with Hanna, his wife of many years who had died only ten months before . . . his walls were covered with mementos of more active days.

He was sitting on the edge of his bed when Yudel came in. His weekend bag that the nurses had packed was next to him. He rose slowly, with some difficulty. "Yudel, my boy," he said. "I thought you'd forgotten me."

Yudel looked at the anxious eyes of his father-in-law and hated himself for all the times he had resented running these errands for the old man. "I never have and I never will," he said. "Don't worry about that."

"But I've been waiting so long."

"Remember I told you I could only come in the afternoon."

"Yes, but I was waiting."

Conversations with Dad often followed this sort of pattern. Yudel let it go. Pursuing it had no purpose. He picked up Dad's bag and helped him up. "Thank you for fetching me, Yudel," Dad said plaintively, as they started down the corridor,

"It's a pleasure, but please don't thank me. It's not necessary."

The route they had to take passed close to the door of the matron's office. She was standing outside her office—lying in wait, as Yudel thought of it. Of all the many people, including thousands of convicts, who Yudel had regular dealings with, there were few that he actively disliked. Matron van Deventer was one of them. "She's a bureaucrat disguised as a nurse," he had told Rosa on more than one occasion.

"Doctor Gordon." He had been trying to slip past, keeping Dad between him and the matron.

The tone of her voice brought him to a stop. "Mr. Gordon," he muttered.

"I thought you were Doctor Gordon."

"Not to my knowledge."

"You would know, I'm sure." She continued without, as far as Yudel could see, even pausing to breathe. "I would like to talk to you about Mr. Yachad. I believe he's very lonely. It would help if you could see your way clear to fetch him every weekend." It was said with the accusatory tone the righteous routinely employ when dealing with sinners.

"We do," Yudel said.

"Mr. Yachad says otherwise." Given the tone of her voice, she might just as well have said, Don't you lie to me, Dr. Gordon.

Yudel frowned at Dad. "Mr. Yachad is mistaken."

"I don't see how he could be. It's his life. He should know."

"Look at your logbook, woman," Yudel was surprised by his angry tone. I should try to perfect it, he thought.

"I certainly shall."

"Good. I'll await your apology." He took Dad by the arm and set off down the corridor at a quick march. He only slowed as they reached the parking lot. "Dad, did you put her up to that?"

"You know me, Yudel. I can't remember when you last came."

"We came on Sunday. We went to the zoo and got one of those

little golf carts and drove around in it. And you had spaghetti Bolognese under the trees."

"Oh yes. Was that last Sunday?"

"Yes. What did you tell her?"

"I don't remember."

You lying old bugger, Yudel thought. On their way to meet Rosa, Yudel deliberately drove slowly to let his agitation subside.

"Yudel," Dad said softly. "Please don't be angry with me."

Yudel glanced at him, ninety years old and feeling remorse for the sympathy-seeking lie he had told the matron. I know, Yudel thought. You were just trying to win a little warmth from that piece of ice masquerading as a woman. Let me not be a jerk. "I'm not angry, Dad. It's all right."

Dad waited a few seconds for the matter to subside. "Yudel, you're a man who knows all about people. You know what they do and why they do it."

Superficially, I'm afraid, Yudel thought. "What do you want to know, Dad?"

"I've heard them say that young women like older men. Is it true?"

"Older men like me, or older men like you?"

"Older men like me."

Yudel looked at the anxious eyes of the old man. His mouth was hanging open slightly and Yudel could see the gaps where two of his teeth were missing. He had not shaved well that morning and odd patches of stubble were visible in irregular patterns across his cheeks and chin. "Certainly," Yudel said.

"Then I don't know why when I try to talk to them, they never seem very interested."

"So what does the matron say about you trying to pick up women?" Yudel tried not to smirk.

"No, Yudel, not like that. I just try to talk to the nurses sometimes."

Oh damn, Yudel thought, don't we ever outlive it? He considered the matter for a moment before being assailed by what seemed to be a moment of inspiration. "I am told that all such problems can be resolved by good marketing," he said.

Dad looked puzzled. "I don't know anything about marketing, Yudel."

But a new thought had been forming in the convoluted patterns of Yudel's thinking. "Perhaps I can help," he said.

Parking was not easy to find near the newspaper office, but after a few times round the block, he saw a car leave on the other side of the street. An illegal U-turn that almost resulted in a collision with one of the city's endless streams of minibus taxis got him into the bay marginally ahead of a luxury four-wheel-drive vehicle. The owner shouted something out of the window, then drove away.

The only person manning an office that was marked "Classified Ads" was a young woman, probably still in her teens. Straggling, bleached hair hung down her back in uneven lengths. She was busy painting her toenails a fluorescent pink. "I'd like to place a classified ad," Yudel told her.

"Why don't you do it on the Internet," the girl said. "It's easy."

"I want to do it now. I came here to do it."

"Anyone can do it on our Web site," she said, carefully examining the glowing varnish she had administered to the small toe of her right foot. "It's easy to do."

"Are you refusing to take my advertisement?" Yudel glared at her. Mariette van Deventer had been enough for one afternoon.

The girl sighed audibly and laid down the little bottle of varnish. "No, I'll take it. We always give good service. It's company policy."

Dad, holding on to one of Yudel's sleeves for support, was following the exchange like a spectator at a tennis match.

The girl passed a printed form to Yudel. "Name and telephone number," she demanded. After he had filled in those pieces of information, she took back the form. "Section?"

"Social," Yudel said.

She looked at Yudel. "So what's it got to say?"

Yudel gathered his thoughts for a moment before starting: "Financially secure older gentleman seeks companionship. I am vigorous, loving, considerate and generous. I am looking for an attractive female companion between the ages of thirty and seventy. I expect her to be well-read, intelligent, industrious and a good cook. Applications from ladies who are physically well endowed and possess a grandfather complex will receive preferential treatment. Applicants please phone"—he thought a moment, in order to get the matron's name right—"Mariette van Deventer at 012-664-3922 to make an appointment with Morrie Yachad."

The girl stopped writing and reread her work. "An older gentleman like him"—cocking her head toward Dad—"or an older gentleman like you?"

"Like him," Yudel said.

Dad smiled at her, revealing the gaps in his teeth.

She made a copy of the form, placed the original in an out-tray and slipped the copy into her bag on the floor under her desk. "Still, I like the part about him being financially secure. None of my boyfriends ever have a buck to their names."

"None of them?" Yudel asked innocently.

"Not one."

"The bastards," Yudel said.

"And this grandfather-complex thing—what's that?"

"Girls who have the hots for men old enough to be their grandfathers," Yudel explained.

"You get that?"

"Certainly."

"A lot?"

"Millions of them."

"Jeez." She sounded stunned. "Some chicks are weird."

"So, are you signing up for a meeting?"

"The next time one of my boyfriends takes me out and I have to pay, I'll phone this Mariette. I swear."

"You won't be sorry," Yudel said. "Take no nonsense from Mariette, though. She can be a bit difficult."

As a result of stopping at the newspaper office, Yudel and Dad were late meeting Rosa in the comfortable, family-run restaurant where they were going to have an early supper. A treat for Dad, Rosa had said. She was sipping from a glass of white wine when they came in.

"We were slowed up by that damned matron," Yudel said. "She accused us of not taking Dad out often enough."

"The cheek of it." Rosa's face colored red at the thought of such impudence.

"And we had to do marketing," Dad said.

"Marketing?" Rosa looked at Yudel.

A barely perceptible shake of Yudel's head was intended to convey that Dad was confused as usual.

"Never mind marketing," Rosa said. "Let's order. I'm hungry. I had no lunch and I've been waiting half an hour for the pair of you."

After they had placed their orders, the proprietor, a man in his early seventies who spoke with a Greek accent and walked slowly between the tables, came to tell them that the kleftiko Rosa had ordered for Dad would take half an hour. If you wanted to get the best out of it, it could not be hurried.

"We'll survive till then," Rosa told him.

"I'm looking forward to this," Dad said. "Since the ANC won the election, they've given us practically nothing to eat in that place."

Rosa looked at her father through half-closed eyes. "Don't talk nonsense, Dad. The government has nothing to do with the food at the home."

"I'm telling you, Rosa . . ."

"The home is a private institution. And the election was months ago. If you'd had practically nothing to eat, you would've been dead by now."

"I nearly am."

Dad was halfway through his life-saving kleftiko when he suddenly put down his knife and fork. Rosa followed almost immediately. It took a few more seconds before Yudel realized that he was the only one eating. Looking up, he saw the panic on the faces of both his wife and father-in-law.

"Yudel," Rosa said, "I need to ask you a very big favor."

Yudel looked from Rosa to Dad. "What's happening here?"

"Yudel," Rosa was pleading, "we're not entirely continent anymore and I can't go into the men's room with Dad."

It took Yudel a long moment to understand. "Jesus, Dad," he said, "have you shat yourself?"

"No, Yudel, I never shat myself. It's just a wet fart."

"Please, Yudel, but you have to go now." Rosa handed Yudel a plastic bag that contained something soft.

"What's this?"

"A pad."

"A sanitary towel?"

"A special kind for this. Please, Yudel."

He took the bag from Rosa. "Come on, Dad, before I change my mind."

On their way to the toilet two waiters watched them with interest. They were accustomed to seeing female clientele approaching the toilets in groups. More than one man at a time was unusual. One of them said something to the other. The second one shrugged. Professionally, it was simply not their business.

Five minutes later, Rosa watched them come back from the toilet, Yudel leading Dad between the tables. "Thank you, Yudel," she said. "You're a kind man."

"Think nothing of it," Yudel muttered.

"I just want you to know that I appreciate it."

Dad added his bit. "I also appreciate it."

"It's all right, both of you. Forget it. I'm trying to." He thought briefly about the classified ad and the girl in the newspaper office and how she would have coped with the situation and whether a measure of financial security was worth it. Suddenly he was not convinced of the kindness of his actions.

"The real problem is I suffer from tenesmus," Dad told Yudel.

"No, Dad. You don't suffer from tenesmus."

"What's tenesmus?" Rosa asked.

The possibility of an answer was interrupted by a distant voice. "Answer your phone," it wailed. "Answer now."

Rosa scratched in her bag and brought out her cell phone. "Answer your phone," the phone itself commanded, louder and more insistent now.

"Christ, is that a phone?" Yudel wanted to know.

"They put that on instead of a ring tone," Rosa explained. Her eyebrows rose as she recognized the voice on the other end of the connection. "Abigail, my dear, how are you?" Then, after a moment of listening, "Yes, of course. He's right here."

Yudel took the phone from Rosa. "Yudel?" Abigail's voice was as clear as if she was in the same room.

"Where are you?" He had already guessed the answer, but wanted it confirmed.

"I'm in Zimbabwe."

"Working on your case?"

"Yes. Have you heard from Robert?"

"No. I've had no contact with Robert since that confusion at the hotel."

"I can't get hold of him."

"Shall I try to reach him for you?" Yudel did not believe that this was the reason for her call, though. "Are you having difficulties?" He was aware of the close attention Rosa was paying to the part of the conversation she could hear.

"Everything seems to be difficult here. I've already had a meeting with one of the CIO top people and I'm serving the papers tomorrow."

Yudel had heard about the CIO from Zimbabwean prisoners in this country, but he had never been convinced of the accuracy of their stories. "Perhaps after you've served the papers you can come home until you have a court date."

"I'm not sure that I can. In fact, I don't feel I can come home till it's all over."

"I think Robert will want you to. I'll try to contact him."

"No, don't contact him."

"I can go to his office . . ."

"No, leave it alone, Yudel. Please leave it alone."

"Abigail," he said, pausing long enough after her name to create the effect that this was important. "Is there some way I can help you?"

"Thank you, Yudel, but no. I don't believe so."

Then why did you call? he asked himself. "You know that if there's anything I can do, you have only to ask."

"I know."

After the conversation was over and Yudel had returned the phone to Rosa to switch off, she asked, "Is Abigail in Zimbabwe?"

"Yes."

"Why did she call?"

"I think she's frightened. She's had the CIO onto her already."

"Those are the horrible people who . . ."

"By reputation, yes."

"You said she should come home. Is she going to?"

"No." Yudel's thoughts were not with Rosa's questions now. His imagination was in Harare, a city he and Rosa had visited only twice, and then many years before, on leave. "She says she can't see herself coming home, until she feels the job is done."

It was a long moment before he looked directly at Rosa and saw the horror in her eyes.

17

The light in Krisj Patel's office came from a single reading lamp. He was working late on the conveyancing of a property in the wealthy security estate of Borrowdale Brooke, just a kilometer from the president's own residence. He had received part payment in U.S. dollars the day before, and was expecting the rest as soon as the deed was registered.

He knew that a portion of his fee would have to go to the staff in the deeds office to encourage them to do their work. Patel did not see it as a bribe. He knew that many of the clerks in the deeds office earned so little that they could barely afford their transport to work. Often there was nothing left for rent or food. Clothing rarely came into any calculation. The clothes you had, had to be made to last. Sometimes, if you were to get the job done, fees had to be shared with others.

He also had to do a will for a farmer. It was being paid for in eggs. Then there was a business contract that would also be paid in U.S. dollars, but over six months. A nurse was suing her employer for wrongful dismissal and Patel had agreed to take the matter on a contingency basis. He had very little hope of collecting anything, even if he won. It was a private hospital, and the word from the staff was that it was not expected to be open much longer.

These were the cases that would help to put food on the table for himself and Suneesha, his wife, at least for the moment. Sometimes her teaching contributed a little. The parents of one of the children in her class had a smallholding outside of town and occasionally Suneesha received a parcel of vegetables from them. Her baking also contributed something. It was not much, but it was regular.

The battle against the dictatorship for the release of the Harare Seven was not going to bring in any revenue, unless the matter came to the attention of an international donor organization. But they were reluctant to release money for fear of it falling into government hands.

Being a member of the Organization for Peace and Justice in Zimbabwe had taught Patel to be careful. The curtains in his office were heavy and overlapped the windows on either side, making it impossible for anyone outside to see in. He had steel doors fitted, front and back. Entering and leaving the building, he first checked the stairwell to ensure that it was empty, then switched off the light and descended in darkness. If anyone was going to take a shot at him, that person would not have his task made easy.

On this evening, Patel had been careless in only one respect. Usually, as night approached and parking spaces emptied around the building, he would fetch his car, which was sometimes parked blocks away, and park it directly opposite the door of the building.

It was only when he reached street level that he appreciated the mistake he had made. He now had three blocks to walk down Nelson Mandela Drive to the car. But he could see no one in the street, except a lone night-watchman in the next block. The night-watchman was sitting on a plastic chair that leaned against the wall of a building. Patel knew him well enough to call him by his first name, Petrus. The watchman always called him Mr. Patel, a habit that seemed impossible to change.

Patel left the building, walking quickly, following a path that would take him right past the night-watchman. The watchman, seeing him approaching, half rose from his seat, one hand raised in greeting. Patel waved back. It was good to be known and liked where you lived and worked. He saw the white of teeth against the brown of the man's face as he smiled.

Neither man heard the click of the rifle's bolt action as the cartridge was slipped into the firing chamber. Neither saw any movement out of the ordinary or suspected that anything could be wrong. Patel had already forgotten fears that were surely groundless.

The first bullet struck his right shoulder before he heard the sound of the rifle. His collarbone shattered and much of the tissue around it was destroyed. It felt like a heavy punch, numbing rather than painful. He thought he had seen a flash, somewhere to his right in one of the windows a block or more away. The nightwatchman was on his feet now, but had not moved toward him. Patel was aware that he had taken one step back. Could it have been the force with which he had been struck? His body felt heavy and he sank slowly to his knees.

The second bullet struck much lower, destroying the joint of his right hip. He was falling to that side. He tried to reach out a hand to break his fall, but the arm was not working. The third bullet penetrated his heart, killing him instantly. The last image he saw was that of the night-watchman coming toward him. "Mr. Patel," he was saying in a voice that betrayed his disbelief. "Mr. Patel!"

Abigail had been in bed for more than an hour when the hotel telephone at her bedside rang. She did not immediately recognize Helena's voice.

"Abigail, Abigail, my God, Abigail . . ." The voice fractured into sobbing.

"Who is this?" Abigail demanded. "Who's speaking?"

"Abigail, I saw him. They called me, my God. Those other people were already there."

"Who are you? What are you talking about?"

"Krisj, Krisj, I saw Krisj on the pavement. He was on the pavement . . ."

Abigail understood immediately that the caller did not mean that Krisj had been standing on the pavement.

The voice went over to screaming. "You told us that you and Krisj would be safe, but the rest of us had to be careful." The hysteria subsided slightly and something about the voice had become familiar. "They got him. Krisj's wife called me. What about the rest of us now?"

"Helena," she said, "is that you?" On the only other occasion when Abigail had heard her voice it had been characterized by a calm so studied that it must have been carefully imposed. Now it was ragged with a hysteria that threatened to make it unintelligible.

"Oh God, Abigail. He was lying facedown. Everything was wrong, the way one of his arms was twisted. The blood on the paving stones made a river in the cracks. I never knew there was so much blood . . ."

The picture the other woman was describing was unbearable, but Abigail had to make sure that she knew who was on the line. "Helena," she said. "I think it's you. Tell me, is it you?"

"Yes, yes, yes." There seemed to be no stopping the outpouring on the other end of the line. "Yes, it's me. Suneesha phoned me. It happened hours ago, maybe seven o'clock. She said she knew it was going to happen sooner or later. The bastards tried with Tony before. She said she just couldn't go. But I couldn't stay away. I had to go. Jesus, I hate those bastards."

"You said those other people were already there. Who did you mean?"

"The CIO. They murdered him and they were standing there pretending they had nothing to do with it."

"Did they shoot him?"

"Yes, yes, yes, yes . . ." It seemed as if she would never stop. ". . . yes, yes, yes. Everything was wrong. I saw his body there. It was not Krisj any more."

"Where are you, Helena?"

"In a friend's car. I'm going back. I'm leaving. I can't be here. I know what Suneesha meant. It's bad enough they killed him, I'm not going to watch them gloat."

"Yes, go home. Go home and stay there," Abigail told her. "Take a sleeping pill. We'll talk in the morning. I know it's terrible, but try to sleep now. Better still, go to a safe place and sleep there. Do you understand?"

"Yes."

"Will you do it?"

"Yes."

After she had hung up, Abigail got out of bed and dressed carefully. She was trying not to hurry, trying above all to maintain the fragile control she had over herself. Once dressed, she left the room, locking the door behind her, and walked the length of the broad passage. She descended the stairs as purposefully as everything else she had done since learning of Patel's death.

Abigail knew that for her the knowledge of his death was not enough. She was like Helena in that way. She would have to go there and see for herself. He was dead, but, for her, that fact would not be real until she had seen the body. Intellectually, she knew it was so and she knew she would have to go on without him now and that they may be coming for her too, but none of it would be real until she had seen his body.

In the foyer, she met Marjorie Swan. "Is it possible to get a cab this time of night?"

The woman's eyebrows rose, questioning the need at so late an hour.

"You know Krisj Patel, of course," Abigail said.

"Of course."

"He died tonight." Abigail looked into the woman's face that was asking a different question now. "He died of gunshot wounds."

"Dear God," the hotelkeeper said.

18

The cab company had said they would send a car and that Abigail should wait inside the hotel. Marjorie Swan had poured herself a brandy and asked Abigail if she wanted one.

"Not now," Abigail said. "Perhaps when I get back."

"I'll leave one at your bedside. You'll be needing it."

"Thanks," Abigail said.

"I'll make it a double."

"All right."

But waiting in the hotel foyer was almost impossible. On her third brief visit to the street to meet the cab, she saw a large vehicle coming hard round a corner a few blocks away. It was one of the black double-cabs Patel had pointed out to her. It came to an abrupt halt next to her, and Jonas Chunga leaped from the door on the driver's side. He came round the front of the vehicle in long strides. "Abigail, have you heard?" His eyes looked wild. His jacket and tie had been left somewhere and the top two buttons of his shirt were open. "Your colleague has been killed."

If this was an act, Abigail would reflect later, it was a very good one.

"I came as soon as I heard. I know you were friendly with him."

"Apparently he was gunned down on the street," Abigail said. Her voice was shaking, but it was impossible to do anything about that.

"Yes." He tried to take hold of one of her shoulders, but she stepped away. She was aware that Marjorie Swan was also on the pavement. So were two men who had come with Chunga. Probably the two who had been with him earlier, Abigail thought.

"We rushed to the scene immediately," Chunga said, "but he was already dead."

The conversation could not be allowed to continue in this vein. "His friends think your people did it," Abigail said.

"It's not so." He was looking directly into her eyes. "It just isn't so. I swear to you it isn't so."

"They say your men killed him and that they were gloating over his dead body."

"Absolutely not. I was at the scene shortly after the first of our men got there. There was absolutely no gloating. I swear it. We see this as a very serious crime—all the more so because government agencies will be suspected of carrying it out."

Her eyes were seeking his, not because of any inner power he possessed, but because of her need to know the truth. Abigail remembered Yudel telling her on another occasion that psychopaths were better able to hold eye contact without blinking or turning away than other people—just as Chunga was doing now. They could often maintain the semblance of truth better than those who were telling the truth. But perhaps Chunga really was just telling the truth.

"Please believe me," he was saying. "If this act was initiated by our organization, I would certainly know about it. And I don't. Please believe me."

"Will you take me there?" Abigail asked.

"To see his body?"

"Is he still where it happened?"

"I believe so. He was five minutes ago."

"Will you take me there?"

"I'd advise against it. It's not . . . it's not good to see. I don't think . . ."

"Will you take me?"

"If you insist."

She started toward the twin-cab. "I'll sit in front with you."

As Chunga had said, Patel's body was still in the same position, just as he had fallen. A crowd had gathered, not the typical joyous, noisy African crowd that might attend a football match or a revival meeting. This was a subdued gathering, drawn from apartments and houses in the nearby streets. Questions were being asked and replies whispered. The people were fascinated by the events of the night. It was not every day that someone was shot dead in the streets of their neighborhood. There were those who knew Patel. He had kept some of them out of jail and helped others in various ways.

A police photographer was taking pictures of the body, aiming from different angles. Abigail saw three men in civilian clothes entering one of the buildings on the far side of the road, perhaps the direction from which the shots had been fired. Another was making notes as he questioned the night-watchman who had seen Patel die. Six or seven uniformed policemen were holding back the gathering crowd. It was not a bad response from the police for one of the poorest countries on earth.

Abigail stayed seated until Chunga opened the door for her. As she got out he was speaking again. "I will not allow this sort of thing. It reflects badly on my country. I promise you we will find the culprit. We will search until we find him."

"Where will you look?" Abigail heard herself ask.

"I beg your pardon."

Was there some small sign of alarm in his face? Abigail wondered. Or did I imagine it? "Where will you look, surely not among his friends?" she asked.

"We will go wherever our information leads us."

And where will that be? she wondered.

A part of the crowd came forward to get a clear view of Abigail. Perhaps she was the widow and they would be on hand to see her reaction to the dead body of her man. Perhaps they would see her kneel beside the body to pray, or scream in agony, or collapse in shock. Chunga moved quickly between her and the crowd, holding up an arm to protect her. "Stand back," he commanded. "Stand back immediately."

A uniformed policeman came hurrying forward to help. "Stand back or we'll have to clear the street."

Patel's body was much as Helena had described it. He was still facedown. The right arm was twisted away from the torso at an angle it would never have occupied in life. The stream of blood on the pavement was largely congealed now, a reddish-black line filling the space between two paving stones until it spilled, spreading, into the gutter. Helena had been right. Abigail too had not expected that much blood.

She bent over to see Patel's face. To her surprise, the violence of his death had left no mark on his features. He looked peaceful, possibly more peaceful than he had in life. And this, finally, would be the end of Smythe, Patel and Associates, that he had been so proud of.

What am I doing in this country? she asked herself. Rosa was right. And Robert was right. The only sensible thing is to get on the first flight home tomorrow. But Tony, what about Tony?

Yes, that's what I'll do, she thought. I'll get out of the damned place tomorrow.

Chunga had the grace to stop his protestations of innocence. Abigail glanced at him. His face was set in what looked to her like an expression of absolute determination. The look alone seemed to be telling her that he would find the killer, no matter what resources it took or how long they worked on it.

She searched the pavements for CIO operatives and found four or five whom she was sure were Chunga's men. Unlike the people in the crowd dressed in a motley assortment of whatever had come to hand, the men were all wearing well-worn suits and ties, or at least jackets and ties. Like so much of the country, they were doing their best to look as good as possible with what they had. They all looked stern and serious, not the gloating mob of Helena's imagination. Where does the truth lie in all this? she asked herself. Only one thing was indisputable. The body on the pavement had once belonged to Krisj Patel.

"Could you take me back to the hotel now?" Abigail asked.

19

When Abigail opened the door of her room, she saw the parcel lying on the only table. Next to it was the brandy Marjorie Swan had promised. The parcel was wrapped in brown paper that appeared to have been used more than once in the past. Abigail drank the brandy and carefully unwrapped the parcel, taking out the affidavits and the application. Everything was there; the originals and three copies of each document. There was even a check for the court fees. She hoped that had not come from Patel's slim resources.

He must have sent them by messenger before he was killed, she thought. It could not have been long before. Everything was there, the affidavits and the application. He must have sent them off, then gone down to the street to become a sniper's target.

Abigail was crying. She had heard the news and she had seen his body, but there had been no tears. Now there was this parcel, the last act of the little solicitor's career. He was not really small, but somehow she saw him that way. Her tears flowed freely down her cheeks and over her lips. She remembered that she had asked if Patel was putting her head into a noose. As things had developed, his head had been sacrificed alone—at least so far.

Any thoughts of leaving on the next morning's flight had disappeared. Patel's brown paper parcel had made that course of action impossible.

She wept for Patel, but Jonas Chunga was the other reason for her troubled state of mind. It could not all be a pretense, she told herself. His reactions were too real. And yet, if it were not a CIO agent who had pulled the trigger, who else would have wanted this ineffective-seeming solicitor dead? Friends of the old dictator perhaps? And if the killer was to be found in that company, would the police be prepared to make an arrest? Would Jonas Chunga and the CIO?

There was no getting Chunga out of her mind. The protective way he had stepped between her and the people in the crowd, the way he had told her that they would search until they found the killer, the way he had hurried to tell her about Patel's death—they all seemed like the acts of someone seeking to protect her.

She thought about the CIO. Its role had always been to find and deal with enemies of the regime. She knew that a certain kind of man, who lusted after uninhibited power, was drawn to such organizations.

And Jonas Chunga, where did he fit into that picture? Was he also drawn to power and did he serve it regardless of who possessed it and how it was used?

Only now, after a day in which her mind had been filled with other matters, did she remember Robert. She took out her cell phone and dialed her home number. As before, her own voice urged her to leave a message. This time she felt no pang of anxiety, no moment of desperation.

Without thinking, she dialed his office number and got one of the security guards. "Vuna Corporation," a heavily accented African voice said.

"Is Mr. Mokoapi still working?" she asked.

"No, nobody's working," the guard said.

"Are you sure?"

"Nobody's working, nobody."

She dialed again without conscious purpose. This time it was the number of Yudel's home. She heard the sound of a single short ring from the other side, then hung up. The whole thing has nothing to do with Yudel, she thought. What the hell would I say to him? And then there was Rosa. What would she think?

She surprised herself by feeling comforted by the idea of speaking to Rosa and dialed the number again. Somehow, it was no surprise when it was Rosa who answered.

"Rosa?"

The older woman recognized her voice immediately. "Abigail, are you safe?"

"No, I don't think so. I don't feel safe."

"How you feel is everything," Rosa said. "You get on a plane and come home. Come home immediately."

"No, I can't come, not now."

"And why not?"

"The attorney who briefed me is dead. He was assassinated tonight."

"Oh." Rosa needed a long silence to give herself the opportunity to find a way to respond.

"Rosa?" Abigail asked. "Are you still there?"

"Yes, my dear. I am simply too horrified to say anything. I think you should speak to Yudel."

"No, I called to speak to you."

"But I'm just not the person for this."

"I just wanted to hear a friendly voice."

Suddenly, as if a switch had been thrown, the friendly voice became authoritative. "Abigail, you listen to me. This whole thing is not your business. You don't belong in that country. You call a cab immediately and get to the airport. Then take the first flight out of there."

"I can't, Rosa. I can't do that now."

Abigail had barely hung up when her phone rang.

"Abby?" This time it was Robert trying to contact her. She could hear voices and music in the background.

Despite herself, she was pleased to hear him. "I tried to get hold of you—last night and earlier tonight. Where were you?"

His response came too quickly and was much too vague. "I've been running all over the place. But how are you?"

"But where were you? I phoned home and the office."

"You know how busy I've been, Abigail. I've had meetings all over the place."

She could hear the lie in his voice. Meetings with whom? she wanted to scream at him. And all over the place? Where is all over the place? Instead she asked, "Are you home now?"

"No, I'm having dinner with Kgomotso. We're going over his marketing plan."

Her watch told her it was almost two. Dinner with Kgomotso at two in the morning? Where in Pretoria did you find a restaurant that was still open at two? Can I speak to Kgomotso? she thought. Let me speak to him so that I know that he is the one you are with. "It's very late for dinner," she said.

"Things are mad at the office. We've been working late. This was the only opportunity."

"Where are you having dinner?" She hated herself for asking.

"Mandrea's."

Mandrea's? she thought. Dim lighting; booths that were pretty private. Without warning, the image of the blond PA rose in her mind. Almost immediately it was followed by one as vivid of Jonas Chunga, his strong arm outstretched to shield her from the crowd trying to get close to Krisj Patel's body. "Is that a good place for a business meeting?" she asked. "The lighting is not good to read by."

"I know," he said. "Perhaps it was a bad choice."

"I think so," she said. Perhaps this conversation had been a poor choice, she thought. But say something to me that means something, she pleaded inwardly with Robert. Above all, say something to drive away the picture in my head of this man.

"But your case. How's your case going?"

To Abigail, he was pretending an interest that he did not feel, or rather, his was an interest that served as a cover for himself. "The case is not going well," she said. "The attorney briefing me was assassinated this evening."

"Jesus Christ, is this true?"

And suddenly the newspaper man takes over, Abigail thought. "Of course it's true."

"I'll have a man on the next flight."

"Why don't you come yourself?"

"I'd love to, Abby. Really. There's nothing I'd like better. But they know about me. Whoever I send will have to pretend to be a tourist. They won't allow a journalist in."

"Won't you try? Please try."

"They won't allow me in. There's no point in my trying. I'll send a man they won't have a record of."

"I wish you would try to come."

"I can't, but tell me about it. Tell me what you can."

Before hanging up, she told him the little she knew. She also told him something about Krisj Patel, the poorly fitting clothes, the nervous mannerisms, and the determination to see justice done in his country. She also told him how she had inspected the body where it lay on the pavement.

She lay back in bed and tried to think about her first full day in Harare. But all she could think about were the last few minutes. Robert would not even try to come. Nor did he once suggest that she should come home, despite what he had to know she was going through.

Lying in bed, her gaze came to rest on the warring tiger and elephant under the window. The tiger's upper lip was curled back, revealing canines that were disproportionately long and pointed. Nice to see a friendly face, she thought.

20

By morning *The Herald* already had the previous night's story. "Government opponent slain," the headline proclaimed. A sub-head expanded on the matter: "Well-known criminal elements suspected by police."

A caption under a photograph of a stern-looking Jonas Chunga read: "Director Jonas Chunga of the CIO has vowed to bring the criminals to justice."

The report quoted Chunga as saying that the fact that Patel was an enemy of the government made no difference to their determination to bring the guilty to justice. It went on to describe how he had been shot leaving his office. A man had been seen fleeing the scene by a night-watchman on duty near the place where Patel had been shot. The method used and clues left at the scene pointed to a well-known gang that had been operating in Harare for the last six months. The police were investigating.

Abigail would have given anything to be part of the investigation into Patel's death, but clearly that would not be possible. The authorities would not have allowed it under any circumstances, but in this matter, in which they were the most likely suspects, joining the investigation was beyond even the wildest possibility.

By the time she had finished her breakfast, her cab, called by the hotel, had arrived. She was at the High Court building in ten minutes. At the registrar's counter, two female clerks were watched over by the same unsmiling photograph of the old dictator that the hotel had on display. They were in deep conversation. One of the clerks was saying how the administration was not fair and that the lawyers and judges got all the money and they got nothing. She looked resentfully at Abigail before getting up from her seat to come to the counter. "Good morning," she said, scowling deeply.

"Good morning," Abigail said. "I have an urgent application here for a hearing."

"Urgent?" the woman asked. "Must it be urgent?"

"Yes, it is urgent."

"What firm do you work for?"

"Bukula and Associates," Abigail said. It seemed to be the Zimbabwean way of giving your firm a name. The woman was screwing up her eyes as if weighing up Abigail's statement. "I am Bukula."

"You're the solicitor?"

"I'm the barrister."

"Oh." The eyes widened. "Sorry, miss." It was clearly not usual for barristers to make the trip to court for this sort of thing. Abigail watched her take out a foolscap-size notebook from behind the counter and page slowly through it. The process clearly took some concentration. Eventually she looked up, keeping her place on the page with an index finger. "Two weeks," she said.

"That's out of the question," Abigail told her. "This is a habeas corpus matter. It is urgent. People are missing and have to be found."

The clerk went back to search through her notebook. "Friday, in two weeks," she said. "That's the best I can do."

"You have to do better."

"Friday, two weeks from today, is the best I can do. The register is full."

"Please try," she said between gritted teeth.

"I can't try. The register, it's full."

The woman who had remained seated spoke up in support of her colleague. "If the register is full, you can't try."

By the time she reached it, everything had changed at the scene of Patel's death. The body had been removed hours before. Only a bloodstain in the gutter and a congealed remnant of his life's blood between the paving stones remained of the night's incident.

The people of the area were going about their business as if nothing had happened. And, no doubt, many were unaware that their local attorney had been killed on that pavement just hours before.

Nothing could be learned from staring at the paving stones where Krisj's blood had run, or at the buildings on either side of the street. The night-watchman who had seen him die would probably be at home, asleep, before his next shift. His plastic chair was nowhere to be seen. Abigail wondered if, after this, he was still going to sit outside on summer evenings.

It was mid-afternoon by the time she got back to the hotel. She was lying down on the bed, debating whether she should call Robert again, when the events of the last twenty-four hours and the little sleep of the night before overcame her and she slept.

The knowledge that she would have to wait two weeks for the hearing and the thought of what might happen to Tony and the others in the meantime ran a tortured race through her dreams. She woke with the sun already low in the sky and the telephone ringing. Reaching for it, she knocked the handset onto the ground. By the time she had scrambled after it and gathered it off the floor, there was no sound from the receiver. Robert, she thought. It must be Robert.

She put back the handset and stood next to the phone, waiting for Robert to call again. In just a few seconds it rang. "Robert?" she demanded of the phone.

"Hello, Abigail."

She recognized Jonas Chunga's voice immediately. "Good afternoon," she said.

"I believe you were at the murder scene today."

"That's right." Is that a crime in this damned country? she wondered, but resisted asking.

"I can't tell you how sorry I am about what happened and how determined I am to apprehend the guilty party."

"The newspaper says that gangsters did it," Abigail told him. Explain that bit of nonsense to me, she thought. "I don't believe it."

"Nor do I."

"I'm sorry," Abigail said. "Say that again."

"I don't believe it was a criminal act. I believe it was a political crime."

Abigail sat down slowly on the edge of the bed. "What are you saying?"

"I believe, as you do, that politics lay behind it."

"And?"

"And it's not a simple matter. Have dinner with me tomorrow night and we can discuss it at length."

"I beg your pardon? I don't think I heard you correctly."

"I said, have dinner with me tomorrow night and we can discuss it."

"Isn't there a Mrs. Chunga?"

"No, there's no Mrs. Chunga. There never has been. There was once a special lady, but there has never been a Mrs. Chunga."

Yes, Abigail thought. I want to do this. I want to do this more badly than I should want it. I need to do this. But what about Krisj? What would Krisj feel if he could see it? Perhaps he can.

"Abigail, are you still there?"

"Yes. I don't think this is a good time, though."

"Are you thinking about Patel?"

"Yes. And my case."

"I understand, but there is so little time to deal with the matter that brought you here. We can talk about that. And we can talk about what happened to Patel. I can share my suspicions with you."

"Just that?"

"I also want you to understand more about my country."

What else? she thought. What else do you want from me?

He answered without her ever framing the question. "And I want you to understand more about me."

Why that? she wondered, but she only said, "I see."

"Will you come, then?"

He wanted her to understand about his country. And he wanted her to understand about himself. This was something real, perhaps something with meaning. He was so different to Robert. If he wanted her to understand anything, it might be why he was doing whatever it was he was doing with his blond PA.

"Will you come?"

What is it that I'm hearing in his voice? she asked herself. It sounds like the uncertainties of a teenage boy. Can it be that it took courage for this powerful man to ask me to dinner?

"Will you?"

"Yes, Jonas. I'll come."

21

The restaurant was in a country club on the outskirts of town. Jonas Chunga steered the Mercedes down a long avenue skirted by sporadic clusters of spreading acacias. The light was still good enough for Abigail to see the beautifully manicured golf course beyond the row of trees. The parking area in front of a low, colonial-style building held more expensive cars than she would have expected, even on a Saturday evening. Nor did she expect the white-jacketed and white-gloved waiters or the maître d'hôtel who came down the stairs to meet them, shaking hands and smiling at Chunga, then bowing to her.

"Andrew is waiting for you, Director Chunga," he said. "He has your table prepared."

If there was a difference between the scene that greeted them on entering the club's restaurant and the one that would have greeted guests fifty years before, it was that now at least half the patrons were black. Most of them were members of the governing elite, dining tonight in the same setting that the colonial elite had once enjoyed. The other guests were probably all members of what remained of the business elite.

The maître d'hôtel had addressed him as Director Chunga. Now Andrew, the waiter, led them to a table on a glassed-in terrace overlooking the golf course and shielded from the main section of the restaurant by a row of potted palms. "I think you've been here before, Director Chunga," Abigail said.

"Once or twice." The waiter attempted to pull out the chair to seat her, but Chunga brushed him aside. He leaned protectively over her now as he seated her. She remembered the same feeling of being protected when she had been crowded by the people at the scene of Patel's death and how he had come between her and them.

He settled into his chair, leaning back comfortably, his hands resting on the edge of the table. He was broad in the shoulders, still more powerful-looking than the image that had remained in her mind since their previous meetings. The gray in his hair was not only at the temples, but spread in little bright tufts across his head. When she had first met him, he had been, for her, the representative of something that horrified her. Now, by some strange metamorphosis, he had changed from being a symbol to just being a man.

"This is a big surprise to me," she said.

"Even bigger to me." The little smile around his mouth and in his eyes revealed genuine amusement. The voice was strong and secure. The hoarseness when she had first met him and the boyish uncertainty over the phone when he had invited her had both disappeared.

"That you asked me. That's what surprised me."

"And that you accepted. That was the biggest surprise of all."

Abigail was aware that she too was smiling. This was a man, a powerful man, an attractive man and he found her attractive. His attention was only with her.

The waiter arrived with a bottle of white wine in an icebucket.

"Do you make all the decisions tonight?" she asked. Damn, she thought—that sounded like a tease.

"Not at all."

"You mean I am allowed to order my own dinner?"

"May I be permitted a suggestion?"

She heard her own soft laugh. "I thought there was a catch."

"There's no catch. It's just that I know the menu well."

"So which delicacy should I order?"

The waiter, who had not gone far since bringing the wine, was back, order-book in hand. "May I suggest the seafood," Chunga said. "The calamari heads as a starter, with the sole to follow. The fish is shipped in from Beira. It takes two or three days to get here, but it tastes almost as fresh as if it were caught this morning."

Even this was comforting, that he was doing the ordering, relieving her of this minor responsibility. It was not something she usually allowed. Abigail did things for herself. She was not even good at delegating to Johanna. But tonight, sitting back in her chair at this man's table, and allowing him to run the evening, she was content.

Unbidden, the thought of why she had come to Zimbabwe entered her mind, and the memory of Krisj Patel and the sight of his body on the pavement. "You're not what I expected," she said.

"And you're certainly not what I expected."

The procedure Abigail usually followed when getting dressed was to lay out the clothing items she intended to wear that day, a process that took perhaps thirty seconds, then slip into them, taking another forty-five seconds or less. Applying the few cosmetic aids she used took as little time as getting dressed. She seldom wore jewelry of any kind. The only ring she possessed was the wedding ring Robert had slipped onto her finger at a ceremony at which only the two of them and two witnesses had been present. She kept her hair cropped close to her head, never once in all her life having resorted to the hair-straightening devices employed by most of her friends and female colleagues. While she was impatient with the female need to look gorgeous, Abigail knew by the average male reaction to her that her appearance did not need artificial bolstering.

Tonight though, she had taken care. She had spent time in front of the mirror and was wearing a glowing crystal pendant set in silver, given to her by Robert, in the years before diamonds had become affordable. She had positioned it to hang just at the point where her cleavage began. Her white blouse was open to halfway between collarbone and waist, and billowed only slightly above close-fitting black trousers.

She knew how fabulous she looked and that Freek Jordaan would have gulped at the sight of her. She was not beyond enjoying the thought that when he told Robert that he was the old white guy lusting after her that it was true. She also knew that she would ensure that Freek's lust would always be exercised harmlessly, from a distance.

Tonight was different. From the time he met her in Patel's

office, Chunga had been unable to disguise the effect she had on him. All the while she had been getting ready for the evening, she had tried not to think about Robert. Despite what she was certain he was doing with that damned PA, she could not think about him tonight. Nor could she think about this strange girl, Helena, or the rest of her clients. This man Chunga was, she had to remind herself, a director of the CIO. But, she persuaded herself, he may also provide the solution to everything.

Thinking about Yudel and Rosa too was not possible. She could not imagine that they would have approved. To hell with them, she thought. Who are they to judge me?

Yet she knew that the only person who knew where she was and who may be judging her was herself. So thinking was not possible. Least of all could she think about the body of Krisj Patel on the pavement, limbs spread-eagled in patterns they would never have adopted in life.

Looking at this man sitting across from her, it was not possible to believe that he had anything to with the evil she had been hearing and reading about. His assurances were so direct and uncomplicated. The sturdy barriers she kept around herself, only ever breached by Robert, had been lowered. As for the matter of the Harare Seven, that too had receded into the distance. She warned herself that there was a real danger tonight that she might lose touch with everything except this man and the moments they were both enjoying.

As they had come up the steps of the clubhouse, she had felt one of his hands in the small of her back. The fabric of her blouse had been between his skin and hers, but the pulse from him to her was as immediate as if the blouse had not existed.

"I didn't think you'd come," he said.

"Nor did I. I didn't even think you'd ask."

"I didn't either. I wanted you to come so that I could explain some things about myself and my work, and to tell you how I can help you. But now that you're here, I'm having difficulty remembering what I wanted to say."

"We can leave those things for some other time," she said. But no, another part of her told her. You can't leave them for any other time.

"We may have to leave them, if I can't remember what they were."

This was a powerful man, a man whom her clients seemed to believe had the power to decide who lived and who died in Zimbabwe. Not only did he have the power but, according to her clients, he exercised it readily. And this man was saying that, just being with her, he could not think straight. It was something Abigail needed to hear and she needed badly to hear it. "Jonas," she said, "you know that we shouldn't be here, talking like this."

"I know."

"I, especially, shouldn't be in your company."

"What if I can help you? What if I can smooth the path for your application to court? What if I can see to it that in a day or two you get everything you want?"

"Can you do that?"

"I think so."

"And will you?"

"I will certainly try and I believe I will be successful."

"And what payment will you expect?" She was aware that a certain flirtatiousness had crept into her voice.

"It's not like that. It really isn't."

The playful tone of her own voice had a sobering effect, bringing her closer to reality. Some part of the cloud smothering her critical faculties lifted. She studied the earnest expression on his face. "Tell me you had nothing to do with Krisj Patel's death. Tell me that."

"I swear to you. Neither I nor anyone else in my organization had anything to do with it. It amazes me that anyone chose to assassinate him. The only effective act of his entire life was to bring you here."

"You didn't think highly of him then?"

"He was nothing, a person of no consequence."

"And you don't know who might have killed him?"

"A man was seen leaving the area, carrying what seemed to be a rifle. We know his name. We'll have him in a day or two."

"Is this really so?"

"We'll have him in custody before you leave Zimbabwe."

"And the missing activists?"

"They may be in prison. I don't know. What I can tell you is that we didn't put them there."

"My clients say they saw your people take at least some of them to Chikurubi prison."

"Abigail . . ." His eyes were holding hers and, as on the previous night at the place where Krisj Patel was killed, if this were an act, it was a wonderfully convincing one. "Abigail, your clients are not the most reliable witnesses. Did they, by any chance, tell you about the explosion they set off at the ruling party's headquarters and how I protected them? Did they tell you about that?"

"Is this true?" Almost everything he said was adding to her confusion.

"I will tell you nothing about it. You ask them."

That too was the response of an innocent man. Ask them, he had said.

Chunga leaned across the table toward her. He placed a powerful hand over one of hers. Abigail's impulse to withdraw it was immediately overridden by the stronger need to be touching him. "What you have to understand is that I also come from a minority group. I am of the Ndebele people. It's true that there are not many of us in the upper levels of government, but just because the Shona people are in the majority does not mean that this country is a Shona dictatorship. I come from a small town in Matabeleland called Plumtree. I started work in the police there."

Plumtree? Abigail thought. Why Plumtree? She remembered that Bizana, where her aunt had died, was not far from the town.

Chunga was still speaking. "My first position with the CIO was there. Did you know that the first director of the CIO after liberation was a white man? He had also been head of security under the old racist regime. I made the same decision as he did. I knew my own people had suffered. I had also suffered. But, like that white man, I decided that resistance would only bring more misery upon my people. I made a conscious decision to work with the government to help build a better country. And the country has changed. It is a better place now. I know the work is not completed. I know the country is far from perfect, but it is improving, and I have no intention of destroying those talented young people who are now missing."

"Talented? Are they all talented?"

He lowered his eyes for an instant. "Tony Makumbe is very talented. I don't agree with all his writing, but the nonpolitical stuff stirs my soul. I don't want to destroy the source of that inspiration. All I'm saying is that I have not personally been responsible for bad things happening, and that I am helping things to improve, and that I will help you reach a satisfactory conclusion to your matter."

"And how will you do that?"

"To begin with, I have the influence to see that it is in court quickly."

"They've given me a date of Friday in two weeks."

"That's disgraceful. Let me see what I can do."

"Can you help?"

"Give me till Monday."

"Thank you." Now, let's forget this subject, she thought. Let's forget all the ugliness. Let me even forget Krisj, at least for tonight.

As if he had been reading her mind, he said, "I also have influence in this establishment. Here is the starter."

Andrew, a young man with eyes that seemed to be permanently downcast, brought the calamari heads. They were as good as Chunga had promised. So was the sole that followed an hour later. The dry white wine, too, was excellent and it was still excellent by the time she had finished her third glass. Andrew was never more than a few paces away, ready to react immediately to the slightest glance from Chunga.

Some of the other diners finished, and she saw waiters dashing back and forth with their credit cards. By the time they finished, only a few were left. Chunga led Abigail through a side entrance of the clubhouse and onto the golf course. Ahead, a fairway, partly lit by the lighting from the parking area and the clubhouse itself, was alive with movement. When her eyes became accustomed to the darkness she realized that what she was seeing was a small herd of antelope. "Impalas," Chunga said. "Aren't they lovely?"

"They live here?"

"There are also wildebeest and some smaller types. Yes, they live on the course. Occasionally a leopard has found a hole in the fence and taken one."

She slipped off her shoes and carried them in one hand. She had found the heels sinking into the fairway's smooth surface, made soft by a heavy dew. The damp grass was cold underfoot.

Halfway down the fairway, Abigail stopped under the spreading branches of a tree. Its trunk was in the rough, but the immense spread of its branches reached across half the fairway. Looking up, she said, "This must get in the way of the golfers."

"It does. I believe there have been many attempts to have it cut down, but the board has always overridden them."

"Good for the board," she said. "I like the board."

Chunga had made no attempt to touch her. She had expected at least a casual attempt to take her hand, but so far there had been nothing. "Abigail," he said, "I don't agree with your clients. I know they will sneer at the idea, but I've tried to protect them from the very serious trouble their activities could land them in. What I really want to say, though, is how much I admire what you're doing. I admire your bravery in the face of all that has happened, and your commitment to your case. I've never met anyone who is like you, in even the smallest way."

Abigail could find no way to answer. They walked on in silence. By the time they reached the green of the first hole they were out of reach of the lights. Now he did touch her, but it was only the gentlest possible contact as he steered her back toward the clubhouse. "Come, there's something else I want to show you."

Chunga tossed a coin to the car guard who had approached to guide them out of the parking area. They passed through the club's gate and he turned the Mercedes away from the city. Two nights before, when he had taken her to the scene of Patel's murder, he had driven the CIO double-cab quickly through the potholed streets. Its big wheels and high ground clearance had almost smoothed out the bumps. Now he drove more carefully, picking his way through the uneven sections of road. It was not long before he left the tarred road to follow a dirt track.

She could see the track rising in front of the car as it twisted through dense scrub. It was not a surprise when he stopped at a thinning of the vegetation and she could see the city lights spreading to the east below them. He got out without saying anything and came round the car to open the door for her.

The hill was not a high one, but standing next to him she could see parts of the city. "Down there," he said, "are the wealthier suburbs, brightly lit and well catered for. I live there too. Despite the state of the country, those people are eating well tonight. Across there . . ." She followed the direction in which his arm was stretched. "Across there, there is an even bigger area. Can you see it? It looks almost ghostly."

"There seems to be something wrong with the lighting. What is it?"

"It's the shack town."

"What makes it look that way?"

"The lighting is by candles and oil lamps. They don't make much light. There's also not much food there."

Chunga was a dark shadow against a still darker sky. "Jonas, why did you bring me here?" Abigail asked.

"I brought you here because I want you to know that I am a Zimbabwean. In addition to that, as I told you, I am of the Ndebele minority. I have been among those who were the victims of a government-sponsored massacre. But I decided that there was no point in resistance. We would all have been slaughtered. Only collaboration made any sense. This is my country, and everything I do, I do only because I believe it to be good for Zimbabwe. My life is aimed at helping to build my country. I am not part of killings or torture or holding people in custody without trial. I brought you here, because I want you to know the real Jonas Chunga."

They had nothing more to say. Abigail was facing him and so close that she could feel his breath. Then he was touching her, drawing her toward him in arms that were powerful, but with a grip of great restraint. He was touching her breasts through the fabric of her blouse, his mouth was on hers, then his body was hard against her and she could feel his erection.

She had no breath and nothing she did was deliberate, but she was aware of the firm crinkles of his hair under her hands. Then one of his hands was inside her blouse, massaging first one breast, then the other.

At that moment the quick flash of a distant headlight reached them. "Not here," he gasped. "We'll go to my house."

He had just started the engine and turned the car around when the other vehicle, a small pickup truck, came bouncing past them. Now Chunga did reach across to take Abigail's hand, holding it firmly but gently in his much larger one.

I'm going to do it, Abigail thought. My God, I am going to do it. Oh, Robert, she asked her distant husband, what in hell has happened to us?

Abigail's chest rose and fell with an almost unbearable excitement, but there was an uneasiness that seemed to have no cause. It was not the thought of Robert, or what her clients may think, or even the possible betrayal of Krisj Patel. Something beyond her ability to comprehend, but more powerful than all other influences, troubled her beyond measure.

The houses they passed were large, some of them almost palatial. Even at night it was clear that the gardens were well cared for. Only the pitted and potholed road fitted what she had seen of the rest of the city so far. Chunga slowed almost to walking pace at times, either to go round potholes or to ease the car through them. At one point they passed a boom at a checkpoint. The uniformed guard saluted. It was clear that the residents of the area wanted access to their neighborhood to be controlled. "What's this suburb called?" Abigail asked.

"Borrowdale Brooke. I'm sorry about the road surface." It was said as if he were personally responsible.

She was watching his face as he drove. His features looked as controlled as ever. Only a slight parting of the lips reflected any excitement he might be feeling. He glanced at her and their eyes met. She thought she saw a degree of surprise there that bordered on alarm.

They reached the front gate of a large house, the garden walls of which stretched away into the far darkness on either side. Chunga activated the mechanism to open the gate. He brought the car to a stop in the driveway.

Abigail remained in her seat until he opened the door for her. Then she allowed him to lead her across a broad patio, a strong hand on one of her elbows, and through a glass door. A tall reading lamp came on in a far corner, but she saw little through the confusion within her. The room was large and a polished wooden floor was covered by a handwoven carpet. Afterward, that was all she could remember of it.

Chunga was close to her. He had taken her hand to lead her toward a doorway on the other side. She reached out to touch him. The muscles of his chest were hard. She found herself massaging the biceps of one arm.

"Come," he murmured. "This way."

She followed him into a short hallway and from there into a spacious bedroom. Chunga had not turned on any other lights. Enough light reached them through the windows for them to avoid the furniture. "I'm glad you came," she heard him say. He dropped his jacket onto a chair.

He came toward her, unhurriedly, fully in control. She felt his hands on her hips.

And then, without warning, Abigail understood the source of her earlier uneasiness. What had only been a disturbing influence, beyond her understanding, had become a reality. No, she thought. No, not now. I can't now. When this is over, perhaps, but not now. Certainly not now.

He drew her closer, but hesitated, perhaps feeling the doubt within her. "Abigail?" He spoke her name as a question. She heard no hostility and no anger in it.

"Jonas, I can't now. I just can't."

"Why? Tell me why?"

"This has to be over first."

"Tell me what's changed in the last five minutes. Just tell me that."

"It's just the case," she lied. "And all the other things that are part of it—your position and mine."

Chunga took a step back. "Something has changed."

She turned quickly and tried to leave the bedroom, but had only taken a single step before he had her hand and had drawn her back toward him. "Jonas, please." She was surprised and almost ashamed at the plaintive sound of her voice.

"There's no need to plead," he said. "Nothing will happen to you against your will, not while you are with me. Do you understand that?"

"Yes, I understand."

"Then listen to me. I am going to help you to clear up this matter. I will show you that the truth has many sides. And that I am no monster. After that, I want things to be different between us."

"After that, everything will be different," Abigail said.

Unlike her first night in Harare, and despite the killing of Krisj Patel, Abigail felt safe in the armchair in her room. On the drive back to the hotel, Chunga had said nothing. Without his almost overpowering presence, she could think more clearly now.

The other matter had started as only a vague uneasiness, but understanding had come suddenly. She had noticed a number of dinner parties in the restaurant finish their dinners, then leave. As far as she remembered, all had paid before they left. Jonas Chunga had not even signed anything. He had led her from the table in a manner that did not acknowledge the possibility of having to pay. Then there was Andrew, their private waiter throughout dinner. She was sure that no one else in the place had a private waiter.

What did this mean? Was this how this director of the CIO was treated wherever he went? And if that were so, then why? Whatever the answer was, Abigail could not imagine herself being at ease with patronage on this level. Was anything ever refused to those close to the source of power?

And yet this was a man who, up on the hillside overlooking the city, had told her what was truly in his heart. And she had given him every reason to believe that she was ready to receive him. But when she withdrew, there had been no force, not even any pressure. He had simply accepted her change of heart.

I swear to you, he had told her, I am not part of killings and torture.

Only time would show how truthful that declaration had been, and whether her change of heart had affected her chance of having her matter heard urgently. She understood why she had not been able to allow Jonas Chunga to make love to her, but nothing else was clear. She fell asleep in the chair, the night within her eyelids swirling furiously with images of Jonas Chunga.

22

The Makwati twins were in the double bed in the front room of the apartment on the building's top floor. Tanya was stretched out on her back, breathing through her mouth. Next to her, Natasha was sitting up so that she would not fall asleep. There were no lights on in the room.

From her position she could see, through a lace curtain, a few hundred meters of the road running down the hill past the prison's main gate. There was no moon, and the wire fence that skirted the trees inside the prison ground was invisible under a dark sky.

The apartment had been a good choice. Some of their members had walked the dark street after sunset to test its effectiveness, but had never been able to notice their presence. Even their selection of the old couple who occupied the apartment had been sound. They were quiet, sympathetic to the cause, willing to help and were always in bed early.

Helena had given instructions on what to wear while they watched. They were not to get within a meter of the window, clothing had to be black and they were to wear no jewelry or adornments of any kind. Even the clips in their hair had to be removed. They could use rubber bands, but nothing else. The color of their skin, a deep mahogany, would do the rest.

Changing shifts took place after dark and through the back door. Tanya had come first, Natasha following ten minutes later. When they were relieved, they would leave separately and go in different cars. "We can't be too careful," Helena had told them many times. "If we are careless in just one small point, it might lead to our undoing."

"But will they care about this?" Natasha had asked. "We are only watching. Is it a crime to watch?"

"It depends on what you are watching," Helena had said.

The precautions had worked well. No one had paid any attention to individual people entering or leaving the building. Watching the street for movement from the direction of the prison, Natasha was confident that they were safe.

The only weakness in their arrangements, and one that had arisen the evening before for the first time, concerned the presence in the apartment of three teenagers, grandchildren of the old couple. The children's parents had died in the cholera, but they had been away from home when it struck and so had survived. Their arrival from the home of their grandparents had been unexpected and, so far, no other apartment had been available to those watching the prison gate.

The young people too had learned to hate the authorities. Their grandparents had told them of the atrocities inflicted on communities and the needless suffering of so many people. A security failure had arisen through the sheer excitement of the thirteen-year-old boy. He had been unable to contain the knowledge that every night, in the front bedroom, the people's spies were watching the prison. He did not understand the purpose of their watching, but he could imagine a few reasons.

"They're checking the front gate and the guards there," he had told a friend, "so they can charge it or maybe plant dynamite and destroy it."

It was a wonderful story and, by noon the day after he had told his two closest friends, every pupil in the school had heard some variation of the story. The most popular version was the one in which they were marking out the spot where an earth-moving machine would batter against the gate and destroy it and those guarding it, to advance on the prison building itself and release the prisoners.

It had been almost four hours since they had relieved Abel. In a few minutes, Natasha would be waking her sister to take over from her. All evening, there had been no movement on the road that passed the prison gate.

Somewhere in the back of the apartment the old couple and their grandchildren were asleep. The old man's snoring was a gentle rumbling, occasionally interspersed with a convulsive roar. "Please, child," the old woman had begged Helena when she first approached them, "be very careful. We are old and can't go to prison. And, if we go, who will look after the grandchildren?"

Some time before, perhaps an hour, Natasha had seen the figure of a man, silhouetted against the headlights of a car. But after the car had passed, leaving the street in darkness, it had been empty. Even once her eyes had again become accustomed to the dark, she had seen nothing.

Natasha did not know that the brief silhouette she had seen earlier belonged to Agent Mordecai Mpofu of the CIO, and that he was part of a team that had fenced off the area. She also did not know that while she was watching the empty street, a team of CIO agents was blocking access to and from the area.

She became aware of them for the first time as the back door of the apartment was smashed in. It was only when the door to the room had been thrown open and three armed agents entered that she rose uncertainly from the bed. Tanya was just waking up.

Natasha tried to stop the first blow from the barrel of the revolver. It landed on her left hand and she thought she heard a bone snap. Somewhere from the back of the apartment someone was crying. The next blow fell behind her left ear. She was down on her knees and nothing in the world was stable anymore. The walls themselves were rotating. She did not see the third blow coming.

23

It was only after Abigail had fallen asleep in the hotel armchair that the city's power had gone down. On some occasions only individual suburbs lost power, but on this night the entire city and a few hundred surrounding kilometers were all in darkness. Only the poorest in the shack villages with their candles, oil lamps, oil stoves and wood fires, and the wealthiest with their standby plants, were unaffected.

Most of Borrowdale Brooke was not as badly affected by the outage as the rest of the city. Within minutes of the power cutting out, the lights were coming back on, one house at a time, as standby plants kicked in. Jonas Chunga's was of the automatic variety, starting within a few seconds of the power failing. As was his way, he had few lights on. Whether or not the power came back was not important to him, but he was glad to hear the refrigerator and the air conditioner buzzing.

He had already received a telephone report about the arrest of those foolish Makwati girls. Agent Mpofu had told him that it had all taken place quickly and effortlessly, without gunfire or excessive violence. The Makwatis were very small fish in a pond that Chunga felt he was drying up fast. A few months in Chikurubi would be a lesson they would not easily forget.

He strode up and down in his den, a spacious, glassed-in room that overlooked a tree-filled garden. The tops of the trees were vague silhouettes against a moonless sky. He noticed neither the trees nor the sky nor even the whiskey, of which he had now consumed a quarter of the bottle. By two o'clock, Jonas Chunga had given up the idea of sleep. The image of Abigail in his mind was both too vivid and too persistent to allow even the possibility of losing consciousness.

He needed something to distract him from this woman and everything she had awakened in him. He found it in a file that had been placed in his hands personally that afternoon by the minister himself. The instruction had been for him to handle this new matter himself the next day. A cabinet minister was interested. Why would he not be? Chunga thought. It was his wife's income that was affected.

Chunga knew the essence of what was in the file, but if he hoped to make sense of it the next day, he would have to at least skim through it. He was working by the light of a desk lamp.

The first item in the file was the minister's note, instructing him to have the matter dealt with as top priority. It was followed by a letter from the chocolate factory, informing the dairy estate, owned by the old man's young wife, that they would not be requiring further supplies of milk. Chunga already knew why, but the matter was further clarified by a clipping from *The New York Times*. The clipping covered a threat by a human rights organization to boycott the company's products worldwide if they continued buying milk from that estate.

There was more in the file, but Chunga closed it and dropped it into his briefcase. He hesitated only a moment before throwing the briefcase across the room. He hated the humiliation of it. They created these situations, then they treated him like their messenger boy, or rather, part messenger boy and part enforcer. No, mostly enforcer.

He knew that the authorities had allowed the farm to be seized from the white owner as part of their land-reform policy, or was it their poverty-relief policy? He had lost track. Then the minister's whore had decided she wanted it.

And now the chocolate maker, with operations in God knows how many countries, cannot afford to buy their milk from them. Somewhere down in the bottom of the file there was probably the new manager's assessment of the effect the chocolate factory's decision would have on the estate and, no doubt, it would be catastrophic.

He was already scheduled to meet the senior black manager at the chocolate company the next morning. Chunga's job would be to explain to him that the white managers would be able to disappear overseas to other branches of the company. They could leave the country as political refugees, while he would be staying. It may not be in his best interests to alienate those in positions of power who would like to be his friends. He should think carefully before choosing the side he wanted to be on.

The matter required little thought. He thought instead about Abigail under that great tree. How long ago had it been? Four or five hours, perhaps. He remembered her breasts. He could still feel them under his hands. Christ, it was torture.

Now, after all this time, there was this face. Of all the faces there could be and all the women there had been, he had been confronted by this one unforgettable face.

He rose too quickly, throwing over the chair, and pressed the intercom button. It took longer than expected before he received an answer, and then it was not the voice he expected. "Send up the girl," he said.

From his window he could see her running from the cottage, her white nightdress just visible against the surrounding darkness. He went down to unlock the back door for her. Once she was inside he locked the door, then led the way up the stairs to the bedroom.

"Wine?" he asked. She had stopped just inside the door, still unsure about what was allowed her.

She nodded and he poured for her. He still had his whiskey. This room was the only place she had ever, in her eighteen years, drunk wine. Chunga's household was also the only place where she had eaten regularly and had money to buy clothes. She had even been able to send money to her mother in the Nyanga hills on the border with Mozambique. Many people ate because she was able to please her boss. She had not lost her virginity here, but she had learned much about what pleased men. And he did seem pleased.

He sat down on the edge of the bed and patted the place next to him. "Come," he said. "There's no need for you to stand there."

24

Tony Makumbe lay on his back, looking up at the ceiling of the cell. Its uneven surface had turned black as the night had deepened. For the first time in hours he was aware of the eight men in the cell with him. The voice had been mumbling on all night, but had become softer, more muffled and altogether unintelligible. Eventually it had stopped.

There was enough light in the cell, a pale gray shaft from the window, to see a man coming across the cell toward him. Tony tried to rise, but it took an effort that was now not possible.

The man bent over him. Tony could see the big square head and a quick glint from the eyes. The face came closer, until it was so close that the features were merging into each other. Tony had heard about the terrible things that happened to young men in prison. This must be the time, he thought. This must be the time and this must be part of the punishment.

But the voice surprised him by its gentleness. "Tony, are you feeling better now?" The speaker had kept his voice low to avoid waking the others.

It was Big Jake. Tony recognized him from the day before. How could I have forgotten? he asked himself. Jake, seeing that he was trying to rise, slipped a broad hand under one of his shoulders and lifted him until he was resting on an elbow. "I'm well, Jake," he whispered.

"Can you stand?"

"I don't think so."

"Do you want to use the shithouse?" The lavatory was in a corner of the cell, not enclosed in any way.

"Not now. Thank you."

"Tell me when you want to."

"Thank you, I will." He looked up at Jake, who was kneeling next to him on one knee. "Why are you doing this for me?"

"We know who you are."

"I see."

"We know who you are, and we are sorry that you are sick."

"I hope I haven't disturbed anyone."

"Just the talking. The talking bothers some of the others."

"I'm sorry about the talking. Ask them to forgive me. At night I can't always control the talking."

"Perhaps you are not eating enough. You have given away too much of the food that was meant for you. They bring it for you, but you give it away."

And yet the hunger was gone. He must have eaten some of it. He remembered his food being brought by the guard, and the murmurings of dissatisfaction from the other prisoners. How often had they brought him food? More often than the others and of much better quality, it seemed. The other prisoners had asked the guards why he was receiving better food than they were, but had received no answer. After that he had shared his extra rations with them.

"If you do not eat enough you will die," Big Jake said.

"I'm not dying yet," he said.

"I have told the others we can't take all of your extra food."

"It's all right, Jake. I'm happy to share."

"You are not strong. Tomorrow you must take more food yourself."

After a while, Big Jake told him to try to sleep now and to avoid the talking, if that were possible. Then he went back to his own sleeping mat.

Tony remembered the bombing. He had placed the parcel just where they had decided. A few bottles of wine had ensured that none of the security guards were awake. He had often wondered what had happened to them afterward. The blast had been heard all the way down to the gated estate of Borrowdale Brooke, where the old dictator himself lived. They had all imagined his sleep being disturbed by it. It had shattered the door of the building, but done little other damage. After that, the police had placed a two-man guard on the door.

He was sure that the bombing was the reason that he had been picked up. And yet it had happened nearly a year before. Surely they must have known sooner?

The members of the group had all expected martyrdom. They had spoken about it on many nights. But when no arrests had been made, the prospect of heroic martyrdom had receded. Some had claimed disappointment, but he had felt only relief. And yet, when they eventually did arrive at his door, he had again felt relief.

Long after Big Jake had gone back to his mat, perhaps an hour or even more, Tony heard two men in the corridor outside the cell. A young, light voice was saying, "How long do we keep them, or is it permanent? And, if it is permanent, why don't they do it and get finished?"

A stronger, older voice answered. "The order came from high up, very high up. Nothing happens to any of them, especially this one. Nothing, you understand."

"Yes, sir, I understand." The lighter voice had lost whatever self-assurance it had held a moment before. "I just thought, perhaps there's no reason . . ."

"You will get your instructions. But you see to it that nothing happens to them."

"And the thing of their extra food. The thing of their special food makes the other prisoners angry. Things are tough enough here without that."

"Food is coming from Beira. The World Food Program is sending it."

"For all the prisoners?"

"Yes, both the politicals and the others."

"Coming when?"

"Soon. It's coming soon. It's already passed through Beira. In the meantime carry on this way."

The voices drifted away and the fog again rose from the floor, enfolding him from every side. It drew back with the sound of breath being sucked in. It came close again as the breath was released, accompanied by a hoarse whistling.

Tony knew that the fog brought with it protection. It insulated him against the violence and brutality that seemed to surround everyone in his country, perhaps all of humanity. And yet fear also came out of the fog. The fear came every night. He had learned to expect it by this time, and he had been waiting. He knew that if he waited very quietly and did not fight it, it would pass. After that the fog would again be his, and he would be safe.

25

On Monday morning, Abigail was woken by her hotel phone ringing. A furious Helena was on the other end of the line. "So you were fucking the enemy last night."

It may have been close, but I never did it, Abigail thought. She adopted her most outraged tone. "I wasn't fucking anybody last night. And your information is out of date. I did have dinner with the enemy the night before last." She had spent Sunday in her hotel room, eating room service sandwiches, drinking coffee and occasionally trying to think. At other times she had tried not to think.

"Why? How do we know we can trust you now?" If Abigail had held the phone a meter from her ear, she would still have heard every word.

"The real question is—how can I trust you? Why didn't you tell me about the explosion at party headquarters?"

"It wasn't relevant."

"Not relevant? You were going to allow it to be sprung on me in court, were you?"

"After this, I'm not sure our people are going to be happy with you representing us." Helena was trying hard to regain the offensive.

"And I'm not happy representing people who hide relevant facts from me. I'll be on the next flight to Johannesburg. Goodbye." She hung up.

Almost immediately the phone rang again. Abigail briefly considered ignoring it. When she did answer, Helena was trying to sound calmer. "You can't expect me to be calm after last night."

"I was not making friends with the other side . . ."

"I'm not talking about that," Helena yelled. "I'm talking about the twins."

"What about the twins?"

"Didn't your boyfriend tell you? His mob picked them up last night after they broke down the door of the flat where they were watching the prison gate. They're in custody too."

After she had hung up, Abigail dialed the cell phone number Chunga had given her. When she heard the recorded voice telling her to leave a message, she hung up and started dressing for breakfast.

The hotel had a small terrace where you could have breakfast served. She found a table that had just enough sunlight filtering through the branches of a tree. The breakfast menu was identical to that of the day before. She ordered two slices of French toast and coffee to come immediately.

She had dealt with difficult clients on many other occasions, and she knew that she was not going to be on the plane to Johannesburg at any time in the next two weeks, at least not before she had done what she had to do at the hearing. The injection of caffeine would clear her head. She could not believe that she would have to initiate the next move, whatever it would be. Something about the events of the last few days indicated that they almost possessed a life of their own. The best she could do was to cling on tightly and try to survive the ride.

While she knew very little about six of the missing activists, she felt that she did know something about Tony Makumbe. And she certainly knew Krisj Patel.

If there was one of the players that she knew nothing about, that person was Jonas Chunga. She admitted to herself that she had behaved like a hormonal sixteen-year-old, allowing him to charm her. She had spent an evening in the company of a man who was not only powerful, but possibly an enemy, and she had been ready to go to bed with him. If he had chosen to take her on the hillside overlooking the city, she knew she would not have resisted.

And if, but this was an unlikely if, she never again heard from any of them—activists, Chunga or the High Court—then she could return and see if there was still anything in her marriage worth saving. Even that was not an uncomplicated course of action.

Abigail was aware of a tension that extended from her hands and arms into her shoulders and back. She closed her eyes and tried consciously to relax the offending muscles. She heard the waiter put down the coffee. Let it be freshly made, she prayed. Please let it be freshly made.

Her attempt at relaxation was largely fruitless. The stress in her shoulder muscles and the pain in her lower back were unchanged. She opened her eyes and reached for the coffee as a shadow fell across the table. She heard the choking sound of shock that came from her throat. Recoiling from the shadow, she lifted both hands to protect herself.

"Abigail, my dear," a familiar voice said, "it's only me."

She looked up into the concerned face of Rosa Gordon. In a moment they were in each other's arms. "Rosa," Abigail gasped. "And this? Are you alone?"

"No, Yudel's still in the restaurant. He'll be along in a moment."

Through the windows that separated the restaurant from the terrace, Abigail could just make Yudel out. He was hunched over the table, a pen in one hand. "What's he doing?"

"Working out the tip."

"The tip?"

"Yudel read somewhere that tips are now fifteen percent in the States. They've traditionally been ten percent in South Africa, so he feels twelve and a half percent might be fair. Do not ask me why. It's not an easy percentage to work out, though. On top of which, he has just discovered that there is no currency below a dollar note in this country. I have no idea what sort of compromise he might reach." Rosa had said it all in a way that suggested she would not be surprised if she was not believed. Perhaps she had difficulty believing it herself. She sat down opposite Abigail.

Abigail found herself laughing for the first time since she had got off the plane, and it at last released some of the tension. "Does he have a calculator?"

"No, my dear. He's doing it by long division on a paper napkin."

"He's a treat," Abigail gasped between chuckles. In a moment, Yudel's particular brand of lunacy had made the world seem a saner place.

"He's a little wearing sometimes," Rosa said.

Yudel appeared on the terrace, looking troubled. He still had the paper napkin in one hand. The picture that greeted him was of the two women sitting opposite each other and holding hands. "Hello, Yudel," Abigail said. "How much was the tip?"

"Two dollars, twenty seven and a half cents," he said.

"And what are you doing about the fact that there are no coins in Zimbabwe now?"

"I gave them three dollars, and they gave me a credit note for seventy two and a half cents."

"Oh, Yudel, I love you," Abigail said. Then, remembering Rosa, she turned to her. "Not in that way, Rosa."

"I know, my dear. I love him in both ways. But you . . . how have things been developing?"

"Not very well. At this stage, it would appear that my urgent application will be heard in two weeks."

The unexpected presence of the Gordons—she dared not hope that it would be support—had all but overwhelmed Abigail. "But what are you doing here?"

"We're on holiday," Yudel said.

"Nonsense, Yudel. How can you say such a thing?" Rosa frowned at him. "After you called us and told us about the assassination of your attorney, I knew Yudel would have to come. I also knew that his contract with the department is coming to an end. On top of all that, they have refused to pay him out for accumulated leave. So I thought he might just as well take the leave. So I booked the tickets."

"Thank you, Rosa. What I feel is beyond gratitude." She looked at Yudel. "You're both so brave."

"Rosa's the brave one," Yudel said. "With me it's a compulsion. Compulsions don't count as bravery."

"This one counts for me," Abigail said.

Rosa looked seriously at the younger woman. "Abigail, Yudel made a solemn promise to me before we left." There was no hint of amusement in what she was saying. "He promised me that every day he would tell me exactly what was happening and that when I felt the need to return home he would come with me."

"I understand," Abigail said. She reached toward Rosa and, in a moment, the two women were holding hands again, looking into each other's eyes. "My parents were killed many years ago. I know we haven't seen each other much, but I have never felt closer to an older couple."

"That's beautiful," Rosa said.

There's the famous Gordon sex appeal going to the dogs again, Yudel thought. "I'm deeply touched," he said.

"One other thing." Rosa was still holding Abigail's hand. "While we're here, I'll be staying with a niece who lives outside of town. Her husband is one of the few white farmers who have been left alone. They run a school for the children of the farmworkers in the area. I don't know if that's the reason they've managed to keep their place. She'll come for me later."

"Now," Yudel interrupted, "you'd better tell us about your visit here, especially the death of your attorney friend."

26

Abigail was not slow to put Yudel to work. Jonas Chunga had left a message for her, saying that they had a suspect in the killing of Krisj Patel and that progress had been made in the matter of the hearing. He would come by to fill her in. "Will you go to see Krisj's widow?" she asked. "Perhaps she can tell us something useful."

Yudel had the name of the school where Suneesha Patel worked, but finding it had not been a simple matter. In his hired car, he picked his way through the potholed roads of a city teeming with people and vehicles, neither of which seemed to recognize the usual rules of the road. Intermittently working traffic lights seemed to provide only a broad guideline to the city's motorists. If an opening existed, only a fool allowed a little matter like a red traffic light to hold him back.

He at last found the school in an apparently unnamed street. A middle-aged woman with tired eyes who manned the administration office directed him to apartments on Josiah Tongogara Drive where Krisj had lived with his wife. "She has a few days off," the woman said. "Her husband was murdered four nights ago. You may have read about it."

The once dignified-looking apartment block was in a part of town that had been dedicated to old African liberators—or dictators, depending on your point of view. Where street signs existed, they carried names like Kenneth Kaunda, Samora Machel, Julius Nyerere, Milton Obote, Kwame Nkrumah and Robert Mugabe.

From what Abigail had told Yudel about Patel, he had expected Suneesha to be a person more interested in principle than in practical matters. As soon as he saw her, he acknowledged inwardly that he had been wrong on that score. She came to the door, wearing an apron that was white with bread flour. Bits of dough still clung to her hands. She frowned at him. "Can I help you?"

"My name is Yudel Gordon," he said. "I'm working with the advocate your husband was briefing on the seven people . . . the missing ones."

Suneesha looked at him, unblinking, from an expressionless face. Eventually she sighed and indicated with a tilt of her head that he should follow her.

The apartment building was old and its rooms, including the kitchen, were large. On a counter, a bowl of dough awaited further attention. She had obviously been kneading it by hand. "You can sit over there," she said, nodding toward a chair. "You don't mind if I go on with my work?"

"Please do," Yudel said, sitting down on the chair.

"What can I tell you, Mr. Gordon?" She glanced at him as she resumed her kneading. "You look surprised. I know I'm not the typical grieving widow. That was what you were thinking, isn't it?"

"That's right. I was thinking that."

"We haven't been close for years." It was said almost defiantly. Could it be that the wife of this hero who had died in the cause of justice was not sorry he had died? To Yudel, she seemed to be daring him to challenge her right to admit that. "No, that doesn't state the position clearly. We were never close."

"You married him, though."

"Obviously." She was kneading the dough as furiously as if it was to blame for the failure of her marriage. "You see what I'm doing?" she demanded. "I'm a schoolteacher, but this is how I've made our living for years—till late every night. There are still a few people who can afford home-baked bread, and I bake it for them. It's a living . . ." She paused to think over that statement. ". . . of sorts."

"There was also the law practice," Yudel suggested.

"Law practice?" Suneesha snorted extravagantly. "Sometimes

what I earned from my baking had to pay the rent for his office. I never saw any money from that so-called law practice."

"These are difficult times . . ."

"Difficult times?" she interrupted him with blazing eyes. "Yes, these are difficult times. They may have been easier for me, if I had only one mouth to feed. Other lawyers at least made some money."

"Is that what drove you apart? That he did not contribute much to the household?"

"Oh, heavens, Mr. Gordon, that and a hundred other things, his friendships among them."

"His friendships with these activists bothered you? Are you saying that?"

"Some of them bothered me, certainly. Oh, some of them did, all right." Yudel heard a trace of bitterness in the laugh that followed.

"I don't understand."

"Forget it, Mr. Gordon. I don't want to speak ill of the dead— not even of Krisj." Suddenly all Suneesha Patel's anger seemed to melt away. "I loved the stupid bastard," she said sorrowfully. "But sometimes I hated him."

And now he's gone, Yudel thought. And you don't know what to feel.

"He was a clever man. Did you know that? He studied in South Africa, and he was in the top two percent of his class. Did you know he was that clever? He could have had a brilliant career if he had taken my advice and we had migrated south."

"You didn't agree with his politics, then?"

"Of course I agreed with him. Every sane person agrees. We can all see what they've done to the country. But you can dissent without getting yourself killed. You don't have to present yourself as a red flag to a bull. You don't have to set yourself up as a target."

"There's something else you might be able to tell me. It has to do with a bomb they exploded." Abigail had asked Yudel to see if he could discover anything about it. "Did your husband know anything about that?"

"Yes, he knew about it. It was a year ago. But he never planted it. A certain Tony Makumbe did. He seems to be the craziest of them all. That damned husband of mine would have done anything for him. He would have done much more for him than for me."

That was the name Yudel least expected to hear in connection with the bomb blast. To his knowledge, it was not the sort of thing writers usually did. "Was Makumbe arrested for it?"

"No." The word was accompanied by a decisive shake of the head. "At least, not until the other day. And we don't know if they picked him up for that."

"Do you know why your husband wasn't arrested? They certainly knew where to find him."

"No." Again, the quick shake of the head.

"Did you know this Makumbe?"

"Slightly, not as well as my husband."

Yudel knew there must be a reason that Suneesha's answers were becoming shorter and more abrupt, but she was a strong personality who would only tell him what she wanted him to know. "Enemies?" Yudel suggested. "Did he have personal enemies?"

Suneesha Patel looked at him, as if he had so far managed to misunderstand their entire conversation. "Only the entire ruling party, the president, the cabinet, the police, the CIO, the armed forces—search for the culprit among their members. That should be just under half the population. Did anyone hate him for any other reason? No. Only me."

"Just one more thing, Mrs. Patel. Have the police been to question you?"

"No."

"The CIO?"

"No. You're the only one."

Yudel drove back to the hotel by a more direct route. Abigail was sitting in the lobby when he came in. She had been resting in an armchair, her eyes unfocused, looking up at the ceiling. She saw him out of the corners of her eyes and sat up as he approached. "Did you learn anything?"

"Only that the police haven't questioned her."

"Not at all?"

"No."

Abigail felt the involuntary twitch of her head as she tried to clear her thinking. "I suppose it's because they already have a suspect."

"No doubt," Yudel said.

"The CIO people are on their way here. They're going to allow me to be present when they take his statement. He's already confessed."

"That was easy."

She looked thoughtfully at Yudel. There was something about his manner that was adding to her own discomfort. "You have doubts?"

"I haven't seen the suspect yet. I'll come with you."

"No, Yudel, I don't think so." It was said too quickly. She was aware that she had averted her eyes. "I am an officer of the court here, but you have no standing. I don't think we should take the chance."

Not take the chance? Yudel wondered. Was this Abigail speaking? By her standards this was no chance at all.

"Here they are," she said. A strongly built African man in a dark suit had stopped in the doorway of the hotel. He was looking at Abigail with an intensity Yudel had often seen in men when looking at a desirable woman. No doubt there had been times when he had looked at women that way himself. The way this man looked at Abigail was no surprise to Yudel. What did surprise him was the hurried, almost frantic way she rose and crossed the lobby to meet him. "I'll see you later," she murmured.

Yudel followed as far as the glass doors. When he reached them, Chunga had opened the door on the passenger side for her. Abigail hesitated a moment, momentarily looking up into Chunga's eyes, before she got in. Yudel saw something surprisingly self-conscious about her movements, something he had never before seen in her. Damn, he thought, this is not going to make things any easier.

27

The police cells to which Jonas Chunga took Abigail were on the southeastern side of town. The cells served more than one township, some shack settlements and a number of suburbs. They had to pass through a spreading tangle of simple dwellings to reach them. An assortment of street vendors plied their trade along streets where buses, minibus taxis and the occasional battered car stirred up the dusty surface. Some of the houses were coated in a layer of reddish dust that was probably a permanent part of their appearance now.

Abigail had seen it all before in other parts of the continent. The food being sold along the road was of the simplest kind, each vendor displaying only a small assortment of vegetables or a few live chickens in cages. The advantage of selling live chickens was that your stock needed no refrigeration. If you made no sales that day, your produce would not go bad overnight.

The police building suited the area. It was an old house, also colonial in style, but nothing like the clubhouse of Saturday night. Like so much of the city, the building had been kept immaculately clean. Porch, floor and windows showed no sign of dirt. It was clear that even the daily dust from the street was swept or washed away regularly. Finding the budget to replace anything that had broken was another matter. Whatever signage may once have proclaimed the existence of a police unit in the building had long since disappeared. So had the front gate, leaving only the rusted frame that once held it.

Chunga asked her to wait in the charge office, while he passed through a door into the back of the building. Two officers behind the desk and a small line of local people, waiting to receive attention, all turned to look at her with undisguised curiosity. A young constable brought a hard-backed wooden chair from behind the counter that separated the staff from the public. "Would you like to sit down, ma'am?" he asked, making only the briefest, most deferential eye contact.

Abigail smiled at the policeman and accepted the chair. Sitting on it was a problem though. One of the people in the line was a woman who may have been eighty or more. Abigail carried the chair to where she was standing. "Sit down, mother," she said. The old woman looked uncertainly at the constable who had offered Abigail the chair. "It's all right, mother," Abigail told her. "You sit down."

The constable was frowning at Abigail, but more in puzzlement than annoyance. The old woman sat down and Abigail returned to where she had been standing at the counter. She smiled at the constable, more as a protection for the old woman than as a gesture of friendliness. He tried to smile back at her. His confusion only lasted a moment. Abigail saw him bend over. When he straightened up he was carrying another chair. This time Abigail had no choice but to sit down.

She reflected on the drive to the police station. She had expected it to be quiet; for Chunga to feel at least some degree of awkwardness after Saturday night. Instead, it could have been that nothing had passed between them.

He told her how pleased he was that they had made an arrest and that they believed the man they were holding was the culprit. He was one of the class of criminals who could not stay out of jail. Before this, he had been convicted of other violent crimes for a variety of motives. He had killed Patel in revenge. Chunga explained how the suspect had been represented by Patel some years before on an armed-robbery charge, but had been sent to jail. Apparently, he had harbored a grudge against Patel ever since. He was a volatile, unstable character and he had been boasting about the killing in a township tavern. An informer had turned him in.

Chunga's reappearance interrupted Abigail's thoughts. He led her to a room in the back of the police station. A man wearing a suit and tie, whom Abigail took to be one of Chunga's men, and a uniformed policeman with a pen and writing pad were seated on one side of a large table. Opposite them was another man in civilian clothes, but he wore no tie or jacket. At the far end, a small, hard-eyed man looked suspiciously at Abigail. He was wearing the sort of khakis that a farmer might give his laborers as work clothes. He had been shackled, both hands and feet. Across from him were two empty chairs. Chunga showed Abigail to one and took the other himself.

"Who this lady is?" The accused man had not turned his head toward Abigail. Only his eyes had moved.

"Shut up. We ask the questions," the man in the suit said. He was not a tall man, younger than Chunga, but stocky, almost as powerful a figure. He was not nearly as well dressed. A collar on the verge of fraying strained to encompass a thick neck that merged almost imperceptibly into broad, sloping shoulders. Only his tie, a glossy, bright scarlet, looked as if it had been bought in the last year. "Does the director want us to begin?" he asked.

"Thank you, Agent Mpofu," Chunga said. He nodded to the other man in civilian clothes. "Please go ahead, Inspector Dzuze."

"I want to know who is the lady." The prisoner's eyes were traveling back and forth between Chunga and Abigail.

"What you don't want is to make us angry," Mpofu said.

"Why I can't know?"

Abigail saw something simultaneously aggressive and servile in the suspect. She could imagine him down on his knees begging on a street corner, but knifing in the back anyone who refused him.

"I want to know who is the lady. Is she Mr. Patel's lady?"

Mpofu moved in his chair, as if ready to attack the suspect. Abigail looked at Chunga and saw the set jaw and firm control she was getting to know.

"Is this lady Mr. Patel's lady?" the prisoner whined.

"This little bastard is looking for trouble." Mpofu's voice had developed a harsh rasping tone. His hands had hardened into fists.

The prisoner was looking at Abigail out of the corners of his eyes, but this time he was wise enough not to continue. Chunga had raised a hand from the surface of the table and was patting the air very gently. The gesture seemed to be aimed at Mpofu.

"My name is Abigail Bukula," Abigail said. "I am an advocate and Mr. Patel was assisting me in a court action against the government. Could you tell me your name?"

"Kleinbooi Mokgareng."

"You're a South African," Abigail said. "Why are you killing people in Zimbabwe?"

She thought she saw his eyes flick toward Mpofu before answering. "Mister Patel let them put me in jail."

"The state put you in jail, not Mr. Patel."

"This lawyer should not be questioning the suspect." Inspector Dzuze made himself heard for the first time since Abigail had come in. He was looking at Chunga. Everyone took his lead from the CIO director.

"The inspector is right," Chunga told Abigail. "Please continue, inspector."

"We already have the motive recorded," Dzuze said. "Tell us what you did on the night."

"I shoot this little bastard, Patel."

"Tell us from the beginning about that night."

The prisoner looked from Chunga to Abigail. "I take the gun from my friend Albert's place." The uniformed policeman started writing. "Then I go to the place where I know Patel works. I go upstairs in the building and wait for him to come out." He was answering Dzuze's question, but his eyes were roving back and forth between Chunga and Abigail. Like a wild animal he had read the situation and knew that the danger was real, but, like an animal that has not yet seen the predator, he could not know just how great the danger was and from which direction it may come. "When he come out, I shoot him."

"So you're saying . . ." Dzuze began.

"What make of rifle was it?" Abigail interrupted. The men in the room all turned to look at her.

"I not know."

"What was the time when you did it?"

"Not late. Maybe eight o'clock. I not know."

"Where does your friend live?"

"There on the other side." He waved a hand. "Kuwadzana."

"How did you get from your friend's place to the place where you killed him?"

"I walk."

"Carrying the rifle—openly—so everyone could see it?"

He stared at Mpofu now. The CIO man saved him the need to answer. "Director Chunga, this is not right."

"Abigail, please." Chunga said gently. "Let our people do their work."

"I'd just like to know which building he fired from and how he gained access to it."

"Please, Abigail."

It took Dzuze a long moment to gather his thoughts before continuing, but the real hostility Abigail felt came from Agent Mpofu. He was taking deep breaths. His eyes were hard. Abigail's interruption was clearly an outrage. Dzuze spoke: "So what happened after you shot Mr. Patel?"

"I run."

Abigail interrupted again. "With the rifle?"

"I take the rifle back to Albert."

Dzuze turned his attention to Chunga. "The rifle is in our possession and it has been fired recently."

"Did you find the spent cartridges or the bullets?" This time Abigail was talking to Dzuze. Mpofu threw up his hands in apparent disgust.

"Abigail, I must ask you not to interrupt," Chunga told her. "You're here as an observer only."

"I'm sorry."

"We found no shells at the scene."

"I throw them." To Abigail it seemed that the prisoner was trying to come to Dzuze's aid. "I throw them by the bush."

"He could point out the spot," she said. "It should be easy enough to recover them."

Chunga put a hand on Abigail's forearm nearest to him. "Abigail . . ."

But she was already rising. "It's all right, Jonas. I'll wait in the charge office."

When Chunga came out, she was waiting for him on one of the straight-back chairs the young police officer had offered her. The old lady had left, presumably having completed her business with the police. Her chair too had disappeared.

On the way back, Abigail was expecting some sort of reprimand, but Chunga only smiled at her. She had seen the same look on Robert's face when he was planning a surprise for her. "A drink?" he suggested.

Yes, she thought, I could use a drink. "Why not?" she said.

The café to which he took her had tables and chairs in a garden you could not see from the road. Chunga ordered a whiskey from a white-suited waiter wearing a red fez. Abigail asked for a Coke. "How many pleasant places like this still exist in Harare?" she asked.

"Not enough."

"And you know them all?"

"There's not much in Harare I don't know. I need to know the city."

"And what do you know about your suspect? Frankly, he doesn't seem to know too much about what happened that night." Abigail said it challengingly, expecting him to defend their arrest.

"I agree," he said.

"You agree?" How was it, she wondered, that he caught her off-balance so easily. "Jonas, why are you so unlike everything I expected?"

"What did you expect?"

"I expected you to defend all government and CIO actions."

He smiled, a warm, playful expression. "Saturday evening you didn't seem to mind my being different."

What was there to say? Abigail looked down at her hands, then back into that smile that seemed to be saying, whatever happens I'll be there to protect you. Or was that truly what it was saying? And how could he so easily create this confusion in her?

With a wrench, she forced her attention back to the man they had arrested. "I have to talk about more serious matters."

The amusement disappeared. "You have my attention." She could see that it was true. There was none of the patronizing of women that, in her experience, was so common in men, especially African men.

"As long as you hold that man, your men will not be looking for the real killer."

"I know. I've already instructed them to question him further to confirm these suspicions. I expect he'll be released no later than tomorrow, unless we find new evidence."

And yet you haven't even questioned Patel's widow, Abigail thought. But she drove the conversation in a new direction. "Also, on Saturday night the Makwati twins were arrested, apparently by your men. Are they also just going to be missing?"

"No. We have them."

There it was again, another of his unexpected admissions. "Are you going to charge them?"

"I am. They were apparently keeping watch on the prison gate. No country allows that." He was speaking seriously, wanting her to understand his position. "You have to ask yourself what their motive could be."

"Perhaps they were looking for their friends."

"If their friends are in Chikurubi, no one is going to see them from the outside."

"Are you going to protect them?"

"Why should I?"

"Why did you protect them after the bombing?"

This time Chunga struggled for a reply. "It was not my decision only." He stumbled over the words. "My director general knew about it." With a visible effort to take back control of the conversation, he directed the discussion onto a new track. "I have a question for you."

"Yes?"

"Who's the white man you were talking to in the hotel?"

"He's a friend."

"Just a friend?"

"You're not jealous are you, Mr. Chunga?" Damn you, Abigail, she said to herself. Why do you go over to flirtation so readily with this man?

"Perhaps," Chunga said. He looked seriously at her, the same look she had seen in Patel's office the day she first met him.

"Yudel Gordon is a criminologist. He's come to assist me."

"That's a very good friend."

"He is."

"I also have something important to tell you." He let her wait for the revelation. She said nothing, only returning his gaze with curious eyes. "A really important something."

Forget it, Jonas, she thought, I'm not going to play your game. He reached into the inside pocket of his jacket, took out a folded sheet of paper and passed it to her. Abigail looked into his eyes without immediately unfolding the paper.

"Open it."

She did as he instructed. The letter carried the national coat of arms. It had been written by someone in the Department of Justice and it announced the date of the hearing. "It's tomorrow," Abigail said. "Why didn't you give it to me earlier?"

"I couldn't do that."

"Why not?"

"Because then you would have stayed at the hotel to prepare. I wouldn't have had your company this morning."

She waved the letter at him. "Jonas, I don't know how to thank you. How did you do it so fast?"

"In Zimbabwe you need connections."

"I can see that." She looked again at the letter. "The letter says it's being held in Chikurubi prison."

"The courts were full and special preparations are being made in the prison."

Abigail thought about what was convenient for the authorities, and how holding the hearing in the prison meant that neither the public nor the press could be present. The hearing could be held in absolute privacy. Perhaps even the court's decision would not be made public. Why, Jonas, she asked silently, when you do something to make me trust you, is there always some reason in it to fuel my distrust?

"I want Mr. Gordon to come with me."

"I'll arrange it."

"Does the judge have a name?"

"It's in the letter."

Abigail glanced at the letter again. Her habit of reading very fast often meant that she stopped reading letters and reports as soon as she thought she had the essential information. It sometimes resulted in her missing facts that she needed to know. "Judge Mujuru," she read.

"An excellent and fair judge," Chunga said.

I hope so, Abigail thought.

28

The afternoon passed slowly for Yudel. Abigail was in her room, preparing for the next morning's hearing. Rosa was in their room, waiting for her niece to collect her. To pass the time she was reading a book about space travelers who had occupied the earth five hundred million years ago. "It sounds like science fiction," Yudel had said.

"Don't attack something just because you know nothing about it," Rosa answered.

Idleness never sat easily on Yudel. Waiting for anything was almost an impossible ordeal. He was accustomed always to be wrestling with some problem. During daylight hours, he was either working on some aspect of his rehabilitation plan, or interviewing individual prisoners. Often there was not time enough in the day to deal with problems arising from the rehabilitation program. On those occasions the problems went home with him. Otherwise his evenings were spent consulting on criminal matters or seeing patients with emotional problems. Reading was done in bed, the book sometimes falling from his hands as sleep overtook him.

The next morning Abigail would come face-to-face with the very reason Krisj Patel had brought her here. Outwardly, there seemed to be nothing he could do to help her. But he knew this was not so. He could feel, somewhere deep inside himself, that there were aspects of Abigail's case that needed his attention, but what they were eluded him. Then there was the death of this Patel. And the investigation into it was being conducted by people who were definitely not sympathetic to the lawyer.

He went for a walk in the streets around the hotel. On a previous visit he remembered almost as many white as African faces in suburbs like this one. Now he saw no white faces at all, the great majority of the white population having sought refuge in other English-speaking countries. Most of those still in Zimbabwe either did not have the educational or financial requirements of the countries they were seeking to enter, or they had found a way to make good money here and had no intention of leaving it behind.

Under the circumstances, the sane thing to do was flee. That was what Yudel's grandfather had done, with his wife and children, when confronted by the realities of Germany in the nineteen-thirties. When faced with the choice between fight and flight, it only made sense to fight if you were the stronger. Anything else was madness.

He found an outlet of an international fast-food brand where he bought coffee for one dollar U.S. The next matter requiring his attention was to work out the tip. It was an easy one, coming to exactly twelve and a half cents. He handed over two dollars. It was only when the girl behind the counter looked helplessly at him that he remembered a dollar note was the smallest change in the country. Yudel accepted his change in the form of a Coke and a packet of potato crisps.

It was late afternoon by the time he got back. Rosa was on the back terrace, drinking tea. "I've just had the strangest call on my cell phone," she said. "That matron van Deventer from the home where Dad stays . . ."

Yudel sat down opposite her. "Yes, I believe I've met her."

"She's the strangest woman. She says that strings of women, strings, she said, have been calling to speak to Dad."

"Obviously she's exaggerating," Yudel said.

"Exaggerating?" Rosa put down her book. "I can't imagine even one woman calling to speak to Dad."

"Companionship is a human need," Yudel said.

"Don't treat me to your psychological gobbledy-gook, Yudel. We're not talking about Dad's needs, we're talking about his sex appeal. And I think you will agree that he doesn't fall into the movie-star category."

"Perhaps not," Yudel said, "but I, for one, am glad he's attracting some female attention. He has many good qualities. Discerning women will appreciate them."

"What are these qualities that discerning women will appreciate?"

"He has a steady income. He's also a man of good character. In addition, he does not have accidents in restaurants too often." Yudel recognized that, even by his own standards, his arguments were becoming ridiculous. He laughed suddenly, with Rosa joining in.

She completed the thought for Yudel. "He's also ninety years old, farts at inappropriate times, is in fact increasingly incontinent . . ." She paused to consider before going on: ". . . has bad breath, missing teeth and had to be reprimanded last year for pinching a nurse's backside."

"No one's perfect."

"I want to get to the bottom of this. I'm going to call this van Deventer woman back and have her tell me what this is about."

"Give her hell," Yudel said.

He looked up to find Abigail watching them from the doorway. "I have to meet the clients tonight, Yudel. Will you come with me?"

This time the meeting was held by candlelight around a kitchen table in a small apartment on Kenneth Kaunda Drive, near the center of town. Rosa had already left with her niece, leaving Yudel more than one number on which to contact her. Helena had arrived to guide them, sitting in the back of the car and making her feelings known. "I hate them, I hate them, I hate them," she was saying. "What they did to Krisj is probably waiting for all of us."

Prince was waiting for them at the meeting place. "I don't think anyone else is coming," he said. "The way they killed Krisj has spooked everyone."

"Candlelight?" Yudel asked. "Do you think meeting by candlelight makes us any safer?"

"The area's out," Prince said. "At least it's not the whole city."

Helena could neither wait on Abigail, nor niceties. Yudel was sitting a hand's breadth farther away from the table than the other three, and in deeper gloom. He saw Helena fix two hostile eyes on Abigail. Her eyes flashed in the light made by the candle. The deep brown of her face was an uncertain shadow in the room's gloom. "You know what happened to the Makwati girls last night?"

"Yes."

"And the old people whose house we were using?"

"No."

"They've also been taken. God knows how long they'll last in there. This morning those kids, their grandchildren, were alone in the flat. In the meantime, you were out again this morning with Jonas Chunga. What the hell is going on here?"

"He took me to see his suspect in the killing of Krisj."

Helena's mouth opened in astonishment. Prince sat forward. "They have a suspect?"

"Yes, but he didn't do it."

"How do you know?"

"He knows too little about the crime."

"I knew it, the bastards. How I hate them. They took some bum, probably a convict, and made a pretense of solving the case." The words poured out of Helena in a stream of uncontrollable bitterness that was aimed at everything in her world. "I hate this damned country. And I hate the people who just take this sort of thing and let the government walk all over them. And I hate these CIO bastards for everything they do. I hate them for parading an innocent man as Krisj's killer. God, I hate them." She turned on Abigail again. "You see? You see what they are? Don't be taken in by this good-guy act of Jonas Chunga's. You've experienced what they are."

"Yes," Abigail said. "But first I need to know about the others. Where are they?"

"After what happened to Krisj, they're too shit-scared to show their faces."

"So you two are my only clients now?"

"I suppose we are. And the missing people, they're your clients too."

"I see." Abigail paused as she took in the two people she was representing. She had, during her career, represented more impressive, and richer, clients. "Unfortunately, they're not in a position to give me the authority to act for them. But there's something I need to know about you. Tell me about the bombing of the Zanu-PF building, and don't tell me it's irrelevant."

"Jesus," Helena snarled. "Whose side are you on?"

"Tell me now," Abigail said. Her voice was calm, but Yudel could see that the calmness took an effort.

"I'll tell you." Prince was leaning forward, his forearms on the table. "There's no secret. We all planned the bomb. Paul Robinson, the farmer, who you met with the rest of us, managed to get some commercial explosives, the kind they use in the mines. The blast was not very powerful. It only wrecked the front door. We decided to let them feel what it's like to be on the receiving end for a change. It was done at night. No one was injured. Only the *Independent* picked up on the story. The government paper never mentioned it. I think they didn't want to admit it had happened at all. That would've made them look weak."

"And no one was arrested?"

Prince had opened his mouth as if to answer, but Helena cut in before him. "Not then. But now they've picked up seven of us."

"How long ago was the bombing?"

"What does all this matter?" Helena's fury showed both in her face and in her voice.

"More than a year ago," Prince said.

"And in all that time no one was arrested?" Both were silent. "And Director Chunga was responsible for the investigation?" Still there was no response. "Why was no one arrested?"

"We don't know," Prince said.

Yudel could see that there was nothing more to be learned by pursuing this. "Let's talk about tomorrow," he said.

"It's being held inside Chikurubi," Abigail said.

"Inside that hellhole?" Helena was staring at Abigail in disbelief.

"That's right. They say the courts are full."

"Do you know who the judge will be?"

"Judge Mujuru."

"Jesus," Helena cursed. "He's bought and paid for. He's in the government's pocket. He does what they tell him to do. He's one of the beneficiaries of the farms they took from the white farmers."

This is the man Jonas Chunga described as an excellent and fair judge, Abigail thought. "Well, he's what there is. They aren't going to change the judge for us."

"Is he also going to be there?" She glanced at Yudel.

"I can speak," Yudel said. "You can ask me directly. Yes, I'm going to be there."

"So will I," Helena said. "I'm not going to let them see how fucking terrified I am."

Prince said nothing.

"I've changed the plea," Abigail said. She was looking thoughtfully at her two clients. "I'm not asking for them to be released."

"Oh?" Helena's suspicions about Abigail and this white South African man who had suddenly appeared with her showed in just the one word.

"If I ask for them to be released, government will simply say that they don't have them."

"So?"

"So, you say that they're in Chikurubi. I'm asking for an order allowing us to search the prison. Yudel has spent his entire adult life working inside prisons. He understands their workings. If we win, he'll help us search."

Helena and Prince looked at each other. It was Prince who spoke. "If we can search the prison I'm also going to be there. If my wife's there, I want to find her."

"Of course she's there," Helena said. At last Abigail seemed to have said something that met with her approval. "I'm in favor. You win the court order and we'll search that damned place. Maybe Tendai Mujuru will do something good for once in his life."

29

The roadblock across Julius Nyerere Drive was tucked away around a bend. By the time they came upon it they had already passed the back-up squad who were waiting in a side street. Turning back was not a possibility.

Two police vehicles were parked at the roadside. A number of uniformed policemen stood in small groups on the pavement. A single young policeman in the center of the road waved a torch for them to stop. Yudel eased the hired car to a halt and opened the window on his side. He could see no one who was likely to be a CIO agent. A police officer approached them, walking slowly. His manner was that of a man demonstrating that he was in charge.

"I've heard about their roadblocks," Abigail said. "Apparently they're not uncommon."

"Identification," the policeman demanded, looking first at Yudel, then frowning as his eyes focused on Abigail.

Yudel took out his passport. Abigail passed hers to him and Yudel handed both to the officer. He shone his torch on the first page of one, then of the other. "South Africans," he said. "Why are you in Zimbabwe?" He was suddenly friendly.

Abigail leaned across Yudel to get closer to the window. "I am Advocate Abigail Bukula," she said. "I am here to represent a client in an important matter. This is Mr. Gordon, my associate."

"Wait here, please." The officer was studiously polite. He

shouted something in Shona then walked to the side of the road where an older man wearing the stripes of a sergeant examined the passports.

"We're not likely to be going anywhere as long as he's got our passports," Abigail said to Yudel.

"The reserves are approaching," Yudel said.

The sergeant and another officer had joined the first one and were coming round the car. "Good evening, sir," the sergeant said. "I'm sorry to tell you that this car's not roadworthy." His two men were standing close to him on either side.

"This is a hired car," Yudel said.

"It's not roadworthy, I'm afraid. The left parking light is out."

"The headlights are on."

"The parking light must also be operational. Under Zimbabwean law this car can be confiscated until it's repaired. I'm very sorry to tell you this." His two juniors clicked their tongues in sympathy.

Yudel sighed. "How much is the fine?"

"Only one hundred dollars. I'm afraid Zimbabwean law is very strict on roadworthiness. And we are sworn to uphold Zimbabwean law at all times and under all conditions. Zimbabwean law does not allow for exceptions."

Yudel considered that at least half the cars he had seen on Harare streets so far had looked less roadworthy than this one. But it had all been done in the most genial possible way. As shakedowns went, it was a truly amiable one. "A bit steep, isn't it?"

"Otherwise, what about a drink for me and my friends, in good faith?"

"A drink in good faith," Yudel repeated. After that sermon on Zimbabwean law?

"A policeman can't afford a drink these days. Most of my men only get paid one hundred and fifty dollars a month."

Zimbabwean law seemed to have taken a backseat, at least for the moment. "How much will that cost me?"

"Only fifty dollars. Cash now."

Yudel's right hand went to his money pocket, but Abigail stopped him. "We won't be paying anything in cash," she told the sergeant.

"They charge more in court," he said. "Three hundred dollars at least."

"We'll see you there."

The sergeant looked disappointed. To Yudel, the faces of the two junior officers reflected the puzzlement that comes when things do not go according to plan.

"Zimbabwean law . . ." The sergeant was trying again.

Abigail leaned over Yudel to get closer to the window and the sergeant who was standing next to it. "I know all about Zimbabwean law," she said. "My friend, Director Jonas Chunga of the CIO, has explained it all to me."

The sergeant's head pulled back as if she had struck him. "You know him?"

"Intimately," Abigail said.

"Get that parking light fixed," the sergeant admonished Yudel. But he was already handing back the passports.

"Thank you, sergeant," Yudel said. As he pulled away, he glanced at Abigail. "Intimately?" he asked.

"Go to hell, Yudel," she said. "You know what I was doing. I just saved you three hundred and forty rands at this morning's exchange rate."

"Thank you," Yudel said.

"And stop grinning at me."

The roadblock had not been unexpected. The country's roadblocks were well known on the African subcontinent. Driving from the border to Harare, travelers sometimes had to negotiate three or four. The purpose of them all was a subsidy for the one-hundred-and-fifty-dollar salary.

The hotel parking was a narrow, gravelled yard down the side of the building. As they got out, Abigail spoke. "Yudel, this schizophrenic thing of Tony's. Tell me about it." They were standing next to the car. The electricity was working in this part of the city, but the absence of functioning street lighting meant that the only light was a faint glow from a few windows on that side of the hotel and the gentle, white light from a clear moon overhead. Even in that light, Yudel could see the intensity in her face. "You said you weren't sure."

"You remember his writing about a fog that seemed to blot out everything except fear?"

"Yes. There's nothing unusual about that, surely?"

"How often do you get misty conditions here?"

"Practically never."

"And he doesn't describe it as other people would describe a fog. He seems to be enclosed by it. It seems to be personal, cutting him off from everyone and everything else. I don't think the mist he experiences would be visible to you or me. This sort of thing is fairly common among schizophrenics. But this is, at best, a guess. I'm not certain."

"If he is schizophrenic, would that have something to do with his being willing to plant that bomb?"

"Suneesha Patel says Tony did plant the bomb."

"Oh, Tony. Poor, poor Tony."

They were halfway down the driveway, making their way to the front entrance of the hotel when a new police officer appeared, spreading his arms to block their way as they reached the street.

"Not another one," Abigail muttered.

"Please, you must stay inside the hotel."

Some distance along the street a car door slammed shut and a man in civilian clothes came hurrying toward them. As he got close, Abigail recognized him. "Agent Mpofu?"

"Good evening, advocate." He stopped close in front of them, the uniformed officer taking a step back. "I have a message from Director Chunga. He asks that you don't leave the hotel after dark."

"Is there a reason?"

"He's concerned for your safety, after what happened to Mr. Patel."

"I see."

"If you do want to go for a walk, the constable and I would like to accompany you."

Abigail thought about taking a walk through the suburb's quiet nighttime streets with Agent Mpofu and his constable as companions. Yudel answered for her. "Thanks for your concern, agent, but we're on our way into the hotel."

"Thank you. We'll be watching the road, and we have a man at the back of the hotel too."

"Thank you," Yudel said.

"Oh," Abigail said. "Agent Mpofu, this is Mr. Gordon. Mr. Gordon, Agent Mpofu."

Yudel shook hands with the CIO man. "Pleased to meet you and thanks again for your concern. These are difficult times for all of us, especially yourselves." They were opposite the hotel's doors and Yudel could see Mpofu's face now.

"I don't understand."

"I mean whatever political changes lie ahead, they may not be good for CIO personnel."

"I know nothing about politics. Nothing." He stared angrily at Yudel. "I just do my work."

"Good night, agent." At the door Yudel looked back. The policeman was close behind, but Mpofu was already retreating down the pavement. "It seems our movements are being carefully watched," he said to Abigail.

"Controlled is more like it," Abigail said. "And not just by the government side. Every time I go out, the other side knows about it too. Maybe this is what drove Tony over the edge."

"I don't think so."

Abigail's thoughts changed direction. "Will I win tomorrow, Yudel?"

"I think you will."

"Why? According to Helena, the judge is a beneficiary of state patronage."

"There's something here that I don't quite understand. Your friend, Director Chunga, has arranged to have the matter heard so quickly, and in the prison where your clients believe their friends are being held. I think it's already been decided that you are to get what you want."

They entered the hotel in silence. We'll know tomorrow, she thought.

Now only hours were left. Abigail scanned the text of her address four times. At first she read fast, reinforcing her arguments. After that she went through it very slowly once, thinking about every phrase and every line. During the final reading she whispered the words for the first time, getting used to the sound of them and practicing the gestures she would be using. Only then was she satisfied that she would be able to read it as smoothly and effortlessly in the next day's makeshift court as if she were speaking without notes.

That Jonas's success in moving forward the court date had given her relatively little time to prepare was not important to her. Since the first call she had received in Johannesburg from Krisj Patel, the matter had been in her mind. And since arriving in Harare she had been making notes at every opportunity.

Abigail knew that her court appearances were good. Even when under personal strain, her thinking was lucid and, on this continent, she was as good a speaker as anyone in the profession. On top of all that, she knew that she looked good.

When waiting to address a court on an important issue, she was always nervous. She often had to clasp her hands tightly to prevent them from shaking. Intense concentration was needed to begin an address in a voice that was strong and secure. But once she had got past the first sentence or two, some other self seemed to take over and the words flowed smoothly and with great confidence. The notes and the prepared speech often lay unused in front of her, as she effortlessly held the attention of the court. She had every reason to believe that the next day would be no different.

It was after two when she put the text of her address aside and closed her eyes for the first time. Her cell phone rang almost immediately. Robert's voice on the other end of the line awakened a mixture of emotions. Anger, pleasure, guilt and frustration wrestled with one another.

"Abigail," she heard him say, "tell me that things are going well?"

"Not so well. Your man hasn't turned up."

"He should be arriving tomorrow morning."

"What time?"

"About eleven, I think."

"He'll miss the hearing. There's no point in his coming, if he's going to miss the hearing."

"Is the hearing tomorrow? Since when?"

Since this morning. "Yes, it's tomorrow."

"Our journalist can still pick up on the main thread of the story. But are you all right?"

Robert, you bastard, she thought. You know damned well that I'm in a hostile country and my attorney has been killed and you ask if I'm all right. "Why are you calling so late?"

"I needed to speak to you."

"You needed to speak to me after midnight."

"No, not after midnight, especially. I just needed to speak to you."

"Okay. That's what you're doing."

"Jesus, Abigail. Don't be so harsh. I'm trying to talk to you."

"I'm listening."

"Look, I need to talk to you about . . ." He seemed to be struggling to find the words he needed.

Is this it? Abigail thought. Is this where a marriage ends? Is this how it happens, on a long-distance call, in a tattered hotel room, after midnight?

"I need to talk to you about . . ." He hesitated again. ". . . you know what I want to talk about."

"You'd better tell me." She could hear the weariness in her own voice.

"What you suspected about me and that young temp . . ." He waited again, as if hoping that she would finish the sentence for him.

You can go to hell, Robert, she thought. I'm not going to help you out.

"I almost had an affair with her." He hurried on. "But it never came to that and she's gone back to the agency. I just want to get our relationship back the way it was." Again he waited, hoping for her to respond. "I just want to repair the damage I've done to the trust between us."

"An affair? What the hell is an affair? Don't tell me you almost had an affair. Tell me you wanted to fuck her."

"All right, I wanted to fuck her."

"And you chose the night before this important hearing to make your confession. That's amazing."

"I just want . . ."

"Why didn't you do it?"

"Jesus, Abigail."

"Well, why not?"

"I arranged to meet her at the Sheraton, but she didn't come. When I got back to the office, her resignation was on my desk."

"So, I owe my marriage to this girl. Are you telling me that?"

"Look, I just want everything . . ."

"Robert. It's after two and I have a hearing tomorrow. I can't do this now."

"Look, I just wanted you to know . . ."

"I don't want to know anything now. I have a big day tomorrow. Good night, Robert."

"Abigail, please, I just want things back to normal."

"That may not be possible. Good night."

She hung up, still dry-eyed and angry. It took a moment before the weeping overcame her. She cried till she fell asleep.

30

Sleep did not come easily to Judge Tendai Mujuru on this night. It was only that day that he had received instructions about the duty he had to perform the next day. During the last year, life had been relatively comfortable. He had dealt with a murder case, a number of civil matters and a serious tax offense. Now, he again had to deal with a political matter. It was not fair. He did not want to do it. There were others who really believed. They should do these cases. Why did it have to be him?

Judge Mujuru liked to have ice in his whiskey. But with the power having been off since early that afternoon, making ice had not been possible. He did have a generator, but fuel was expensive. He only used his standby plant to heat up the water every evening and to provide two or three hours of lighting. Cooking on bottled gas was also a damned nuisance—you seemed to spend a lot of your life buying bottles, disconnecting used ones and fitting new ones.

But the worst inconvenience was drinking his whiskey at room temperature. It was much less expensive than the brand favored by Jonas Chunga, but it was greatly improved by a few blocks of ice. And, on a warm summer night like this one, room temperature seemed almost lukewarm. Given what you paid for whiskey, you should be able to drink it the way you liked it.

The whiskey did serve to dull the sharp edges of the discomfort he felt at the hearing he would be presiding over when morning came. He had seen the documentation and knew that this South African woman was going to be asking to be allowed to search Chikurubi. He also knew that the old man himself would be interested in this matter.

And whose bright idea was it to hold the hearing inside the prison? It was madness.

He knew where it had all begun. This Paul Robinson had been ejected from his farm by some of the party men, the so-called war veterans. They were faithful supporters of the president who had to be rewarded, he had been told. As for Robinson, he was just another white leech, taking for himself and giving nothing to the people. That was what they had told him the night before he heard Robinson's plea to have his farm restored to his ownership.

It was also not fair that Robinson and his lawyers had expected him to rule against the government. After all, the new owners had their letter of offer for the farm, issued by himself, that gave them full right to the land. Robinson knew he had no choice but to vacate the farm.

It was also not fair that when Robinson refused to vacate the land the matter had to come before him and he had to find Robinson guilty. And when he handed down a suspended sentence there were those in government who cursed him for being a weakling and others overseas who said he had no respect for human rights. Human rights groups in three European countries had said that he had better not try to visit their countries. If he did, things would get hot for him. None of it was fair.

And when they offered him a farm, how could he refuse it? If he had, where would he stand with government now? And he was a man with a family after all. He had never asked for the farm. They had instructed him to issue the letter of offer to himself and he had simply obeyed. It was their idea, and his reward for patriotic judgments.

The damned thing stood fallow now. He had left some workers with instructions, but the moment his back was turned they had left with whatever farm implements and seed they could carry and sold them in the city. How was he supposed to see that the farm stayed productive? It was two hundred kilometers away. If he went once a month, that was all. The damned thing had been a liability until he sold the tractors, pumps and a harvester. At least that way he had gotten something out of it.

We look after our own, they had said. You've looked after us, we're looking after you. We understand loyalty. In time to come, your new farm is going to be worth a fortune, they had told him.

And now he was their man. Refusing them anything had become impossible. But he had asked for none of it. He had wanted none of it. And this woman who wanted to be allowed to search Chikurubi—she had been made to think that such a thing could be allowed. What was she doing here anyway?

His glass was empty. It had been for some time. He poured another double from the bottle and again cursed the absence of ice. He had just started it when his phone rang.

Very little was required of him during the call. The caller did most of the talking in a call that did not last long. At the end of it, Tendai Mujuru understood perfectly what he had to do and the burden that he had been wrestling with had been lifted. Perhaps it was true. Perhaps they did look after their own.

31

The sun rose early on the morning of the hearing in Chikurubi prison, long before any of the day's protagonists were awake. The light it threw over the Nyanga hills some four hundred kilometers away was always beautiful, but especially at this time of the year, and more especially this year. There had been a fire during the winter which had burned away all the old dry grass. As a result, there had been no impediment to the new green shoots. The hills, as far as Bino D'Almeida could see, were a bright green.

The border had not been easy. There had been more trucks coming up from the coast, and Customs had been even slower than usual. At least he had got through without having to pay anyone, and his load was still intact. He calculated another six hours of driving, definitely not more than eight, before he reached Harare and Chikurubi prison. A few hours to offload, then on to Bulawayo.

With an empty truck and trailer, the down run would be much easier. Without a load, Customs also would have no excuse to hold him up. In the old days, the other drivers had told him, there were always full loads going down to Beira. Now that the Zimbabwean farms had been destroyed, it was only every second or third truck that carried a load on the down run.

Bino's own country had not been good to him. He had struggled to find work and had never been able to hold on to the jobs he did find. But in Mozambique he had found this job, driving the big trucks between Beira and Zim. He had his own place in the world now. It was not much, but it was more than he ever had at home. A cousin had told him about Mozambique. The cousin had been intending to go to Africa, but in the end he had stayed home and Bino had gone.

And the other drivers had accepted him readily. They all spoke Portuguese, his home language, which from the beginning had made contact with them easier. There were also the women—African women. They were less complicated than their European sisters and more eager to please, both in bed and in the kitchen. He had told a Portuguese friend that the people back home would never understand about his having black women. The friend had said that he should not worry. In Mozambique, mulatto was the national color.

He loved his job and was determined to do it well. This cargo especially. It was a World Food Program shipment, intended for Chikurubi prison. It did not take much intelligence to realize that things could not be too good for the guys in prison. But that was all right. He was coming with their food. He was glad to be doing something good for people, even a bunch of convicts.

I'll get it to them, he told himself. It may not be fast enough for the head office, but I'll get it there.

He was out of the hills and rolling easily over a good road surface toward Rusape. He saw the roadblock from a long way off, but he knew there was no practical way around it. This time paying them would probably be unavoidable. He hoped twenty dollars would do it. He knew not to offer it too soon. The thing to do was to feign reluctance. That usually kept the payment within sensible limits.

The only police vehicle was parked across the road. There seemed to be five or six officers. They never worked alone at the roadblocks. The driver they were stopping always had to feel outnumbered. That was how they worked. He also knew enough to know that the UN markings on the load were not going to be of much help.

Two officers had moved into the road. One had raised both hands, his palms facing Bino. That was no surprise. Only some of the locals would be allowed through without stopping. "Good morning," one of them said, approaching the driver's window. "Where are you going, my friend?"

"Harare."

"Where in Harare are you going?"

"Chikurubi prison."

"Chikurubi? What's the load?"

"Officer, I don't know about the load. I just drive the truck."

"Well, Mr. Truck Driver, do you know how to switch off the engine?"

Bino switched off the engine.

"The keys." The officer held out a hand to take them. "Get out. We'll see what's in this load you know nothing about. Maybe it's arms or drugs."

Bino followed the police officer to the back of the truck. The second policeman had fallen in behind him. The others, who had been standing together at the side of the road, were also moving closer. The one who had done all the talking so far plucked at the tarpaulin covering the load. "Open," he said.

Bino held up both hands in a gesture of helplessness. "If I open it, the food falls out," he said.

"Food? What food? Now you know what's in the load."

"The boss never told me. I think it's food."

"Open. I want to see this food."

The policemen had all gathered around by now. "Don't worry, Mr. Portuguese," a new voice said. "All we want is to look at your food."

Bino climbed the two steel steps at the back of the trailer. It took him ten minutes to loosen the binding enough to free one of the ten-kilogram bags and pass it down. Then he climbed down.

One of the policemen cut open the top of the bag. He allowed a handful to spill into his cupped hands and tasted it with the tip of his tongue. "What's this shit? It tastes like sawdust."

Bino shrugged.

"How do you eat this shit?"

Bino shrugged again. "You make porridge, I think."

One of the other officers, an older man, had come forward. "Chikurubi, amigo?" he asked.

"Yes, Chikurubi."

"So why do those prisoners get the food? Nobody here has food. Why do you take food to criminals and dissidents?"

Once more Bino shrugged. "I just drive the truck. What do I know?"

"What do you know? First you didn't know what was in the load. Then you knew it was food. And you did know to make porridge from it. Tell me what else do you not know."

"I know nothing about the load, sir. I know nothing." He could see that this time twenty dollars would not do it. Perhaps a few bags would be enough. Perhaps a few bags and twenty dollars.

"You think it's right for prisoners to eat while good people starve? You think that's right?"

"I don't think. I drive the truck."

The older officer had approached to within an outstretched arm of Bino. "That's the problem, amigo. You don't think. Mr. Portuguese, this is the time to think. You go sit in your truck and think about what is right and what is wrong. I'll keep the keys."

"Please, sir, officer. I have to deliver this load. I'll lose my job."

"You sit there and think. You think about what is more important, your job and food for criminals, or the starving people of Zimbabwe. You think about that."

"Please, Colonel."

"Not yet. I'm not a colonel yet. And I'm finished talking. You go back to the truck and think."

Bino went back to the cab and slowly climbed the three steps of the ladder that led into it. He knew that sometimes they let you wait, just to show who was in charge. When enough time had passed, they let you go. That's what they did sometimes. At other times, things did not go that well. In any event, there was no other way. He would have to wait and think.

32

Chikurubi was gray. Many people who had seen it, or even been inside it, having been asked what it was like, had described it as big and without color. Abigail saw it as a forbidding, lifeless presence.

Tucked away behind a low ridge and a dense fringe of blue gums, and set well back from the fence of the outer perimeter, it was invisible from the road. A sign proclaiming its presence was so badly rusted and weathered that it now served little purpose.

Helena and Prince had traveled in the backseat of Yudel's hired car, with Abigail next to him in front. They arrived twenty-five minutes before the scheduled start of the hearing. At the outer gate, a guard in prisons department uniform met them and asked them to wait while they were identified.

Entering Chikurubi was not easy for Abigail. She had been telling Yudel about the form she expected the hearing to take, but had stopped talking as the building appeared through the trees. Even Yudel, who had spent much of his life inside the walls of prisons, felt the wave of oppressive energy that swept toward them from beyond its walls. For Abigail, it was much worse. She stopped in the pedestrian doorway as if repelled by everything that resided within. There was never any possibility that she may take a step back, but she had to gather strength before continuing.

Like all prisons, Yudel knew the outstanding characteristic of this one would be the gates—heavily guarded access points that barred the way to every part of the building. They passed through three gates, each of which had to be opened by a guard on the inside, before they reached a large hall with unpainted concrete walls and floor. It may at one time have been a gymnasium. The court had been set up in a corner of the hall. The rest stood empty. Yudel had the impression of crossing a plain to reach a distant oasis. The sound of their footsteps, especially Abigail's leather heels, echoed off hard surfaces as they approached the corner in which the hearing would take place. Two rows of plastic seats at the back of the makeshift court had been provided for a small group of observers. So far the only people occupying them were three officers in the uniform of the prisons department. A pile of backless wooden benches stacked in a corner revealed the nature of the room's usual seating. The only windows were shallow and set close to a high ceiling. Most of the light came from overhead fluorescent lights.

The prison officer who accompanied them showed Abigail and Yudel to their seats at a wooden table. The two government lawyers were already seated at a table to the right of them. The judge's table stood in front and in the center on a slightly raised platform. Just in front of the judge, the court registrar had his own table. He was cleaning his fingernails with the sharpened end of a match. The room's two doors were guarded by uniformed policemen. Because they could be called as witnesses, Helena and Prince had been left in a corridor just outside the hall.

As Abigail and Yudel arrived at their table, the two government men came to meet them. They introduced themselves as Barrister Gorowa and Solicitor Moyo, and said that it was a pleasure to meet Advocate Bukula and Mr. Gordon. Abigail returned the compliment and Yudel said, "Hello."

Gorowa was very young. Too young for this, Abigail thought. Moyo was trying to look bored. A glance at the two of them gave Abigail the impression of insecure, lower-level civil servants. It was a reflection of her view of herself that, although she was a civil servant, she never saw herself as that. Among her colleagues, she thought of the outstanding ones simply as good lawyers. The ineffective ones she saw as civil servants.

He's not here, Abigail was thinking. He made this morning's hearing possible, but he's not here. Surely he'll come? Not that it'll be easier with him here.

Thinking about Chunga and whether he was going to attend turned her thoughts toward Robert. Abigail had a way of never looking back once she had said goodbye to someone. At an airport or on a train station, she said her goodbyes and then walked away. This morning she had not once thought of Robert. Until this moment, only the hearing had occupied her thoughts. He had promised a journalist, an idea that had pleased her. With wider publicity she would have felt safer. She asked herself why she had not contacted the *Independent* about the hearing. Having a newspaper present that really did live up to its name would have been comforting, but it seemed that even *The Herald* was not present. To help her, Chunga had seen to it that the hearing was arranged quickly. But perhaps other reasons existed. Perhaps the suddenness of it all had also made it possible to keep it out of the press.

It was still five to nine and Judge Tendai Mujuru had not yet appeared, when the door by which Abigail and Yudel had come in opened and Jonas Chunga stepped into the hall. Abigail saw him stop in the open door and look for her. She made no greeting and did not smile, but as long as he held her eyes she could look nowhere else.

Sitting next to her, Yudel looked first at Chunga, then at Abigail. What he saw in her face looked like an anxiety that came close to panic. Chunga's face wore no clear expression. It was just a look between a man and a woman, and Yudel would rather he had not seen it.

As suddenly as the moment had arrived, so abruptly did Chunga break it, walking quickly across the hall, followed closely by Agent Mpofu. They joined the prison officials on the plastic chairs behind the two legal teams.

The registrar disappeared through a second door. When he came back it was to step aside to allow Judge Mujuru, tall, heavily built, shortsighted and balding, to enter. His eyes were red and his nose carried the glow of the heavy drinker. Abigail could not know that he had already consumed two warm double whiskies that morning, and that they had probably not improved his powers of concentration. Everyone rose as he entered, and all sat down when he did.

Just as she did whenever she said goodbye to anyone, so Abigail's awareness of Chunga's presence disappeared in a moment. She looked at the judge and saw what she believed was a weak and dissolute man. She could not believe that having this man presiding would be good for her or her case, but she remembered something her father had told her when she was in her early teens. She had been complaining about some aspect of her life that was important only to herself. He had waved her away with the words, "In life, you have to play the cards you are dealt. You have no other choice." Since that day, she had lived accordingly. Regardless of what she saw in the judge, she was going to play her cards as well as she knew how.

"We have only one matter before the court today," the registrar was telling his small audience, all of whom already knew that. "This is the matter of Ndoro and others against the state."

He sat down. Mujuru nodded to him, then spoke for the first time. "Who appears for Ndoro and the others?"

Abigail rose. The judge was looking down at the notepad in front of him. She waited until he looked at her before speaking. "I do, your Lordship. My name is Abigail Bukula."

After Barrister Gorowa admitted to his part in the proceedings, the judge continued. "This is a matter of great importance," he began. "There are matters of principle here and precedents that may be established and may affect Zimbabwean and even international law for generations to come." He had spoken slowly, every word carrying a heavy emphasis, as if each were equally important. It seemed that to Judge Mujuru, this was the way a judge should dispense legal wisdom. Now he looked directly at Abigail. "It's very stuffy in here. Isn't it very stuffy in here, Miss Bukula?"

Abigail was surprised by the question, but if his Lordship wanted to socialize with her in court, she had no objection. "I must say I also find it so, your Lordship," she said.

"I agree," Mujuru said, using the same heavy emphasis that he would have given to a legal pronouncement. "Officers, open some of those windows," he told the two policemen.

To reach the windows one of the policemen had to climb onto a plastic chair, while the other held it. Even then, the task was not easily accomplished. The latch on the window resisted the officer's first few efforts. At the fourth attempt, he put enough energy into the action to overcome the resistance of the latch. The window flew open and he fell backward onto his colleague, the two landing in a tangle of arms, legs and uniforms on the concrete floor.

For Judge Mujuru, this was the best possible result. He laughed heartily, slapping his hand on the surface of the table. Everyone in the court dutifully joined in the merriment, while the policemen scrambled to their feet.

The judge's amusement lasted only seconds, though. A breeze coming in through the window carried on it a rich, animal smell. Yudel remembered having experienced such a smell only once before. Taking a walk in a forest, he had come upon the distended corpse of a baboon. It was lying on its back on a sandspit in the center of a stream. The maggots were already devouring it. To Yudel's memory, this smell was much like that one had been.

"Close it, close it." The look on Mujuru's placid face had become agitated. "What an awful smell. Close it immediately."

This time the policeman succeeded in following his orders without entertaining the court. The judge took an added moment to compose himself. "This is the first time in the history of our country, perhaps of any country, that a plaintiff seeks an order to have the cells of a prison thrown open to search them for prisoners that the government has declared are not being held. If this petition succeeds, it will have an effect that may prove to be historic on our continent and throughout the world." He looked pleased at the idea of making history. "Miss Bukula, please proceed with your opening address."

Because her audience was gathered into a corner of the hall, there was no reason for Abigail to raise her voice. She spoke softly, almost conversationally, but clearly, as was her way, every word perfectly enunciated. "The principle that is involved here is the most basic in our law. Habeas corpus is the remedy against unlawful detention that is applied in all civilized countries. Its provisions ensure that people do not disappear off the streets, that ordinary citizens cannot be taken by the authorities and held without trial at the pleasure of their political masters." All her attention was concentrated on the judge who was nodding sagely at every point. "In this matter, we are able to produce witnesses who have seen their loved ones and colleagues brought to the place in which we are gathered this morning. They are willing to testify to the circumstances of the abductions and the manner in which the missing people were taken and delivered to the very premises in which we find ourselves."

Abigail had read the first few lines. Now the inner force, as she thought of it, had taken over. She had stopped glancing down at her prepared text and spoke to the judge as if only they were in the room. The words flowed without hesitation.

"The crime of these individuals was to disagree with policies and actions they found tyrannical. They are brave young patriots, who sinned only by having the courage to stand against what they believe to be wrong." For half an hour Abigail reasoned with Judge Mujuru, offering legal precedents, building arguments that she told him were self-evident, raising issues of Zimbabwean law and begging him to remember the many brave judges who had gone before. She and Mujuru both knew how many injunctions ordered by those brave judges had been ignored by the government. "But this can surely not be the case here. If this precedent-setting judgment is made today, we are here in this place. The order of the court can be carried out immediately."

She knew that African patriarchs rarely liked to have women, especially younger women, prescribe their actions to them, but the opportunity was too great for her to resist. "Your Lordship, this is your opportunity to deal with a matter today that will establish, once and for all, the personal rights of the citizens of your country." But Mujuru showed no sign of irritation at her reminding him where his duty lay. He continued to nod, seeming to agree with everything she was saying.

So far, Abigail's gestures had been restricted to only the smallest movements of her hands. As her address drew toward its end, she raised both hands in what was almost a supplication. "I am speaking of a country in which I lived for years and that I love dearly. The dilemma of the courts is to dispense justice in a country in which the national government has, on many occasions, ignored the basic rights of its citizens. This morning, your Lordship, this dilemma is in your hands."

When she sat down, Mujuru nodded one more time, as if there was certainly food for thought in what she had said. He looked sternly at Gorowa. "Mr. Gorowa, your opening statement please."

Gorowa rose, managing to spill a sheaf of papers onto the floor in the process. "If it please your Worship . . ." Abigail heard a tremor in his voice. ". . . if it please your Lordship, the Zimbabwean people see the logic in the arguments of my learned colleague. We see no reason to oppose the application."

"What the hell?" Abigail murmured.

Yudel leaned toward her. "They're not here," he whispered. "We aren't going to find them, not today."

Judge Mujuru was nodding yet again. Would the corrupt old bastard ever stop? she asked herself. She wanted to scream at him to stop this charade. But she admonished herself in her father's words: play the cards you've been dealt. And, for the moment, these were the cards.

"Since there is no objection from the state, I can find no reason to refuse the application," Judge Mujuru said in the thoughtful tone a man would use while making history. "I will give my reasons in writing at a later date. Will the representatives of both parties approach the bench to discuss implementation of this order?"

Gorowa was already at the judge's table when Abigail reached it. "In the interests of justice, my client is willing to do it now," Gorowa said.

"Director?" Mujuru had raised his voice. He was looking in the direction of the men at the back of the court.

Abigail turned, quickly, thinking that the judge was talking to Chunga. But one of the prison officers had risen. "Yes, your Lordship."

Chunga, who held the same title, had not moved. The whole damned thing is choreographed, Abigail thought. And I've been the prima ballerina.

"Do you see any reason why this inspection should not be conducted now?"

"No reason, your Lordship."

Mujuru banged down his gavel once. "The inspection of this prison by Miss Bukula, her assistant and her two clients will commence immediately within the provisions of the Official Secrets Act as it applies to our prisons. They will be accompanied by the director and other staff members of the prison and, because this is a matter of national security, representatives of the Central Intelligence Organization." He took a deep breath and looked round the room with obvious satisfaction. "I further order that if any of the complainants in the pleadings are found in this facility, they are to be released to Miss Bukula immediately. And let those who criticize our Zimbabwean system of justice take note of this judgment."

33

The group which, according to the judge's order, was to conduct the search gathered in the passage outside the hall. "Shall we let the director of the prison lead us?" Chunga said to Abigail.

It sounded to her like a tea-party suggestion. She could imagine Chunga saying, "Shall we ask Auntie Martha to pour?" It was an offer no one would think of refusing. But this was not the way she saw it. You did not let the criminals decide where to search for the hidden loot. She was still looking for the right answer when Yudel spoke.

"Thank you for the offer, director, but that's not necessary. I'll lead the way."

Chunga sighed ostentatiously. "With respect, the director of the prison knows it better than you do, never having been here before."

"I know many prisons," Yudel said. "I'll lead the way."

"But this is not one of them." Chunga turned his attention away from Yudel. "Abigail?"

Helena had moved close to Abigail. "Don't let the bastard get away with it." She tried to keep her voice low enough that only Abigail would hear her.

Chunga's eyes had gone cold. "I heard that, Miss Ndoro. There's no need for that. You are being treated with respect here."

Abigail placed a hand, both comforting and protective, on Helena's nearest shoulder, but she spoke to Chunga. "Jonas, I apologize for Ms. Ndoro's outburst, but please support me in this. I want Mr. Gordon to lead the way."

"But he doesn't . . ."

"Please, Jonas."

"Very well. Let's have Mr. Gordon take us on a tour of our prison. Let's also hope that he doesn't miss half the cells." He was making no attempt to hide his irritation.

Abigail smiled at him. "Thank you, Jonas."

Mpofu came forward and spoke softly to his boss. This time no one else heard.

"One more thing," Chunga said. "We have forms here which all visitors need to complete. No interviews with the media on the state of our prisons may be conducted. Please understand that the state of the prison is not what any of us desire, but ours is a country in which many people do not have enough to eat. We do not have the resources to feed the prisoners the way we would like to."

Mpofu handed a form each to Abigail, Yudel, Helena and Prince. It swore them all to secrecy for everything they saw in the prison. All signed without comment.

Chunga waved an extravagant hand toward the door. "Mr. Gordon, please."

Yudel was not one to be affected by sarcasm. "This way," he said.

The principles on which prisons are constructed are much the same everywhere. The cells are divided into groups, usually called blocks or floors. Once you have identified these groups, ensuring that you cover all the cells is not difficult. After that come the various common areas, the storerooms and the offices. In anticipation of the hearing's outcome, Yudel had already formed an idea of the prison's geography. He was certain that, if Abigail's clients were here, he would find them.

He found the entrance to the first block where he expected it to be. It led off to the right of the main passage from the front entrance. The group went slowly through the block, Yudel and Abigail leading, followed by Helena and Prince who stopped at every cell, taking turns to study the inmates through the inspection holes in the cell doors. The five officials walked behind. It took over half an hour to complete the block. Chunga tried to draw Yudel aside.

"For God's sake, Gordon. This is a big prison. Do you know how long this is going to take us?"

"The rest of the day," Yudel said.

"Exactly."

"We have the time. I'm sorry if it inconveniences you."

Abigail, who had been listening to the exchange, directed her warmest smile at Chunga.

The group moved on, from block to block and cell to cell. Helena and Prince studied every face, occasionally asking someone to turn round to be identified. The reasons that the visitors had to be sworn to silence were everywhere. Cells that had been intended for six now held twice, even three times that number. Some of the prisoners wore ragged clothing that had obviously not been replaced for years and may not have been washed for months. The others wore the clothing they had been wearing when sentenced. Yudel could see no sign of reading matter or any other sort of diversion. The dirt floor of the exercise yard showed no signs of having been disturbed by human feet in the last week. Against its farthest wall, a sewage outlet seemed to have burst, spilling a trail of its contents onto the dirt.

It was the condition of the prisoners themselves that disturbed Abigail most. The bodies of some were covered with sores—evidence of kwashiorkor, brought on by severe malnutrition. Almost everyone was desperately thin. Most of them were sitting or lying down on the mats that provided the only furnishings in the cells. They showed little interest in the visitors, many not even turning to look at them.

As far as Abigail could see, Chunga never once looked into a cell. He walked in silence behind the prison officers, his face set in the stern expression she had come to associate with his displeasure. Mpofu walked a step behind him.

It was after the second block that they found themselves in the part of the prison directly behind the hall where the hearing had taken place. They turned a corner, and now the smell that had entered the hall when the policemen had opened the window was everywhere. The change was so great that a valve may have been opened and the smell pumped into the air around them. Yudel turned toward it.

"There are no cells there." Chunga's voice had taken on an urgent tone.

"We both know what that smell is," Yudel said. "We have to look there. One of our clients may be among them."

"What is it?" Abigail, who had fallen a few steps behind Yudel, caught up to him.

Yudel was looking at Chunga. "It's the prison morgue."

"It's not necessary. None of your people are there."

Abigail had stopped. "Dear God," she said. "This never occurred to me."

For the first time since they had started searching the prison, Prince spoke. "We have to look." The thought that his Joyce may be among the bodies was frightening, but if she was, he wanted to know. "We have to."

Abigail steeled herself for what she knew had to be done. "The order is for us to search the entire prison, not part of it."

The director of the prison had made his own decision. He led the way to the door from which the smell was issuing. A ring of keys had appeared in the hands of one of his men. The director stepped aside for him to unlock the door. Yudel looked at Abigail. "You can do nothing in here. You don't need to come."

"At last there's a point on which I can agree with Mr. Gordon." Chunga had positioned himself between Abigail and the door. "You don't need to go in there."

But Abigail was there for the search, all of the search. "I have to," she said.

Yudel followed the prison director into what seemed to be an old solitary-confinement cell. Abigail was close behind him. She reached out and took hold of one of his sleeves. It was not much, but it provided some reassurance. Behind her she could feel the presence of Helena and Prince.

The morgue had only one window, set high like those in the other cells, but it had been covered by newspaper. The heat of the African day penetrated all of the prison, but in this confined space it had no way to escape. The heat and the smell together were an assault on the senses that even Yudel had not expected. There was perhaps a quarter of the light in the other cells. It took almost a minute for Abigail's eyes to become accustomed to the semidarkness. She was holding Yudel's arm just above the wrist.

At first glance, what she saw looked like a mound of elongated sacks, piled in layers. Only as her eyes became accustomed to the darkness could she see the face of a woman on the top layer nearest to her. It was smooth, unlined and expressionless, at peace now with the world that had consigned her to this place. There seemed to be three layers, four or five rows deep. The bodies were all in the ragged prison uniforms they had died in. "How long have they been here?" Abigail heard Yudel ask.

"Four days or less." The prison director's voice carried no inflection that may have indicated what he was feeling.

"These are the people who died in the last four days?"

"Yes, since Monday. But you have to remember that the World Food Program's food hasn't come yet."

"They died of starvation?" Yudel asked.

"No. We don't have medical resources. You may not believe it, but I try to stop people dying of starvation."

"How many inmates do you have?" Yudel asked,

"One thousand three hundred, more or less."

With that mortality rate, no one could be sure, Yudel thought. At the rate of three a day, more than half the prison population would be dead in a year.

Abigail turned to look for Chunga, but he had not entered the cell. "How can our people examine them to see if their friends are among them?"

"The bodies will not be decomposing yet. We can lift them. We'll bring a torch."

"Are you able to do this?" Yudel asked of Prince and Helena.

Prince was a motionless shadow against the light from the doorway. "I have to," he said.

"Jesus Christ," Helena said. "Me too, I also have to."

"Cover your noses with your handkerchiefs," Yudel said. "It'll help." Abigail felt him draw her close. "Go outside," he said softly. "There's nothing for you to do here."

Abigail stumbled through the door. Once in the passage, she again looked for Chunga. A man in the uniform of the prison staff was waiting in the passage, as if to guard the corpses. "Did you see Director Chunga?" she asked.

He waved a hand in the direction of the main entrance. "He left."

"He's left?"

"Yes, he left. He's gone."

After a warder had gone to fetch a torch and returned with it, the shuffling of feet and muted voices reached her as the group in the cell searched through the bodies. It was taking too long, she thought. How could it take so long to look at fifteen or twenty faces? Oh God, fifteen or twenty since Monday. And Tony, where is he and what, if anything, is he getting to eat? What diseases is he being subjected to? And how far is he from a situation like this?

At one point the warder who had fetched the torch emerged, muttering something about batteries. The others came out to wait in the passage until he returned. Helena leaned against a wall with her eyes closed. Prince stood a little distance away, as if he was no part of this matter.

"How many still?" Abigail asked Yudel.

He looked pale. "Still a way to go. They have to be certain."

"Jonas has gone."

"When?"

"He never came into the morgue."

After the warder came back, having fitted the torch with better batteries, and the group had gone back into the cell, Abigail was again alone with the warder. "Is it always like this?" she asked. "So many dying?"

He shrugged. "The doctor only comes on Fridays."

"One doctor, to see all the sick prisoners?"

He shrugged again. This was clearly not his business.

"Why do you keep the bodies here?"

"There's no space in the city morgue."

"The morgue there is full?"

"Too much," he said. "It's the cholera."

And Jonas? She asked herself. Did he not have the stomach for this aspect of his country? The makeshift morgue in Chikurubi prison was a long way from the country club with its toadying waiters, wildlife on the fairways and bills that no one expected you to pay.

When they did emerge, even the prison officials looked as if they may be close to puking. "Nothing," Helena said. "Not a damned thing. I don't know who those poor people are, but none of them are ours."

Eventually they had been through all the cell blocks, all the stores and even the offices. The director who had followed Yudel patiently through his own prison turned to Abigail. In a tone of voice that revealed nothing, he said, "Ms. Bukula, they are not here. I don't know where they are, but they aren't in my prison." Abigail looked at Yudel, who seemed to her as if he were trying to remember something. He turned toward the main entrance, then suddenly turned back to face the director. "Is there anything else, Mr. Gordon?" the prison director asked.

"The solitary-confinement cells, where are they?"

"I think there are three prisoners in them at the moment, just three."

"We'd like to see them, please." Yudel almost added "if it's not too much trouble," but this man had already gone to great trouble, and sarcasm would not be helpful.

"This way."

The cells they were looking for were in a separate part of the building on the side farthest from the main entrance. The first two were empty. The next held a man who was sitting on the far side of the cell, his head between his knees. When the warder called his name and he looked up, both Helena and Prince shook their heads. In the next cell, a prisoner who had probably heard them coming was standing at the inspection hole in the door. "Am I going back to the others now?" he asked of the first face he saw. It was Helena's, and she shook her head. "Am I going back?" His voice followed them as they went on to the next cell. "Am I going back now? When am I going back?"

In the last cell, what looked like a pile of rags was unmoving in a far corner. The light in this cell was worse than in the others, and

Abigail was not sure that this was a person. Then something twitched and a small foot emerged from the anonymous heap of rags. Prince maneuvered his way forward, all but pushing Abigail away from the door. "Joyce?"

"Prince?" A young female voice answered uncertainly. Then, in a moment, the bundle of rags had come to life and a figure was dashing toward the inspection hole. "Prince, oh, Prince."

"Joyce."

"No, it's me, not Joyce." With her face framed by the inspection hole, Abigail recognized Natasha Makwati. "Have you come to fetch me?"

"Have you seen Joyce?"

"No. Have you come to take me?"

Abigail had to push Prince aside. "Where's your sister?"

"She's somewhere else in this place. They put me in here because I got into a fight with another girl."

Abigail left the inspection hole to Prince. "Director, this is one of them. This woman is one of them."

The director raised both hands, as if to defend himself. "No, she came in after the others. Her name is not on the court order."

"After the others?" Abigail's voice rose. She was immediately the prosecutor who had found a weakness in the defense of the accused. "What do you mean—after the others? When were the others here?"

There was nowhere left for the director to shelter, but he had done what the court had ordered him to do. "This visit is over. None of the people on the court order are in my prison. Please come to . . ."

"When were they here?" Abigail shouted. "Tell me—when were they here? And where is this woman's sister?"

From the cell, she could hear Natasha Makwati. "Don't leave me. Please don't leave me here."

34

In his rearview mirror, Bino D'Almeida saw the trailer swinging heavily from side to side. He slowed right down, bringing the rig to little more than walking pace. The potholes were causing it. If you hit one hard and the trailer was heavily laden, it could throw you off the road. He had once had a rig jackknife on him on a road like this one. The load of liquor he had been carrying had been thrown across the road in a mix of broken glass and pungent liquid. The incident had taken place not long after he got his heavy-duty license. It had cost him his job, and nearly his license as well.

The road from town to Chikurubi went through a well-kept, comfortable-looking suburb. Only the surface of the road spoiled the picture. A few kids playing football in a side street allowed the ball to come bouncing into the path of the truck. It struck just below the windscreen and cannoned across the pavement.

I made it, he was thinking. I lost a bit of the load to the crowd in Marondera, but only a few bags, maybe one bag in a hundred, no more. That was not bad going. And there was no way you could get past that many hungry people and not give away something. As for the police, having sampled his load, they had lost interest in it. Getting past them had cost him fifty, but that too was not bad. The boss would be all right with that.

The outer perimeter of the Chikurubi complex drew into view. It was a great sight, he thought. The end of every journey across national borders was a relief, but this one had been harder and slower than most. Carrying food could be tricky, but he had made it with his load almost intact.

The guard who approached the truck had been expecting him. Bino handed over the documentation, and another man disappeared into the guardhouse. Five minutes later he and two others came out to search the vehicle. Bino climbed down. He had been through this before. They searched him and the cab, they peeped under the tarpaulin in a few places, pretending to approve the load, then one walked round the truck with a mirror mounted on the end of a pole. With that they inspected the bottom of the truck for limpet mines. The whole procedure took no more than fifteen minutes. The gate opened and he climbed back up and drove through.

From a distance, Bino saw cars parked outside the main entrance to the prison building. The gate seemed to be open, and people were moving through it onto the verge of the road. He allowed the rig to roll to a stop next to the entrance. As he got down, an attractive black woman, wearing a dark trouser suit, walked quickly toward him. A small, gray-haired white man with both hands in his pockets was following her from a distance. "What's in that load?" she demanded. This was someone accustomed to giving orders and demanding responses.

"Food, ma'am," Bino said. "World Food Program delivery."

"You're too damned late," Abigail said. Then, seeing the look of surprise and dismay on his face, she checked herself and spoke more gently. "You're too late for my clients. But this may save the lives of others. You did well."

"I hate them, I hate them. Christ, how I hate them." Helena was leaning forward in the backseat of the car, her hands clasped together.

"Be quiet, you foolish woman." Abigail's mind was elsewhere.

"Don't you hate them? I do. You were in that damned morgue with us. You saw the Makwati girl in that hellhole, and why wasn't she on the court order?"

"Because she was arrested after our pleadings were filed."

Helena was not yet finished. "You should hate them too. What's foolish about hating them?"

"Be quiet, damn you." Abigail had turned in her seat. "How much you hate them is not important. What we do about it—that is important. For you to sit here whining about how much you hate them only serves to bore the rest of us."

Yudel could see Helena's face in the rearview mirror. It seemed to swell with the humiliation of Abigail's rebuke. He spoke before she could. "Security checkpoint," he said. "Let's give them no reason to hold us back." The guard who had taken Bino's documents now took Yudel's. He counted the number of people in the car and waved for the gate to open. "Since the twins were arrested, has anyone else been watching the prison?" He was looking at Helena in the rearview mirror. He could see the effort it took her to desert her argument with Abigail.

She still sounded as angry as ever, but she answered the question. "Paul has been watching the road from a house he still owns on that side of town. He does his best, but he's not that close to the prison and he's the only one, and he's out for an hour or more every day. While he's away nobody watches. He doesn't sleep much, and sometimes he wakes when a conveyance from the prison is passing. It's a hit-and-miss affair."

"Something else," Yudel said. "Where is Tony's sister?"

Prince answered. "We don't know. None of us do."

"Did he ever talk about her?"

"Never. We didn't know about her until Krisj told us."

"How did he know?"

"Tony must have told him."

Yudel glanced back at Prince. "How well did you know Tony?"

"Not well. We didn't see him often. He sometimes came to meetings with Krisj."

"You trusted him, though?"

"Jesus," Helena broke in. "You should read his writings."

"I have. Did anyone know him well?"

"We knew enough," Helena said.

"There was someone else," Prince said. "There was a caregiver."

"A caregiver?"

"One who looked after them as children."

"She knows nothing about politics," Helena said. "She's just an ignorant old woman."

"We'll need to meet her."

"She knows nothing." Helena was leaning forward, aiming all her furious insistence at Yudel. "There's no point. She's an old wet nurse."

"You know where to find her?" Yudel asked Prince.

"I'll write it all down for you."

"Jesus," Helena said. She was having a bad day.

"One more thing," Yudel said.

"I can't wait to hear it," Helena told him.

"Is there anyone who knows Director Chunga well and will talk to us?"

"Ask your buddy, sitting next to you. She knows him better than anyone else." Helena's natural bitterness had given way to jeering.

Yudel felt Abigail's bridling at the intended insult. "For instance, a disaffected CIO operative?" he said.

"Any disaffected CIO agent would either be dead or in jail."

"There is one," Prince said. "He fled south last year, lives in Johannesburg now. I know his name, nothing else."

"Write that down as well," Yudel said.

"What the hell is all this for?" Helena demanded.

For all her fury, her bitterness and her easily aroused hatreds, Yudel recognized that this was a brave woman who was ready to go through hell to find her friends. Already this morning they all had a fair taste of hell. He was still framing his answer when Abigail spoke. "Do you want them back or don't you?"

They reached the place where Helena and Prince were to get off. Abigail took the piece of paper, the margin of a newspaper page, from Prince. He had written down the name of the former CIO agent and the name and address of the woman who had cared for the Makumbe siblings. "Thank you," she said. "I'm sorry it wasn't Joyce who we found."

Prince got out quickly. Answering was impossible.

As they drove away, Abigail looked at Yudel. "Where are you going with all this?"

"I have a feeling that we are missing too much. There is too much that we don't understand. We have to begin where the story starts. I think the answers may lie there."

"We have little time."

"I know."

Abigail was not one to linger over anything. Too much needed to be done in her life for her to spend excess time on anything. This principle applied to showering as much as to any other activity. But on this occasion she stayed in the shower much longer than usual. She needed to wash away any remaining vestige of Chikurubi. She soaped her body again and again, allowing the streams of warm water to flow over her. She hoped they would cleanse even the memory of the place.

From the single high window of the shower, she could see the western sky. It was still blue, but a deeper color now and fading to white-gold near the horizon. When she switched off the water, a few street noises reached her. Somewhere in the middle distance a woman's pleasant contralto was singing what Abigail recognized as an African lullaby.

The air temperature on this lovely African evening seemed to be almost that of the human body. Abigail felt that she was contained by a medium that was made for her, or that she was a part of. At any other time, on any other evening, that sky and the wonderful air would have allowed the sounds, the sights and the red wine that was waiting for her on the room's only table to spread a calming net over mind and body. But this was not such an evening, and Abigail already feared the night that was approaching. At least Yudel was just a few doors down the passage, but then how much could she expect from him? She feared that she had dragged him into something that was too big for either of them.

Answering a knock at her door revealed the waiter who had earlier brought her glass of wine. He had an envelope for her. She opened it absentmindedly. It was a note from the proprietor, saying that a Mr. Robert Mokoapi had called three times during the day and that he would be at home this evening. Her home telephone number was written underneath.

She dressed slowly, then went to stand at the window. The short twilight was deepening fast. As on other evenings in this place, the window had drawn her with an almost irresistible force. She opened the curtains, but stood a full stride back from the glass so that she would be in deep shadow and all but invisible from the street.

Abigail had been there for five minutes before she saw the uniformed policeman step out of a shadow and pass slowly in front of the hotel. In the semidarkness she could not make out his face, but judging by his size, he could have been the policeman of the night before.

She stood there, unmoving, for almost twenty minutes before the black CIO double-cab stopped outside. This time there was no doubting who stepped out of the cab and into the light from the hotel's front door. This was the first time she had seen Agent Mpofu without a jacket. He scowled in the direction of the guard, then looked up and down the street. Abigail had the strong impression that this was a man unconvinced of the necessity of spending his evening this way.

Abigail only drew the curtains closed after Mpofu had left. She did not look at her watch to see how much time she had spent that way, or what the time was now. She again read the note that told her Robert had been looking for her. Then she crumpled it into a ball and threw it into the wastepaper basket. The front desk answered at her first ring. "Please hold all calls for me," she said. "I'll be asleep and I don't want to be disturbed."

"A Mr. Mokoapi . . ." the girl at the front desk started.

"If he calls again, tell him I'm asleep."

What did you do about a good man who had made a mistake? she asked herself. Did you forgive him? Might he make other, future mistakes?

Abigail knew that the problem was not that Robert was a good man who had made a mistake, but that he was a good man who had lifted her from desolation to exultation, and then made this mistake, this awful, most serious of all mistakes. She could not speak to him now, not tonight. Maybe she would be able to speak to him some other night. But she was not even sure of that.

And what did you do about a different kind of man—one you did not understand, in whose presence, if you were alone with him, you could hardly breathe? And nor could he? How different was he? Perhaps he was not personally responsible for any of the evils she had heard and read about, and seen today. But they were all around him, everywhere. If he was not responsible for them, at the very least he seemed to ignore their existence.

He had been unable to enter what passed for a morgue in Chikurubi. What did that say about him?

She had heard him talk about Zimbabwe and his life and where he came from, how he too was from the Ndebele minority, that he too had suffered. And she had felt his body against hers and she remembered the grace with which he had stepped back when she could not continue. Perhaps a good man could be trapped in a web from which he could not escape. She could not believe that Jonas was an evil man. She had come too close to him. He was still the one who was able to help her. He was the one who sought to protect her. She needed to believe it.

35

More than twenty-four hours had passed since Tony Makumbe had been brought from his cell in Chikurubi and put into the truck. But it was now nearly two weeks since his arrest. He had not heard about the arrest of the others. This was the first time since then that he had seen them.

He had struggled to climb the ladder at the back of the truck. At the second attempt he hung by an arm hooked over one of the rungs. By that time even the prison staff could see that without help they would never get him loaded. All the others had managed to climb the four rungs without assistance.

"Why's this man so weak?" he heard a voice say. "Has he been eating?"

"We gave him the food."

"You know what the instructions are."

"Yes."

"Enough?"

"Yes." It was true that he had been receiving it, even if he had not been eating it.

Tony missed the mumbled response, but he felt a strong hand take hold of his waistband and lift him. The hand released him and he tumbled into the truck between two rows of seats. "Tony," a voice said. "It's Tony. Tony, have you seen my sister?"

It was one of the Makwati girls. He could never tell them apart. "No, I haven't seen anyone else." He looked at the other faces in the truck, all of whom were watching him closely. "All our people," he said, as much to himself as to the others. "Is it only our people?"

"Just our people," someone else said. "Just us."

Tony looked at the faces of the others. They were all watching him with a singular expectancy. What is it? he wondered. Is it my weakness? Can it be that? They don't look too good either.

One of the men was speaking. Tony struggled to make sense of the words. "Tony, we have something to tell you—something bad."

They were all still looking at him in the same peculiar way. So this is it, he thought. But what worse news could there be than being in the hands of these people?

"It's Krisj. He's been killed. We heard it on the prison grapevine."

After an hour's travel it was clear that they were not on their way to the cells in the Supreme Court building. Despite this, some of the others continued to talk as if that was their destination. By the time another two hours had passed, no one could be deluded into believing that they were going to the court building. "I think they're going to kill us," Tanya Makwati sobbed. "They're taking us into the country to kill us."

Tony did not believe that. The voice he had heard had been angry that they had not been fed and that he had appeared weak. Surely he did not want them to be in good shape just to be killed? That made no sense.

He believed he knew why Krisj had to die. Had he thought about it, he would have come to expect it before the event. But the death of someone you loved was not something you thought about.

Tanya Makwati was still sobbing. Tears that she made no attempt to hide were streaming down her face. Those Makwati girls reminded him so of Katy. It was not the way they looked. Katy had a round face, while theirs were long. The similarity had to do with their personalities. The Makwati twins showed their emotions, crying and laughing readily; quick to anger, but equally quick to forget the reason for it. Katy had been just like that.

He remembered how much he had loved her, how much they

had shared, and what effect her death had on him. The only one he had loved as much as Katy was Krisj. He had loved them both more than anyone else he could remember. He had often thought about it, and he knew too when the mist had first appeared in his life. It had started on the day Katy died.

36

The Ponte was tall, circular and hollow. The apartments were arranged facing outward, while the hollow center provided a clear fall to a courtyard at ground level. Within months of being opened for tenants it had become known as Johannesburg's suicide center.

The building's depressives did not seem able to resist the opportunity that the hollow center presented. All you had to do was slip over a waist-high wall and, for you, the problems of life were over. So bad was the effect on the building's reputation that a screen had been erected on every floor to block the residents' access to the hollow center. Renting only to suicides was not a policy with a long-term future.

It had been intended for young, upwardly mobile white people, but they had tired of the Ponte at about the same time that the country's restrictions on where black people were allowed to live had fallen away. Within a few years, the nation's disenfranchised majority had also rejected the building and its beckoning chasm.

By the time Freek Jordaan, deputy police commissioner for Gauteng province, invited the building's security personnel to step aside or spend a long time thinking things over in prison, the Ponte had been filled almost exclusively by immigrants, both legal and illegal, for more than ten years. Other Johannesburgers thought of it as the headquarters of the Nigerian Mafia in the city, but in truth it was filled with a mixture of the citizens of almost every African country south of the Sahara. Freek knew this, and he also knew where to find Ephraim Khumalo, the CIO operative who had fled south a little more than a year before.

Yudel had spoken to him the previous night and given him the man's name. It had taken a team of Freek's officers most of the morning to establish his whereabouts. A battle with Immigration to establish whether he was in the country at all had been followed by calls to a foundry where he had briefly done heavy manual labor; a restaurant where he had been employed as a waiter; and a casino where he had trained briefly as a croupier. After the croupier job he had disappeared, but an enterprising lieutenant had discovered a recent conviction for possessing an illegal substance in quantities large enough for the authorities to charge him with dealing. He was currently out on a two-thousand-rand bail.

Freek knocked softly on a door on the Ponte's twenty-seventh floor, then stepped aside to be out of the range of the peephole. He had to knock a second time before the door first opened a crack, then a little wider, then a head peered round the corner of the doorway. In the same moment that the occupant peered into the corridor, he was seized by the front of his vest and dragged out. "Ephraim, my man," Freek whispered, "I'm so glad to see you."

"What the fuck . . ." Freek's victim was a small man. At this moment the whites of his eyes were the most prominent part of him.

"I need to talk to you, Ephraim," Freek murmured seductively.

"Fuck it, man." He whispered. "I'm not Ephraim."

"Where is he?"

"He's inside with the others."

"Let's go and find him." The small man stumbled ahead of him into the apartment's tiny lounge. Four other men, all very much larger than the one who had come to the door, were rising from their chairs. "I'll talk to Ephraim. The rest of you clear out."

Freek flashed his official identification at them much too fast for them to focus on it. "Freek Jordaan," he said. He had already picked out his man. The sudden widening of the eyes had been a giveaway. The alarm in the other faces was of a different sort. "Clear out now," Freek said. He had made no move toward the automatic that rode in its holster under his left shoulder, but all of the men in the room had already looked in that direction.

One of the men, a blank-faced individual, wore a T-shirt from which the sleeves had been removed. The object was to show off biceps that had taken many hours in the gym to develop. "There's a lot of us and there's just you. Why should we go?"

Freek looked at him without the smallest glimmer of amusement. "I can see three possibilities," he said. "You can leave this flat now, you can be on your way back to the countries you came from an hour from now, or maybe you won't leave this room alive. You decide, but decide now."

T-shirt spent no time thinking it over. He tilted his head toward the door as a gesture to his friends and started in that direction. The rest followed. When they were gone, Freek turned the key in the lock.

"Mr. Jordaan, I never did nothing, I swear. Only a little bit of dagga." Ephraim Khumalo was also a big man, but he looked a lot smaller now that his friends had left. He was a long way from the CIO and the authority of those days. "But who the hell are you, man?"

"I'm the deputy police commissioner for the province."

"Shit. Don't you take muscle with you at times like this?"

Freek smiled for the first time since entering the room. "Only when I need it," he said. "But sit down, make yourself at home." Freek waved a hand in the direction of Khumalo's own couch. He imagined that Khumalo's mind was racing as he tried to guess just which of his many transgressions had caught up with him. "You don't keep a job long, do you?"

"I'm trying, man. I'm trying. I just had bad luck so far. I'll have a job soon, I swear." A line of sweat was forming along Khumalo's forehead.

"Relax, Ephraim. You tell me what I want to know, and I'll do what I can to keep the immigration authorities off your back."

"What do you want to know, man?"

"I want you to tell me about Zimbabwe."

"Zimbabwe?" His relief was obvious. "What you want to know?"

"I want to know everything you can tell me about Director Jonas Chunga of the CIO."

"He's defecting?"

"Is that what you call it—defecting?"

"I call it like that."

"No, Chunga's not defecting. I just want you to tell me about him."

Khumalo thought about this for a moment. "And what do I get?"

"You get to stay here. I don't send you back to Chunga."

"Shit, you can't do that."

"You want to try me?"

Khumalo said nothing. He did not seem to be enthusiastic about trying Freek.

"How long did you work with this man?"

"Ten years, plus-minus."

"How closely?"

"I was his main man. I worked with him every day."

"I believe there's an officer called Mpofu working with him now."

"Mpofu was nothing in those days. I did everything for Jonas."

"But you don't want to go back?"

Khumalo shrugged. He had decided on the role he should be playing. "I can go back. Jonas and me, we're all right . . ."

Freek rose quickly. A pair of handcuffs had appeared in his hands. "On your feet," he said. "Let's go."

Khumalo was struggling to his feet. "Jesus, man, what you doing?"

"You don't want to cooperate with me, so you can cooperate with Jonas Chunga."

"Wait. Wait, man. Wait!" He raised his hands in protest, trying to keep them away from the handcuffs. "I'm cooperating. Whatever you want, I'm cooperating with it."

Freek sat down slowly, motioning Khumalo to do the same. "Now, why are you afraid of going back to Chunga?"

This time the answer did not come easily. "With Jonas everything is about loyalty. If he thinks you not loyal to him, you dead."

"Dead?" Freek asked.

"Maybe not dead, but you outside, you nothing."

"But not dead?"

"Something you got to understand about Jonas . . ." He was

leaning forward and for the first time he was speaking earnestly to Freek. ". . . he tries to keep his hands clean. He tries to stay away from the killing and he tries never to give the order to have someone killed. Some of the top guys in the CIO don't give a fuck. They'll give the order to rub some small opposition politician out. It's nothing to them. They even pull the trigger themselves sometimes. I think some of them like it."

"But not Chunga?"

"Not Chunga. Jonas does his best to be a good man. But in his book, if you not loyal to your country, you a bad man."

"And being loyal to your country means being loyal to Jonas?"

"Some'ing like that."

A wire-bound book had appeared in Freek's hands and he had started making notes. "But you don't want to go back to this good man?"

"Man, it's not personal. I like Jonas. I admire him. Jonas got principles. I seen Jonas bring food to a poor village where the people were starving."

Freek knew that in a country as poor as Zimbabwe, where so many people were starving, the reasons for such gestures often did not have simple answers. It was impossible to feed everyone. "Where did the food come from?"

"We took it from a World Food Program shipment."

"Did he charge the people for it?"

"Never, not Jonas. He's a good man. The others woulda sold it, but not Jonas. Jonas didn't do that stuff."

"So he's a good man?"

"He's a good man." Khumalo was nodding emphatically.

"Not violent?"

"Never, not usually."

"Never, or not usually?" Freek asked, speaking slowly. "Which is it? Explain it to me."

"I seen him crack."

"And then?"

"It's not something that happens a lot."

"You've seen it?"

"I seen it once. An' I heard about it."

"What did you see? What happens when Jonas cracks?"

"I heard about it before, but I only seen it once when I went with him to a farm where the white farmer was getting kicked out—part of land redistribution, you know. It was not the stuff we normally did, but someone high up who was getting the farm asked for us to come. When we got there the farmer was gone, but twenty or so of his workers were still there. The new owner wanted them gone too. Jonas told them to get out, but they said no. He showed them the letter of offer from the magistrate, giving the new owner permission to occupy the farm, but they wouldn't listen. So he warned them to be out the next day and we went back to Gweru and booked into a hotel. That night he gets a call from our minister. I was there when he took it. The minister wants to know what's going on, are the workers out? Jonas says, not yet, and the minister goes mad, screaming at him. He tells him the order came from the very top and if it is not carried out some head is going to roll. No prizes for guessing which head. The next morning we go back to the farm and the workers want to argue. They tell Jonas they won't go. Jonas explains to them very nicely that it's not him personally, it's the government. They got to leave and they got to leave now. He says we'll come back after lunch and they got to be gone. So we come back that afternoon and they still there. One a them, a youngster, comes right up to him. He brings his face right up to Jonas. He's right in Jonas's face and he screams as loud as he can. We not fucking going, he screams. This kid makes two mistakes. He didn't show respect for Jonas and he was doing some'ing that woulda meant Jonas coulda lost his power. Jonas shoots him right there. He went down like a sack a potatoes. Deader'n a mackerel. Two others come forward too fast and Jonas shoots them too, himself, but not to kill. One takes it in the thigh, not too far from the main attraction either, and the other loses a knee. We not waiting longer, he says. They were out ten minutes later, goods, dead boy, their wounded and all. An' they didn't have much goods. With Jonas, you got to do what he says and you got to be loyal and you got to respect him and don't mess with his power."

Freek had listened carefully to the story. It sounded real to him. Ephraim sat back now, exhausted with the telling of it. "You spoke about other occasions?"

"Two others I heard of. One with a trade-union problem and one with interrogating a activist."

"He also did the killing himself?"

"No. They say he gave the orders, but I dunno."

Freek was looking past him. "Any others?"

"No, just them. But listen, commissioner, I don't want you to get the wrong idea about this guy. He saved lotsa people too. Sometimes, even when you on the wrong side, maybe he saves your life."

"Give me an example."

"The bombing of the party offices last year was big news, that's a example. In Zimbabwe that sorta stuff is treason. All involved can get death. Jonas knew who done it, but he destroyed evidence and they got away. They never even arrested them."

"He destroyed evidence? You sure?"

"I swear. I was working with him at that time."

"Do you know why?"

"Compassion. He was like that. Like those people at Madikwe Falls where he took food. That was Jonas. He was like that. An' if he thought someone was not guilty, he never pushed for conviction. Never, not like the others."

Khumalo waited for another question from Freek. When it did not come he made as if to rise, hoping the interview was over. Freek was not finished, though. He was thinking about this man, Chunga, and what it was that Yudel most needed to know. "How high in the CIO is he?" was the question that came eventually.

"One below the DG."

"So he's next in line?"

"Maybe, but there's about six on his level. And I don't think the others ever try to save anyone. They know their job. Maybe Jonas thinks too much."

"One last thing. Have the CIO chiefs ever in your experience used snipers to do their business?"

"No, why would they? They can take whoever they want. Make them disappear, if they want to."

Freek studied the face of the other man. And you, he thought . . . what was your position in all this? "Why did you defect?" he asked.

"I read the papers, Mr. Commissioner. I know Mugabe and them can't travel anywhere in the world. I know what the world says about Zim. I don't want to be tried for crimes against humanity. When the shit hits the fan, I want to be here in Jo'burg." His voice took on a wheedling tone. "I helped you today. Maybe if immigration comes looking for me, you can also help old Ephraim."

"Maybe," Freek said.

Downstairs, in a parking garage that was almost completely empty, Freek tried to raise Yudel on Rosa's cell phone. He was looking at his notes in between keying in the number, then keying it in again. He was getting no response from the Zimbabwean telephone system—no busy tone, no number-unobtainable signal, nothing at all. He had made only two pages of notes, but he knew there were points in Khumalo's story that Yudel would want to hear about. Before starting the engine, he tried one last time. Still there was nothing. That country may as well have disappeared off the planet.

37

Yudel had seen a lot of the back terrace of McDooley's Inn. On many occasions, Freek had made him aware that listening devices were more effective inside than out of doors. Now, with the power down for the third time since he had been in the city, he had ordered a glass of wine. On the table next to him was a copy of *The Herald*. It carried a report that the government had not opposed an application to court for a search of Chikurubi prison. The search had been conducted, but the applicants had not found what they were looking for. The confident face of Jonas Chunga looked back at the reader from the picture that accompanied the text.

Yudel had considered ordering coffee, but two factors decided him against it. He may be embarrassing the management by asking for something they could not deliver . . . In fact, he had forgotten that one of the waiters had already explained that, because of the city's regular power outages, the hotel used gas in the kitchen.

The other factor was Rosa's constant explaining that caffeine was bad for barely controllable sugar levels, like his. The wine also contained sugar, he had been told. So to minimize its effect, he had asked for and received an extra glass filled with ice. Sip by sip, as the wine level dropped, Yudel replaced the wine with ice. By the time he got to the bottom of the glass, he would be drinking water, with only the faintest taste of wine.

Sitting opposite him, Abigail was fascinated by the process. "Why do you do that?" she asked.

"Do you know how homeopathy works?" he asked.

"No."

"Apparently, they take a tiny portion of whatever is ailing you and dilute it by a million or so to one to cure you."

"Does it work?"

"I've no idea. But I like wine and it's not good for my blood sugar. So I drink it in homeopathic style, hoping that just the faintest vestige will cure my desire for it."

Abigail looked intently at his face for a long moment. "Jesus, Yudel," she said eventually. She chose not to explain what she meant, and he never asked.

She picked up her bag from the chair and excused herself, saying that she was going to shower and that after that they should discuss their strategy for the next few days.

Yudel had spent the day following her from one office of the Department of Justice to another. It had been almost five in the afternoon before they got back to the hotel. "I'm not leaving until I have that judgment in writing," she had told numerous government officials. The day had ended at Judge Mujuru's private residence where Abigail, following his dictation, used his computer to type the order onto a departmental letterhead.

As soon as they were out of the judge's earshot, Abigail had waved the envelope triumphantly in the air. "I've got it," she said. "I've got it. I've got it!"

"We still have to find them," Yudel had said.

"When we do, I'll be holding in my hand the authority for their release."

He was using a teaspoon to drop more ice into his wine, when the phone Rosa had left for him demanded his attention. "Answer your phone!" the recorded voice said.

"Freek?" Yudel said into the phone.

"I beg your pardon," a female voice said.

Yudel recognized the voice as belonging to Mariette van Deventer. "Gordon here," he said, immediately wishing that he had just hung up.

"Professor Gordon?"

"Mr. Gordon," he said.

"Mr. Gordon," she agreed. "I have a woman in my office.

She's carrying a newspaper clipping and she wants to see Mr. Yachad."

"No harm in that," Yudel told her.

"And she is very insistent. She says Mr. Yachad was in her office at the newspaper with another old man, not as old as Mr. Yachad though, she said."

"Young woman?" Yudel asked. "Long, rather ragged blond hair?"

"That's right. Do you know her?"

"No, I don't, but I understand that she works for the newspaper."

"What I would like to know is where does this advertisement come from?"

"It comes from the woman who wants to see my father-in-law. You just told me that."

"I don't mean . . ." He heard her take a deep breath. "I asked Mr. Yachad and he said something about marketing that I did not understand."

Go away, Yudel was thinking, I have more important matters to deal with. He had glanced toward the dining room and could see a light burning inside. The power was back on, so that was how the van Deventer woman had got through. "Marketing is a complex subject," he told her.

"I know nothing about marketing." Mariette van Deventer's voice had risen a few notes. "But I do know that my name is in an advertisement in the newspaper."

"Your fame is spreading. I suggest you introduce this lady to Mr. Yachad immediately."

"I have already introduced twenty-three to him."

"Well done," Yudel said. "It's been wonderful chatting, but I have to go. I have important Zimbabwean government officials waiting for me, members of the Central Intelligence Organization. Goodbye for now." He cut the connection.

He only waited a moment before dialing Freek. The answer came almost immediately. "Jordaan."

"Freek, it's Yudel."

"Good. I've been trying to reach you."

"The power's been down in the whole city."

"I found him."

"And what did he say?"

"Listen, Yudel . . ."

"I am listening."

"Listen well. You and Abigail need to be careful. You need to be very careful in dealing with this man."

As soon as he had broken the connection, Yudel went in search of Abigail. He knocked on her door, then called her name, but there was no response. He looked at his watch and saw that it was almost dinnertime. In his own room, he found that the keys of the hired car had been removed.

It was not usual for Yudel to hurry over anything, but now he went down the stairs too quickly, stumbling on the landing. Abigail was not in the restaurant, nor on the terrace that he had left only two minutes before. Christ, he thought, we only just got back. He found Marjorie Swan in the hotel lounge, talking to one of her guests. She looked curiously up at him. "Is everything all right?" It was said in a way that suggested the expectation that perhaps everything was not all right.

"Do you know where Abigail is?"

"She took your car. I hope that's all right?"

"No, it's not all right. Do you know where she went?"

The hotel owner looked anxiously from Yudel to her guest. Emotional disturbances were not good for business. "I didn't give her permission to take the car. I thought you two were . . ."

"Do you know where she went?"

"No. She said something about an important meeting. I asked if she didn't want you to accompany her, but she said this was something she had to handle herself. Shouldn't she have taken your car? I know men are often touchy about their cars."

"Damn the car," Yudel said. "The car is of no importance. Did she say nothing more?"

"She said she may be a while. Is it serious?"

"I don't know. I hope not." As he was turning away, the phone called to him again. This time it was Helena.

38

Abigail remembered that to reach the club, Jonas Chunga had taken the car through a number of turns. She had to stop twice along the way, once at a liquor store that had a stock of only two lines, a cheap brandy in half-liter bottles and a popular beer; then once more at a residence where she asked a woman, probably in her early twenties, to direct her further. The woman called her ma'am, told her where to go and offered the use of the phone if she needed it.

She had contacted Chunga by using the cell phone number on the card he had given her. Waiting while the ringing signal reached her, she had recognized all the old uncertainties. It was just like her early days with Robert.

What are you doing, girl? she asked herself. You want to know about him. You want to be certain. But what you know so far should be enough. You don't want the truth. You want to discover that everything you've learned so far is wrong. It can't be so, you're telling yourself. And that's what you want to learn.

He has to be what he says he is, Abigail thought. I can feel it. And yet, since I've been in this country there have been so many times I've known he's not. So many times and so many indications that nothing he says is true. And yet his eyes say something different. Oh God, Abigail. You sound like a fourteen-year-old. What's happened to the other twenty-odd years of your life?

When he had answered, she had heard something in his voice

that she was certain was relief. "I'm so glad you called," he said. "After yesterday, I thought there would be nothing more."

And after she asked him to meet her, he had said, "Yes, of course I'll meet you. Can I fetch you?"

Her cell phone rang. Jonas, she thought. Oh, Jonas, don't say you can't come.

She slowed the car and, glancing down at the phone, recognized the calling number as Rosa's. For a moment she hesitated, then switched off the phone. No, Yudel, she thought. This is not for you. I'm not discussing this with you, not now, maybe not ever.

At the boom of the estate in which the country club was situated, a uniformed guard came up to the car. "Member?" he asked without smiling. His demeanor said that he was the man in charge of the gate and she had better have a good reason for wanting to enter.

"No," Abigail said. "I'm a guest of Director Jonas Chunga."

As she had expected, the man's manner changed. Was there any place in this city where his name would not have that effect? "The director is expecting you, ma'am. He said you'd know where to find him." He waved her through.

Abigail drove slowly now. There were only a few hundred meters to the clubhouse. She did not want to hit one of the animals that roamed the property. She was not sure that she should have come at all. And in a few minutes she would be facing him again.

No, it was not that she was unsure about the wisdom of coming. Somewhere deep within her, not as an officer of the court, but as a woman, she knew that she should not be here. But she also knew, as a woman, that she had to be here. Turning back had become impossible.

Abigail saw him the moment she stepped onto the fairway. The day was over, but the African twilight remained. Fringing the horizon ahead of her, the sky still glowed with the warmth of the sun. Chunga was a silhouette under the tree that spread across the fairway, just where he said he would be. His feet were apart and his hands seemed to be in his pockets. She saw him for what he was—a man of power, an alpha male in the center of his territory, a physical presence that drew her toward him. It was only with the greatest restraint that she did not run to him.

She compelled herself to walk slowly and stop all of twenty paces from him. He had not moved since she had first caught sight of him where he stood, waiting for her. "There are things I have to know," she said. She had raised her voice just enough to reach him across the distance between them. "There are certain things I just have to know about you."

"Ask me anything and I'll tell you."

"Do you know where the seven are?"

"No, I do not." His voice was strong and calm, reaching her without any apparent effort.

"Were they abducted by members of your organization?"

"As I told you before, not as far as I know."

"Did you have anything to do with the arrest of the Makwati twins?"

"Yes, I orchestrated it. You can't have people observing the movements in and out of a prison. You have to ask yourself what the purpose is."

"Did you know about the conditions in Chikurubi prison?"

"Yes."

"But you did nothing?"

"I am not all-powerful, Abigail. Ordinary working people have little to eat. The country is starving. I know the prisoners get too little, but a World Food Program delivery has just reached Chikurubi. The prisoners ate better today. They will in the weeks ahead."

"Do you know who killed Krisj Patel? Tell me again."

"No. The arrest we made was clearly a mistake. Our agents are not as skilled as I would like them to be. They are all desperately underpaid. We are still searching for the killer."

"Have you ever personally killed anyone?"

"Yes. Twice I've killed criminals in self-defense."

"The Gukurahundi killings, of which my aunt was a victim— were you involved in them?" This question was a surprise to her. It had arisen from somewhere within her, unplanned and perhaps unwanted.

"I was just a boy of twenty when they started. I had only left school the year before. I was already a police officer, but I was a victim of the Gukurahundi, not one of the perpetrators. I was beaten and left for dead by members of Five Brigade. I saw what happened in Bizana. I was there right after the massacre. The people who died were my people. After that, I decided that it was impossible to resist the government. Since then I've worked from the inside to stop even worse things from happening. At Plumtree, where I grew up, I was the youngest station commander in the history of our police. It was there that I was recruited by the CIO."

"Why did you leave us at the prison? Why didn't you stay?"

"I've seen it before. I couldn't bear to see it again."

"So you left?"

"Yes."

"Someone had been trying to kill Tony earlier. Was that the CIO?"

"First of all, we have no real evidence that anyone was trying to kill him. His friends say that someone was, and they blame us. In any event, Abigail, have you any idea how many enemies those people have made?"

"And what about the CIO? Everywhere, in the world press, from activists, Western politicians and others, the stories are the same . . . and the CIO is at the center of it. How can I believe that you have no part in it? Or at least that you don't know about these things?"

"Look at me." He had spread his arms wide, a defenseless posture. "Do I look like a killer? What you have seen of me so far, does that look like a killer? Do I behave like a killer?"

"No, you don't behave like a killer." It was true. At that moment, looking at the man before her, she could not believe that he was part of murders and assassinations. But then, how do killers behave while they're not killing? she asked herself.

"Good God, woman, you were in my arms a few evenings ago. Did I feel like a killer then?"

Abigail's next question was for herself. Why am I here? I knew the answers before I came. I knew what he would say before he spoke. She turned, as if to leave, uncertain of her next step, knowing that she had learned nothing.

Afterward, Abigail was never sure when Chunga had first moved, or how she came to be lying in his arms on the grass of the fairway, or at which point her own passion had ignited. She felt his hands in the small of her back, pressing her against him. Breathing was difficult, and yet the racing of her breath and his merged so that all other sound was eliminated. Her hands were clutching the fabric of his jacket. She heard his voice, barely audible through the sound of their breathing. "Why did you ask me to come? Not to answer those damned questions. I don't believe that."

"Jonas," she heard herself gasp his name. "Jonas, please, Jonas."

"Please what? What are you asking of me?"

"Jonas, please." Her voice was no more than a whimper. She hated the weakness she heard in it. "Jonas."

Then she was lost in the whirling vortex of her passion. She was unaware that there was still enough light for them to be seen, if not from the clubhouse, certainly from a hundred paces down the fairway. She was not aware of exactly what he was doing, he seemed to be everywhere. "Jonas." Again the whimper, the pleading, "Jonas, please."

"What do you want from me, woman?"

"I don't know. What do you want from me?"

"I want everything. I want your soul. I want every moment of your life. I want your body now, this moment."

She had lost her jacket. She saw it on the grass, beyond her reach. Her brassiere had been pushed up. She lifted an arm to try to cover her breasts. They were not very big and perhaps he would not like them, seeing them as too small. God, what am I thinking? she asked herself.

The arms that she had tried to use as protection had been swept aside and she felt his lips on her nipples, first one, then the other. "Jonas, please." Surely I can find something else to say, she thought.

Then suddenly he was holding her at arm's length. "My God, you're beautiful." He was looking at the very naked breasts she had been ashamed of just a moment before. "What is it, Abigail? You know what I want of you; what do you want from me? Why did you bring me here tonight?"

"Jonas, please." How many times had she said that since she had been in his arms? Her voice sounded as weak as it had before.

"Do you know how easy it would be for me to take you now?"

"Yes, I do."

The passion between them stopped as if a valve had been shut, cutting off the torrent that a moment before had been consuming her. He rolled away, rose and helped her to her feet. While she covered herself, he picked up her jacket and handed it to her. He was still no more than an arm's length from her. His chest was still rising and falling with the force of everything that had just passed between them.

"Please tell me this," Abigail was saying. "You were married once. What happened to her?"

"No, not married. I loved a woman once, but she died long ago."

"Have there been many women since then?"

"Yes, there have been many women; some of them very attractive women. There have been black women who I knew were paying homage to power. They would have done anything to be close to the people who give the orders in our country. And there were white women hoping for protection, feeling vulnerable, one of them trying to avoid losing a farm. And there have been overseas visitors, mostly from Western countries, looking for an exotic experience. There were even a few I took by force, out of desperation, while I was looking everywhere for you."

But you didn't know that I existed, she was thinking.

"I'm telling you all this because you want to know the truth. The real truth is that I have only once before felt this way about any woman. That was the one you asked about. Twenty-seven years have passed, and no one since has had this effect on me. Until I saw you for the first time in Krisj Patel's rat hole, I had thought no woman would ever affect me that way again. I can't bear the thought of any other man having you. At least I knew that wouldn't happen with Patel."

"Jonas . . ." God, Abigail thought, let me try to say something that makes sense.

"Then there was you, and why did you have to come to my country under these circumstances?" He was again standing against the last brightness of the evening sky and she could not see his face. "Couldn't you have come some other way? Did it have to be as defending counsel for these unruly kids? Couldn't you just have come as a tourist? Or for any other reason?"

Then Abigail remembered the other question she had wanted the answer to. "That explosion at party headquarters, Jonas, did you know who was responsible?"

For the first time she heard anger in his voice. "I don't want to answer any more of your questions, Abigail. I could hardly breathe as I watched you walking the length of the fairway. And I've been answering your damned questions since you arrived here. I've had enough of them."

"Please tell me if you knew."

"Yes, I knew."

"Then why did you do nothing?"

"I don't know. Because I'm a fool who always hopes that people will change."

For the first time Abigail knew that he was lying. Some of the other things he had said may also have been lies, but she knew beyond any doubt that this one was.

"I have to go," she whispered.

"Why did you come? Why did you ask me to come?" The tone of his voice was somewhere between a demand and a plea.

"I had to know the truth." She was backing away in the direction of the clubhouse.

"What truth did you have to know?"

"I just had to be sure about you." She had turned to go.

"Why?"

"I don't know."

"And what have you learned?"

"I don't know that either."

"And what happens now that you know some of the truth?" She was backing away and he had raised his voice to reach her.

But I don't, she thought. I don't yet know the truth. "When you brought me to this club, everyone seemed to be bowing to you. You were charged nothing. Why were you charged nothing?" She was far enough from him that projecting her voice to him took effort.

"Did you consider that they may have put it on my account?"

"Did they?"

"No. The way I'm treated here is simply a sign of respect for a senior person. It's the African way."

Not in my Africa, Abigail thought. She had started to run for the car.

39

The hotel passage was in darkness. In order to save power, all the globes had been removed from their sockets. Abigail saw the familiar figure sitting at the far end. He was no more than a faint outline in an uncertain glimmer of light from somewhere outside, but she recognized him immediately. "Hello, Yudel," she said.

"Hello, Abigail." He waited for her to come closer before he rose. "You and I need to talk about Mr. Chunga."

"I know, but not now, Yudel. I can't do it now."

"It must be now. There is no time. You know that we don't have time."

She opened the door of her room and switched on the light. For the first time, she could see him. He was looking at her with the sort of concerned expression she had rarely before seen on his face. Its effect was so much greater, because she could see that his concern was for her. "Do we have to do it now?"

"I believe so," Yudel said.

"In my room?"

"No. We need to get out of the hotel."

"In the car?"

"Yes."

"Can't we just stay in my room?"

He drew her close. His voice was barely above a whisper. "The rooms may be bugged."

Oh, Jonas, she thought. "Please don't tell me this," she said to Yudel.

"We can't be sure, but I think we should go."

Yudel knew that there was always the chance that Mpofu would be outside in one of the CIO double-cabs, ready to give chase and stop them, but there was no alternative. The car bumped out of the driveway and into the street. He saw the startled face of the policeman whose job it was to protect them and thought he heard a shout of protest. In a moment they had swept past him. Yudel turned the car at the first intersection. "Where are we going?" Abigail asked.

"I don't know. Somewhere we can be alone."

"He'll be on the phone to Agent Mpofu."

"I know. We need to get off the road."

Three corners and a few hundred meters down the road, Yudel saw what looked like the answer. The gate to a sports field stood open. He swung the car through the gate, onto a gravelled track and stopped behind a wooden hut.

They had just got out when the door of the hut opened. An old man wearing a pair of shorts much too big for him and a gray vest that had once been white, shuffled out. He was carrying an electric torch that he shone into Yudel's face. "Good evening, sir." Then the torch flashed onto Abigail's features and he chuckled softly.

"Oh, Christ," she muttered.

He shuffled across to Yudel in his old felt slippers, taking hold of a piece of Yudel's shirt and drawing him away from Abigail. "The girl is damn good-looking," he said. "This is worth ten dollars, easy."

"It's not like that," Yudel said, passing him ten dollars American at the same time.

"Sure," he chuckled again, digging an elbow into Yudel's ribs. "There's nice flat benches up the top of the first pavilion. They should be all right. Enjoy yourself, my friend."

"It's not . . ." Yudel started, but gave it up. What the hell, he thought.

The caretaker had not yet let go of Yudel's shirt. He brought his mouth right up to Yudel's ear. "I'm going to be right here in my hut. Stay as long as you like. The wife will never think of looking for you here." As an afterthought, he added, "Tell your friends. Ten bucks is not much."

Abigail glanced back at the caretaker once and he waved to her. "Yudel, you make the most interesting friends. I don't want to know how you discovered this one. This is the first time I find myself in this sort of situation and it's not even for the purpose he thinks it is."

"It's not possible to control what other people think."

"What a wonderful piece of wisdom," Abigail said.

Yudel led her on a climb that took her to the top row of seats in the pavilion and into its deepest shadow. Clouds parted and a night that had been almost completely dark was brightened by a half-moon. The gray-black of the playing field became green and the white lines took on a luminous quality. Abigail could see Yudel now. She knew how strongly he supported her. She also knew the look on his face that said he would wait if necessary, but that now he needed to learn everything. "Where do we begin?" she asked.

"Have you had sexual intercourse with this man?" It was said altogether dispassionately. He may have been a scientist inquiring about the behavior of a species of insect.

"No." Yudel waited for her to expand. "No, I have not. But only because he did not push very hard. When I left him tonight, part of me was crying out to turn and go back."

"I'm glad you didn't."

"Why?"

"I'll tell you later. For now, know that it would have been a terrible mistake. What happened with you and Robert? It had nothing to do with that nonsense at the Sheraton, I trust."

"That was just a symptom. The problem lies with a pretty blond temp."

"I see."

"Not pretty, Yudel. She's beautiful and fifteen years younger than me."

"Is it over?"

"Robert says so."

"Then it's over. If Robert says so, then it is over."

"He also says it never really started. Oh Jesus, Yudel. It brought out all the worst in me. I found myself thinking, little white slut,

and other things like that. I've never seen myself that way. I hated
having those thoughts."

"It's all right. Robert's not perfect and neither are you. He's a
good man, though, and you need to forgive him. Jonas Chunga is
not a good man, and you need to be rid of him."

Abigail was a proud woman who did not easily accept the advice
of anyone unless she asked for it. But this was different. At times in
the past she had seen the intensity of the hunter in Yudel's eyes, and
she had seen the distraction of deep thought there, too. Now she
saw something else in this strange man who cared deeply for her in
a way that most people would not understand. "As soon as this is
over," she said. "I will only see him until this is over."

"If we have to see him, let me do it."

"That may not be possible." She was crying. Whether for her
relationship with Robert, or because of what there had almost
been with Chunga, or because of what Yudel was giving her, she
could not tell. "We'll discuss it next time, if there is a next time."

"I think there might have to be. There are still answers that he
is going to give us." She felt his eyes on her as he spoke again.
"The thing between yourself and Chunga—did it happen because
of the problem with Robert?"

"Only partly, Yudel. There seem to be no barriers between us.
This is prim, monogamous Abigail speaking. A moment ago you
said I may have to meet him again, and immediately I was excited. Oh God, Yudel, it will be best if I never see him again, not
even for a moment. He told me tonight that there were women he
took by force. Why does a man use that sort of terminology?"

"You mean why didn't he say he raped them?"

"Yes, why didn't he say that?"

"He chose that way to tell you because he's hiding from himself that he raped them. It suits him to pretend that forcing them
is not the same as raping them."

"Oh God, Yudel. What have I got myself into?" She paused and
seemed to shake herself free of Chunga's confession. "But this isn't
why you brought me here."

"No, it's not. We each need to know what the other knows about
Jonas Chunga. You go first and tell me everything, no matter
how small. We can take as long as we like." He allowed himself a

faint smile. "You heard the caretaker. Afterward, I'll tell you what Freek found."

The crying stopped and Abigail spoke slowly at first, trying to do as Yudel had said and remember everything. Gradually the flow of words took on a life of its own, much like the force that seemed to grip her when making an opening or closing address in court. The restless energy within her could not be contained in their grandstand seats, though. The clouds again closed, plunging the field into darkness, and they walked the perimeter of the field while she spoke. And she did tell him everything. Every piece of information she could remember, both desperate passages in Chunga's arms, her thoughts at the time, what she thought that Chunga had told her and was true, and what she believed was not: all of it passed into the recesses of Yudel's near-perfect memory. When she finished, her forehead was wet with sweat and she was breathing unevenly.

Then it was Yudel's turn to talk. He first told her that Helena had called to say that Paul Robinson had seen a prison truck leave Chikurubi on the night before the hearing. He had not been able to see if anyone was inside. It had returned nearly fourteen hours later, meaning that, if her clients were in it, they may have been taken far away. After that he told her what Freek had passed on from his notes. When he came to the killings, Abigail stopped walking. They stood on the edge of the field and Yudel told her what he knew as gently as he could.

"Oh, Yudel." The crying had started again and now she was in his arms. "I've been on the edge of a precipice. I came so close."

"It's all right. It's over now."

"It's not, it's not over. It's not nearly over."

The caretaker came out of his hut as they neared the gate. He swung it open with what was intended to be a gallant gesture. Yudel saw his conspiratorial wink in a shaft of light from a nearby house.

As they drove back to the hotel, Abigail asked the question that was filling her mind more than any other. "We seem to be lost. Is there anything left for us to do? Tell me that."

"We must talk to the caregiver they spoke about, the one who looked after Tony and his sister.

"How will that find the seven?"

"We are missing something. I feel it strongly. We may find it there."

"I hope so," Abigail said. "There's something else I want to talk to you about. The thing of Tony being schizophrenic. I don't think that's so. I remember one of the passages in his writing. It said that all of life is pretense, that everything we do is aimed at misleading others . . ."

"'All of life is only a pretense,'" Yudel quoted. "'We spend every hour of every day pretending to others that we are more than what we really are. Everything we do, every word we speak—all are aimed at misleading others as to our virtue, our bravery, our competence, our attractiveness. Truth and honesty are beyond the grasp of any human being.'"

"Good God, Yudel, you memorized it."

"I reread it six or seven times, and it stuck."

"Could that really be the view of a mentally ill person? There's so much truth in it."

"There is much truth in it, but it's not a worldview that helps one to survive. The people we see as mentally ill often have a clearer view of the less attractive aspects of the human condition than the rest of us do. It may be that truth and honesty are practically beyond the grasp of any human being, that we are always presenting ourselves, as to our virtue and so on, in ways that mislead others. But we need our hypocrisies in order to survive. The people we see as schizophrenic often don't possess those hypocrisies."

"You mean to be completely truthful, you need to be crazy?"

"Something like that."

The police guard saw them from a distance and came running to meet the car. Yudel drove past him, but he followed them down the driveway. He was out of breath when he reached them. "Where have you been?" he wanted to know. "I can go with you if you want to go out."

They got out of the car, Abigail looking disdainfully at the policeman. "It seems to me that you haven't been doing your job very well. You allowed us to slip away. I hope your seniors don't find out." They started toward the hotel entrance.

The guard hurried alongside. "Where were you?"

"Summer evenings in Harare are beautiful," Abigail said. "We were inspecting the soccer pitch."

"You like soccer?"

Abigail answered as they passed through the front door of the hotel. "We love it."

The proprietor was in the lobby. She nodded in the direction of the lounge. Seated in a chair at one of the coffee tables in an otherwise empty lounge was Agent Mpofu. The CIO man rose, frowning. "I'm glad you're both safe," he said.

Any reason we shouldn't be? Abigail thought. "How nice of you to drop in," she said.

Mpofu looked at Yudel. "I wonder if I can have a word with you in private, Mr. Gordon."

"Of course."

"Perhaps we can go outside." He led Yudel across the terrace, through the narrow garden and into the parking lot. Glancing back at the building, Yudel saw Abigail at the window on the upstairs landing. The moon had again come out from behind the clouds, and she would be able to see them clearly. Yudel waved and she returned the wave. Now there was a witness to the scene and Mpofu knew it. "Mr. Gordon," he said. "I might have information for you."

"You might have?"

"Yes." He was looking at Abigail who was making no secret of her presence. "But you must understand that we are very poorly paid in this country." He had turned away from Abigail. He was also careful not to look at Yudel. "It's impossible for a man of good taste to afford even a bottle of whiskey."

A man of good taste? Yudel wondered. "What is the information you have?"

"I may know where the seven are."

Yudel took a step back. That the information may be offered to them in such a direct way was not what he had expected. "First I need to know if they're all still alive."

Mpofu's eyes narrowed. "That's part of the cost."

"No, my friend. No one is going to pay to find dead bodies."

"All right. They are all alive."

"Are they all in one place?"

"Yes."

"And what will this information cost us?"

"Five thousand."

"Five thousand U.S. dollars?"

"That's what I said—five thousand American."

"We're also civil servants," Yudel said. "That's nearly forty thousand rands. We don't have that sort of cash."

"You want them alive, or don't you?" The CIO man was staring at Yudel, an almost unbearable tension in his face.

"Are you telling me you'll kill them if you don't get the money?"

All the uncertainties inside Mpofu came bursting out. "I never said that. Don't you pretend I said that."

Yudel was already moving back toward the hotel building.

"Wait." Mpofu managed to keep his voice down, but the urgency was unmistakable.

Yudel looked back over his shoulder. He remembered what Freek had told him about Ephraim Khumalo's fears. "Something else you should think about," he told the CIO agent. "This country may soon have another government. Where are you going to be then? Who's going to protect you from a new regime?"

"I just do my job."

"I'll pay you one thousand U.S. dollars," Yudel said, "at twelve noon tomorrow. We'll hand over the money when you give us the information."

"Two thousand."

"Good night." Yudel said. He was moving again.

"All right, one thousand." The words came as a strangled shout. This time Yudel did not stop until he reached the terrace. He stood at its edge, looking down at Mpofu who was still in the garden. "I'll see you here at noon tomorrow."

"No. Come to this place. Follow these instructions." He passed up a small piece of paper to Yudel.

So, Yudel thought, you have it all worked out. "Just one more thing," he said, "if you take the money and we don't find them, I will declare you to Jonas Chunga. We are protected by our government. No one is protecting you." His last view of Mpofu was of a truly frightened face.

But how far our government can protect any of us against a sniper's bullet is a different matter entirely, Yudel thought.

40

"I'll talk to Robert about the money. I'm sure he'll do it." Abigail was seated on the edge of her bed. "But I don't want to do this other thing now." By agreement, they had remained in the building. What they were discussing was safe enough, even if someone was listening, as long as they stayed away from names, times and other specifics.

Yudel was resting against the windowsill, facing her. "I think we should. It may be very important that we do."

"Why? Let's get some sleep. We can do it tomorrow." She was searching the expression of his face. "Or am I facing a Yudel Gordon intuitive moment? I know about them. Logic doesn't stand up to them very well. Why can't it wait?"

"I feel strongly that we are running out of time here."

"Any reason?" Abigail was looking helplessly at him.

"No single reason. Something in Mpofu, something in the air, if you like." He spoke softly, his mind seeming to be elsewhere. Abigail had seen him in this state on other occasions, and knew better than to ignore it. "I feel that the sort of investigation we are undertaking cannot continue for long in this country. There is a sort of communal patience in government that is wearing thin. I feel it."

Abigail rose. Yudel's final argument had persuaded her. Now that she had decided to do what Yudel wanted, the weariness seemed to be slipping away. "Let's hurry. It's nearly midnight."

————

It took almost an hour and six or seven inquiries—Abigail lost count—to find the room where Grandmother Loise Moyo lived. It was on the level directly above the ground floor of a building in which the lift had long since stopped working.

The door was opened by a young woman. Two small children, still rubbing their eyes after being woken, were pressing close to her. "I want to speak to Mama Loise," Abigail said in English. She had taken the precaution of buying food along the way. The smell of the fried chicken was already having an effect on the woman and her children. All three were looking at the parcels Abigail was carrying. "I brought food for all of us," Abigail said.

The woman turned her head and called the old woman. "Grandmother." She followed that with something in Shona. Abigail understood it to be "There's a rich woman here."

A curtain divided the room down the center. It moved and an old woman appeared; her hands outstretched in the way of someone whose eyesight was either very poor or had disappeared entirely. She was wearing a crinkled cotton dress she had been sleeping in.

"Mama Loise, my name is Abigail Bukula." None of Abigail's usual assertiveness was present in her voice.

There were elements of African culture that Yudel deeply admired. Abigail's gentleness and the respect she showed when dealing with this old woman reflected some of that.

"The white man with me is my good friend. I have come to talk to you about my family."

"Your family, child?"

"And the food?" the young woman inquired. One of her children, a girl who came up to her mother's mid-thigh, had reached out to touch the warm parcel with the tips of her fingers.

"I'm afraid I can't see very well these days, my child," Loise said. "The eyes are old. I think your voice is young."

"Not very, mother. I will never see thirty again."

"Your voice sounds younger."

"What about the food?" the young woman asked again. "The children must go to sleep."

Abigail smiled at her, but spoke to Loise. "Yes, mother, I have brought food."

"Thank you, my child," she said. "Come into our room, but we have no chairs."

"I'll sit with you, on your bed. My friend will not mind standing."

The old woman turned in Yudel's direction. "He is not very big. I can see that."

"He's not big at all, but very clever," Abigail said.

And foolish, Yudel thought. Let's not forget foolish. Any sensible man would have been at home in Pretoria tonight, where the only dangers come from criminals.

"Ah." Loise nodded. Clearly, being clever was something she admired. "Does he speak?"

"Haltingly," Yudel said. "With some difficulty."

This drew a short laugh from Abigail and a chuckle from Loise. "I think you are joking with an old woman, sir."

Abigail handed the food parcel to the young woman. "Mr. Gordon and I have eaten. Please share it with the children and with Mama Loise."

"Thank you, sister," she said, but her eyes were on the food parcel.

The curtain had been drawn aside, revealing the whole room. Each side had a single bed, one for the young woman and her children and the other for Loise. A row of cardboard boxes along one wall served as cupboards. Abigail could see no dust anywhere. There were places where tears in the flawlessly clean bedding had been mended with needle and thread. While the others sat down, Yudel took up a position, leaning against the door.

"Mother, my name is Abigail Bukula."

The old lady raised a hand to her mouth. "I know the name, Bukula. Who are you, my child?"

"I think you knew Janice Makumbe."

"I knew her. Yes, I knew her. And her name was Bukula before she got married."

"She was my father's sister."

Bending forward, Loise covered her face with both hands. "You have come about unhappy matters, I think. Why are you here?"

"I think you looked after her children after she died."

The old woman was rocking back and forth now. She had not

yet touched her share of the fried chicken. From the other side of the room, her three roommates were eating noisily. "Is the lady very rich?" the younger one asked her mother in Shona.

"Be quiet, child," the mother said.

"I came to find Tony. Mr. Gordon and I want you to tell us a few things. After that we'll go away and not bother you again."

The rocking stopped long enough for her to speak. "I know where Tony lives. I can give you his address. He still comes to see me sometimes."

"No, he's gone from there."

This was even more distressing. The rocking started again, with greater intensity. "Oh, my poor child. Then I don't know and I can't help."

"Please, eat while we talk," Abigail said. "We just need to talk a little, then we'll go."

Loise groaned aloud, but before she could protest further Abigail placed a packet of the fried chicken in her hands. "Eat. Please eat."

Loise began eating with her fingers. Her eyelids flickered furiously over eyes that could barely see.

"Tell me, mother. Did Tony and his sister come to you soon after their mother died in the Gukurahundi?"

"Don't speak of those times, my child. Please don't speak of them."

"But that is right, isn't it?"

"I only knew they'd died when the children arrived."

"Who brought them?"

"The police. The police from Plumtree brought them."

"Plumtree, mother?"

"That is the main police station in that part of the country."

"And you had to look after them? Why you?"

"I don't know, my child. Perhaps because I also come from the same village. Its name is Bizana. I am also Ndebele. My own husband had died and I was alone. First the social services came to see me, then the police brought the children."

"It must have been a burden."

Loise shook her head. "There was money. Every month there was money. Postal orders came every month. There was food. We lived quite well. Once a year the social services came."

"My Uncle Wally sent the money, but he never came to see the children?"

The rocking, that had eased, started again. "Wally was dead, my child. Your uncle died the same night your auntie did."

"I thought he survived that night."

"No, my child. He died. I saw his body the next day. He was still in his van. The soldiers of Five Brigade killed him there."

"So who sent the money?"

"At first, I thought the government, but other people never got it. I don't know who sent it. But whoever sent it didn't want to have the children, just wanted me to look after them. I asked the social services lady once, but she said she didn't know. But I was getting money, so I should be happy, she said. And I was. I only ate because I had the children."

Despite the distraction caused by the fried chicken, the young woman had been listening to the conversation with growing interest. "They bring no money now," she said. "We are struggling."

Abigail glanced at the children's faces. The area around the mouths of both were gleaming with the fat of the fried chicken. How many other hungry children are there in this damned place? she wondered. She lay a hand on the old woman's shoulder nearest to her. "Where is Katy, Tony's sister?"

The old woman turned toward Abigail, reaching out with chicken-oily fingers to touch her face. Abigail made no attempt to avoid her. "My child, where have you been? You know nothing about your family."

"I was overseas, and I was in South Africa, mother."

"You have been away too long. The girl is dead. She killed herself, in my house. We had a visitor who had a gun and she shot herself in the kitchen of my house."

Abigail took the old woman's hands in hers. "When did this happen?"

"Long ago, my child. Katy was still a young girl, maybe seventeen, maybe eighteen, when she killed herself."

"Do you know why?"

"No, I never knew. She was not a happy child."

Yudel raised a hand as a signal to Abigail. "Did anything happen just before that, a visit perhaps?"

"No, my quiet friend. I remember nothing."

"A visit perhaps from social services?" Yudel was surprised by the question. He had not intended asking it. It seemed to have come from some place outside of himself.

"Social services?" Loise's thoughts seemed to go back to those days. "Yes, I think so. They took the children away once and brought them back a day later. It may have been then."

"And what effect did her death have on Tony?"

"Oh, Tony." She seized upon his name, as if relieved not to be talking about Katy. "He was always a beautiful boy. His face was beautiful and his soul too, but other spirits, sad spirits, lived inside him, like his sister—from the beginning, when he was small."

"And that got worse when Katy killed herself?"

But she was shaking her head, as if to brush away the collected dust of so many years. The memories were old, and no longer in sharp relief. "Perhaps, sir, perhaps . . . I don't remember."

Yudel knew that they had drawn close to something, but not what it was or how close they were. "You don't know what made Tony the way he is?"

Something close to anger flickered across the old woman's face. "I don't think it's wrong to be like that. I know many men do not like it. They see shame in it, but I don't think it's wrong. I don't think he could help it."

Yudel was trying to grasp this new idea; that there was something deeply wrong with schizophrenia, something men hated. He looked at Abigail, but she looked equally puzzled. "Do you think he was happy at home, before his parents were killed?"

"Oh yes, he was happy. Wally was a very good man. Tony loved him."

"Didn't he love Janice, his mother?"

"Yes, I think he did."

Loise had gone back to eating the chicken and potato chips, finishing her portion with a smacking of lips. She leaned toward Abigail. "I am tired, my child. It's very late. Perhaps you and your friend can come to see me some other day."

Abigail had seen Yudel's interest in Janice. "Why didn't he love his mother as much?" she asked.

"Boys have special love for their fathers, my child."

"Is that the only reason?"

Again a brief moment of anger appeared in the old face. "Janice was a good woman, and very beautiful. I have a picture. I'll show it to you." She opened a small cardboard box, the top one in a pile next to the bed. She scratched inside it, but closed it almost immediately. "It's too dark and my eyes are not good. But don't think your aunt was not a good woman. She died trying to protect her children. They found the children with her body the next morning. And it's not true that she was a bad woman."

"We never thought she was a bad woman," Abigail said.

She continued as if she had not heard. "You have to know that Wally was not a strong man. He didn't have much manly strength. And in some women the flame of being a woman burns too fiercely. But now I am tired. I can't talk any more. Come back another time, my child, and we will talk again."

Abigail again laid a hand on Loise's. "Mama Loise, when did you leave Matabeleland to come here?"

"Long ago. I wanted to get away from the Gukurahundi. Janice and Wally were killed. My husband was killed, my only child, my sister. I thought they wanted to kill us all. I could speak Shona well, so I left. I went first to Madikwe Falls, then I came . . ."

"Madikwe Falls?" Yudel echoed her.

"I lived there for a few years before . . ."

"Mama Loise . . ." Yudel used the form of address he had just learned from Abigail. "Mama Loise, were the children with you in Madikwe Falls?"

"Yes, yes. But I am Ndebele and I grew up in Matabeleland. My husband was a Shona. That's how I came to have the name, Moyo. That is, of course, not my childhood name."

Yudel felt a tingling that filled every part of him. He knew there was no rational reason for his excitement, but containing it was not easy.

"Now you must please go." The old woman slid into a horizontal position on her back and closed her eyes.

"Will you bring more food?" The young woman and her children were all looking inquiringly at Abigail.

On the stairs, Abigail stopped Yudel. "Jesus Christ, Yudel. What the hell is going on here? What does it all mean?"

She could see the intensity of concentration in his face. But she saw confusion too. "I don't know," Yudel said. "But it's not far away. I can feel it. It's only just out of reach."

"Jonas Chunga knows everything. He holds the key."

"He's not going to tell us."

"Perhaps he will tell me."

"No. Stay away from him, at least for now. Please stay away from him."

41

It was comforting for Abigail to have Yudel in the room next to hers. She was still afraid, but she was no longer alone in her fear.

Too much had happened in just one evening. In her mind, her meeting with Chunga at the country club, her confession to Yudel, the deal with Mpofu and the revelations, whatever they meant, of Mama Loise, had become a churning maelstrom of unstructured information.

Yudel had told her what Mpofu had said. He had also said that they should be prepared that the CIO man might try to take the money and not fulfill his end of the bargain. That had also been her thought. She had nevertheless told Yudel that she would try to get the money from Robert's paper in exchange for an exclusive. It was not a lot of money if the paper wanted it. She corrected herself—if Robert wanted it.

Abigail switched on her cell phone. Except for the brief periods in which she had been making calls, the phone had been switched off since she had last spoken to Robert. Now it showed that he had tried to reach her three times during the evening. She keyed in his number. The answer was immediate.

"Abigail."

"How are you, Robert?"

"I've been trying to get hold of you for days. Your phone has been switched off." She knew Robert better than anyone else she had ever known and the anxiety she heard in his voice was real.

"Robert, I need money."

"Money? Of course. How much?"

"One thousand U.S. dollars. And I need it not later than mid-morning tomorrow."

"I'll get it to a bank there by not later than ten-thirty. Leave your phone on. I'll call you to tell you where."

Hearing his immediate agreement, she recognized for the first time the sound of relief in his voice. "Aren't you going to ask what I need it for?"

"I wasn't going to, no. I'm just happy to be talking to you."

"I'm glad to be talking to you too. I'm going to use it to pay a bribe."

"A big one. I should think a thousand U.S. dollars will go far in that country."

"Pretty far."

"But please keep your phone switched on. Will you do that now?"

"Yes."

"How are you? Tell me how you are?"

"I'm fine, Robert."

"And Yudel. I know he's there. Is it helping that he's there?"

"Very much. Rosa's here too."

"Rosa too?"

"She came with Yudel."

"Abigail." He waited while he searched for a way to continue. "The things I said at the Sheraton . . . at the launch of the exhibition. I don't know . . ."

It was wonderful to hear his voice. It was even more wonderful to hear him talking to her in words that had real meaning. "It's all right, Robert."

"It was my relationship with that girl. That's what was talking."

"I know."

The relief she heard in his voice was no stronger than her own, but it was difficult to find words to convey feelings too complex for either of them to express so soon. "I'm glad," she heard him say. "I'm glad to be talking to you."

"Me too, Robert. I'm also glad."

Later, after she had hung up, she thought about what Yudel had said. That Robert was a good man and that she should forgive him, and that Jonas Chunga was not a good man and that she should be rid of him. Perhaps Yudel was right. She knew he was right about Robert. But Jonas, it was impossible to be sure about Jonas. Perhaps it was not as simple as Yudel made it seem. After all, men fighting in wars killed others. The world did not see them as criminals.

Oh God, she thought, where is my mind going? This is not a war. According to the information that came from Freek, Jonas had killed because his victims had chosen not to obey him.

Robert was again in her thoughts; a good man, endlessly reliable, an unbelievably good provider, her rescuer from a brand of fear that struck whenever she was alone with any man except him and, in recent years, Yudel. He was the only lover she had ever known. He was everything she knew she should desire. And yet, he had not come. Under these circumstances, he had stayed in the relative safety on the other side of the border.

Shouldn't he have come? she asked herself. She did not even expect it of him, but if he had come, it would have been wonderful. Had it been unreasonable to hope for that?

And there was Jonas Chunga, a man of power who had released an unexpected torrent—no, a cataract of passion in her. People around him, from waiters to women, rushed to meet his every desire and to do it immediately. He was also the man who had the restraint not to take her when he so easily could have.

And I still have unfinished business in his territory, she reminded herself, in the heart of the country he thinks of as his own, this place where nothing is refused him.

Sleep did not come easily to Abigail that night. While on other nights in this place her thoughts had been filled only by Chunga, now Robert's presence was the source of still greater confusion. She believed him that the affair was over and that the girl had gone back to the agency. But did it have to be that kid's decision? They were friends again. But it was still too early to know whether they would ever be lovers again.

But most confusing of all was the matter of Mama Loise Moyo. She had become tired too suddenly. Had her weariness been brought on by the thought that perhaps she had already told them things she should not have? Perhaps she thought there may be things they should not know. And had she told them the truth all the time, in every detail? That was unlikely.

And Yudel? On the way back from Mama Loise, he had fallen silent. Barely responding to anything she said. She knew this meant that his facile mind was hard at work, but he had shared nothing with her. "Tomorrow we meet Mpofu," he had mumbled as he left her at the door of her room. Working with him was not always easy.

A visit to the window on the landing between floors revealed a police guard inside the fence at the back of the hotel. Was he something new, or had she just not noticed him before? From the window of her room she saw the guard on the pavement in front. Within the limited range of vision the window provided, she could see no sign of a CIO double-cab or of Agent Mpofu, who had arranged that tomorrow he would sell them the whereabouts of Tony and the others.

Turning to go back to bed, she stubbed the toes of one foot against something hard. She had to open the curtain wider to see the battling tiger and elephant. From that angle, the tiger was certainly the aggressor, a thought that seemed reasonable given their respective public-relations images and appetites.

42

He thought he had dismissed the memory of that morning in the village permanently. Perhaps he would have, if it had not been for Abigail. If he had been able to bury the incident, out of reach of his conscious memory, the way he had always tried to, perhaps then he would have been free of it. He knew this was not true, though. It was not just Abigail who had brought the memory to life again. Since that day it had never been far from him. The grave in which that one morning in his life had been buried had been a shallow one.

A whiskey bottle was open on the kiaat tray, an empty glass next to it. The morning in Matabeleland, twenty-seven years before, was everywhere. For the moment, nothing else existed. Not even the whiskey helped.

He remembered the police truck and the long drive there. He also remembered the place in the reed-fringed hollow where he had stopped. The other officer, twenty years older than he was, but his junior in rank, had refused to enter the village. It had not helped to assure him that Five Brigade had left hours before and that they were already in Solusi. Word had come from the people there. "They will not be the ones to die if that information is wrong," the other man had said. "In any event, I know what we will find and I can't go into the village. I've seen it before and I can't see it again."

Making the decision to go had not been difficult. "I must go," Jonas told the other officer. "They are my people. I have friends and relatives there. I must go."

"Are you sure there is no danger now?" the other man had said. "Maybe there's still danger."

"No," he had said, "there's no danger. They've left. I've heard it from people in the area."

"I'll come with you." That had been his intention and his will had only failed at the sight of the first body. They were still a few hundred meters from the village. The body was that of a teenage girl. It was clear that she had been fleeing whatever had happened in the village. She was lying face downward and her body was cold. There was blood, and there must have been wounds, but he did not look for them.

Why he had stopped there to continue on foot was never easy for him to explain afterward. He felt somehow that by driving into the village he would be desecrating it, like walking over a grave.

From the place where he had left the truck, he could see the roofs of the huts. They were partly obscured by the scrub and nothing seemed out of the ordinary. It was true that there was no sign of cooking fires, but the morning was well advanced and the time for cooking was over. If they had torched the huts, the thatch grass would still be smoking, but there was only the silent scrub, the blue sky and the girl's body.

Everything was so silent that perhaps the girl's death was an isolated incident. Perhaps the reports had it wrong. Perhaps the people who had phoned in had confused one village with another. Perhaps when he reached it he would find that all was normal. Perhaps people were going about their leisurely business today, as on any other day, and perhaps the girl who had died was part of an altogether separate matter.

Let it be so, he prayed. Let it be that the report was a mistake. I will do anything, if it never happened. I will devote myself to the service of humanity. I will give my life. Just let it be so.

And yet he knew that this was unlikely. The night before, they had already heard that Five Brigade was on the move. When they traveled at night it usually had only one meaning.

The people here know every village and every person in them, he told himself. There can be no mistake. Such a mistake is not possible.

It was only when he reached the flat, straight section of the track immediately below the village that he got his first clear view of the huts. He had been walking, but now he broke into a trot. The other man had already fallen behind. If it had not been for two bodies toward the far end of the village in the center of the track, the place would have looked innocent. But the bodies, even from a distance, were clearly lifeless. Before that time of his life, he had little experience of death, but the untidy spread of the limbs set them apart from any living creature. There was no creature, human or animal, that slept with so little concern for how its limbs were spread.

He slowed again. The trotting became a walk, then even the walk slowed. Over to his left, at the edge of the huts, a burned-out car was leaning at an angle the manufacturers could never have intended. Behind it, another body lay facedown, much like the girl he had passed on the track.

To his right was the house where the woman had lived with her husband and the children. The front door stood open, but there was no sign of movement. The pickup truck, too, was gone. That's what had happened, he thought. They had fled in the truck, and she was still alive.

He climbed the steps of the house slowly and stopped in the front door. Then he made his way slowly from room to room. As far as he could see, there was no sign of disturbance. The beds had been slept in, but otherwise nothing had been disturbed. Certainly no one had died there.

They're alive, he thought. They got clear away. It's obvious they're alive.

Going back to the veranda, he looked into the house one last time. Somewhere he could hear the buzzing that he recognized as being made by the big bluebottle flies.

That the truck was gone was a sure sign. If they had a start of just thirty seconds and had headed into the bush, no one would have found them, certainly not a bunch of soldiers. If they were out of sight by the time Five Brigade entered the village, then there would be no stopping them. And her husband knew the bush and he knew how to handle the truck on bush tracks. When they ran out of track they would continue on foot, and be safe. He was not much of a man, Jonas thought, but he could drive and he knew the country for many kilometers around.

Jonas had not wanted to see it. At the first glimpse, he had turned his head away, but it was there, protruding from the door of one of the huts ahead. The hand was perhaps half the size of one of his. Its owner must have been no more than five or six when he died. Was it a boy? He would have to go closer to look. He would have to know sooner or later who the child was. But not now. For now it could wait. She and her family had gotten clear away. He was sure of it.

Ahead the track dipped and he came to a stop at the edge of a slight rise. The dip in the track had hidden the bodies. Bluebottle flies rose from them, but only for a moment.

It was then he saw the truck. It had ridden high against the sloping trunk of a thorn tree. There was no one on the back. The people who may have occupied the back as they tried to escape were spread around it on the ground. Their limbs were trapped in the ungainly contortions of death. Hanging partly out of the driver's cab he could see the body of a young man. His shirt was stained by his own blood. Without going closer he knew that it was her husband.

He made his way slowly round the tangle of bodies, staying clear of them. He saw no children, and only two women. Both looked older than she was. But there was the truck, and there was her husband. Now he could see stab wounds. Each wound looked like a small mouth, the tissue puckering up like lips where it burst through the slit made by a bayonet. Hands too were damaged, as the people had tried to defend themselves.

In the distance, beyond the last line of huts, a man was approaching. He was wearing a shirt that was torn and shorts that came down below his knees. He was walking very slowly and wandering from side to side as he made his way in the general direction of the village.

"Hello," Jonas called. "Hello." Then he recognized the man as old Makaleka who lived with his daughter. "Father," he called. "It's me, Jonas."

The old man showed no sign of having heard him, turning away, then sitting down heavily in the grass. To reach him, Jonas would have to pass next to the bodies around the truck.

How many bodies were there? He tried to count them, but

they were close together, some of them partly covering others. He was not seeing clearly. Something about his eyes made the bodies all merge into one another.

Old Makaleka was stirring. From his position next to the truck and close enough to her husband's body to touch it, Jonas could see the old man's head just protruding above the tall thatching grass. His head moved first one way, then the other.

He would have gone closer, but it was then that he heard the crying. It was clearly the sound of small children, but weak and plaintive. They may have been crying for most of the night. The sound was coming from the direction of the old pigsty, but there were huts in the way.

He ran, stumbling on the uneven pathways, once colliding heavily with a clay wall and almost falling. Unexpectedly, he broke clear of the last hut. He saw the form on the ground between himself and the pigsty, and knew it for what it was. Approaching it was impossible, but avoiding it was also impossible. From ten paces away he could see where the bayonet that had killed her and the child inside her had entered her abdomen.

Remembering that day in later years, he never knew whether he would have gone closer or simply fled the scene. But it was then that he heard the children cry. They were on their feet and peering at him through the light scrub skirting the pigsty. The boy was wearing underpants, but the girl was naked. They had not moved from the place where their mother had hidden them.

No more, Chunga thought. He was pouring from the whiskey bottle again. With a great effort he drove the images away. He could bear no more of it. The part after that was beyond recollection. It was beyond his ability to approach it.

And now, after all this time, there was this face. Of all the faces there could be and all the women there had been, he was again confronted by this one unforgettable face.

He drank from the glass without emptying it and left the bottle and glass on the tray. His wristwatch told him that it was almost three o'clock. The time hardly mattered.

43

The body shop was located just south of the city center, among other small industries and buildings that had once housed store-rooms or workshops, but which now stood empty. Yudel followed the instructions on Mpofu's note, driving slowly to avoid the seemingly aimless crowds that filled the streets. He parked as Mpofu had instructed, next to the gate of what seemed to be a dis-used warehouse. "We go in by the back door, down there," Yudel told Abigail.

The door at which he was pointing was made of steel and set into a corrugated-iron extension of an old brick building, clearly the back entrance. They had brought Helena as back-up "in case of unpleasant surprises," as Yudel had put it. "She may be a pain in the ass," he had said to Abigail, "but she's a tough guy." Now he turned to her where she was sitting in the backseat. "You move in behind the steering wheel. If we have to leave in a hurry, be ready. On the other hand, if we don't come out, you'll know where we went missing and who we came to see."

"I should also come in," she said.

"No," Yudel said. "This is why you're here."

"Yes, sir, Mr. Boss," Helena said.

They walked the half-block to the door unhurriedly. Nothing in the narrow back street, fringed with service businesses, looked unusual. Yudel had the thousand U.S. dollars in ten-dollar bills that Robert had sent. He was carrying it in the money belt inside his shirt. Larger denominations had not been available. Abigail raised the question that was occupying both their minds. "Do you suppose this is real?"

"It looked like it, when he made the offer," Yudel said.

The door was slightly ajar. It yielded to the gentlest push. Yudel led the way through the door. Inside, the body shop smelled of fresh spray paint. Two workmen in overalls were rubbing down a car that had just received a new undercoat. On the far side, the double-garage door of the shop's main entrance was standing open. A bicycle passed outside. One of the men pointed to a small, glass-enclosed office without saying anything.

Mpofu was seated behind the desk on an office chair. He sat forward without rising. "I thought you'd be coming alone," he told Yudel.

"I am Ms. Bukula's assistant in this matter," Yudel said. "The money is hers, not mine." As an extra thought, he added, "We also have people waiting for us outside in the car." Just so that you don't get the wrong idea, he thought.

Yes, you little prick, Abigail thought. Why don't you talk to me? She and Yudel sat down on the two chairs that were intended for visitors.

"I thought you were going to be alone," he said again. "I made the deal with you."

"If you're unhappy, we can leave now." Although he had only met him once before, Yudel knew his man. Mpofu wanted the money too badly to let it slip away now.

"Have you got the money?" Mpofu's eyes had narrowed with the abiding suspicion all dishonest people carry with them as part of their character makeup.

"Yes," Yudel said.

"I'd like to see it."

"Not yet." Abigail took over the negotiation. "Where are my clients being held?"

"How do I know the money is here?"

"It's very simple," Abigail said. "Mr. Gordon and I are well-known as honest people. You are everywhere suspected of being dishonest. We are the only people in this meeting who can be trusted."

Clearly put, Yudel thought. Perhaps not the most diplomatic way, though.

Mpofu bridled under the insult. "I'm not used to being spoken to like that." He moved in his seat, so that his right shoulder was facing them, his jacket hanging open enough to give them a view of the holstered firearm in his left armpit. Neither Yudel nor Abigail could avoid seeing it.

"You're not a CIO agent at this meeting," Abigail told him. "At this meeting, you're a traitor, selling your organization's secrets."

It seemed that the thought of the money had caused some confusion in Mpofu's thinking. This may have been the first time that the idea of his being a traitor had entered his mind. He made as if to rise, glancing in the direction of the body shop's front entrance, but sat down again. His position in the CIO may have been under threat, but the gun, resting against his chest, had always been an effective way of settling disputes. "I want to see the money."

"While two of your thugs are just over there, pretending to be mechanics?"

"That's my brother and his helper. This is his business. I wouldn't be such a fool as to bring other CIO people."

Unless you're all in it together, Abigail thought. "How do I know you've even got our people?"

"I know everything about it. I know where they're being kept. I know that they get better food than the others."

"They do?" Abigail was interested.

"That's Jonas Chunga. You never know what to expect from him."

It was not the main issue, though. "I want to know what you've got. Tell me what you've got." He had not changed position. The handle of the gun pointed forward, perfectly positioned for his right hand.

Another glance at the front entrance confirmed to Mpofu that none of his CIO colleagues were coming in to arrest him. "They were taken away in a prison truck that came back fourteen hours later. I heard one of the drivers complain about the long drive."

"Are you serious?" Abigail demanded. "You think it's worth a thousand dollars to know that they may be six or seven hours' drive from here? And even that's not certain. They could be anywhere."

"I've got more."

"Let's have it." The contempt Abigail felt for this man was now mingled with the humiliation she felt. He thought they would be easy to handle, that he could flash his gun and they would be cowed into doing his bidding.

"I got the telephone number of the place they're being held. I overheard Director Chunga giving the number to someone else, the DG, I think."

"What did he say to the director general?"

"The DG asked for the contact number, and they were definitely talking about those prisoners."

Abigail knew that, at the very least, the telephone number would reveal which town they were being held in. "Why didn't you just ask where they are?"

"In the CIO you don't ask those sorts of questions."

That was understandable, she thought. "Where's the number?"

"I've got it. It's hidden. Give me half the money now, then I'll take you to it." And still the gun was on display.

Yudel was trying not to look at it. He stifled an artificial yawn. "Time for us to go." He glanced at Abigail, moving in his seat as if to rise. "This fellow doesn't know anything."

"You want a lot of money for very little information," Abigail said.

"I hid the number at my mother's house. You know you don't have any other choice. This is your only chance."

Abigail was not sure whether he was pleading with them or threatening them, but, despite herself, she knew that he may be right. His weakness was how badly he wanted their thousand dollars, but his strength was this information that could be their last best chance of finding the missing seven. "We'll go to your mother's house now. You'll give us the number and I will call it. The answer I get will determine whether you get paid."

"You think they'll tell you?"

"I know how to get the answer I want. It's that or nothing." Abigail looked at Yudel who was already on his feet, glancing at his watch and stretching extravagantly. "Goodbye, Agent Mpofu," Abigail said.

Mpofu rose more quickly than they had. His jacket was hanging in the normal way. Advertising the gun had not worked. "All right," he said. "Let me write out my mother's address. Meet me there in two hours."

44

The township where Mpofu's mother had her home lay on the northern side of the city. Its inner core had been started in colonial days as a neat network of tiny identical four-room brick cottages. But over the years, the resources of succeeding governments, first that of white settlers, then of black liberators, had shrunk. Idealism had also dissipated, with very few brick cottages being added. Shacks of every possible shape, size and building material had spread beyond the original township. The dwellings followed no town-planning regulation, along tracks that appeared to have more to do with accident than intent.

"Down here," Helena said. "I think it's down here, past that tavern, the one on the right. Do you see it? There's an opening in the shacks there, an alley. Stop there and we'll see if we can get through."

Yudel did as she instructed, but the gap between the two shacks was blocked by another, bigger one set farther back. "Wait here for me. I'll go into the tavern and ask."

He and Abigail watched her go. Through the open door they could see her engage in conversation with a man, perhaps the proprietor. Abigail and Yudel got out and waited next to the car. It was a miracle to Yudel that anyone could be traced in this place. There were no street names, no house numbers, no formal way of finding anything. There was probably no postman for the township either.

The signs of commercial activity were equally miraculous to

Yudel. Every second or third shack carried a homemade sign advertising some kind of enterprise. Barbers who operated in front of doorways, tiny convenience stores that carried only five or six of the most basic foods, wedding-gown-hire agents, ladies' hair salons, tire repairmen, exhaust-system repairers who displayed their stock of five or six used exhaust pipes in conical piles alongside the track, woodworkers, a baker who claimed to make cream cakes and wedding cakes, a prepaid phone service under a hessian awning, a pickup truck that could be hired either as a taxi or to transport goods, taverns like the one in which Helena was looking for directions—all of them advertised their wares in this impoverished place.

To Abigail, it was a wonderful advertisement for the resilience of the African spirit. The country's economy had been destroyed beyond the worst of nightmares, but the residents of this ramshackle place had not given up.

While the signs on the buildings gave notice of a surprisingly active community, there were few people in the streets. At the bottom of the alley, two children were playing a game that involved using one stick to flick another into the air and then strike it before it landed. Two old women, dressed entirely in black, were sitting on armchairs that had lost much of their stuffing. They were talking in undertones and looking in the direction of the strangers and their seemingly new car. In the direction the car was pointing, a teenage couple were strolling in the purposeless way of people in the grip of sexual attraction who have no place to exercise it. He had an arm wrapped around her neck and she had both of hers around his waist.

From a distance they could hear what sounded like crowd sounds, the rising and falling of many voices. "Do you hear that?" Abigail asked Yudel.

"What is it?"

"They're certainly excited. I can't make out if they're happy or angry."

"I hope we don't have to find out," Yudel said. "Things could get uncomfortable for us."

Abigail grinned at him. "This is the point where I'm supposed to say, what do you mean—us—white man?"

"You'll forgive me, if I don't laugh," Yudel said. Abigail chuckled briefly, though.

Helena and the tavern's proprietor stepped out of the hut, squinting into the brightness of the sun. "I think I understand," she was saying. "Right at the school, then past the football field, then it's left and when we reach the tavern in a green, corrugated-iron house we are close and we must ask again." She was speaking Shona, but Abigail understood enough of the language to follow it.

The tavern owner, a short, broad-shouldered man who walked with a stoop, was nodding. Abigail went closer. She spoke to the tavern owner in English, her Shona not being good enough for the purpose. "There's hardly anyone in the streets. Is there an occasion?"

"Political meeting, opposition to the government."

"You didn't go?" Abigail asked.

"I'm too old. Politics is for young people."

"Aren't they scared of reprisals?"

He shrugged. "Last night they chased the police. You see the smoke." He pointed across the ragged line of rooftops. In the distance, a few thin wisps of smoke were blending into the distant hills. "They burned houses. Maybe policemen stayed in those houses."

"They aren't holding this rally at the football field, are they?"

"Yes, they always hold meetings at the football field."

"The one we've got to drive past to get to the green tavern?"

"Of course. You want to go there, you've got to pass the football field."

Ever since they had entered the township, Yudel had driven slowly along the uneven potholed surfaces of the township roads. Now he drove even more slowly. In the distance they could see the crowd. In the rearview mirror he saw only the puffs of dust churned up by the car's wheels.

"Stop, Yudel," Abigail said. She turned to Helena who was in the backseat. "We have to find another way. We can't go past that football field. I'm not sure we should be here today at all."

"That's a movement of the people." Helena's voice held the angry tone Abigail had heard too often before. "You have nothing to fear from the people."

"Helena, we need a different way. We need at least a few rows of shacks between ourselves and the political meeting, no matter whose side they're on."

"Turn here, if you must." She seemed to be gritting her teeth as she spoke.

"That's barely a track," Yudel said.

"Tell her," Helena said. "This is what she wants."

Yudel looked at the way Helena had indicated. He brought the car to a stop. The rough, grassless track they had followed so far was a highway by comparison. Ahead, although still a distance away, the crowd seemed to be a loose gathering with people moving back and forth aimlessly. He opened the window on his side and the sound from the football field grew in intensity. He heard the ill-defined chorus of many voices, united only in their excitement.

"There's something wrong about this," Yudel said. "That's not a crowd at a political meeting."

"What the fuck are you talking about?" the voice from the backseat muttered in disgust.

At that moment, two teenage boys, dressed in unwashed T-shirts and jeans, burst out of a side street, running fast. Both faces held expressions of hard-eyed excitement. Yudel saw a breathlessness about them that had nothing to do with how hard they were running. Neither seemed to notice the car. They fled across the track and into one of the alleys between the shacks.

Now there were others, coming from the front, younger people running and older people scampering as quickly as they could. A red-eyed man in rags, who used a stick to walk with, was coughing and laughing as he hurried past the car. Helena yelled something at him in Shona, but he only shook his head and kept moving.

Not all were running, though. Some of the crowd in the middle distance was still gathered across the track, possibly opposite the football field. "The police must be there, maybe shooting at people," Helena said.

"If the police were there and shooting at people, they'd all be running and we'd have heard the shots." Abigail glanced at Helena. To Yudel, she said, "Let's go on."

"Do you think it's safe?"

"Nothing we've done here so far has been safe. Let's go on."

Yudel let out the clutch. His right foot barely touched the accelerator pedal. The car eased forward at little more than walking pace. Another group of teenagers, this time both boys and girls, were running toward them from the front. One of them turned to look back, then another, then they were running again. Yudel saw in their eyes the same excitement he had seen earlier. One of the boys stopped next to his window. Yudel brought the car to a stop. The boy shouted something to one of the others in Shona. Seeing Yudel looking at him, he shouted in English, "Now we are all together. Now we are all one. We are united."

Abigail leaned past Yudel and called to the boy. "What's happening down there?"

He brought his face close to the open window. Yudel could see the whites of his eyes all the way round the irises. "We are united. No more will we have dictatorship, no more, not in my country." Then he was gone, still fleeing in the direction away from the football field. From where they had stopped, Yudel could see only a corner of the space that passed as a football field. Unlike the well-kept one in town, the field seemed to be almost entirely without grass. The absence of a watering system and the relentless sun had destroyed whatever greenery may once have existed.

Down at the field the crowd seemed thinner, as people either drifted away or fled headlong. A man and a smaller figure, perhaps a boy, were kicking something on the ground.

"I think we can go, Yudel," Abigail said. "Whatever the threat is, I don't think it's aimed at us."

He agreed with her, but he allowed only gentle acceleration. In the rearview mirror he caught a glimpse of Helena's face and thought he saw the same hard-eyed excitement there that he had seen in the eyes of the kids fleeing the football field. "I don't think this is good," Abigail was saying. "This is not good at all."

The smoke pointed out by the tavern owner had not come from a burning house, as he had thought. Its source was a smoldering bundle on the edge of the grassless football field. Others had joined the man and boy to kick the bundle on the ground. There were five of them now, one of whom was a woman.

The people still on the field could not now be described as a crowd. They were a scattering of individuals, edging away from the scene in which they had participated. "Not in my country," the boy's voice shouted. "Not anymore in my country will they do what they like."

Yudel had stopped the car again and was getting out. He started toward the bundle on the ground. Abigail was running ahead of him. "Stop, brothers and sisters, please stop. This will bring reprisals on us all. Please stop." It was only now that Yudel could see the shape of the thing on the ground. He saw a single hand with fingers spread-eagled that for the first time identified it for what it was. Smoke was rising from the blackened corpse. The clothing, or was it the flesh, was still glowing in places. There was not enough smoke to be visible from far.

Most of those who had been kicking the body had stepped back with Abigail's approach. Only one man and a boy who Yudel thought had not yet reached his teens were still attacking the figure on the ground. Abigail was shouting. "No, please stop. This will not help." She pushed hard against the man. He stumbled and went down on hands and knees.

"It's too late, Yudel." She knelt next to the body. "It's much too late."

"The clothing," Yudel said. Enough of the clothing had survived the fire to make it identifiable. "Look at the clothing. He's wearing a suit. How many people in this place are wearing suits?"

"Never in my country will this happen anymore." They heard the teenage boy's voice faintly, from a distance. Farther away a woman ululated and was joined by a second, then a third and perhaps more.

By the time Yudel straightened up, it was clear that Agent Mpofu would not be selling them information of any kind, not ever again. From somewhere behind him the ululations were continuing.

"Dear God," Abigail said. "Let's get out of this ghastly place."

Yudel could hear Helena. "It's the will of the people. The people have spoken." When he looked at her, her jaw was set and her eyes were shining. "It's not your country." Her eyes met Yudel's. "It's our country. You can't feel the way we do."

Helena's eyes suddenly widened and she drew back. Yudel looked for Abigail, but could not see her immediately. He felt the blow on the back of his head as a heavy, blunt-edged concussion. Abigail's scream reached him through the swirling confusion of a consciousness that was no longer functioning. He felt his face make uncontrolled contact with the dusty surface of the field and tried to rise.

45

Very slowly Yudel became aware of the walls and ceiling of the cell. He was on his back on a mattress so thin that it may not have existed at all. At least it provided some insulation from the cement.

His head seemed to have swelled to double its usual size. Even the smallest movement started the beating of a bass drum inside his skull. Consciousness came and went a few times. He was aware of skimming along just below some part of the afternoon. He was on a pillow of light, floating somewhere beneath the surface—but the surface of what?

Eventually the floating stopped and he was in the cell, his head aching. He levered himself up on an elbow, but the bass drum in his skull started again and he sank back. "How blind I've been," he thought. "It was all there. I can't believe how long it took."

For the first time he wondered about what may have happened to Abigail. Someone shouted from the solid steel door. The face of a uniformed policeman had appeared at the inspection hole. He shouted again. Yudel did not understand the language, but he imagined the shout was a signal that the prisoner had woken.

The inspection hole closed and moments later an officer who wore the stripes of a sergeant entered the cell. He was a small, lean man, in a uniform made dusty by the day's activities. His hollow cheeks and bulging eyes made him look like a hungry insect, perhaps a mantis. He stopped next to Yudel. "So, my friend," he said.

"What were you doing here helping to kill the people of our township?"

Yudel tried again to rise, but his head remained a problem. He settled for resting on one elbow and spoke softly, trying to keep the drum in his head quiet. "First of all, I'm not your friend. Second, I'm not going to answer your questions."

"Oh, yes?" Fury flared in the sergeant's eyes. "You think so?"

"I'm quite sure of it. If you have any doubts, you'd better check first with Director Jonas Chunga of the CIO." It was a device that had worked for Abigail, and Yudel thought it was worth a try now.

The sergeant's chest was heaving with indignation. "Are you CIO?"

"That's not your business. My name is Yudel Gordon. You'd better tell Jonas Chunga that your men assaulted me and that you're holding me." The sergeant backed away to the door. Containing his anger had just become easier.

The sound of many voices reached him from the window. Then a single voice shouted what sounded like a military command. The other voices fell silent. Yudel maneuvered himself carefully onto all fours, trying not to jolt his head as he rolled over. From that position he rose unsteadily into a crouch, then to his feet. Yudel found that by pulling himself up by the bars, he could just see out of the window. He had never been an athlete, and only managed to stay in that position for a few seconds, but it was long enough for him to see a group of twenty or thirty township residents, their heads bowed in submission. He let himself down as the hammering in his head started again.

The steel door of the cell was just a few paces away. He walked carefully to it and, with great care, beat on it with his flat hand.

The inspection hole snapped open and the guard's face appeared. "Yes?"

"Who are those people in the yard?"

"Suspects."

"Suspects for what?"

"Suspects for killing the CIO man."

Yudel had not expected the reprisals to start so soon. "There were two ladies with me," he said. "Were they also arrested?"

"No ladies, just you."

"Do you know what happened to them?"

"No ladies were arrested."

"Was I the only one arrested at the football field?"

Almost as he asked the question, a murmuring of many voices, a subdued rumbling, reached him. "Twenty, maybe thirty were arrested. We got them outside."

"So why am I alone in here?"

"You must be the mastermind, the sergeant says."

"I'm the mastermind?"

"Sergeant says you're the mastermind."

Thanks awfully, Yudel thought. "The ladies I was with are not in the twenty or so you arrested?"

"All are men and only one township lady."

"Thanks."

Yudel heard the inspection cover snap shut as he turned away. It was nice to be thought of as the mastermind, much better than being seen as just part of the mob. It earned you a little status. Although how much masterminding it took to burn someone alive was another matter.

His appearance was not something that ever took much of Yudel's attention. His clothing was, without exception, made up of fairly neutral colors and he selected what he wore each day by the simple device of taking the items that came to hand first. But now he looked down at his clothes. Having spent some time face-down in the thick dust of the football field had not improved their appearance. He tried to dust off his trousers, but was only partly successful. After a minute or less he gave up and went back to the plastic foam sheet that passed as a mattress, sitting down with his back resting against the cell wall.

In the distance he heard what sounded like the rolling of a great drum. Through the only window, set high in the wall, he could see the clouds that had gathered over the city. While he watched, a sharp flash of chain lightning snaked across the sky, the roll of thunder following a few seconds later. The rain had not yet started.

Yudel was confident that what he had said to the sergeant would reach Chunga soon and that the director would not be able to resist his curiosity as to what Yudel was doing at the scene of Agent Mpofu's death. He was surprised though at just how quickly that reaction took place. Within half an hour the cell door was being unlocked, and the guard indicating that he should follow.

A middle-aged man wearing a tie, the jacket of a suit, faded denim trousers and sneakers was waiting in the charge office. "Mr. Gordon," he said. "Director Chunga is waiting for you." The station sergeant was nowhere to be seen.

Yudel followed him outside to an old Honda, the upholstery of which had worn through in places. Waiting behind the car was an armored personnel carrier. Through the vehicle's narrow windows, men in combat fatigues were visible.

The afternoon was growing darker, the gathering clouds having blocked all sunlight. As they drove, lightning flashed over the city and to the north, but the ground was still as dry as before. For a short distance the armored vehicle followed close behind, churning up a column of dust that was spread by a gusty wind to settle on shacks on either side. As Yudel watched, it stopped at one of the alleys between the shacks and troops armed with repeating rifles started to disembark. In the middle distance, another personnel carrier was patrolling the football field.

The offices of the CIO on Samora Machel Drive were far simpler than Yudel had imagined them to be. Chunga's own office was large, but simply furnished and without the paintings and statuettes he had expected. The director was seated behind his desk. He did not rise or offer a hand to Yudel, but he did nod to a chair.

Yudel sat down and looked into the director's unsmiling face and unblinking gaze. He was not in a hurry to start. He seemed to be appraising the man sitting across from him, making up his mind before he even heard Yudel's explanation. "This is altogether unexpected," he said. "To find you, a visitor to our country who is on a legal mission, seemingly involved in the violent death of one of our agents. Perhaps you would care to explain."

"Of course," Yudel said, "but before I do, could you tell me if Abigail is safe? She was with me and . . ."

"She's at the hotel. She's been making a nuisance of herself, trying to discover what happened to you. I phoned her and told her that you are now in CIO custody so there is no need for her to be concerned and that I would keep her informed."

"Thank you." Yudel felt certain Chunga did not really believe he was involved in the killing of Mpofu. He was also certain that this would be the last chance to learn anything of value from the CIO man. He knew he would have to go very carefully, but he also knew that the excessive enthusiasm of the township police had given him an opportunity he had no reason to expect.

"Perhaps now you would care to explain what you were doing next to the body of one of our agents."

Yudel could see no obvious hostility in Chunga, but nor could he see anything that may benefit him. Nor could he be sure how Chunga's obsession with Abigail may affect this meeting. The other man's tight control was securely in place, as always. Perhaps not always, though. What Freek had told Yudel about the times when that control had cracked was foremost in Yudel's mind. "I went there with Abigail to meet Agent Mpofu, but when we arrived there we found that he had already been killed by the mob. I was attacked from behind. I don't know who did it. Probably someone who thought I was one of your men."

"There was a reason for you to be meeting him there, I presume."

"Yes." Yudel knew that only the truth made any sense in this matter. "Agent Mpofu had offered to tell us where we could find our clients. We were to pay him one thousand American dollars for the information."

"So you were there with the purpose of bribing a government official. Is that correct?"

"No. Agent Mpofu invited us." And now it was necessary to lie. "It had never been our intention to pay him the money. We had intended to try to get the information from him without giving him any money."

For the first time, the slightest smile reflected something of what Chunga was thinking. "Congratulations, Mr. Gordon." He let Yudel wait before telling him why congratulations were in order. "You lie beautifully." He reached into one of his desk drawers and brought out Robert's one thousand American dollars in ten-dollar bills and laid them on the desk. Inadvertently, Yudel's hand went to his waist. The money belt was still there. Now Chunga smiled more broadly, with real amusement. "I'm sorry to say that your belt is empty now. This is what was in it. Now tell me again what you were doing at the place where my agent died."

Yudel looked at Chunga. The little smile of satisfaction told him that this was something he would have to give Chunga. He had made the most basic mistake. Chunga had won the point and he would have to leave it there. He knew he would simply have to let the dice roll. "All right. I was going to pay him the thousand dollars for that information. But he solicited the bribe."

"You were nevertheless a party to it."

"And yet it was not a real bribe. He was probably going to take the money, and we would get nothing from it. In truth, it was extortion."

"Because he never knew where they are?" This time Chunga laughed loud. "Mr. Gordon, are you suggesting that you are guiltless because of your stupidity?"

"It could be seen that way."

Chunga laughed again. "I doubt that a court would see it that way." The laughter diminished until it was no more than simple amusement. Yudel saw it as the amusement a cat may feel at the attempt of a mouse to escape. "I do believe that you had nothing to do with the death of my agent. And I will accept that he solicited the bribe. He was a fool. Getting himself killed that way was also the act of a fool." The amusement had retreated to his eyes. "Would you like a drink, Mr. Gordon?"

What does this mean? Yudel asked himself. Are we friends now? "What would we be drinking?" he asked.

"Whiskey, imported."

"Thanks," Yudel said. "Half a tot."

"Half a tot?" Chunga's eyebrows lifted. "This is the first time I've heard a man ask for half a tot. Doubles often, nothing but water occasionally, but half a tot is new to me."

"I have a blood-sugar problem."

"Ah." Chunga nodded. "Half a tot, then. With water, I suppose, to dilute the sugar further?"

"Please."

Chunga poured the drinks at a table in a corner of the office. Yudel waited in silence. He knew that this was not the time to be raising any of the matters that interested him. He would have to let Chunga direct the conversation and wait for an opening that may not come. "Mr. Gordon, what exactly are you doing here?"

"Do you think you could call me Yudel?"

Chunga raised his eyebrows, this time in mock surprise. "Are we friends now?"

"I hope so."

Chunga laughed again, no more than a brief chuckle this time. "I'm sure you do. No, I think you will remain Mr. Gordon and I will remain Director Chunga. But please answer my question. What are you doing in my country?"

"Well, we came for this matter of these missing people."

"No. Abigail came for that reason. Why did you come?"

"To assist her."

"Is she paying you?"

"No."

"Are you her lover?"

Now Yudel could see no sign of amusement in the other man, but he did see the smallest weakness in Chunga's defenses. "No."

"What are you to her?" It was clear that this was something Chunga needed to understand, and that it had nothing to do with the dead CIO agent.

"I can't describe it exactly. I can't even describe it inexactly."

"Give it a try."

"No."

"You refuse to describe your relationship with her? Why?"

"I prefer not to examine it. I choose not to."

"I see," Chunga said, only to correct himself a moment later. "No, I don't see at all."

"You know that my wife is with me here?"

"Of course, but that tells me nothing. So there is nothing sexual in your relationship with Abigail?"

"Not overtly."

"Not overtly?" Chunga had said it thoughtfully, seeming to weigh up the meaning of the words.

"I'm aware that I would probably not have had this relationship with her if she had been a man. But our relationship is not typically that of a man and a woman. Of course, I like her company and she is both a brilliant and a good-looking woman. The picture of her that *The Herald* carried does not begin to do her justice."

"No, it doesn't."

Yudel could see that Chunga was thinking and that it was probably about Abigail, possibly realizing that Yudel was no threat to his need for her. "So you came for Abigail, because you have this unusual connection with her?"

And at last the opportunity had presented itself. It was a slim one, but he had to take it. "I also came because of my fascination with Tony Makumbe." He only saw the reaction in Chunga because he was looking for it, but it was clear and it had been immediate. The eyes had narrowed and the face had tensed. "He suffers from a form of schizophrenia that interests me."

"You have no schizophrenics in South Africa?"

"Of course we do, but none that I know of who write beautifully. And none that I know of who have been plunged deeper into their illness by the suicide of his sister." Again Yudel thought he saw a reaction, a tensing of the face, no more than a muscular twitch.

"You seem to know a great deal, Mr. Gordon."

"Not as much as I would like to." This was the time to press forward. Whatever the dangers, if he wanted to know the truth, this was his opportunity. "Especially one who had that reason for suicide."

Yudel waited for the response he knew would come. "And what was that reason?" It had come slowly, but his eyes had never left Yudel's face.

"She couldn't face Wally, her father, going over to the side of the government who had murdered her mother."

Chunga's face turned away from Yudel with an expression of disgust. "What the fuck do you know, Gordon? Wally never went over to the government's side. He died the night Tony's mother died."

"Not according to my information." Yudel prodded the matter a little further. "I've been told that Tony's father hated his son's homosexuality."

"Where do you come up with this shit?"

"Few heterosexual men are at ease with a homosexual son."

"Christ, Gordon, what the hell are you talking about? The man died when Tony was two or three, a small child. Wally could know nothing about his homosexuality." Chunga was looking at Yudel through disbelieving eyes.

It was time for Yudel to backtrack. "I can't vouch for my sources."

"You're damned right you can't."

"I also wondered if the manner of his mother's death had caused his schizophrenia," Yudel said.

Chunga had turned his head slightly to one side, so that he had to look at Yudel out of the corners of his eyes. It was an expression that said that he had overestimated this man. He had been dealing with a fool all along. "I have to hear this. Please enlighten me."

"Well, I understand that Janice Makumbe was a beautiful woman. Some would say an irresistibly beautiful woman."

"What has that got to do with anything?" And yet he seemed to be agreeing.

"I think that may have added to the horror of the way she died. How Five Brigade killed Tony's mother in front of him and raped the dead body while he was watching."

"Jesus Christ." It was with an effort that Chunga stopped himself from rising. "What the fuck are you talking about? Nothing like that ever happened."

But you seem to know so much about what did happen, Yudel thought. And where were you at the time? "Perhaps her death was what they call bad karma. She was not faithful to Wally, you know."

This time Chunga could not stop himself from rising. His eyes were blazing with both fury and panic. He had snatched a sheet of paper from a tray on his desk. "Here, this is for you." He handed the sheet of paper and the thousand dollars to Yudel. "Now get the fucking hell out of my office and out of my country," he roared.

From the door, Yudel looked back. Chunga was swallowing down his whiskey. The hands that held the glass were shaking. His own half-tot remained untouched.

46

Chunga had been wrong, perhaps deliberately, about Abigail being at the hotel. She was waiting on the pavement, next to the hired car. At last the rain had started. It was still only a scattering of big drops, though, not yet enough to bring real relief to the dry Zimbabwean earth. High above, a bolt of lightning crackled and roared through a late-afternoon sky which, under dense cloud, was already in deep twilight.

Abigail waited for Yudel to approach, as if she might not be sure of a friendly welcome. She was clasping her hands together. "I didn't desert you. I didn't. They escorted me out of the township and . . ."

"And since then you've been making a nuisance of yourself. I know. Our friend, Director Chunga, told me."

"Our friend?"

Yudel had his sheet of paper in one hand. He waved it at her.

"What's that?"

"Notice to leave the country in twenty-four hours."

As she read the order, a few large drops of rain splashed over it, causing some of the ink to run. She handed it back to him. "So it's over, then." And yet, looking into his face, she saw an excitement that did not fit the circumstances.

"Perhaps not," he said.

"What is it, Yudel?"

"We have to go somewhere now. Immediately."

"Where?"

"To old Loise Moyo."

"Why?"

"Just do this with me."

Abigail drove quickly through the city streets, skilfully dodging the uneven places. Something in Yudel had conveyed to her this unexpected urgency. "Has something happened? Have you learned something?" She had to repeat herself to break through the barrier of thought that had suddenly enclosed Yudel. "What have you learned?"

"Not yet. The old lady first."

By the time they reached the building where Loise Moyo lived, the rain's intensity had increased, but Abigail found parking right in front of the door. They had to avoid children playing in the lobby and on the stairs, but the old woman's door stood open. She was sitting on the edge of her bed and singing softly to herself. The young woman and her children were nowhere to be seen.

"Mother . . ." Abigail began.

"Oh. I think it's my wealthy young friend again." She looked in Abigail's direction through eyes that could not focus.

"Yes, it's me."

"Is your friend with you today, the one who speaks little?"

"Yes, Mrs. Moyo, I'm here. We want just one more thing from you."

The old woman shook her head. "I hoped you wouldn't come back. Last night I could hardly sleep after your visit."

"This time it's a small matter," Yudel said. "We would like to see the photograph you have, the one of Janice Makumbe."

She reached toward the pile of boxes next to the head of her bed and lifted the top one to put it on her lap. "I think I still have it. But I can't find it for you. My eyes . . ."

Abigail, who had been looking at Yudel as if he may finally have stretched her belief in him too far, took the box from Loise. "We will look, but how will we know it's her when we find the picture?"

"Don't worry about that," Yudel said.

Abigail unpacked the cardboard box carefully, placing each item on the bed next to Loise. The first was a plastic Madonna whose eyes were turned piously heavenward. After that, she removed a tin box with a hinged lid. The lid carried an advertisement for the toffees it had once contained. A tiny winged fairy, of the sort found in music boxes, was wrapped in tissue paper. A creased and battered school report card carried the name Katherine Makumbe. The last item was Loise's Bible, its cover cracked and its pages well-thumbed.

"There are no photographs, mother," Abigail said, "none at all."

"Oh my. I was sure there were pictures." She turned her face toward the sound of Abigail's voice. "Have you looked inside the Bible, child?"

Abigail lifted the Bible and shook it gently. A few photographs fell onto the bed. The first one she touched was an old and cracked head-and-shoulders of a beautiful young woman, perhaps in her early twenties. Her chin was raised in a way that gave the impression of haughtiness. She looked boldly into the lens of the camera. Neck and shoulders were naked. Abigail dropped the photograph and walked unsteadily to the door.

Yudel caught up with her on the stairs. "My God, Yudel, what does it mean?"

"Come. We must go."

"Wait." She was holding him. "That's me in the photo."

"I know."

She started unsteadily down the stairs with Yudel trying to steady her, then she stopped again. "Do you still have the thousand dollars?"

"Yes."

"Give it to her. Give it to Mama Loise."

47

Abigail drove, distracted, through the Harare streets. Within a block, the car had gone heavily through more than one place where the tarred surface was eroded away. The rain that had been no more than a shower was now coming down with the intensity of a real African storm. Sheets of big drops swept across the streets, hammering on the roof and windscreen of the car. Visibility had been reduced to perhaps a block. The crowds that not long before had filled the streets had now miraculously disappeared. Only a few people remained, huddling in the doorways of shops or office buildings.

Abigail switched on the headlights. It did little to improve visibility, but at least the car could be seen from the front. Out of the corners of her eyes she could see Yudel, hunched forward in his seat. He still seemed unsure about how the welter of information they had gathered fit together. She felt rather than saw him turn toward her. "I pushed him too far. At that moment he didn't realize what I was thinking, but he is no fool. When he does realize—and it may be soon—I shouldn't be close at hand. None of us should be."

"Yudel, tell me. You tell me now."

"He's the father of both Tony and Katy. He was Janice's lover. Do you remember Mama Loise saying that Wally didn't have much manly strength?"

"Yes, I do."

"And that the flame of being a woman was strong in Janice?"

"Yes."

"I believe she meant he was impotent. As for Janice, she was drawn to Chunga in a way that she couldn't resist. They would both have been in their early twenties at the time. Remember, he was a policeman in Plumtree and she was just down the road in Bizana."

Abigail knew that what Yudel was telling her was the truth. "And where do I come in?"

"He saw your photograph in *The Herald*. This is why he's been trying to be close to you ever since you got here. Any one of his men could have done what he did. He just wanted to be with you, and it was because you look so much like her."

"My God, Yudel, you can't be sure of this."

"You remember what Ephraim Khumalo told Freek about the way Chunga provided food to the starving community of Madikwe Falls? And old Loise told us she and the children were there. Now in the prisons, according to Mpofu, the seven have been eating better than the other prisoners, and this is not a country in which political prisoners are treated kindly. In each case a kindness . . . no, a father's caring . . . is camouflaged by helping others too. First the tiny community of Madikwe Falls, and now the other activists who were picked up with Tony. And all down the years, when money had come for the children, Loise had never known where it was coming from. On top of this, the Plumtree police brought the children to her. And Tony knew. I don't know how, but he knew. There's a passage in his writing that reads: *The corrupt seed, too, results in a harvest—but what is the value of such a harvest? Look only to the seed, for that is where the guilt lies.*"

Yudel fell silent for a moment, still in thought. "Is there more?" Abigail asked.

"Jonas Chunga knew that Tony had planted the bomb at party headquarters. Freek told me how Ephraim Khumalo had said that the CIO had enough evidence to prosecute, but never did. Helena told us that someone had tried to kill Tony. Soon after that, seven of the group were picked up by the CIO. Helena would snort at the idea of the CIO protecting them. And she would be right. It was Jonas Chunga's way of protecting his son. Picking up the others as well masked what he was really doing. His daughter had already killed herself, at least partly because of his politics."

Abigail had allowed the car to coast to a stop. "Yudel." Speaking had become very difficult. The wheels scraped against the pavement in front of a marble-faced building, one of the city's few with corporate pretensions. "I need you to drive now." The rain was thundering against the roof and windscreen of the car. She opened the door on her side.

"Should we change over now?" Yudel had to shout to make himself heard above the sound of the rain.

"We have to." Abigail struggled to get the words out. "I can't drive now."

Yudel and Abigail got out into the rain to change places. She stopped him in front of the car. Their clothes were already saturated by the torrent. Above the noise of the rain and with water cascading over her face, she shouted to Yudel. "He wanted Janice, not me? Are you certain?"

"Nothing in all this is certain, but I believe so."

"How terrible," she gasped, "but how wonderful, how damned liberating to know that I'm not really the one he wants."

Yudel's own confusion had been as great as Abigail's. Only since his meeting with Chunga had the confusion begun to clear, and only since seeing Loise's photograph had his thoughts crystalized.

In Yudel's view, one more matter could be left untouched, but it was not so for Abigail. "Did Jonas kill Krisj?"

She was reaching out to him with both hands. He took them in his. "We'll never be able to do anything about the killing of that man," he told her. "Let it go. Nothing can be done about it now."

She had brought her face right up to his to be able to hear him. "I can't let it go. Tell me."

There was no avoiding this woman. "I think he ordered the killing."

"Why? For what possible reason?"

Yudel could feel rainwater running down his back. In the light from the headlights he saw it pouring over Abigail's face, as if she were in a shower. "Helena and her friends all assumed that there is a connection between the attempts on Tony's life and the killing of

Patel. But the two had nothing to do with each other. I misunderstood Loise when she was unable to say directly what men saw in Tony that brought shame upon him. She thought there was nothing wrong with being that way, but that she knew men did not like it. I thought she was talking about his schizophrenia. Suneesha Patel had come much closer, telling me how she hated Tony's relationship with her husband. And Chunga's contempt for Patel had been clear. The idea that this Indian man of no importance was his son's lover would have been something Jonas Chunga would never be able to bear. If his finger was not on the trigger the night Patel died, then I feel sure he gave the order."

At last they got back into the car. "There's more, isn't there?" Abigail's voice sounded more secure now. A new strength had appeared with the powerful release of emotion.

"Yes. In my anxiety to learn everything, I've endangered us all. I tested all this by imputing his actions to Wally who, like Chunga, was also a police officer. I told him that I knew that Wally had gone over to the government side and that his daughter had killed herself for that reason. His reaction was profoundly enlightening. I thought he was going to attack me. I also lied to him about what the Five Brigade soldiers had done to Janice."

"Why, Yudel? For heaven's sake."

"I needed to see his reaction to try to establish that my thinking about him and Janice is right. But I fear that I went too far. He's no fool. Once he calms down, he'll realize what I was up to. I hope it's not before tomorrow."

Reaching the hotel, they ran through the rain for the entrance. The lobby was lit by candles. Perhaps the standby plant had failed. They crossed the lobby toward the stairs still running, scattering rainwater with every step. They were just starting up the stairs when the lights flickered briefly, then came on. "In this weather," Abigail said, "it's a miracle."

She stopped Yudel on the landing. Her face was filled with the wonder of a new discovery. "They're in the police cells in Plumtree, aren't they?"

Yudel looked into her excited face. "I believe so," he said.

In the gloom of the stairs, her eyes were bright points of light. "Jonas comes from that area and was in charge of the police station there. He would know the local police. And Plumtree is almost on the Botswana border, some five hundred kilometers from here. The length of time Paul Robinson says it took them to be delivered and for the truck to return is about right. They must be there, Yudel."

"The only way to find out is to go there."

"No," Abigail said. "There is another way."

48

There were no attendants on duty at the first filling station to which Helena guided Yudel. She had answered at the first ring when he called her. "We need your help," he had told her.

"Have I seemed reluctant so far?"

"Not in the slightest."

A wind had come up, sweeping the rain in long bursts under the roof that covered the pumps. The glass-fronted room where the attendants normally sought shelter was in darkness.

At the second, a handwritten sign read, "No petrol during power failures."

"Even when the power's on, it seems," Helena said. She stared at the lifeless pumps for only a moment. "I have an idea. I know a transport operator who owes me a favor. He has his own tanks."

"Let's go there," Yudel said. He was thinking about Rosa and whether Abigail had contacted her. He knew that this weather was their greatest ally. It was surely going to keep even Jonas Chunga and his CIO indoors. Few crimes were committed on such nights as these, few rebellions conducted and even fewer arrests made. Such matters were usually kept for better weather.

The transport operator's dwelling was in a few rooms behind his yard, where two small trucks were parked. Yudel could see the two-hundred-liter fuel tanks mounted on steel frames at above head-height. At least it was a gravity feed. If the power went off, the force of gravity could still be relied on. He could see no shelter anywhere. The dirt of the yard had already turned into a swamp. Water was pouring down the sides of the tanks. Yudel wondered if refuelling was possible without getting as much water as fuel into the car.

At the hotel, Yudel had ignored his damp clothing, saying he would change when there was a chance of it remaining dry. The water running down his back, which was only a little below his body temperature, had since been soaked up by his clothing, but he had cooled down with the relative inaction in the car. The fabric clung damply wherever it touched skin.

The motor gate was closed and padlocked, but a side gate stood open, hanging crookedly on its hinges. "I'll go," Helena said. "I know him." Without giving Yudel the opportunity to debate the matter, she was out of the car, leaving the door open, and splashing across the yard to bang on the door with her flat hand.

Yudel leaned across to close the door. The rain was already swirling through the doorway onto the passenger seat. He saw Helena bang on the door a second and third time. There were lights inside, but Yudel could see no movement. It was only after the fourth attempt that she tried the door handle. It opened immediately and Yudel lost sight of her as she tumbled inside and out of the rain.

He was still watching the door when she appeared again and waved for him to join her. As he ran across the yard, the thought came to him that the African thunderstorms of his experience were almost always violent, but short. This one did not seem to know the rules.

The front room was part storeroom, part lounge. It contained shelving on which sat cans of oil, spare oil filters, a few battered box files, a monkey wrench, assorted screwdrivers, a large bunch of keys and other necessities of life for the fat African man who was sitting on the linoleum floor. He was staring at Helena through glazed eyes. An empty bottle of cheap brandy, lying on its side next to him, made clear what had reduced him to his current state. A television set with bunny-ears antennae was producing nothing more than a vigorous snowstorm on its tiny screen. The man's face and hair were wet.

Helena was leaning over him. She had a wet kitchen cloth in

one hand. Her pointing finger was so close that, in Yudel's view, the transport operator risked losing an eye. "Ezekiel, I have an emergency. I must fill up from your tanks."

Ezekiel turned his head away to avoid the finger. With or without it blurring his vision, he was going to have difficulty focusing on Helena. "One hundred American, to fill up."

"Are you crazy? You want to get rich from me on one sale?"

He seemed to be trying to concentrate. "Eight hundred rands South African."

"You're out of your mind."

Ezekiel raised a finger of his own. "No discount," he said. He tried to rise, but instead lurched to one side and lost consciousness.

"Gordon, help me search for the keys to the gate's padlock." Helena was already looking around the room.

"Are we going to take the fuel without his permission?" Yudel felt uneasy at the thought.

"Do you see any alternatives?"

Ezekiel woke suddenly and blinked at his visitors. "Hard times," he assured them before his eyes again closed.

"You're telling me," Yudel said. He found the padlock key in one of Ezekiel's trouser pockets. Just like a small operator, he thought, keeping the important things close. "Now, how do we fill the tank in this rain?"

"I've seen him do it. He throws a tarpaulin over the tanks, the truck and everything. Then he runs the petrol in."

"It sounds jolly," Yudel said.

"If you've got fifty American dollars, that will do."

Yudel slipped it between two fingers of Ezekiel's right hand. The tarpaulin was in plain sight, rolled up on the floor next to the television set. Yudel looked at Helena for suggestions. "You'll have to get up on a chair," she said. "I'll hold it steady. Then you have to the throw the tarpaulin over one of the tanks and I'll pull it over the car as well."

"In this rain?"

"Can you think of another way?"

49

Abigail knew that the presence of the prisoners in Plumtree police cells was based on nothing more than a likelihood. She had the number she wanted from the Matabeleland directory, and she keyed it in. A surly voice mumbled, "Plumtree."

"Good evening," Abigail said. "This is Advocate Abigail Bukula. I would like to speak to the officer in charge."

"Not on duty," the voice said.

"Who's in charge now?"

"The inspector is in charge now."

"What's his name?"

"Inspector Marenji."

"Let me speak to him."

"He's outside." Nothing in his tone suggested that it might be possible to call the inspector.

"Go and get him."

"He's in the garage, checking vehicles."

"What's your name?"

"Charles," the voice said.

It was not exactly what Abigail had wanted, but it would do. "Constable Charles, I am a barrister of the High Court. Do you know what that means?"

"Yiss." The word slid out in an expulsion of air. "I know."

"I'm not calling at this time of night for a small matter. Get Inspector Marenji immediately. I'll wait."

"I'll get him."

"Thank you."

The handset was put down heavily, perhaps with unnecessary force, but Abigail could hear the sounds of voices and movement in the background. It was almost five minutes before a new voice came onto the connection. This one was lighter and sounded younger. "Good evening, ma'am," it said. "Inspector Marenji here."

"Good evening, inspector. Advocate Abigail Bukula here."

"Yes, ma'am, what can I do for you?" The inspector sounded friendly and businesslike.

"You have seven of my clients in custody. I have a High Court order for their release. I will be with you in a few hours to take them off your hands."

This time there was too long a pause before the inspector spoke. "Do you have their names?"

Abigail had the list of the seven before her. She read the names into the telephone. "Please prepare them for release by the time I get there."

Again the long pause, while the inspector thought about this. "Where are you now?"

"Not far away. I'll be with you shortly. I trust I won't have to wait."

"I'll have to talk to my sergeant."

"Talk to anyone you like. Just see that they're ready for me. I'll have the court order with me, signed by Judge Mujuru. Good evening." She hung up. For the first time she realized that her hands and face were both wet, this time with sweat. "They're there," she said to herself. "My God, they are there."

Abigail knew the country well enough to estimate that ordinarily it would take perhaps six hours to cover the four hundred and fifty kilometers to Bulawayo, and another hour from there to Plumtree.

She knew that her calculations were based on good weather and daytime driving. But now, at night and in this weather . . . The rain was drumming on the roof as insistently as before. She acknowledged that it could take twice that long, if they got through the roadblocks and if the rain had not washed away sections of the road. She looked at her watch and saw that the time was seven o'clock. I'll give us ten hours, she thought. If we're out of here in an hour, we'll be there before the local police or the CIO people are out of bed tomorrow morning.

One other critical matter remained. She already knew the answer, but she had to try. If flying were possible, that would change everything. A friendly voice from the airport answered at the first ring. "No, ma'am. Tonight's flight to Bulawayo has been canceled. Nothing is coming in or going out in this weather. The incoming Jo'burg flight has turned back to wait for morning."

"Thank you," Abigail said. "What time is tomorrow's first flight to Bulawayo?"

"O-nine hundred hours."

"Arriving there?"

"Eleven hundred, if there are no delays."

"Are there often delays?"

"Not always, ma'am, but sometimes," the friendly voice said.

I'll pray for delays, she thought. "Thanks."

Abigail hung up and started packing. It was a process that would take less than five minutes. Apart from clothing and the single file containing the documentation of the matter that had brought her to this place, there was only her laptop and its few accessories.

Something had changed in the storm, possibly the wind direction. The rain was beating against the window now. Streams of water flowed down the pane on the outside. Nothing was visible through the glass.

There was still no guarantee that Yudel and Helena would return with a full fuel tank, or when they would return. The only thing that was guaranteed was that they could not afford even the slightest delay.

Abigail was crouched in front of the cupboard, reaching for her spare pair of shoes, when she heard the door open, then close immediately. "Yes?" she asked.

She had the shoes in one hand and was starting to rise, still facing away from the door. Yudel must have arrived back sooner than she had anticipated. "You ready to go?"

"No, I'm not. It's a surprise to find that you are." The rich tones of Jonas Chunga's voice were unmistakable.

For Abigail, it would take a while before speaking was possible.

"Leaving now in this weather?" The voice was calm, but carefully controlled. Abigail could see none of the gentle amusement she had seen in his eyes before. "I understand there are no flights tonight. The storm has ruled them out."

"Is that so?" Getting the words out was not easy.

Chunga had moved to the bed. He sat down. "I'm afraid it is. You may as well unpack. It's not possible to go anywhere tonight. Or were you thinking of changing hotels?"

"No; this one is quite satisfactory." Her voice had risen a few notes. But where the hell was Yudel—and would he rush in, wet, expecting that they would be ready to go?

"I thought so. By current standards it's a pleasant enough place." Chunga leaned back on the bed in a posture of exaggerated relaxation. His eyes were cold, or were they pleading? The fingers of one hand beat a silent rhythm on the bedspread. He gestured vaguely in the direction of the stairs and the lobby. "I asked the manager about you and she said that you were booking out, but I corrected her. I told her that booking out on a night like this was not feasible. She must have misunderstood you."

"Thank you," Abigail said. I don't know where this is going, she thought, but don't come in now, Yudel. Stay away a little longer while I deal with this. This is something I have to handle myself. I don't know how, but I have to.

"Of course, that may prove to be a problem for your friend, Mr. Gordon. As I understand it, he has to be out of the country by tomorrow afternoon."

"I'm sure the weather will be better tomorrow." She hated the breathless, almost apologetic tone she heard in her voice. "These tropical storms don't usually last long."

"Quite so. I'm sure he'll be fine. I'll just sit here while you unpack."

"That's not necessary," Abigail said. She had control over her voice now. "We will be leaving in the morning, after all."

"Of course. Then why not sit down next to me?"

No, Abigail thought. I'm not sitting down next to you or across a dinner table from you, not ever again.

"Please." He was patting the bed next to him. "It's a comfortable bed. But you know that. You've been sleeping in it for a few nights now."

"Yes." But where do I go from here? she wondered. Should I be the regretful lover who never quite became a lover and has now realized that her heart belongs to her husband? Or the indignant advocate who orders him out of her bedroom? Or do I buy safe passage by giving him what he wanted all along? Or do I tell him I know that he never wanted me, that he still longs for my aunt?

"Where is Mr. Gordon, by the way?"

"He went out."

"Any particular destination?"

"I'm sure there must have been one, but he never shared it with me."

"What a pity. He is a very clever man, I have to admit. He almost succeeded in deceiving me this afternoon. I only realized what he'd been up to after he'd left. He and I have unfinished business. I'd best wait here until he returns."

But you aren't in his room, she thought. You're in mine. Then again, perhaps it's better that you aren't in his room.

Abigail had decided on her strategy. She did not have great confidence in it, but it was at least based on the one strength she knew she had. It was possible that her face, so like that of her Aunt Janice, still left him vulnerable. It had on every occasion so far. But then she knew nothing about his relationship with her aunt. With an effort, she produced a smile. "You know," she said, "you have had a powerful effect on me. I came very close to forgetting my marriage vows."

"Close, but not quite."

She could still see no sign of softening or flirtation in his face. "Especially last night."

"That's interesting. Everything about you has been interesting so far."

"I should think it has been more than just interesting," she said. How far can I go with this?

"It was interesting for me, but perhaps for you it was just a game, a tease. I think that's the commonly used word."

"It never was that." This time Abigail was telling the truth.

"A tease, because you thought you could use me in the quest for justice—what a word—for those clients of yours."

"No, Jonas. It was not that. For a few days I almost reached the point when I would have done anything for you."

"Almost."

"Yes, almost."

"But that's over, so there's nothing for me to do but to leave, I suppose."

Abigail knew at which moments silence provided the best argument. And she knew that this was one of them.

"I suppose it would be best if I left, and then tomorrow you and the Gordons can board your flight to Johannesburg. That seems like the obvious solution."

There was still no sense in replying, but now she knew that he did not intend leaving soon, at least not before Yudel returned. And what did he intend to do with Yudel then?

From beyond the wall, the sound of a heavy object falling to the floor reached them. Chunga's eyebrows rose in a bored imitation of surprise. "Rosa Gordon is a careless packer."

You bastard, Abigail thought, how do you even know her name? "That can't be her. She's not here; hasn't been for a few days."

"So you've had her husband all to yourself?"

Forget it, she thought. I'm not going to play your game. There was always the option of racing him to the door. She was closer than he was. But what would she do once she was on the other side of the door, if she even got that far? And perhaps he had a man waiting for him in the passage.

"Well, that's all I have to say." He rose and stretched, the picture of a middle-aged man waking from a slumber. "Good night, Abigail."

It was too easy, much too easy. To respond in any way would be to invite a reaction.

"Are you not going to bid me good night? How about a last kiss?"

The hand that reached out to take her behind the neck moved much too fast for her to avoid it. She was pulled toward him with sheer physical power that she was not able to resist. In the same movement, she was thrown onto the bed and pinned there by one strong arm pressing into her solar plexus.

This time there could be no pleading with him. The pressure of his hand eased a little as he changed position and she tried to roll free. A hand was at her throat, cutting off the air to her lungs. Her left hand was free. Its fingers found one of his eyes. "No," he cursed. A large hand flashed and she was pinned down again.

"Why, Jonas?" her voice rasped painfully. "There's no point to this."

"I think there is."

"Don't do this. You'll regret it later."

"No; you're the one who may regret it later." He was on the bed with her. The weight of his body made it impossible to break free. The hand at her throat moved and she could breathe again. She felt her blouse torn away in a single movement. She got one of her legs free. She aimed the knee at his testicles, but found only a fleshy thigh. "Before you struggle any further, know that you can't win." One of his hands was on her forehead, pressing her head down into the pillow. The other was at the zip of her trousers. She heard the fabric tear. "Abigail." In saying her name, the tone of his voice had changed. She heard something close to pleading in it now. "Abigail, I never wanted you this way. I wanted you to be my woman. Even now, I can give you so much." She was pinned down, but it was clear that he had stopped trying to hurt her. "It's not too late. It's still not too late."

"Jonas, it makes sense for us to stop and talk about this."

"You mean it makes sense for me to stop."

Her left hand found the hotel's reading lamp and she swung it hard, making sharp contact with the side of his head. For just a moment his grip weakened. She saw his right hand rise and the beginning of its descent. She ducked her head forward, pressing her face against his right shoulder. The punch scraped the back of her head. The second smashed against an ear. With her head burrowing into his shoulder, she was protected from his right hand. He tried with the left, but missed entirely. "I'll fucking kill you," he cursed. "I would have done anything for you."

She felt her trousers being torn away. The protective warmth of the fabric had disappeared. One of his legs was between hers, prying them apart. The fingernails of one hand found the skin of his face. She dug them in with the fury of desperation and heard his grunt of pain. Her fingers moved, finding new flesh to dig them into.

With a violent jerk he lifted both her hands above her head and pinned them there with one of his, leaving his other free. She felt him tear away whatever protective clothing remained.

I'm sorry, Robert, she thought. I know I got myself into this. Oh God, Robert, I'm sorry.

"You forced me into this. You've been looking for this ever since you got here." His face was pressed against hers, his mouth seeking hers. She could feel his erection against her upper thigh. Oh, Robert.

A loud crash and an avalanche of plaster shards that sprayed around her and into her face made her turn her face away. Her eyes closed involuntarily under this new assault. Chunga's body, so powerful a moment before, had become a deadweight. She pushed at him. Someone else was also pulling. The CIO director's body rolled to the side, falling heavily to the floor.

Abigail turned her head to one side to shake off the plaster dust and the pieces that seemed to be everywhere. Wiping it away to clear her eyes, her fingers closed around a larger piece. She opened her eyes and found that she had in her hand the still snarling head of the plaster tiger. One of the elephant's tusks rested in the hollow at the base of her throat.

Rosa was standing over her. "My dear, are you all right?" she asked.

"My clothes have seen better days, but I'm fine." She had rolled to the side and was sitting on the edge of the bed. "That's more than can be said for the tiger and the elephant. Christ, Rosa, I don't suppose it seemed to be consensual?"

"No, it didn't look terribly like it." Rosa sounded excited. She was staring at the unconscious body of Jonas Chunga on the floor. She had never before assaulted anyone, let alone rendered an officer of the law unconscious. It was the first time that Abigail had seen her composure shaken. It looked to her as if Rosa was having difficulty in believing that she was responsible for the state Chunga was in. "Men don't usually tear your clothing, when it's consensual. At least, Yudel never did."

Abigail was hanging on to Rosa and laughing softly in a state of barely controlled hysteria. "No, I don't suppose he did."

"And you're far too sensible a person for it to have been consensual," Rosa gasped.

I wish I believed that, Abigail thought. "We'd better get out of here. Where's Yudel?"

"I think I heard the car arrive downstairs as I was coming in here. Get into something else, but do hurry." Her chest was rising and falling furiously. "He's not dead, is he?"

"No. He's breathing."

"Then we must hurry. He's not going to be in this condition indefinitely."

50

Yudel had little interest in matters of a mechanical nature, but he did know how to remove the valves from car tires. He removed all four from the CIO double-cab that Jonas Chunga had parked in front of the hotel. To get it moving again would not be the simple matter of changing a tire.

It was still raining hard, but without the earlier violence, and this time he was sheltered by the hotel proprietor's umbrella. As he drove away from the hotel, he threw the valves, one at a time, into the yards of houses they were passing.

Helena had shown great enthusiasm for the sabotaging of the tires on Chunga's vehicle, encouraging him with assurances that she would never underestimate him again, and that she had never imagined him to have such street smarts. "Where can we drop you?" Abigail asked her.

"Like hell!" Even her agreement was couched in hostile terms. "I'm coming with you to Plumtree. You're going to need me."

Yudel drove toward Samora Machel Drive, the main artery that he knew led to the Bulawayo road. Rosa was in the seat next to him, with Abigail and Helena in the back. "Not this way," Helena said. "If he does know what we're doing, like maybe the Plumtree crowd may have called him, then there may already be roadblocks. We've got to stay away from Samora Machel for as long as we can. Once we're on the Bulawayo road there's nothing we can do about roadblocks. But in town, that's where they're likely to stop us."

The wipers were running at maximum speed, keeping the windscreen clear enough to give Yudel reasonable visibility. Ahead the road looked clear. A single pair of headlights, one of which was blinking intermittently, was approaching from the front. The pavements were empty. "I don't think they'll have roadblocks yet," he said.

"I hate it when you think you know my own country better than I do." Helena was leaning forward in her seat, her lips almost touching his ear. While she was speaking, a black double-cab moved out of a side street at an intersection almost a kilometer ahead, at which both the red and green traffic lights were burning brightly. Her voice dropped to a whisper. "Now, for Christ's sake, Gordon—go right here!"

He did as she instructed. The street they had entered was narrow. It passed the back of a sandstone structure that seemed to be a government building. "Left in front of the park there," Helena said, "but go slowly. Stop on the corner and let's look."

He stopped. The street sign told Yudel that they were in Josiah Tongogara Avenue. It was altogether empty. The light of a single working streetlamp showed the rain being blown at what was almost a forty-five-degree angle to the ground. He considered that the storm would have one clear advantage. It would make things more difficult for their pursuers, if they were being pursued. On the other hand, it had almost emptied the streets.

Two blocks ahead he could see the lights of what seemed to be a hospital. As he was pulling away, something in the electricity-supply system could no longer carry the load expected of it. The streetlights and the hospital lights went out together. The darkness was broken only by the headlights of their car and one other, approaching from the opposite direction. He could see no other signs of movement.

Abigail had her cellphone out. "No signal. Is that because of the power failure?"

"Maybe. I think so." Helena was nodding. "Straight ahead, Gordon. You're doing great . . ." After considering that statement, she added, ". . . so far."

They crossed street after street, stopping at each corner to look for signs of CIO or police presence. Twice they saw the headlights of vehicles, but both times they were at some distance and passed without any interest being shown in them.

Ahead, the road ended against what seemed to be open ground. "Stop just before the corner and switch off the headlights," Helena said.

Rosa turned to look at her. "My dear, we won't be able to see."

Yudel was bringing the car to a halt. As he switched off the lights, he reached across and placed a hand on hers. "What Helena means is that, in this weather, the only way they will be able to see us is by our headlights."

"Right on, Gordon. You're almost a Zimbabwean already."

Helena threw open the door on her side. "I'm going to look." Marjorie Swan's umbrella snapped open as she stepped into the rain.

From the car they could see little more than her silhouette; a dark form against the still deeper darkness. The road to the left fed into what was probably a main artery. A car came past from the right, its headlights a weak yellow. Helena had stepped back into the shelter of the street where they had stopped. They saw her briefly in silhouette as the car passed.

"I can't stand this." Abigail was opening the door on her side. "I have to see."

By the time she reached Helena, the activist had moved back into the shelter of the nearest building. Abigail reached out to touch her, but the other woman leaped at the touch, in the same movement turning to face her. "Christ, don't do that."

"I'm sorry." She had stopped next to Helena.

"Down there," Helena whispered.

In the distance, all of ten blocks from them, two sets of headlights were maneuvering back and forth in the road. While Abigail watched, the headlights of one fell on the other. For just a moment they could see the now-familiar shape and color of a CIO double-cab. Helena brought her lips right up to Abigail's ear. "Even if he came round as we left, they couldn't have gotten organized so fast. They're a bunch of incompetents."

"Jonas Chunga's not," Abigail said. "He didn't know he'd find us at the hotel. This is a precaution. He doesn't intend to let us out of Harare tonight."

"He can screw off," Helena said. "I hate the bastard."

"Don't switch on the lights till we've turned round," Helena said. "We need to go back a few blocks, then turn right again." The route she took led them back to Samora Machel Drive. "Go straight across it this time. When you're across, switch off the lights again."

"You're taking us around them," Yudel said. Some traffic had appeared on the artery. There were now a few cars and trucks, the drivers of which had braved the rain. They came past slowly, trying to avoid skidding, almost coming to a halt at a place where a blocked stormwater drain had caused a shallow lake to form across the road. Down the nearer gutter a torrent of rainwater was pouring over the pavement.

Yudel waited until the road was clear of all traffic, then crossed, staying in low gear through a stream of water in the nearer gutter. The engine note dropped for a moment as the car's tailpipe was submerged. Then they were through. On the other side the car bumped over a second gutter, splashing through water that was also running strongly, but not as deep. Most of the road was under water.

He switched off the headlights and stopped. "Where are they from here?" he asked Helena.

"A bit in front and a few hundred meters to the right, but that wasn't the roadblock. That's just a patrol. I've got to get out again."

This time both Yudel and Abigail followed, stopping next to her on the veranda of an old retail building. She was pointing in the direction of the Bulawayo road. "You see up there, at the top of the rise? That's Heroes Acre, where the heroes of the liberation struggle are buried. The road curves to the left there and drops behind the rise. There's also a hedge." A light flashed in the direction she had been indicating. "Did you see that?"

"Yes," Yudel said. He glanced at Abigail.

"I also saw it."

"That's probably the roadblock."

"And this will take us around them?"

"A track I know will take us past them. We'll cut back across to the main road once we've passed them."

"A dirt road?"

"There's no other way, unless we try to go through the roadblock."

"A dirt road will be swamp by now," Yudel said.

Abigail had been listening to the exchange. She felt it was time for her to enter the discussion. "There is no other way. If we try to go through the roadblock, that will be the end of our journey."

They hurried back to the car, splashing through puddles. Yudel moved it gently forward. Without headlights and with the rain still beating strongly against the windscreen, visibility was down to a few paces. At least the sound of the rain might drown out the engine noise, he thought.

"We have no choice but to go back to Samora Machel for a few blocks." Helena was still sitting forward, her head between Yudel and Rosa. "Just a little way. Leave the lights off."

There was no sign of the CIO patrol now. Light traffic was moving slowly in both directions. To their left, the shining tower that was the ruling party's headquarters and the scene of Tony's explosion looked down on Harare. On the rise that was now perhaps half a kilometer ahead, a car was slowing. Its brake lights reflected brightly off the wet road.

"He's stopping for the roadblock," Helena said. The car's lights faded from their field of vision as it passed behind an obstruction. They could see no other sign of the roadblock. A car coming from the front flashed its lights to warn them that theirs had not been switched on.

They traveled the next block as slowly as before. Away to the right, farther than Yudel thought the roadblock would be, something flared and flickered, the light a fire would make. To survive the rain, it would need to be under shelter.

"Go left here, at the end of the block," Helena directed him.

Yudel guided the car around the corner and onto the promised dirt road, moving even more slowly than before. The houses had fallen away, and they were passing through a maize field where the plants were more than head-height. The roadblock would be ahead and to their right, but the maize blocked their view in that direction. It would also give them shelter from the roadblock. The dirt surface of the road had turned to mud, just as Yudel had prophesied. It was smooth and slippery, even when traveling slowly.

The maize cover broke as they crossed a makeshift bridge of fuel drums and concrete over a stream that was now flowing strongly.

The car crept forward at walking pace. They had a view, partly obscured, of stationary headlights that were still burning. Yudel thought he saw the roof outlines of two double-cabs. One seemed to be parked across the road, cutting its usual width. The other may have been facing away from them in the direction of Bulawayo, ready to give chase if anyone tried to jump the roadblock. In the briefest flash he saw men in rainwear, carrying torches. A torch was being shone into the face of the driver whose car had been stopped. The driver was gesticulating with both hands as he tried to explain something to the men manning the roadblock.

The rain was a still a steady downpour, angling toward them. Yudel edged the car forward. He wondered what the men at the roadblock would see if they looked in their direction. There may have been a reflection off the windows, except that with the city's power down, there was so little light.

The track dipped, and the screen of maize cut off their view of the road. Yudel only saw the turn in the track as the stalks of maize swept toward him. He swung the steering wheel, but the car broadsided gently over the edge of the track. He tried to compensate, but it kept going in a slide so slow that it might have been a television replay on a sports program. The wheels reached a fringe of hard veld grass. The maize was brushing against the windows on his side. The car lurched to a stop and the engine choked off. Somewhere to the right, above the sound of the rain, Yudel could hear the sound of running water.

Helena was patting him anxiously on the shoulder. "This is not working. If we hit plowed land here we won't get the car out tonight."

"You want me to switch on the lights?"

"No. I'll walk in front and you just follow me."

Rosa sounded horrified. "In this rain?"

"I've got the umbrella." She opened the door and was already getting out. With her head bowed and the umbrella held low, sheltering her from the wind, Helena made her way to the front of the car. First she guided Yudel back onto the track, then she started down the trail. To Yudel she was only a vague figure in the darkness, but one he could follow. He stayed close, keeping the center of the car directly behind her.

"That umbrella will only shelter her above the waist," Rosa said. "Perhaps not even. She's going to catch her death."

"She can be such a pain, but, heaven knows, she's got guts." Abigail sounded admiring. "She's probably right. We couldn't have made it without her."

Yudel was squinting into the darkness beyond the rain-washed windscreen. "We haven't made it yet."

The track twisted to the right and rose toward higher ground. "I can see them." Abigail was on her knees, looking out the side window.

A glance over his right shoulder gave Yudel the view she had. The double-cabs were barely visible, but the beams of their headlights were shafts of bright light. "Is there traffic through the roadblock?" he asked.

"A small truck, I think. That car has either been let through or turned back." While Abigail watched, the driver of the truck got out, shielding his head with what looked like a newspaper. One of the CIO men was walking to the back of the truck. "They're taking no chances. It looks like everyone gets out and every car and truck gets searched."

Along the crest of the rise, a sudden screen of scrub cut off their view of the road and again gave them shelter. Underfoot, the track had hardened and flattened. The rain was lighter now. Helena had broken into a jog. She had folded the umbrella and was holding it in one hand. The maize had fallen away and they were passing through a small village of laborers' cottages. After a flat stretch of perhaps another hundred meters, Helena stopped and stepped aside. Yudel brought the car to a halt next to her and she got in, shivering and gasping for breath. With a bump, the car was back on the tar of the Bulawayo road. Yudel stopped on the verge. The roadblock was a few hundred meters behind them, and clearly visible. The headlights of the double-cab that was facing in their direction had been switched off. "What now?" He found himself whispering.

"Just go and keep the lights off," Helena said. "And hope that they don't look our way and, if they do, that they don't switch those headlights on."

Uniformed police officers at the roadblock were busy with two cars they had stopped. The CIO men too would be more interested in the cars they had stopped than in what was happening on the road behind them. From their point of view, it should have been empty.

Yudel moved the car smoothly forward. In the rearview mirror he could see the lights of the CIO vehicles. Helena's teeth were chattering and she had both arms wrapped around herself. "The road will drop down into a depression a bit further on. Then you can switch the lights back on."

From behind, the weak light of distant headlights reached them, momentarily casting the shadow of the car onto the road in front of them. It lasted only a few seconds, then the road dipped and the headlights were no longer reaching them. The roadblock too had disappeared from sight.

51

He had been trying to drive the girl from the cell he shared with three of the men, but could not. Tony Makumbe heard her weeping as from a distance, faintly, the sound slowly growing in volume.

He could see her now. She was no more than six or seven, and small for her age. He could also see the body of his mother where she had fallen when they killed her. He knew that they had been fleeing through the bushveld night. His face had been scratched by thorns and dry branches. His hands were bloodied where he had touched the scratched places. They had fled and hidden, but when the soldiers came their mother had told them to sit down and be quiet, and she had gone to meet them alone.

And now Katy was crying in the cell. It seemed she would never stop.

He remembered the time when she said that now she knew everything, and he remembered also that everything had been too much for her. And he remembered finding her after she had fired the single shot, and what it had done to her face and head. Every moment of his life since then had been dominated by the memory of her dying.

The sound of crying subsided. Katy had not left the cell, but she was farther away, standing pressed against the far wall. He expected to hear her crying all his life and beyond this life, if that were possible.

She had been quiet that night until the soldiers left. Then the crying had started.

He remembered the bayonet at the end of the rifle barrel and how a light from the village had reflected from it. And he remembered what the soldier had done with it.

The next morning that man had come and taken them away.

And the story had not ended there. Now Krisj was dead, and the story had not yet ended. He knew how it had to end. He was as sure of it as if it had already taken place.

The others were all asleep. Tony rose from the mat and walked across the cell to stand below one of the two windows. He felt stronger than he had for some time. A few days before, he had not been able to walk at all. Through the opening he could see the stars. It had been raining, but the rain had stopped hours before and now the night was clear and cool. He loved such nights as these, when the heat of the day was gone, but there was no cold, only a richness of the air that made you feel part of the night itself.

They had brought all eight of them, the original seven plus one of the Makwati twins, to this place. At one point during the afternoon he had been taken from the cell and brought to Sergeant Mafuta's office. Since he was a boy he had known the sergeant, who was an old man now. The sergeant had told him about the court order for their release issued by Judge Tendai Mujuru. He also told him that very few government people even knew that the members of Tony's group were in custody.

He had told Tony that he expected that many government people would believe that the court hearing and everything that went with it had simply been part of a plot to discredit the country. It was the first time that Tony or any of the others had heard of the court order. The sergeant had also told Tony not to be too optimistic. He had orders to continue holding them. He was sorry, but there was nothing he could do about it.

The last thing he said was that he would try to contact Tony's father to see if he could help.

"My father is dead," Tony had told him.

"You know who I'm talking about," the sergeant said.

"My father died long ago. That man you are talking about is not my father."

"But he is interested in you. I'll try to speak to him about your release. He has seen to it that you and your friends are well fed." Tony had said nothing more. He knew the sergeant meant well, but he had no more to say about the man Sergeant Mafuta called his father. "I'm glad to see that you are well, Tony," the sergeant had added. "I know you've been sick, and it's good to see that you are well."

"Yes, I'm very well, thank you, Sergeant Mafuta."

Tony knew that the sergeant had also lost relatives in the Gukurahundi raids and that he had refused promotion to Harare because he did not want more authority than that of a local station commander. Tony expected that he would hold them no longer than he had to, but as he had said, there was nothing he could do. Tony knew that he meant well, but also believed that the old sergeant was simply excusing himself. Like so many others, he had found that it served the chances of survival to keep your opinions to yourself and to obey orders from above.

Looking up at the stars, Tony felt that he was in control. He was confident now, sure in the knowledge that he was ready to meet what he knew lay ahead. As for the man the sergeant had referred to as his father, for the first time he knew he had the strength to deal with him too. It had not always been so, and he was still uncertain of what he had to do, but he was sure that he would know when the time came and that he would be able to do it.

The stars were lovely, the night was fine and gently warm, and he felt stronger than he ever remembered feeling, all his life.

52

The car jerked violently, but Yudel steadied it without much difficulty. It had been going at no more than eighty kilometers an hour when they hit the pothole. The road surface had been almost perfect until then. He brought it to a stop with two wheels on the tar and the other two on the gravel verge.

Unlike holes in dirt roads, those in the tar easily destroyed tires if you hit one wrong. Even if you were going slowly, the sharp edges of the tar around the pothole could tear right through a tire. And once you were using the spare you had to slow right down. Losing a second tire disabled you completely. Some farmers carried three or four spares on their Land Rovers.

The pothole had been filled with water, making it harder to spot in the headlights. Yudel had rarely allowed the speedometer to climb above ninety at any time, but had still hit it with more force than the tire could handle. It had been all but shredded. "Stay in the car," he instructed the three women, as he got out.

Of them, only Rosa obeyed. "Do you know how to change a tire?" Helena was almost pushing him out of the way to get a better look. "Otherwise we should look for help."

"I can do it," Yudel said. It was a matter of manly pride.

The rain had all but stopped. Only a light drizzle remained of the storm. He found the jack and wheel spanner in the trunk where they were supposed to be. Where he had stopped the car, the damaged tire was just off the tar on a muddy verge. Yudel managed to position the jack so that it was anchored on the edge of the tar. The place where they had stopped was on a slight incline to the front. He packed small rocks in front of the tires to stop the car rolling forward. By his calculation, the incline was not steep enough to affect the working of the jack.

It was a good hydraulic jack. Soon the car was rising with relatively little effort from Yudel. "Good stuff," Helena said. It took the car's weight and the tire was just lifting clear of the ground when the patch of tar on which the jack rested, undermined by the rain, broke free and slid away. The car came down hard, throwing Yudel onto his back. "Shit," Helena said.

"We'll have to move it deeper onto the tar," Yudel told her.

He removed the rocks that were steadying the wheels, got back in behind the wheel, restarted the engine and maneuvered the car another handsbreadth further onto the tar. Visibility was still poor, and he was afraid to go any deeper into the road. If there was any traffic from the rear, they might not be seen until it was too late.

This time the jack would not cooperate. The fall, with the car's weight descending on it at an angle, had bent its shaft. "This is not going to work," Helena said. "I saw this happen to a jack once before."

Abigail was looking down the road in the direction they had come from. On the right-hand side of the road, not far ahead, some white-painted walls were just visible. Another car came past slowly, without stopping. Its headlights revealed a sign that announced the presence of Halfway Motel. A glance at her watch told her that it was nearly midnight.

Yudel had the jack in his hands and was looking at it, as if willpower alone would repair it. He looked very tired. "I'll go to the motel," he said. "They'll be able to help us."

"Yes," Helena said. "I'll also come."

The rain had stopped being an issue. The gate of the motel was standing half open, as if someone had passed through it on foot and forgotten to close it. Even across the distance from the gate to the reception building, Yudel could see that some of the window-panes were broken, and that there were no curtains. "Shit," Helena said. "I hate it when it's like this. Is nothing left of my poor country? I don't suppose we'll find any tools."

Yudel was peering in at a window. The room was empty. A few broken pieces of plaster were scattered around the floor. "They would have taken the tools when they left," he said. "Let's go back."

As they reached the gate, a heavy transport rig, pulling a trailer, lumbered up the incline from the front. Its headlights revealed Abigail, waving both hands in the light rain. The truck rumbled to a stop next to their car, blocking the road. They could see the driver climbing down, leaving the engine running. Abigail was talking to him and pointing toward the offending wheel.

Yudel was too far away to hear her saying, "I've seen you before, a few days ago, outside Chikurubi prison."

"Yes, ma'am," Bino D'Almeida said. "You told me I was late."

"My name's Abigail."

"Bino." The drizzle was forming little globules on his mustache. They glistened in the light from the car. He was grinning at Abigail.

"What are you doing here?" she asked.

"I had to make a delivery in Bulawayo after dropping off the load at the prison."

"It took you a long time."

"Ma'am, deliveries sometimes do take a long time in this country."

"I'll bet they do," she said. "We have a problem, Mr. Bino."

"Mr. D'Almeida," he corrected her. "But I'd prefer it if you called me Bino. What's the problem?"

"We have a flat and a faulty jack."

"Can I help?"

Abigail could not help returning his rain-wet grin. "Would you?"

Bino brought his rig round the car to park behind it on the Harare side. The hydraulic jack he fetched from his cab was big enough to lift wheels of the rig off the ground. It took him only a few seconds to have the side of the car where the problem existed lifted well clear of the ground, and not much longer to change the tire.

On his return from the deserted motel, Yudel watched Bino with the slight embarrassment of the amateur for the professional. Bino came up to him, still smiling, not as warmly as when he was talking to Abigail. "You were driving, sir?"

Yudel nodded. "I'm afraid so."

"Did you see the pothole you hit?"

"No, I didn't see it."

"The ones to watch out for are the ones that come sneaking across from the side of the road. They're harder to spot than the others. There are usually some of them after heavy rain."

"Thanks. We really do appreciate what you've done."

"The potholes are also harder to spot when they're full of water."

"Thanks a lot."

"That's okay."

Abigail had come closer and was about to thank Bino again, when the first black double-cab came past. The light above its registration plate was working perfectly, and it was impossible to miss the CAM registration. Abigail stepped closer to the car, as if seeking shelter. The double-cab slowed sharply. She saw that Yudel too had seen it. The way Bino's rig was parked, they would not have seen the car as they approached. Now they would have to turn or look back before seeing it.

The double-cab came to a stop opposite the gate of the deserted motel. At almost the same moment, a second, identical vehicle came past, braking hard when the driver saw that the first one had stopped. The stop lasted no more than a few seconds, then both vehicles were moving again, their tail lights shrinking quickly into the distance.

Bino had noticed the reactions of the people around him. He spoke to Abigail. "Do you have problems with those people?"

Abigail looked into a concerned and innocent face. She asked herself if there was any reason to trust this man with even a small part of the matter that threatened to consume all of them. She spoke before she had received an answer. "Yes, we do."

"That's the CIO, ma'am. You want to stay away from them."

Abigail stepped forward and kissed him on one cheek. "Thanks, Bino. We'll do our best to stay out of trouble."

"Please," he said. "I'd hate to think of you getting into trouble with them. They're very strict. Good luck. I got to go now."

"You also take care," Abigail said.

They watched Bino's rig disappear in the direction of Harare. "Shall I drive for a while?" Abigail asked Yudel.

"Are you up to it?" He was looking at her through tired, blinking eyes.

"Yudel, I'm so strung out, I couldn't possibly fall asleep at the wheel. You and Rosa get in the back and sleep for a few hours."

Rosa, who had been no more than an interested spectator, felt that this was at last her territory. "Yes, Yudel, you need to rest. Come on."

"Jesus." Helena's hands were facing the heavens in mock supplication. "I can't believe we're discussing seating arrangements. Did you people see who came past us? Our friend, Director Chunga, is in one of those. Aren't we interested in that?"

Abigail put an arm around her shoulders. She was beginning to feel warm toward this restless, combative woman. "Yes, we all saw it. And we all guessed that he may be in one of them and that they are most certainly going to the same place we are, and that they're traveling faster than we are. We also saw that they're looking for a place to spend the night. While they're sleeping, we'll keep traveling."

Helena looked at Yudel, who was nodding in agreement with Abigail's assessment of their situation. "I hate it when you two communicate like this without saying anything. How's a person supposed to know?"

53

This new roadblock was no more than five kilometers outside Plumtree in the harsh bush country they had been traveling through for the last hour. Yudel was driving again, with Abigail in the front passenger seat. As far as she could see, it consisted of a single police van and six or seven policemen. None of the CIO double-cabs were in sight. It was seven o'clock, later than she had anticipated, but before most of the town would have risen.

A small truck laden with watermelons was just being allowed through. Three of the officers had stepped into the road to wave them down. "We're expected," Abigail said.

Yudel brought the car in slowly and stopped at the side of the road, as directed. The officers approached Yudel's window. One came right up to it and the others stopped just behind him. "Driver's license, sir." Yudel got the card from his wallet and handed it over. "South African?"

The driver's license made that clear. Yudel saw no reason to answer the question.

As for the officer, he gave the impression of studying the license before asking his next question. "Is a Mrs. Abigail Bukula traveling with you, sir?"

"Have we committed some offense, officer?" Seated behind him, Rosa was wondering how serious an offense it was to knock out a senior member of the CIO, using a garish plaster ornament.

But Abigail was already getting out on her side. She walked

briskly around the car, holding out a hand of greeting. "Good morning, inspector." She had read his rank on his shoulder badge. "I'm Advocate Abigail Bukula." Her manner was both friendly and businesslike. To Yudel's astonishment, despite having had only an hour's sleep in the relative discomfort of the car's backseat, she looked as fresh as she had the previous morning in Harare. "I suspect you're looking for me."

The inspector took the offered hand. He swallowed as he shook it. "Ma'am, I've been instructed . . ."

Abigail waved a hand dismissively. "I can imagine, inspector. You don't need to tell me. I'm on my way to the police station. Perhaps you'd like to follow us."

The inspector seemed to be a reasonable man. If his orders were to bring her in, but she was going in of her own accord, there was nothing more to say. "All right, I'll drive behind you," he told her. Then he added uncertainly, "You are going directly to the police station?"

"We have no other stops, inspector."

In the car, Helena was sitting forward on the edge of the seat as was her way, her chin almost touching Yudel's shoulder. "Jesus, she's got style. I'll give her that. What are we going to do when we get there?"

"We're not going to do anything," Yudel said. "Abigail's going to do it."

Plumtree police station was housed in an old single-story building, and had not seen maintenance for many years. It had the spacious veranda, wide doors, big rooms and broad passages of those times, but it had never been much more than a fairly humble dwelling. Most of the guttering was missing, only the brackets intended to secure it remained in place. The result was a chain of shallow pools of water along the walls of the building. A wire fence of more than head-height surrounded the property. The police station was in the center of the loose scattering of shacks and old houses of which Plumtree consisted.

A line of four officers was waiting on the veranda. Yudel drove through the open gate and stopped the car in the unpaved parking area. In the rearview mirror he saw the police truck arriving, but they parked in the street outside. The car had barely stopped moving when Abigail was out and advancing on the four officers, briefcase in hand. "I need to speak to the commanding officer." She approached them in the same businesslike manner she had used at the roadblock.

"I'm in charge," a young officer said. He glanced in the direction of the other officers, but took a step back as she reached the veranda.

"Good. Let's go to your office."

"This way," he said, backing into the charge office.

Abigail feigned surprise. "You don't have your own office? You just told me that you're the officer in charge."

"Look, ma'am. I have instructions . . ."

"Don't tell me about your instructions." She was already taking the court order from her briefcase. "They don't interest me. Here is an instruction from the High Court." She handed it to him.

The officers who had been on the veranda had followed them in. Two more were behind the counter. Yudel, with Helena following, was forcing his way between two officers.

The young officer was reading the court order, doing his best to look and sound like a man in authority. "Who says these people are here?" Around him his juniors frowned, their jaws clamped tight. They were, after all, the law in Plumtree.

Abigail did not seem to have noticed them. "I say so, Judge Mujuru says so, and Director Jonas Chunga of the CIO says so. By the way, are you Inspector Marenji?"

His retreat was sudden and complete. "Yes, I'm Marenji. I'll have to call the sergeant."

Abigail adopted her surprised look. "You said you were in charge here."

"I am, but the sergeant . . ."

Having seen the first signs of weakness, Abigail instinctively went on the attack. She pointed a finger at the officer. "Do you know what you're holding?"

"Yes, I understand . . ."

"Then deliver my clients to me immediately. This court order does not leave any room for you or your sergeant to make decisions on the matter." Yudel was close behind her now, trying to look as angry and determined as Abigail sounded.

"Yes, I know, but my sergeant is the one who must decide."

"There's a telephone number on that document. Call it and speak to Judge Mujuru."

The inspector had probably never in his life addressed even a single word to a judge of the High Court. "My sergeant . . ." he said and let the thought trail away. To one of the officers behind the counter, he said, "Get Sergeant Mafuta on the line and tell him to come."

The man started dialing the number. But Abigail was not yet through with the men of Plumtree police station. She waved a hand in a circular motion intended to take in all the men around her. "Do we need all these people in the room? Don't these officers have anything to do with their time?"

The number of officers in the room started to thin out immediately, apparently having decided that they did indeed have other things to do with their time. The officer at the counter succeeded in making contact with the sergeant. The young inspector took the phone from him. "She's got a court order, signed by Judge Mujuru, saying those prisoners must be released."

Thank you, Abigail thought. At least you seem to understand.

Inspector Marenji hung up and looked worriedly at Abigail. "He's coming."

"I hope this is not going to take too long," she said.

The inspector's chin lifted noticeably. He looked straight into Abigail's eyes. "Look, ma'am. I've done my best. I've treated you with respect, and my sergeant is coming. I've done everything in my power. I can't do more."

Having taken her authority act as far as it would go, Abigail turned to her other major weapon. She smiled and took a step closer to the inspector. "I know you have. Thank you for your efforts."

"The sergeant lives close by, very close. He won't be long."

From a corner of the room a radio crackled into life. "Plumtree. Come in, Plumtree."

The sound of the voice was overlain with static and there was too much treble in the sound, but Abigail recognized Jonas Chunga's voice immediately. She tried to distract the young inspector. "Yes, I do appreciate what you're . . ."

But this time her intervention was not effective. "Excuse me," the inspector said. "I have to get this."

"Come in, please, Plumtree," Chunga called again, the noise level rising around his voice.

"Plumtree here. Over."

"Who's that? Who'm I speaking to?"

"Inspector Marenji here. Over."

"Listen, inspector, this is Director Jonas Chunga of the CIO. I am well-known to your sergeant. You have . . ." The noise level rose again and engulfed what remained of the sentence.

"Bad reception?" Abigail suggested.

"It often happens. It just depends where you are. If you're in a dip, you sometimes lose contact."

Out of the corners of her eyes Abigail saw Yudel moving forward. "What's its range?" The question sounded innocent, even to Abigail.

"Thirty, forty k's—no more than that."

Twenty minutes, Abigail thought. Half an hour if we're lucky. The crackling from the radio started again. Maybe not as long as that, she thought.

"Plumtree, damn you . . ." And then Chunga's voice was gone again.

The inspector looked at the offending radio as if it were responsible for the problem. When he turned back to Abigail, his eyes widened. "Here's Sergeant Mafuta."

The sergeant, a broad-shouldered man carrying far more weight than he should have been, was coming laboriously up the veranda steps. He paused to catch his breath. By now, the only other officers in the charge office, apart from the young inspector, were the two behind the counter. He went past Abigail to his inspector, and took Judge Mujuru's order from him.

Abigail could not know about his talking to Tony during the night, or how well he knew Tony. She saw him as the kind of African man she had known all her life, taking charge, sensitive about others invading their territory, wanting recognition, but equally ready to give it. She said nothing. It was just possible that this man might be an ally. But it was only a possibility. It would be a rare police sergeant who dared stand up to a CIO director.

Sergeant Mafuta read the court order. He spoke to the inspector. "Have you established the authenticity of this?"

"No, sir, I have not . . ."

"Phone the number of the judge's office and do it immediately."

And how long will this take? Abigail wondered. Silence was now not possible. "Sergeant, my name is Abigail Bukula. I am an advocate of the South African High Court and a barrister of the Zimbabwean High Court. I . . ."

The sergeant looked sternly at her and held up a hand to stop the flow of words. "If this document is genuine, you may have your clients. This will not take long."

"Thank you, sergeant."

Behind the sergeant the two-way radio again burst into life with Chunga's voice. "Plumtree, come in immediately."

The inspector started toward it, but the sergeant grabbed hold of an arm, stopping him. "And this?"

"It's Director Chunga. I think it's about these people."

"Plumtree, where the hell are you?"

Sergeant Mafuta went to the radio and turned the volume down to zero. Chunga's demanding tones faded, then disappeared. He tapped the inspector on the chest with a thick finger. "The judge's office."

"Sir." The word was a verbal salute. The inspector keyed in the number of the judge's office. The sergeant's arms were folded across his chest. His face seemed to be puffed up by some inner pressure. "May I speak to Judge Mujuru?" the inspector said into the phone. "It's Inspector Marenji of Plumtree police station. I need to talk to him about some prisoners we're holding. He has issued an order for their release." He turned to the sergeant. "They're calling him." The sergeant nodded.

Abigail turned to look through the open double doors of the charge office. It gave them a good view of the police station yard and the dirt road beyond the fence. There was still no sign of the two CIO double-cabs. Could they possibly have been on their way to some other place? But the range of the radio was no more than thirty or forty kilometers, the inspector had said. Bulawayo was the nearest town, and it was over a hundred kilometers away.

"Good morning, sir. Inspector Marenji of Plumtree police station here. We are trying to verify the authenticity of a court order that has your signature on it."

"Speakerphone," the sergeant grunted. "I want to hear the old bastard."

The inspector activated the speaker phone, and the judge's voice burst into the room. ". . . court order is this? When was it issued?"

The inspector told him. "Shall I read the names? Joyce Mawere, Petra Jones . . ."

"I know the matter," the judge cut in. He cleared his throat. "This is a particularly delicate matter. I would appreciate you calling the office of Director Jonas Chunga of the Central . . ."

The pressure inside the sergeant seemed to have increased since he first heard the judge's voice. "Are you saying this court order is invalid, judge?" he roared.

"Who's this? Who's this? This is a different voice."

"This is Sergeant Mafuta. All I want to know—is this a valid court order? Is this your signature?"

"Yes, yes. But I'm saying all I want you to do is . . ."

"I want to know if this order is valid, that's all." The sergeant's chest was rising and falling with indignation. To Abigail he was reacting like a man from the Ndebele minority who had put up with too much from senior government people. "Did you issue it?"

"Yes, of course . . ."

"And have you issued another order countermanding it?"

"But what I'm saying is—this is a delicate matter. You should discuss it first with . . ."

The sergeant's voice dropped to a lower level. "I'm not a politician, judge. You've given me a court order, and I'm going to act on it."

"I think it would be wise . . ."

"Goodbye, judge."

"You need to consider the repercussions for your career." The judge was trying without success to hide his anxieties.

The sergeant hung up. It could be that all his life he had considered too many repercussions, and that now it was impossible to consider any more of them. "Release the prisoners," he said to the inspector.

The inspector took a step toward the entrance to a passage that led deeper into the building. "Shouldn't we call Director Chunga?"

The sergeant pointed toward the passage. "Get the prisoners." He waved the court order. "This says they must be released. I've got nothing to do with the CIO."

The inspector's eyes were wide with alarm, but he did as he had been ordered. The sergeant turned to Abigail. "Wait here, please. Your clients are coming." He left by the same doorway as the inspector.

"Jesus." Helena was bobbing up and down on the balls of her feet. "I can't believe this. Should I get a taxi for them?"

"Perhaps that's not a bad idea," Abigail said. She had also noticed the one lone minibus taxi parked just off the highway. The taxis seated at least twelve people. There would be plenty of room for the seven and for the Makwati girl. Helena ran for the door.

"This is so wonderful." Rosa was standing just inside the door. "Congratulations, Abigail. What an achievement."

One of the policemen behind the counter crossed to the radio and turned up the volume. Immediately Chunga's voice was in the room. "Where are these people? Plumtree? Come in, over." This time there was no static, and the signal was strong.

"Plumtree here. Over," the officer said.

"Who's in charge there?" Chunga demanded, adding "over" as an afterthought.

"Sergeant Mafuta. Over."

"Get him for me. Get him for me now."

As the officer ran for the passage into which the sergeant had disappeared, the phone on the counter rang and the remaining policeman behind the counter answered. Abigail saw Yudel move quickly to the radio and reach behind it. He jerked hard at something, then stepped away, turning his back on the radio. "What?" she whispered.

"Antenna." His voice was so low that she could barely hear it.

Now there were voices from the passage, the mumbled sounds of more than one person. A female voice was asking, "Where are we going?" A male voice answered that they were going to the Harare Holiday Inn, at government expense.

The inspector came into the charge office first, followed by the eight activists. Tony Makumbe, who came in last, was the only one Abigail recognized. "Good morning, people," she said. "I trust you're ready to travel."

"Who are you?" a small yellow-skinned woman asked.

"My name is Abigail Bukula. I'm your legal representative. This is my colleague, Mr. Gordon."

"We're going to court?"

The inspector had stepped between Abigail and her clients. "The court hearing is over. You are all free to go." He passed a sheet of paper to Abigail. "I need you to sign this, ma'am."

"Thank you, inspector," she said.

It had taken a moment for the seven to comprehend the reality of their position. "We're free," a voice said. "Is that right? Who hired you?"

"Krisj Patel contacted me, but we have to go."

"Krisj? When?"

"Krisj did it," Abigail said. This was no time for explanations.

The yellow-skinned woman was hugging one of the men. Others were shaking hands. One of the women kissed Yudel. But their voices stayed low. The celebration was real, but there was a subdued element to it. Perhaps it was just possible that the reason for the celebration may not be real. Freedom was not yet complete.

Of the seven, only Tony showed no emotion. He was still in the doorway that led to the cells, leaning against the wall. Abigail made her way through the muted happiness. She took one of his hands in both of hers. "Tony, I'm your cousin."

"I'm pleased to meet you." She was not sure that what she saw on his face was a smile. "Thank you for all you've done."

Abigail moved her grip to his arm. "We must go." She looked at his face, but could not read the expression. He was looking past her.

With Abigail leading and Yudel coming behind to herd the stragglers, they arrived on the veranda. There was no sight of Helena and the taxi. Abigail looked for Yudel, but her eyes caught the figure of the sergeant. He was at a window, observing the scene, his arms folded across his chest.

54

Abigail was still looking at the sergeant when, at the end of the street, the two double-cabs turned the corner and accelerated toward them. They passed the police station and continued to the next intersection, where they both swung hard to the right, then reversed, blocking off that exit completely. They had barely stopped when two more double-cabs entered the street from the same side. They stopped almost immediately and blocked off the street at that intersection.

No one on the veranda spoke. Down in the street, the four black double-cabs were in position. There was no immediate movement from any of them. Then the front passenger door of the nearest one opened and Jonas Chunga stepped out. Now doors were opening on all of the vehicles, and CIO agents were following the example of their boss. He came as far as the gate before stopping. Four agents fell in behind him. At the other end of the street, six more agents had spread across its width.

Chunga said nothing and showed no sign of coming closer. Yudel looked for Inspector Marenji, but he had retreated into the charge office. Abigail was first to move. In a corner of her vision she saw Yudel step forward. The finger of one hand fluttered. "No," she said. "I have to go alone."

Abigail stepped carefully off the cement apron of the veranda and onto the dirt of the yard. Jonas Chunga was no more than fifteen or twenty meters away, surrounded by the evidence of his power, the agents who would follow his orders without question.

They may have seen him kill and may have killed for him. She started slowly across the uneven surface, picking her way. To fall, even to stumble, would be a sign of weakness. And weakness was not something she could afford.

Abigail picked a spot that she guessed to be halfway between herself and Chunga, a patch of cement that may have been the remains of a structure that had once stood there. She stopped at her chosen spot and waited for him to come to her.

His face was clearly visible to her now. The determined set to the jaw, the direct gaze, the complete stillness of features and hands: she had seen it all before. But I will come no closer, she thought. You will have to move too, my friend.

And will you move? she wondered, watching his motionless form. My aunt's lover, she thought . . . almost my lover, almost my rapist.

Chunga was coming toward her, moving even more slowly than she had. His arms were partly outstretched, signaling to his men to stay where they were. Neither he nor Abigail dared show any eagerness to get this done. Hurrying was out of the question.

He stopped within arm's length of her. "Good morning, Jonas," she said, deliberately keeping her voice low.

"Good morning, Abigail. Every time I run into you lately, you seem to be leaving." He, too, spoke very softly. It seemed that by mutual agreement this was between just the two of them. But now that he was close to her, she could see the movement of his eyes. He was struggling to give her his full attention. Something on the veranda was drawing him to it.

Tony, she thought. Yudel was right. "Just bad luck, I suppose. I'm told everything in life is about timing."

"Yes." His eyes again darted in the direction of the veranda. "Ours does not seem to have been too bad this morning."

"And what do you intend doing with your good timing?"

"I haven't yet decided." He was looking at her, forcing his attention away from the young man behind her. His eyes had narrowed and any playfulness that may have been present in his voice was gone. "You didn't really think you could get away with this. Or did you?"

"I have a court order. My clients are free."

"No. You have a piece of paper and your clients are on the veranda of the Plumtree police station."

"You're not going to ignore a court order, are you? You were there when the judgment was made."

"I'm going to do what's best for my country." But he was not looking at her. She could see how he was struggling to keep his mind on her.

A cry came from behind her. Abigail recognized neither the voice nor the single word that had been called out. It was only when the cry came a second time that she heard the word "Father!" clearly, and knew the voice was Tony's.

"Father," it came again. And for the first time since she had first met him, Jonas Chunga's composure was shaken. "Father."

This was not the time to look round or to allow her gaze to falter. None of Tony's friends, nor any CIO members would understand. Chunga was trying to keep his eyes on her, but could not. They flickered again toward the young man on the veranda behind her. The pretense could not be maintained. His attention moved from Abigail and he was looking past her. At last she turned to look back. Tony was standing at the edge of the veranda. "Father." The cry came again. Abigail could not say whether it was a plea, a cry for help or simply an acknowledgment of their relationship. Then Tony was coming toward them, uncertainly, not with the sort of care she had shown, stumbling as he stepped off the cement.

"Father." Abigail heard a wildness in the sound, the call of an animal in pain. "Father." If there was more he wanted to say, the struggle to articulate it was too great. Now he was stumbling toward them. In a momentary glance, Abigail thought she saw fear in Chunga's eyes. "Father."

The distance was not great, but later, as she remembered the incident, she could not decide whether it had taken very long for him to reach them or perhaps no time at all. He stumbled again on the uneven surface. Then he was in his father's arms. His own arms were round Chunga, holding him close, perhaps the only time he ever had. Chunga seemed unable to move. Abigail knew that there was nothing else that could have had this effect on him. "Father," Tony sobbed.

The embrace lasted only seconds. Tony burst away, stopping

within an arm's length of Abigail. It was a moment before she realized that he was holding his father's service revolver in his right
hand. Chunga's jacket had been thrown open for an instant and
Abigail saw that the shoulder holster was empty now. Tony was
standing just a few meters away from his father and pointing the
revolver at him. Almost immediately firearms had appeared in the
hands of all the CIO men. "No," Chunga shouted. "Put away your
weapons. Put them away."

Almost any other command would have been obeyed instantly,
but this one was different. This political lunatic was pointing a
firearm at the director. The bastard was clearly mad.

"Put them away," Chunga commanded again. "Any man who
fires his gun will be the next to die. Put them away."

Tony had found a target in the center of his father's chest. On
either side of Chunga the guns were being put away—slowly, reluctantly, one agent at a time. "Tony," Chunga spoke gently. "Tony,
it's all right. It's all right. Just put down the gun. No action will be
taken against anyone, just put down the gun."

"Father . . ." The word hung in the space between them. It was
clear that there was more to be said, but that saying it was not
possible. "Father." Tony raised the hand that was holding the gun.
The angle of his wrist twisted. He had found a new target, one
he could not be denied. A finger was searching for the trigger.
The single report of the gun seemed to be amplified by the quiet
of the rural morning. The bullet struck the boy just below his
right ear. He fell heavily on the spot where he had been standing.

None of the CIO agents had moved. Yudel was the first to reach
Tony's body. His fingers searched for the carotid, then for the artery
at his wrists, but in neither place did even the smallest flicker of life
reveal itself. He found the position of the entry wound. The brain
stem must have been blown away, and with it any chance of the
body's functions continuing. He rose to look at Chunga. The director was sinking to his knees. It was clear that he did not need
proof that his son was dead. Abigail had moved back a few steps,
putting that small extra distance between herself and the now lifeless body of her cousin.

––––––––––

To Abigail it seemed later that every moment of that morning had been etched permanently in her memory. Afterward she would remember the unevenness of the ground as she walked toward Jonas Chunga. She would remember the look on his face, first as he approached her, then when he heard his son calling to him.

If one moment was blurred in her mind it was the fraction of a second that it took for Tony to turn the gun away from his father and toward himself. It had happened so fast that perhaps there had never been even an instant when the picture was clear to her.

She remembered too the long moment, far too long at the time, before Chunga, consumed by his private hell, was able to give direction to his men. Without him giving the orders, none of them knew what should be done with the remaining seven dissidents, or with Yudel and Abigail. It was only when Chunga waved a hand, still without rising, and snarled, "Let them go, let the bastards all go," that the group on the police-station veranda moved uncertainly into the street.

Equally clear in her memory was the horror on the face of Helena, who had heard the shot from the front passenger seat of the minibus taxi she had gone to fetch. Her first words on seeing Tony's body were: "So the swine are open about killing us now." Yudel had intercepted her to quiet her and tell her what had happened, and how silence was the best option.

Abigail could also never forget the brief meeting, that she later described to Yudel as bizarre, with Helena and her seven colleagues. They were in their seats in the taxi. She suggested that they make the short run to the Botswana border post. She said she was sure she could get them into that country as political refugees. The post was poorly manned, and there was no boom. If they left the taxi and walked across in a loose group, they would be in the office on the Botswana side before the Zimbabweans realized what was happening. Botswana would take them in. It was the continent's country that had greatest respect for personal freedom. They always accepted political refugees.

But the group in the taxi had already held an impromptu caucus among themselves. They had looked at one another, and Helena spoke for them all. "We are very grateful for what you and Yudel have done. Also Rosa. She was very brave too. But we're staying. We believe our country is changing, and we are going to stay here and help it change."

"You're not serious," Abigail had said.

"We are serious. We are very serious."

But the image that would return to her most often and most clearly of all, as the months passed, was that of Jonas Chunga kneeling next to his son's body, his hands clasped together and pressed to his chest. Of all that had passed between them, that was the picture that she knew would never disappear from her memory.

55

It was early afternoon before Abigail, Yudel and Rosa reached the Bulawayo airport. That the car Yudel had hired in Harare was going to be returned to the car-hire company in a different city, so far from where they expected it and where they seemed to have no office, only troubled Yudel briefly. He was sure that they were understanding people and would not penalise him unduly.

Their flight would take off three hours later. They were still waiting for it when Rosa's cell phone rang. Yudel listened to her side of the conversation. It was made up of "Oh yes, how are you? . . . You don't say . . . I see . . . Yes, I see . . . When did this happen? . . . Oh, I see . . . And how is he? . . . And thanks for the call, Mariette . . . Yes, we will . . . I see . . . We certainly will, Mariette . . . We are very much in favor."

What the hell is all this Mariette business? Yudel wondered. How did they suddenly become old friends? "What did that old cow want?" he asked after the call ended.

"Don't talk about her that way," Rosa said. "She's younger than us. All she wants is what's best for Dad."

Yudel was less than certain about the accuracy of that statement. "So what does she want?"

"She says there's now a woman in Dad's life."

"The old devil," Yudel chuckled. "It just goes to show that marketing does pay."

"It shows nothing of the sort. It didn't come about as a result of that stupid advertisement. He and one of the ladies who live at the home, whom he has known for years, have decided to pool their resources and are moving in together. Mariette is giving them one of the flats there. She asked if we had any objections, and I said we are in favor. I trust that you have no objections, Yudel."

"Certainly not."

"Apparently she and Dad have each sold their single beds and bought a double bed. Mariette says this matter of their double bed is the talk of the place. She says there has already been a delegation to see her, suggesting that if they really wanted to do something that extreme, they should have kept it quiet, perhaps had the bed delivered at night. Apparently they felt that such an act of rampant sexuality was not in keeping with the mood of the establishment."

"Rampant?" Yudel said. "I'm not sure that I understand what the word means in this context?"

"Neither do I. It's Mariette's word, not mine."

It was deep twilight when the cab Yudel had hired dropped Abigail at home. She asked the driver to stop at the motor gate. "Just leave me here. I'll walk up the drive."

"Why? Let us take you to the front door," Yudel suggested.

"No, Yudel. Please. I'll walk the last little bit. I want to."

She watched the cab with Yudel and Rosa in it drive away, until it turned the corner at the end of the block. How long do you have to be together to fit together in such an effortless way as they seem to? she wondered. Now perhaps she and Robert would never find out. For Abigail it was good to be home—in a place where, despite the closing down of the Scorpions, the law was not overridden by government whenever it suited them.

It was Saturday morning, and Robert would be at home, or should be at home. Perhaps not should. But why would he not be at home? Where else would he be? And when last had they had contact, the time when he told her that the thing with his temp was over? Or when? Her talking to Robert had disappeared into the jumble of more pressing matters.

That sounds terrible, she thought. More pressing matters? And yet, that was the truth of it.

The motor gate opened at the first touch of the remote's button.

This was her home, or was it still that? It was so absurdly big, so far beyond any imaginable needs she and Robert would ever have.

The front door and all the windows were closed. It was unlike Robert to be inside the house and not open any windows. Could he have moved out? she wondered. Perhaps, after all, he had disappeared with the temp.

But Abigail was tired. It was two weeks, or close to it, since she had caught the flight to Harare, and now all she wanted was to sleep. The night in the car had been less than satisfactory. More than anything else, she wanted her own bed and enough time to enjoy it.

She let herself in at the front door and wandered through both lounges, dining room, kitchen and family room. Everything was impeccably neat, as if someone had spent the day before preparing the house for a magazine shoot. There was not even a used coffee cup in the sink.

Upstairs in the bedrooms, the condition of the house was the same. Nothing was out of place, nothing left lying around, not even a book on his bedside table. It was clear that the bed had not been slept in.

He's left me. Abigail was sure of it now. He's gone and left me the house. After more than ten years, it ends this way . . . not with ugly words and shouting, but with a perfectly tidy house, a perfectly empty house. And no Robert anywhere—not even a note. Maybe there would be an e-mail waiting for her. That was probably the way these things were conducted these days.

She sat down on the edge of the bed, slipped off her shoes, then stretched out and closed her eyes. She was very tired. The phone rang almost immediately. She lifted the handset and mumbled into it, "Abigail Bukula."

"Abby, what are you doing there?" It was Robert's voice, coming from far away, almost as part of a dream.

In an instant Abigail was fully awake. "Hi, feller," she said. "You may have noticed that I live here. What are you up to?"

"I've been looking for you?"

"What are you talking about? Where are you?"

"I'm here."

"Where is here?"

"McDooley's Inn, Harare."

She was sitting upright on the edge of the bed now. "What are you doing there?"

"I came to see if you needed help. It sounded as if you and Yudel were in trouble."

Abigail was laughing. The whole thing between her and Robert was all so funny now. There he was, her knight in shining armor, more than a little clay-footed perhaps, but still coming to her rescue. He was a few days late as it turned out, but at least he had turned up for the battle. "Damn, Robert, you bastard, I love you," she said.

"I suppose I can come home now. I feel a bit foolish."

"Don't feel foolish. Just come home."

The combined funeral of Tony Makumbe and Krisj Patel was a muted affair. There had been some uncertainty about the sort of occasion it should be.

Patel had been brought up a Hindu, but had converted to Catholicism when the Catholic Bishops' Conference had been the only body, religious or otherwise, to speak out about the Gukurahundi massacres. With the world media silent, choosing not to believe that the hero of his country's liberation struggle could be a tyrant, and with his own religion showing no interest in the fate of the Ndebele people, Patel had decided that Catholicism must be the one true way. However, as the years passed, he had wearied of the rituals and chanting, and the stories of priests molesting young boys. He had not been to church for a decade or more. His own priest had not demonstrated nearly enough vigor, in his mind, in attacking the government's excesses.

As for Tony, he had never shown any sort of interest in religion. In fact, Helena remembered him having once told her that he wanted to be cremated without ceremony and have his ashes scattered over CIO headquarters in Harare. Apparently he felt that such a course of action would have infuriated them. And that would have been satisfying to him, if satisfaction is possible after death.

Finally, the decision fell on a young Presbyterian minister who was a member of the Organization for Peace and Justice in Zimbabwe. At least they knew where his sympathies lay. Suneesha

Patel had shown little interest in the occasion, agreeing readily to the arrangements, simple as they were, that were made by her husband's political friends.

She had attended, though, and listened to the minister read a verse from the Bible that said something to the effect that David's love for Jonathan surpassed that of women. She sighed at the thought. She had loved Krisj, but his love for Tony had surpassed the love she could offer. Damned fool, she thought. And finally the two of them were together, in one ceremony. The bastards. She wondered if even their ashes had been mixed by their friends.

Helena Ndoro was one of the first into the chapel, holding the hand of her partner, Petra. She also thought about the young minister's text. She would have chosen a different one. There was a verse in Ecclesiastes that said there's a time to live and a time to die. At least Krisj and Tony had lived. They had risked comfort, success, their very lives. And they had done it every day. They had lived.

Most of those who attended the service in the chapel that morning were members of their organization. One of the few who was not a member was old Mama Loise. She had cried for Tony from the time she came in till long after it was all over.

A thick-set, graying man, wearing dark glasses and an expensive suit, arrived after everyone else and sat in the back pew. He was also first to leave. Few of those who attended even noticed his presence. What he thought about the funeral of his son being combined with the funeral of the one who had to die because of their relationship was never known.

Helena had torn a page from that morning's *Herald*. She had it in her bag, intending to show it to the others at the funeral, but, distracted by the emotion, had forgotten it there. On the front page, the government paper carried a short report about the retirement due to ill health of Jonas Chunga, one of the CIO's directors. He was a man, the newspaper said, who had been tipped to be that body's next director general. The minister had been quoted as saying that the nation could not afford the loss of so dedicated a senior executive. "He is a man who has devoted his entire life to the pursuit of justice."